THE
COMMONWEALTH
OF
BOTH NATIONS

Poland and Lithuania

THE
COMMONWEALTH
OF
BOTH NATIONS:
The Silver Age

by
PAWEL JASIENICA

Translated by
ALEXANDER JORDAN

THE AMERICAN INSTITUTE OF
POLISH CULTURE
Miami

HIPPOCRENE BOOKS
New York

1987

Hippocrene Books, Inc.
171 Madison Avenue
New York, NY 10016

Printed in the United States of America.

ISBN 87052-394-5

Contents

CHAPTER 1

THE SILVER AGE

The king died heirless: but God wanted
This crown to prosper.
Though without heir, he left us freedom.

Jan Gluchowski,
Interregnum, 1572

The confusion at Knyszyn castle was shortlived and the excesses of the court clique were soon curbed. A few days after his death, the body of Zygmunt August, appropriately attired, was on display in the castle hall. Insiders openly hinted that the crown on the king's head was a substitute of Hungarian origin. The last of the Jagiellonians had inherited it a year earlier from the king of Hungary, John Zygmunt Zapolyi, who was his nephew.

The official in charge of Wawel castle firmly refused to release the regalia of the Polish crown. The end of the dynasty initiated a period of crisis, which had been anticipated with anguish for years.

Precautions had to be taken to prevent any attempted usurpation and the best place for the crown of the Piasts and Jagiellonians was under lock and key in the Wawel treasure chamber.

It was inevitable that the crown would soon rest on the brow of a foreigner. The simplest and seemingly most rational solution was ruled out, for the idea of a native monarch—though appealing—was wholly unrealistic. That term would mean different things in Cracow, Warsaw, Wilno, or Perejaslaw in Ruthenia.

The second article of the constitutional statute enacted a year later began "Under that noble crown of the Polish, Lithuanian, Ruthenian, Courlandian, and other nations. . . ."

The "other nations" requires comment.

The leading political writer of the time, John Dymitr Solikowski, explained to the gentry that even if a Pole and a Lithuanian could be miraculously fused into one, their unity would not be enough, as a Prussian might stand in opposition—even if his name was Dzialynski, his native language Polish, and he disliked the Germans.

It was impossible to elevate one part of the Commonwealth at the expense of others, risking the destruction of a delicate balance built over centuries.

In the country loosely described by its own citizens and foreigners as "Poland," with an occasional mention of Lithuania, the dominant magnates at the end of the Jagiellonian era were Ruthenian princes of the Orthodox faith. The most powerful clans were the Ostrogski, Zbaraski, and Slucki, whose princely titles—confirmed by the Lublin Union—derived, if not from Ruryk, at least from the heirs of Gedymin. The Radziwills, with their vast estates around Birze, Olyka, Nieswiez, Szydlowiec, and Pacanow—recently elevated by the emperor to princely rank—came next. Lower down the feudal hierarchy came the native Polish nobility, perfectly at ease in Renaissance Europe, which accepted them as a culturally developed nation.

The Princes Wisniowiecki could adopt the Polish language and custom, later even the Catholic faith, but they could not accept as their monarch some lesser lord from central Poland, on whom even the impoverished Princes Woroniecki looked down as one not descended from ancient rulers and no better than a country squire.

Poland proper was then at the apogee of its history. Politically, it was a partner in the state described by the simplified term of the Commonwealth of Both Nations. Two coequal states formed in

Lublin a definitive union, hence the name. But everyone realized that the Commonwealth actually comprised three nations. Even if Ruthenia was formally part of Lithuania, no one could deny its separate identity. The day on which the official record of parliamentary proceedings would include the name of the Ukraine was close. In the meantime the *voievodship* (province), with its capital in Lwow, comprising the castellan districts of Lwow, Halicz, Przemysl, and Sanok, was called the province of Ruthenia.

The problem of Ruthenia—the Ukraine—was Poland's greatest historic challenge. The Lublin Union had not resolved it, but merely set out a path to be followed, under pain of death.

There were later many who regarded the state stretching from Silesia and Poznan to Polock and the Ukrainian steppes as simply the kingdom of Poland. They looked upon Wilno and Kiev as politically equivalent to Sandomierz, Kalisz, or Sieradz. Their vision was one of a unified empire and its memory the greatest prize of all. Their view was actually in step with those who perceived imperialism and expansionism as the worst sins of the Poles. Eulogy and criticism coalesced into a single though errant voice.

The greatest contribution of post-Piast Poland to the history of the continent of Europe was the creation of its first multinational, multicultural state. Poland cooperated in that task with Lithuania and Ruthenia, but it was the leading and the most persistent architect of that common home, as well as the keystone of its structure. Owing to its greater density of population and superior economic and cultural development, it was also the leader. If it had at any time witheld its support, the eastern wall of the structure would have collapsed immediately. Poland could neither withdraw nor impose its primacy over the Commonwealth by installing a native Pole on the throne. His way to Wawel castle was barred, precisely because Poland actually controlled the Commonwealth even when it was ruled by a Lithuanian dynasty. Another step toward consolidating that power would have broken the still fresh bonds holding the whole together.

A quarter of a century after the extinction of the Jagiellonian dynasty, much confusion was caused by a plan for an exchange of dignitaries, of which more later. A Lithuanian was to be appointed bishop of Cracow and a native Pole bishop of Wilno. The first part of the deal was carried out without much trouble; the second, never—despite the efforts of the king and even the pope. Cardinal Jerzy

Radziwill became bishop of Cracow, but Bernard Maciejowski, a future primate of Poland, never reached Wilno. This was a case involving an ecclesiastic office, somewhat cosmopolitan by reason of the universal character of the church. One can imagine what would have happened if the dispute concerned a secular office reserved for native sons.

The guardian of the Wawel treasure chamber, who watched so closely the coronation regalia in 1572, was surely not afraid of any attempt on them by his countrymen.

At the time of the interregnum the principal, immediate obstacle was at the same time the greatest achievement of statecraft. The candidate to the throne had to be sought among foreigners. That was the desire of the Lithuanian magnates, while the Ruthenians were not yet thinking about the crown for one of their own. The first native monarch of the Commonwealth was Michael Korybut Wisniowiecki, a Ukrainian prince—but not until the end of the next century.

Immediately after the death of Zygmunt August, pamphleteers argued against the election of a native son, because "when an owl turns into a hawk, it wants to fly higher than a falcon." Later, when a new and not too welcome dynasty had established itself on the throne, even serious writers blamed the envious nature of the Poles, which prevented one of them from reaching for the crown. They seemed to overlook the fact that mutual envy and ferocious competitiveness for advancement are the typical features of the aristocracies of all nations at all times. But at the time when the country faced its first free election of a monarch, its political leaders confronted realities. They had to reckon with the pluralism of the Commonwealth, a political body that did not seek ethnic unity or the domination by any single member nation. It was a state that was never an empire but rather its opposite, a federation.

In the preceding volume of this work there is frequent reference to the disruptive practices of the Lithuanian magnates. They were certainly not farsighted, but were guided by excessive ambition and were lawless in their pursuit of selfish goals—characteristic features of societies without deeper cultural traditions. They were often oblivious of geopolitical realities and believed that a strong will could change them to their liking. That is why they cared little for strengthening the only power that could ensure Lithuania's survival—Poland—ignoring the obvious fact that without Polish sup-

4

port the Grand Duchy of Lithuania was doomed to be conquered by Moscow.

The list of their sins was not exhausted in the preceding volume but it is time to mention also their virtues, bearing in mind that we are speaking of a time only three years after the Lublin Union.

The Lithuanian magnates guarded the separate identity of their country. The Radziwills acquired vast estates in Poland proper; they held high offices there and took first place at the court of Wawel. Yet none of them denied their Lithuanian origin or turned their backs on the country of their ancestors. This was eloquently expressed in a letter written by Radziwill the Red to King Zygmunt August (in Polish): "Your Majesty, please do not show this letter to your secretaries, for they are Poles and I am a Lithuanian."

The gentry of the Grand Duchy also guarded its identity but wanted to achieve full union sooner. In the feudal structure of that era, however, it was the voice of the great lords that counted. That is why it was the attitude of the Lithuanian Gasztolds and Radziwills, the Ruthenian Chodkiewiczes and Sapiehas, as well as the art of compromise of the majority of the Poles that made the federation possible. The notion of the simple annexation of Lithuania by Poland was ruled out and the Grand Duchy lost neither its autonomy nor its identity.

The Union of Lublin started a historical process that, had it not been frustrated by a series of wars and political upheavals, would have made a significant contribution to European civilization. A new, pluralistic nation was being born through a voluntary association of states retaining their independence.

Let no one be deceived by the fluent Polish of the Radziwills of Hlebowiczes. The official language of the Wilno chancery was still the old Ruthenian, which later evolved into the present Byelorussian. That language continued to be spoken by the overwhelming majority of the population.

In January 1576 Prince Melchior Giedroyc was appointed bishop of Samogitia (Zmudz). He found his diocese in a sad state: seven Catholic priests and a resurgence of paganism. There were also forty Calvinist churches in his territory. The Radziwills of Birze had joined the Helvetian creed and that determined the religious character of the region for a time. Bishop Giedroyc started his work from scratch, following the example of his predecessor of two centuries before. He organized missions and baptized adults.

Wladyslaw Jagiello had the main Christian prayers translated into the language of his people. Melchior Giedroyc did the same, but on a higher level. He was not content with seeking priests speaking Lithuanian, but induced Father Mikolaj Dauksza to translate into that language the catechism and the *Postilla* of Father Jacob Wujek, a Polish religion writer, which he had printed at his own expense.

Zygmunt August was still alive when, at the time of the most fervent debates on the completion of the union, an unknown publisher printed and disseminated the political pamphlet "Conversations of a Pole and a Lithuanian About Freedom and Slavery." Its author was probably Augustyn Rotundus Mieleski, mayor of Wilno and a staunch patriot of the Grand Duchy, though himself a native Pole from Wielun. Speaking about ancient pagan times, he repeated the then widely held opinion that since "Lithuania started to speak Ruthenian, because the Ruthenians were warlike men and well liked in Lithuania," its own language went into disuse, except along the sea coast "where we now have Prussia, Samogitia, Inflanty, as far as the Wilia River."

The Lublin Union determined the new boundaries of the Grand Duchy, which reached the river Prypec in the south. Towns such as Pinsk, Mozyrz, and Dawidgrodek were then considered Lithuanian. The official documents reaching that country from Cracow invariably started with: "We by the grace of God, King of Poland, Grand Duke of Lithuania and Ruthenia, Prince of Prussia and Samogitia . . ." in Ruthenian.

When the turmoil of the interregnum died down, Janusz Zbaraski, a magnate of southern Ruthenia, sought the office of *voievode* of Wilno. It was denied because he was not a native of the Grand Duchy. High office there was open, however, to Benedict Wojna, a squire from the Minsk region who had just disawowed the Orthodox faith, as did Zbaraski. The Commonwealth recognized him as a Lithuanian and he considered himself one.

The nationalist manias of the nineteenth and twentieth centuries were then still far away. Lithuania gave the Grand Duchy its name, but only a part of its actual content. It was one, and not the largest, of its ethnic components. The same was true of Poland, whose name was often used to describe the entire Commonwealth, although it was a federation of several nations.

The Commonwealth never indulged in any form of discrimination, chauvinism, or attempts to impose a language or culture by coercion. It was a unique and remarkable structure, deserving close study and respect. A state comprising two coequal partners was about to increase its area through acquisitions for Lithuania, approaching the staggering total of a million square kilometers (385,000 square miles). The Grand Duchy, which kept its own administration and treasury, was a separate economic entity. Its citizens remained deeply attached to their culture and tradition as Lithuanian patriots. No one objected to that, but they unfortunately sometimes went further and tried to conduct a foreign policy of their own, not necessarily in accord with that of the Commonwealth as a whole. The impressive structure was not fully completed.

After the Lublin Union, Poland acquired for its own crown the region of Podlasie, by then thoroughly polonized (though the Lithuanian *voievode*, Kiszka, remained in office), as well as Wolyn and the Ukraine. In Gdansk and the Baltic province of Inflanty, the German residents kept their municipal autonomy, confirmed by King Zygmunt August. The provincial legislature of Royal Prussia conducted its debates in Polish but guarded jealously the autonomy of the region.

The last male of the dynasty that brought together the multinational mosaic of the Commonwealth died in Knyszyn, near the border between Poland and Lithuania. He "left no heir but freedom." It was not only the freedom of the individual citizens—the gentry; during the interregnum the Wilno rulers guarded firmly also the rights of "our nation and the Grand Duchy of Lithuania." The freedom bequeathed by Zygmunt August to the Commonwealth was also that of its member nations, that is their equality within the federation.

Politically sophisticated men with experience in public affairs shrugged off simplistic suggestions of a "Piast" (meaning Polish) monarch. They knew that the sovereign of the Commonwealth had to be acceptable to all its component nationalities.

The year was 1572. The parchment of the act of union signed in Lublin was still fresh, its seals gleaming. The federation was exactly three years and a week old. The union was concluded in July and the last of the Jagiellonians died also in July, three years later.

Andrzej Frycz Modrzewski, the eminent political writer, also died in 1572 and another one, Mikolaj Rey, three years earlier. The names of the great writers of the Polish Renaissance were passing into history, but others continued their work. Jan Kochanowski, the poet, had just left the court to settle at his country estate. His most brilliant poems were still to come. The works of Polish writers were published in many countries of Europe. Only twenty years before, the youthful Stanislaw Warszewicki of the Paprzyca crest caused a literary event in western Europe. He translated from Greek to Latin the *Ethiopica* of Heliodorus, a romance of the third century A.D., which had enjoyed wide popularity in Byzantium. A wave of other translations and adaptations followed. Stanislaw Ilowski translated the works of Dionysos of Halicarnassus and those of Basil the Great. But when he translated from Greek to Latin the textbook on rhetoric of Demetrius of Faleros, he had an unpleasant surprise. Another translation of that work appeared in the same year in Padua, its author was Franciszek Maslowski. Krzysztof Warszewicki, a half-brother of Stanislaw, undertook an unusual task: He translated from Italian to Latin, at the request of its author, the treatise *Della Perfettione della vita politics*, by Paolo Parato.

It was a strange phenomenon—a theoretical work of an Italian scholar presented in the language of Cicero by a squire from Warszewice, located on the Vistula, close to Czersk. The book of Marcin Kromer about the origins and customs of the Poles was published in Basel and aroused considerable interest in France and Italy.

The western section of the Jagiellonian federation had joined the circle of the makers and propagators of universal cultural values.

In the eastern part of the Commonwealth the high office of grand marshal was held by the first Lithuanian to produce a literary work that withstood the test of time. It was the *Travels to the Holy Land, Syria and Egypt*, by Nicholas Christopher Radziwill, called "the orphan." Four centuries later it still makes enthralling reading and testifies to the fact that Lithuania produced a writer fully equal in talent to his contemporaries in France.

Radziwill wrote his book in Polish, but it would be an injustice to classify it simply as part of the literature of Poland. Its author considered himself a Lithuanian, but a citizen of the Commonwealth. *Travels* is written in beautiful and flawless Polish, but it is different in spirit from, for example, *Farewell to the Greek Envoys*, an outstanding Polish literary work of the period. The Lithuanian magnate and patriot used the language of his home and society, choosing it as an instrument of his art, but not as a declaration of national identity.

Radziwill "the Orphan" was an opponent of the Lublin Union

and favored its abrogation. He even went so far as to participate in a secret plot that could have damaged seriously the federal bond.

Political maturity is evidently slower in coming than cultural assimilation. A European class writer behaved in the execution of a political scheme like a child. The Italian diplomat with whom he was cooperating looked at him with pitying condescension. The "Orphan" was joined in his scheme by another Lithuanian magnate, but not of the literary variety. It would seem that the political primitivism was due not to the naivete typical of artists, but was common to all the leaders of the Grand Duchy.

Seventeen years after the death of Zygmunt August, a certain castellan of Smolensk in Lithuania was alleged to have delivered in the Seym in Warsaw a speech recorded for posterity in somewhat garbled form:

> Leaving my home I prayed to God that I would reach you whole and find your lordships in good health. I have to confer with you, but I never before attended any such meetings or sat down with His Majesty, for under our dukes of Lithuania there were no debates. They just spoke from the heart, did not bother about any politics and told the truth good as gold; if someone even joked about it he meant it in a friendly way.
>
> King Henry, he came to us from overseas by way of Germany, but when he saw that we would not allow him to play games or let his Germans get out of line, he quietly skipped away by sea, though frankly he was not to be blamed as much as our native tricksters, who hover around kings, befuddle everyone, and are the perdition of the Commonwealth; it's because of them that we lost Podlasie and Wolyn. We walk benighted because we are afraid of them, we flatter them with sweet talk. Oh, if only one could punch them with the fist on the nose, they would quit their meddling!
>
> And what about this craze of women in fancy clothes. We never knew before the portigals or fortingals, the ruffles and courtiers like crested cockerels with feathers to pick. I would advise womenfolk to dress as before, well laced and secure. Also if it was not for the German breeches, we would be safer from the amorous coxcombs, they could not get as quickly at the lewd parts and now the devils can't be kept away even if one stands guard with a halberd.

It was, of course, a parody whose author betrayed its apocryphal character by mentioning by name persons absent from Poland at that time. Nevertheless even parody reflects reality, though as in a distorting mirror and with exaggeration.

It is true that the parliament of the Commonwealth of Both Nations comprised the opposite poles of the European political culture of its time.

Among the senators were such men as Wawrzyniec Goslicki, whose writings were respected throughout the continent and in England; Jan Zamoyski, a statesman of the highest standing; and other representatives of the Renaissance at its best. Their new colleagues from the east had been brought up in a different tradition. Shortly before the Lublin Union it was reported that:

"In the Grand Duchy there are no local legislatures as in Poland, for the gentry do not attend any. The *voievode*, castellan, or sheriff get together and after making their decisions send the document to the gentry to sign and seal. If they do not sign, the are threatened with the stick."

Which of the two models would take the upper hand? The answer to that question could decide the future of the state, even its survival.

The last Jagiellonian missed an opportunity for reform. Zygmunt August did not leave any guidelines. The Lublin Union did solve some problems of long standing, but it created others just as thorny. There were many obstacles, but none of then unsurmountable.

Rationality was the only way out—the kind that inspired the political treatises of Ostrorog, the debates of the parliaments under the reigns of the last of the Jagiellonians and the behavior of the Polish Catholic gentry, which elected mostly protestants as its deputies, judging them better qualified. Rationality differentiates between a policy and an act of faith; it counsels a statesman to place political strategy ahead of ideology and warns against extremism.

The teaching in schools and in the areas forming public opinion was of the utmost importance, for it could determine the mental attitudes of the nation.

The name of politicians was invented for those who give to peace within the realm precedence over the salvation of their souls and religion; those who prefer peace without God to war on His behalf. The politicians say: under a single faith, all of France will be at war; under two faiths it will rest in peace.

These were the observations of Gaspard de Saulx, seigneur de Tavannes, an author of the same period. Speaking of "politicians," he was referring to a party using that name, which endeavored to conciliate the two camps intent on slaughtering each other.

The Polish pamphleteers of that time seldom reached the Gallic levels of precision of expression, or cynicism. Yet the evolution of the Jagiellonian Commonwealth followed in practice the precepts of the seigneur de Tavannes.

In 1564 a young member of the Arian protestant sect, Erasm Otwinowski, was charged before the court of the Seym (parliament) with snatching the monstrance with the Holy Host from the hand of a priest in a religious procession in Lublin and trampling it under his feet. He was defended by Mikolaj Rey, an eminent political writer, who said that Otwinowski should pay for the damage to the precious liturgical vessel and the Lord, if He felt offended, could inflict his own penalty. He convinced the deputies and won acquittal for his client. It might seem to us today that the provocative speech of Rey could have caused a violent conflict between the Catholics and the Protestants, but the Primate of Poland, Archbiship Uchanski, was not at all perturbed by the Lublin incident.

The Commonwealth soon reaped the reward of its tolerance, religious indifference, or lackadaisical attitude. Whatever the phenomenon might be called, its results counted more than its definition. The day of March 1, 1562, is recognized by historians as the beginning of the religious wars in France. The men of the Duke de Guise killed on that day in Vassy twenty-three Protestants and wounded more than one hundred. According to French scholars, in the following twenty years, nine thousand clergy, thirty-two thousand noblemen, more than six hundred and fifty thousand commoners, and thirty-two thousand foreigners lost their lives in religious wars in France. The elite of the knightly estate nearly exterminated one another, as they were the most skilled in the use of arms.

Poland enjoyed at the same time domestic peace, even though the Reformation had gained much ground. The great poet Jan Kochanowski wrote:

How shall we pay you, Lord, for your rich bounty,
For blessings you shower upon us without end?

He was right, Poles often envy nations that modern history has treated more kindly. But the Commonwealth also had its happy age. It came early, passed, and was forgotten.

Fiction writers created a false image of the past. They convinced their readers that the nobility of that period thought of little else than martial valor. Actually its interests were bucolic rather than military. It is true that the gentry responded to a call to arms and declared proudly that the nation's best defense was not the walls of castles, but the breasts of its valiant citizens. Nevertheless, military service was also often regarded as just another way of making a living and rural husbandry was considered a far more desirable occupation. The model citizen was well born, prosperous, and settled on his estate, not necessarily campaigning somewhere far away. Deploring the sad consequences of the Tartar raids in Podole, Jan Kochanowski urged his countrymen first to turn their silver plate into *thalers*, that is to raise funds for hiring mercenaries.

"Give and give first. Ourselves,
We shall keep for a more pressing need."

The frontiers had to be guarded, but that did not mean that one had to abandon the good country life. There were other ways of fighting evil.

Few Poles who had tasted war thought it the only calling worthy of a nobleman. The hum of hussar wings in a cavalry charge intoxicated the bourgeois readers of Sienkiewicz's historical novels, but the crested citizens of the old Commonwealth were less enamored of its tune.

In the next century these problems were dealt with by Maximilian Fredro in his excellent, though forgotten book, *The History of Poland Under Henry de Valois*. Fredro was a writer known throughout Europe and deserves credence. He had access to sources and documents of which no trace remains today and dealt with long-term trends. He insisted that it was widely believed at the time that "wars are waged more by the whim of the rulers than in the interest of the Commonwealth."

In the fifteenth century the gentry participated in the Bukowina expedition of Jan Olbracht, but looked upon it—according to contemporary writers—as a private enterprise of the Jagiellonian dynasty.

After the dynasty's extinction, Fredro wrote: " . . . it was perceived that it was time to stop the expansion of the Commonwealth, bordering on the Baltic in the north, the Black Sea in the east and the Carpathians in the south. It was thought that guarding present possessions was more important than seeking new ones . . . for both too small and too large states have their disadvantages."

Similar sentiments are to be found in various other writings of the period. Andrzej Frycz Modrzewski expressed the same view when he warned Zygmunt August that those who coveted neighboring kingdoms often jeopardized their own. The translation of *Ethiopics*, by Stanislaw Warszewicki, was dedicated by him to the monarch.

The printed dedication condemned wars and conquest, praising peace. Stanislaw's half brother, Krzysztof, published later a book about diplomacy in which he wrote, "We are all citizens of the world and our duty is to help one another."

Such attitudes worried the papal nuncio, Julius Ruggieri, who anticipated serious problems for the Commonwealth, since its eastern part, the Grand Duchy of Lithuania, had been engaged for centuries in conflict with Moscow, "whose laws and customs have mostly war as their goal."

The deeply rooted pacifism of the gentry set the tone of history and exerted a major influence on its course. It was the desire for peace that had dictated to the Poles their union with Lithuania. It was also the main criterion at the time of royal elections, when candidates were graded according to the risk of war they were perceived to present.

The Commonwealth had been a constitutional state for a long time and the government had to respect the will of its citizens. Most of the wars known to history would never have been fought if the decision had rested with a popular referendum rather than with general staffs and political rulers. The pacifism of the Commonwealth was not due to any particular inclinations of its Polish, Lithuanian, or Ruthenian components, but to the constitutional system. Under the Jagiellonians the king could declare a war, but he had to wage it with mercenary troops paid from his own treasury. He could not raise new taxes without parliamentary consent or proclaim a general levy for military service. With the Jagiellonians no more, the gentry had to define the future constitutional structure and policies of the state.

The pacifism of the gentry was one of the main causes of the subsequent downfall of the Commonwealth. It had many enemies, but was incapable of mounting the best form of defense, which is often a preemptive offensive. This was the way to ultimate disaster.

Jan Kochanowski was not alone in singing the praises of the good life enjoyed by the citizens of the Commonwealth. Others were also making comparisons, as the Poles and Lithuanians traveled extensively in Europe. The reports of those who recorded their impressions were succinct: in Spain, tyranny and servilism; in France and Germany, massacres; in Bohemia and Hungary, oppression; in Moscow, the bestial cruelty of Ivan the Terrible.

In the united kingdom of Poland and Lithuania the magnates flourished, the middle gentry did well, and even the peasants fared better than elsewhere. The cities, enjoying wide autonomy, enjoyed a period of growth and prosperity that was never repeated again.

Moralists deplored the license of the powerful lords, abuses and coercion. They were surely right, but later, when conditions had deteriorated, an Italian returning from Poland instructed his countrymen that two things were to be avoided there: carrying a stiletto and bragging about people one had killed. Neither was tolerated in Poland.

Father Stanislaw Gorski, deceased in 1572 and the author of the famous historical compendium *Acta Tomiciana* and others, anticipated the future great preacher Piotr Skarga as a prophet of doom. He predicted the demise of the state because of domestic laxity. Similar prophecies were also made at the time in France. Apocalyptic political forecasts have always been popular, especially among the Protestants, whose study of the Old Testament provides them with an ample supply of prophecies. Some of their large number may eventually come true. Father Gorski deplored the decline of Catholic orthodoxy, the weakening of the influence of the clergy and the Reformation movement among the gentry.

He was not alone in that opinion. The papal nuncio, Aloysius Lippomano, described Poland as simply "hell." Sent there as the first pioneer of the counter-reformation, he soon became highly unpopular and feared for his life. The Commonwealth could hardly please people repelled by such notions as freedom of thought, conscience, and speech.

They flourished in Poland and Lithuania, occasionally assuming rather odd forms. The Lutherans and Calvinists were at the time in strong opposition to the Arian sect. The Catholic bishops, however, opposed their plans for the expulsion of the anti-trinitarians, reasoning correctly that such a move would amount to legitimizing the other Protestant denominations. "War among heretics means peace for the church," said Cardinal Stanislaw Hozjusz. Suddenly the powerful Mikolaj Radziwill the Black, a leading Calvinist, became a protector of the Arians. He corresponded with Calvin himself, but at the same time invited the "Polish Brethren" as the Arians were called, to his town house in Wilno and permitted them to establish a place of worship and a school.

The Polish Catholics followed a similar line. On February 7, 1571, the burghers of Lublin assembled in a town meeting, at which a royal decree banning the Arians from that city was read. Further ordnances voted at the meeting prohibited the lending of premises for heretic meetings and services, or any intercourse with them. An additional measure was the prohibition of the employment of Arians as house tutors, because of the nefarious influence they might exert on the young. Citizens violating these rules were to be expelled from the city and their property confiscated.

None of these regulations was ever observed. At the same time a particularly militant group of Polish Brethren made Lublin its headquarters. They included one of their leaders, Marcin Czechowic, and Jan Niemojewski, a remarkable personality. A prosperous squire from Wielkopolska, he attended parliament "in very simple and worn out clothes, without a sword, servants or attendants." He emphasized his democratic principles by resigning from the bench, returning to the crown lands granted to his ancestors, and working in the fields with his hands.

Few were inclined to persecute people like Niemojewski.

The citizens of that strange state were aware of their achievement. "No nation in the world enjoys more liberties and freedom than we do," wrote a pamphleteer after the death of Zygmunt August. Unfortunately he was also one of those who believed that "our country has been so wisely constituted by our ancestors that it surpasses the republics of Lycurgus, Solon, or Romulus."

The forecasts of imminent catastrophe were definitely premature and the eulogies of the system frivolous. Nevertheless, some of the content held within its frail framework had lasting value.

CHAPTER 2

THE GENTRY AT THE HELM

"It is more important, my lords, to reform the Commonwealth than to elect a king," observed a political writer during the first interregnum, outlining the program of the reform party. It was true that the election presented a serious but immediate problem, while the reform was a far more complex, long-range project.

Foreigners marveled: You are ready to elect without having first set out the rules of the election? "That is right," replied the magnates, "for if rules existed wicked men would have found ways of bypassing them."

The response was not as absurd as it sounded. The magnates deliberately rejected the Seym's proposals concerning the election, as they were linked with plans of reform. The situation created by the extinction of the dynasty—a political vacuum in a state of vast size—did not endanger the position of those wielding power. The senate comprised the highest secular dignitaries and all the bishops. The interregnum did not affect their standing.

Three years before the death of Zygmunt August, Mikolaj Rey, the leading political writer, submitted a set of suggested rules for the forthcoming election. It seems that the author of the *Life of an Honest Man* was belligerent and arrogant only in religious matters. His political views were guided by the golden rule he recommended for the management of domestic life. His suggestions could hardly offend the senators as he wanted them to be the electors, together with the members of the Seym. To ensure balance, he even advised that the number of the latter be reduced. His proposal was ignored and Providence soon called him to eternity, thus sparing him the despair of witnessing political disarray.

The reform party was led by the lower chamber of the Seym, which comprised also the senate and the king. In the absence of a monarch it was not clear whether the full Seym could be convoked before a king was elected. The convention of the gentry could either confine itself to the election or enact constitutional laws. An acrimonious debate over the limits of its authority broke out immediately.

This was conducted in an atmosphere of unease and even fear. It had been known for a long time that the dynasty was dying out and the country was heading for a major crisis. Now it became a reality. The Commonwealth had been ruled by the Jagiellonians for two centuries and their demise left the people apprehensive and bewildered. There had been squabbles with the kings, even feuds, but the nation was essentially a monarchy. An empty throne disturbed the basic order on which everything else depended.

> Weep with me, Sarmatians, draw over your head
> Black hoods and the garb of mourning.

The poet's words expressed the mood of the moment. Only the magnates were free of the existential anguish and hardly missed the "Lord and Father of the nation."

The news of the king's death triggered a significant shift in market trends. The price of weapons and military equipment soared and those of luxury goods declined. The gentry sensed instinctively that a crisis was at hand and prepared for action. Danger was looming particularly in the east.

A truce with Tsar Ivan was signed only two years earlier. The envoy from Moscow, sent in 1571 for the ratification of the treaty, had firm instructions not to sign if King Zygmunt August were to die in the meantime. His death made questionable the validity of all the international agreements signed on his behalf.

The castles guarding the Dnieper and the Dzwina were pitifully inadequate. "They have no infantry, few guns and mounted men," reported a contemporary. Moscow, on the other hand, fortified Polock, which it had taken recently.

The truce had been signed two years earlier. Since that time, scores of thousands of ducats were spent on the royal mistresses and even more plundered by the court clique at Knyszyn. The treasury of the personal property of the royal family was well guarded at Tykocin. The Muscovite garrison of Polock threatened Wilno directly; all that barred its way were the small forts of Dzisna and Druja, poorly equipped and stripped of mercenaries, as there was no money to pay them.

The situation was judged harshly by contemporary observers, who did not hesitate to call Zygmunt August a "poor monarch." The heritage he left inspired among the gentry plans for a more responsible government.

But why did Ivan the Terrible not strike? Why did he wait for a warrior king on the Polish throne? It was perhaps one of the errors that shape history.

The lords of Wilno played a skillful game, hinting to Ivan that he might become the grand duke of Lithuania, perhaps even king. Ivan hoped that the disarray of the interregnum might break up the union and give him Lithuania.

Alarmed by the threat, the gentry took prompt action. Within a week of the king's death the knights of the province of Cracow proclaimed the first "captur," that is a provincial confederacy for the defense of the country and the enforcement of public order during the interregnum. A network of such bodies soon extended all over the country. Jan Zamoyski, the sheriff of Belz, who was just starting his ascent to power and statesmanship, declared, "Whoever disturbs the peace, robs or kills, will be proclaimed an outlaw, slain, and his property confiscated." Every province established courts to guard law and order. Zamoyski demanded that all penalties of the law be doubled for the duration of the interregnum. Squadrons of mounted gentry and detachments of the magnates' private troops patrolled the highways. It was not a good time for foreign visitors, for they were stopped and searched without regard to rank, even the clergy.

No outside enemy attacked Poland, as every one of the neighboring Christian monarchs aspired to the Polish crown for himself or his son. The Sultan of Turkey did not want war and had no hostile intentions, but wished to see a Frenchman on the Polish throne.

Domestic peace was ensured by the citizens, unanimous in their determination to defend the borders and their respect for the law within them. There was little agreement, however, on other issues. The arsenals amassed in the country castles and mansions never harmed anyone; to the amazement of foreign observers, there was no internal conflict or bloodshed.

Yet a political contest for power and the direction of national policy was in progress, with the "party of reaction," as it was called by later historians, particularly active.

Actually it would be inaccurate to speak about parties in the modern meaning of the term, as they were rather class groups with their own goals. The reformist gentry continued its momentum, mindful of earlier disappointments and frustrations. The "execution" movement had peaked earlier, under Zygmunt August. Nevertheless the older leaders and their younger followers were still calling for a "correction of the laws." The most jealously guarded among them was religious freedom. It divided the nation into two factions, opposing each other without resorting to violence. The bishops, hostile to the principle of religious tolerance, were ready to frustrate the program of reform and call to the throne a monarch likely to enforce orthodoxy and the dominance of Catholic faith. On the other hand, the defense of religious tolerance inclined some Protestant magnates to side with the reform-minded gentry.

In July 1572 the papal legate, Francis Commendone, was on his way from Poland to Rome. The news of the king's death reached him when he had already left Cracow. Commendone immediately changed his plans and turned back, in order to be able to direct personally the "party of reaction," of which he was the moving spirit.

The Commonwealth was participating in the strife that was shaking all of Europe. Nine years earlier the Council of Trident concluded without enunciating any new dogmas, but strengthening considerably the organiztion of the church. A campaign for recapturing the ground lost to the Reformation (and earlier the "Schism") was waged throughout the continent, including Poland. The throne of Cracow was an important strategic position in that war of ideas. To place on it a militant Catholic, to curb the ideological laxity of the gentry and win a major state for the counter-reformation—these were the goals in the pursuit of which Cardinal Commendone postponed his return to Italy and remained in Tyniec, later in Sulejow. He dispatched to Vienna, however, one of his diplomatic aides, Anthony Mario Graziani, whose mission was to induce Emperor Maximilian II to take strong action, mainly by assembling considerable funds and a military force in Wroclaw. The best way to achieve the objectives of the Holy See was to install at Wawel Castle a Habsburg monarch.

The situation had changed radically since the time when Jacob Uchanski, excommunicated by Rome for seizing his diocese by force, responded to the pope by excommunicating him in Lowicz and burning his effigy. The Polish clergy abandoned the idea of a national church, which would have enabled them to keep at least some of their privileges and estates. Rome was now taking a tough line, witness the harsh treatment of Bishop Drohojowski, guilty of insubordination. The reform at the head of the church inspired the clergy with new militancy, in the hope of restoring the age of the powerful princes of the church, such as Cardinal Olesnicki. The episcopate opposed the reform movement of the partly Protestant gentry, finding natural allies among the magnates. The program of the "execution of the laws" had reduced somewhat the holdings of the clergy, while the leading lords were alarmed by the rising ambitions of the parliament of the gentry. In the countries under Habsburg rule the aristocracy held a position privileged under the law above the rest of the nobility. The democracy of the gentry, proclaiming the equality of even the humblest squire and a magnate with vast estates, was unacceptable to the lords. Some of the magnates even acquired estates in Habsburg lands and moved there permanently. The Rozrazewski clan, for example, did so and its younger members even abandoned the Polish language.

Peace at the borders and within the country did not mean domestic harmony, and a confrontation was approaching between the two camps, both of them bearing swords. The clergy, prohibited from doing so, had armed men in their service.

Before electing a king, it was necessary to decide where and how the election was to be held. The immediate problem was the choice of a regent who would assume provisional power prior to the election. The two candidates for that position were: the primate of Poland, Archbishop Jacob Uchanski, and the grand marshal of the crown, Jan Firlej, a Protestant. The positions were clearly polarized. The elevation of a Protestant to the office of interrex would emphasize the Commonwealth's independence and set the political climate of the election.

The contest caused some feuds among the magnates, focusing not so much on the rivalry itself as its side effects. The grand marshal was opposed by Piotr Zborowski, himself a Protestant, who aspired to the *voievodship* of Cracow. Shortly before his death, Zygmunt August appointed to that office Jan Firlej. Zborowski, deeply offended, withdrew his support for Firlej and even made some friendly gestures toward the primate. The balance of power shifted in Uchanski's favor.

An ongoing contest for personal advancement is a perennial feature of the political scene in all countries at all times.

The conventions convoked by Firlej at Cracow and Knyszyn designated Bystrzyca near Lublin as the site of the election, scheduled for October 13. But other decisions were made at Lowicz and Kaski near Sochaczew, where meetings were held under the auspices of the primate Uchanski. In Kaski the senators of both parties voted for the capital of Masovia, Warsaw, as the election site. The Zborowski diversion weakened the position of Firlej, who had to recognize Uchanski's primacy. The convocation Seym was to open its session on January 6, 1573, and the hope of a brief interregnum was abandoned.

The dispute over the location of the election was not merely formal. According to some, Europe ended at the line of the Vistula. That may have been true prior to A.D. 1500, but not after it. In the period under review the province of Lublin, east of the Vistula, shared in the cultural life of the whole European continent and was its integral part. Historians find evidence to that effect in many documents of the period, among them the papers of Jan Osmolski, a squire and member of the Seym. There are among them letters from Calvin himself, the elders of the Italian Protestant church of Geneva, an official act of faith of the Lublin Calvinists addressed to their brethren in Zurich, and many others.

Lublin was at the time the geographical center of the Commonwealth. The region was prosperous and was developing rapidly. There were several schools, among them the Calvinist college of Lubartow, later taken over by the Arians to achieve wide academic renown. There were in the Lublin province many foreigners, mainly

Dutchmen and Scotsmen exiled from their countries as religious dissidents. The local Jewish community was entering a period of cultural growth, with a Talmudistic academy founded in Lublin in 1567 and headed by the famous Solomon Luria. In many small towns and villages, now insignificant and forgotten, Protestant synods were held, conducting debates of interest to the whole country and perhaps to other European nations. Belzyce and Bychow were among the centers of such activities.

At one of the synods theorecticians boldly proclaimed that:

> It ill behooves the gentry to feed upon the sweat of the brows of their subjects and they should labor themselves. It is also improper to live on land granted to your forebears for spilling blood. Sell such estates and distribute the proceeds to the poor.

Such principles failed to get unanimous support, but both their champions and their opponents "parted in love without reaching any conclusions."

It is open to doubt whether the Arians could have saved the state. They were divided as to the proper behavior of Christians in time of war. The moderates held it permissible to participate, but only as noncombatants in the rear. Actual fighting should be left to the papists, the Orthodox, Calvinists, and Lutherans.

More significant than the particular doctrines advocated, there was the general moral climate of the Lublin region, selected by the reform movement as the election site in the expectation that the convention would be attended by most of the local gentry. They were people receptive to pluralist ideas, open debate, and discussion of first principles. They accepted opposition and criticism in accordance with their doctrine of free expression. Only fifteen miles west of Lublin, at Babin, a group of satirically minded political writers and politicans founded a mock "Babin Commonwealth," with its own Seym and Senate. The speeches delivered there were a parody of those in the real parliament. It was also called the "Republic of Jesters" and was a unique example of political wit and tolerance, as it included Catholics and Protestants of all denominations, sharing a keen sense of humor. Zygmunt August once asked the founder of the "Republic of Jesters" when it would elect one among them as their king. "As long as you are there, Sire, we don't have to," was the reply.

Lublin and its region were a lively center of intellectual ferment and free debate, but the Kaski convention decided to hold the election in Masovia.

That province was unique in having a "viceroy," Stanislaw Pobog Lawski. None of the other provinces had such an office, but Masovia had joined the kingdom fairly recently, under Zygmunt the Old, and the survival of its viceroy was not the only trace of its status as a recent member of the Commonwealth. After the death of the last of the Jagiellonians, the other provinces started promptly to hold *capturs*, a kind of primaries. Some did so already in July, but Masovia waited until November.

It was a province with little initiative, passive and submissive to its leaders. It had not yet fully assimilated the freedoms of the Commonwealth and certainly did not contribute to them. The pastor of the Plock cathedral, to say nothing of the bishop, was such a powerful dignitary that the office was sometimes sought more eagerly than some dioceses. Even the gentry had to submit to his will and the enforcement of the decree of Zygmunt the Old, prohibiting the residence of "heretics" in Masovia, was responsible for the banishment of the only Protestant in the province.

In the following year the *voievodship* of Plock protested violently against the legislation on religious tolerance. It did so after the election, but the action reflected the attitudes which influenced the selection of Masovia as its site.

The Masovian declaration of protest claimed that the principle of freedom of thought and expression was sure to bring about divine wrath in the form of the nation's downfall.

> Should we, peaceful people, treasuring the welfare of the Commonwealth above everything else, permit something that is certain to bring about the decline and fall of the Polish crown? What could be more shameful than to mete out punishment to one who steals a cow, pig, or goat, letting go free those who desecrate churches, drive out priests, dishonor the saints and the holiest Virgin, Mother of God? Those guilty of blasphemy in concert with evil spirits will go unpunished!

The declaration went on to argue that freedom of religion allows the Protestants to believe only the words of the Gospel and asked, "In which of the psalms did King David promise the knights pay-

24

ment of five *grzywna* for serving abroad? If everyone will be free to take whatever religion he chooses, the king may also change his faith and renege the coronation oath to stop paying five *grzywna* per lance."

The speech of the castellan of Smolensk quoted earlier reached us in the form of a parody by one of the jesters of the "Babin Commonwealth." But the text of the Masovian protest is authentic. Even though central Poland was culturally well ahead of the rest of the Commonwealth, it also had its enclaves of backwardness.

The Kaski convention, controlled by Commendone, determined that the election Seym would be attended by more Masovians than delegates from more distant provinces, such as the progressive Lublin region.

Yet there were similarities between Masovia and Lublin, for both had large contingents of petty nobility, who had never had any serfs but tilled their own holdings. Thus historical background rather than social structure proved to be the decisive factor.

The Convocation Seym held its session at the appointed date in January 1573 in Warsaw. The election was set for April and its site was to be the village of Kamien, near the Praga suburb of Warsaw. The primate was confirmed in his position of interrex or regent. The Seym also set down the rules of the royal election, adopting the "viritim" principle proclaimed under Zygmunt the Old and never abrogated, owing to his son's culpable negligence and despite attempts by the Seym. "Viritim" meant that every member of the nobility of the Commonwealth was entitled to participate in the election and vote. The emphasis it placed on the multinational character of the Commonwealth was the only positive feature of that provision, for the mass attendance of the gentry counterbalanced the centrifugal ambitions of the magnates. The proposal to make attendance compulsory was rejected as obviously impractical. Consequently it was clear that the Masovians, whose province hosted the election, would attend in the largest numbers.

Jan Zamoyski has been thought, erroneously, to be the author of the "viritim" concept. The future chancellor had actually suggested election by an electoral college and received immediate support from six provinces. It was Piotr Zborowski, endorsed by Firlej, who proposed election by universal referendum and unanimity. Both magnates were seeking popularity among the gentry.

In Lithuania the powerful clans of the Radziwill and

Chodkiewicz were in total control, as was the case to a large extent in Royal Prussia. In Poland proper this was impossible; there the magnates had to pretend to be very democratic and indulged in demagoguery. Zborowski and Firlej were endeavoring to win over the mass of the gentry, away from the primate's influence.

When the "viritim" slogan caught on, Zamoyski changed his tactics. The graduate of the university of Padua, learned in history and law, was also a skillful politician who would not let anyone outbid him. He supported the "viritim" principle, with the provision of election by majority vote, but the proposal failed. It should have been adopted earlier, at the regular session of the Seym, which anyway had always counted votes, but the interregnum fever did not favor sensible proposals. It is all the more remarkable that despite the restless atmosphere so much was achieved.

The convocation Seym opened its session on January 28, 1573. The act of the Warsaw confederacy was drafted and adopted by majority vote.

"Living in this dangerous time without a monarch to rule us," the document stated, "all the estates of the one and indivisible Commonwealth hereby resolve to elect jointly their king. None of the provinces has any priority in that respect. The new monarch will have to swear not to drag us outside the boundaries of the Commonwealth, either by royal entreaty or by payment of five *grzywna* per lance, nor to call a general levy without the Seym's consent."

The gentry thus institutionalized pacifism by law. It was very anxious to avoid the paths of war.

The section of the act which gave it durable historic importance read:

> Since there is in our Commonwealth much dissent in matters of the Christian religion, eager to avoid harmful strife among our citizens, such as we clearly observe in other realms, we pledge ourselves and our successors, under solemn oath and upon our honor, that those who are *dissidentes de religione* will keep peace among them and neither spill blood nor penalize anyone by confiscation, prison, or exile for reasons of difference of belief, nor assist any office in such actions.

At the same time—to be exact, five months earlier— on August 28, 1572, a royal decree in Paris banned any Protestant meetings, sermons, or services in France. It was issued four days after Saint

Bartholomew's Night. The decree confirmed the edict of Compiegne, enacted sixteen years before, which ordained only one penalty for the open or clandestine profession of heresy: death.

The authors of the resolution of the Warsaw Confederacy did indeed "observe clearly" what was happening in "other realms."

The Confederacy was supported by the majority of the gentry and the secular senators, while the episcopate was in opposition. The act of religious tolerance was signed by only one bishop, Francis Krasinski of Cracow. The gentry of Silesia also protested vehemently against freedom of conscience for heretics, using the arguments quoted earlier. Tolerance did not enjoy universal approval and had to be fought for. At any rate it was the will of the majority, though no actual vote was taken.

No country in the world had enacted up to that time any legislation comparable to that of the Warsaw Confederacy. In France it was not until 1788, just prior to the Revolution, that religious pluralism was legalized, though without granting full equality to the Protestants. In Denmark religious freedom was granted to the Jews in 1824 and to Catholics in 1849. In England, Catholics were granted equality of political rights in 1829.

The equal rights legislation of the Warsaw Confederacy was so far ahead of its time that it should have brought Poland more acclaim and glory than a dozen battlefield victories, but Europe paid it little heed since the Commonwealth began to lose its battles.

Domestically, the policy of religious tolerance served well the national interest, by bringing to the fore moderation and sober rationality. Respect for other faiths curbed ideological demagoguery and favored a conciliatory settlement of other social and political problems. Speaking of the Commonwealth, we often call it simply Poland. But in that vast state stretching from Pomerania to the Ukrainian steppes ethnic Poles accounted for no more than 40 percent of the population. While the act of religious tolerance addressed mainly the Protestant denominations, the problem of its citizens of the Orthodox faith was perhaps even more vital for the Commonwealth. It was not acute, because even in the absence of specific legislation, the Orthodox faith had been traditionally respected by the Polish crown. That was the case until the fanaticism of the counter-reformation exacerbated the situation, triggering a reaction by the Orthodox population, which shook the Commonwealth in the seventeenth century.

In the area of international relations, the spirit of the Warsaw

Confederacy could offer chances of salvation. Europe was then progressively splitting into two camps: the Catholics and the dissident denominations. The Commonwealth adjoined the predominantly Catholic Habsburg empire along only a small fraction of its borders—in Silesia—while it was surrounded elsewhere by non-Catholics. Poland was thus a candidate for the role of a bastion of papacy encircled by "heretics"—a situation hardly conducive to peace or even to the Commonwealth's survival. Its neighbors were, starting from the west: Brandenburg, Ducal Prussia – with Sweden in the background, Moscow, the Tartars, Turkey, Hungary – where the nobility was mostly Calvinist, and traditionally dissident Bohemia. These nations of diverse faiths were nevertheless capable of uniting against a militantly Catholic Poland. As a nation open to all faiths, Poland stood a better chance of coming to an understanding with at least some of her neighbors and thus surviving. Religious fanaticism almost insured destruction. The question whether the Commonwealth was to be a pluralistic society or an outpost of Rome was one of life and death.

The act of the Confederacy contains an article which was sometimes misinterpreted. The research of Joseph Siemienski dispelled the doubt when he discovered the original document with many seals, but "so faded that only shadows of letters or strokes of the pen could be discerned." This was not surprising, as already an inventory made in 1730 mentions "a parchment instrument, defaced by water, because it was on the floor since the fire at the castle of Cracow." The law of 1573 ruled out failure by the peasants to perform their duties of servitude on religious grounds, but it also prohibited the landowners from imposing any religious faith on their subjects.

The ink on the parchment of the Confederacy was still fresh when, in January 1573, the sister of the deceased monarch, Anna Jagiellon, still a spinster at about fifty, came to Warsaw from her estate. The senators were quick to pay their respects to the royal princess whose dynasty had reigned for two centuries.

The country was humming with political debate, which reached even the most remote villages. The first election of a king was the heyday of political pamphleteering. The right to publish freely even the boldest political views and engage in lively polemics was the uncontested privilege of every citizen. Poland was at that time perhaps the most democratic nation in Europe. The pamphlets, treatises, poems, and proclamations of that period were collected by Jan Czunek and published recently in a large volume of seven hundred pages, *The Political Writings of the First Interregnum.*

The Poles were then still free of many complexes that the future was to bring. A squire from the Kalisz district in western Poland insisted in his publications that "Moscow is good and can set everything right," a view shared by many in the provinces distant from Russia. Lithuanians, especially the magnates, did not accept such illusions. In western Poland, however, many believed that an association with the eastern power could help Poland to recapture the territories lost in the west since Lokietek's reign: Silesia, Pomerania.

Their dream was that of another union, a repeat performance of one that had worked well. But another writer warned of its dangers: "Poland, Lithuania and Russia joined together? Who could rule such a giant? Give us Theodore, not Ivan; the son instead of the father, who is old anyway."

The Moscow candidacy had a good chance, but it was turned down by the tsar himself. Ivan the Terrible did not want the Polish throne and proposed conditions unacceptable to a Catholic nation. He demanded to be crowned at the Wawel not by the primate from Gniezno, but by the Orthodox metropolitan from the Kremlin. That was what he told the Lithuanian envoy, Michael Halaburda, himself of the Orthodox faith. He conveyed to him through the boyars, as a parting message, that he would gladly accept the rule of Lithuania and even promised that he would then regain for it the provinces lost through the Lublin Union: Wolyn, Podole, and Kiev.

No promises could seduce the Lithuanian lords, who were well aware of the treatment received at Ivan's hands by the Russian boyars. Many Poles also knew what to expect of Ivan the Terrible. Only two years earlier the first Polish embassy to negotiate with the tsar in Moscow returned home, bringing with it strange tales. During a formal banquet Ivan suddenly ordered one of his princes to "bare his arse" and jump around the hall on all fours. This was one of the mildest ways the tsar used to subdue his boyars.

No one denied these facts, but it was argued that Jagiello had been not only a pagan, a savage and cruel ruler, but also a patricide, since he had killed his uncle. Yet he mellowed after settling in Poland.

"It is clear" wrote Andrew Maximilian Fredro, "that a monarch becomes kind and just, or savage and brutal, depending on the education and character of the people who called him to power."

The Commonwealth believed in the ennobling power of freedom and the rule of law, citing its own history as an example.

Ivan the Terrible told Halaburda that if Poland and Lithuania decide to maintain their union and choose a joint monarch, they would do best by electing the emperor's son, Ernest Habsburg. The tsar's advice suited well the sentiments of most of the Lithuanian magnates and some Polish ones. In the spring of 1572, when Zygmunt August was still living, the papal legate, Commendone, and his aide, Anthony Maria Graziani, met secretly with Mikolaj Krzysztof Radziwill ("the Orphan") and Jan Chodkiewicz. The Lithuanian lords proposed that upon the death of King Zygmunt August, Ernest Habsburg be proclaimed grand duke of Lithuania, without prior consultation with the Poles, who would be compelled to recognize the *fait accompli*. If they should refuse to recognize Ernest, the union would be dissolved. That idea did not appeal to the Vatican, which wanted a Catholic Habsburg at the head of the vast Commonwealth and did not favor its breakup to satisfy the ambitions of the Lithuanian magnates.

Commendone soon afterward sent Graziani to Vienna, advising prompt action and the readying of troops and funds. He knew that the defense of the Wawel against a German candidate was perceived by the Polish gentry as a sacred duty. It was the subject of ardent debate throughout Poland. It is significant, though seldom recollected, that the example of Bohemia played a key role in shaping Poland's policies then and on many subsequent occasions. "Look," it was said, "what happened to that fraternal nation under the Germans. One city in three at most remained Czech. Their arsenals were dismantled, their defense walls demolished, the emperor tore up their charters and oppresses the people. The same is true of Hungary. Do you want this to happen to us?"

The gentry was convinced that under a Habsburg the Commonwealth would not only lose its civil rights and freedom, but also its political independence. Though ostensibly still a sovereign state, it would be ruled by foreigners and serve their interests. Such fears were well founded.

The hatred of the Germans for the Slavs was also cited, with their record of invasions, atrocities, and depredations.

There was no doubt that a Habsburg on the throne would mean

war with the sultan of Turkey, but what alarmed the Polish and Ruthenian gentry was viewed by the Vatican as a desirable goal. It wanted the Commonwealth to fight against the infidel. Accordingly, the Polish episcopate, influenced by the papal legate, favored the Habsburg candidate.

Fortunately another candidate came to the fore, bringing with him counter-reformation credentials no one could match. He was the younger brother of Charles IX, king of France, Henry d'Anjou of the Valois line. On March 27, 1570, the prince, then only nineteen, received from the pope a sword and hat in recognition of his victory over the French Protestants at Moncontour. The standards taken in that battle were hung in the Lateran palace in Rome. More recently, just after the death of Zygmunt August, the prince won honors as one of the organizers of the terrible massacre of the dissidents, known in France as the Huguenots. The slaughter started in Paris at 4 A.M. on August 24, 1572, and passed into history as Saint Bartholomew's Night.

The advocates of counter-reformation could hardly fault such a candidate for want of Catholic fervor. Fortunately for the Commonwealth, the rivalry between him and Archduke Ernest became a personal political contest, without ideological overtones, since both princes were militant Catholics.

Already three years earlier the court of Istanbul decided to promote the French candidacy to the Polish throne. Henry's country was called the senior daughter of the church and its king was styled the archcatholic monarch. Nevertheless, France, oblivious of religious considerations in foreign affairs, was Turkey's ally.

Ivan the Terrible had ominously told Haraburda that if the Commonwealth should elect a Frenchman, "I will have to give you some thought." The tsar also wanted to embroil his neighbor in a war with Turkey.

Two other men aspired to the Polish crown: the king of Sweden, John III, husband of Catherine Jagiello; and an insignificant minor prince, the ruler of Transylvania and a vassal of the Sultan (and secretly of the emperor as well), Stefan Batory of Somlyo. Both had minimal chances, while the tsar ruled himself out by failing to send even an ambassador, so the princes Henry and Ernest were the only two serious contestants.

The election was to be held on a vast field, in the center of which a huge tent was erected to serve the debates of the senate and the delegates of the gentry. Around it other tents were placed, one for each of the thirty-two administrative districts of the Commonwealth. The electoral field was placed on the right, sparsely populated bank of the Vistula, so that most of the participants had to cross the river. In February and March workers were busy completing the construction of the impressive first permanent bridge on the Vistula, started by Zygmunt August. It was completed by Anna Jagiello, using her own funds. Her already great popularity was enhanced by that gesture.

Anna Jagiello was in the eyes of the overwhelming majority of the gentry the only lawful moral heiress of the royal dynasty. People wanted to see at the Wawel castle a king's daughter, born there, as the only person capable of ensuring the continuity of the crown and the Commonwealth. Attachment to the dynasty had taken deep roots in the Commonwealth and became a moral imperative superseding written laws.

Under law the sister of the deceased king was a private individual. The easiest key to the throne was a wedding ring. The candidate who married the royal princess would be assured of unanimous support. The princess was twenty-eight years older than Henry de Valois and thirty years older than Ernest Habsburg. The archduke was a grandson of her cousin. Aging and plain, the princess ardently desired marriage, the more so as it would bring her to front stage for the first time in her life.

The senators—men beyond the reach of mystical traditionalism—were aware of the hazards of the situation. Everyone remembered Zygmunt August's erratic matrimonial behavior and it was feared that the princess might follow her brother's example. "You shall not choose our lord, Your Highness, for our eternal perdition and we will not spare our blood in fighting against it," said Bishop Stanislaw Karnkowski (who had been worrying only a few months earlier about the king's demented plans of marriage with Barbara Giza).

The royal princess was compelled by the senators to keep away from the election in Blon, and later in Plock and Lomza. Nevertheless, both the French and Austrian envoys managed to reach her secretly. Both proposed marriage to their respective candidates. It was then decided to send her further away, to Krasnystaw or Leczyca, but the tough lady refused to comply. She went of her own accord to Piaseczno and then returned to Warsaw, where the royal castle had long been her residence. She meant to take an active part in the political game. The senators knew that she had the support of the gentry and the princess herself was well aware of her strong position.

The ambassadors of the powers concerned had been in Poland since the fall, but they were kept away from Warsaw. The papal legate was assigned a residence in Sulejow, but Commendone sneaked away secretly for his meetings with the princess.

The best public relations move of the emperor was to appoint as his envoys two Czechs. One of them, William of Rozemberk, became so popular that a group of Polish gentry unexpectedly proposed him as a candidate. Both Czechs were well disposed toward the Commonwealth and, when drinking one night with the senators, they actually warned them against the Habsburgs.

Recent historical studies ascribe a key role in the election to bribery. This seems a superficial view of history. Accepting money for political favors was common, even universal at the time. The papal legate Francisco Commendone, the stalwart champion of counter-reformation, was on his second assignment in Poland. He had left it before as inflexible as when he came, but with a lifetime pension from Zygmunt August, whose actions he was supposed to oversee on behalf of the Vatican. Citizens of the Commonwealth accepted gifts from foreigners, but also gave them. They were neither more nor less virtuous than all the other politicians of sixteenth-century Europe.

Economic considerations did play an important role in the election. Philip Erlanger, a modern French historian, summed up succinctly the appeal of Henry de Valois: "The dazzled Poles visualized their grain, salted meat, leather, and other goods reaching through the Ottoman empire the rich market of the queen of the Adriatic, where any merchandise found a buyer." The French connection promised the possibility of peaceful cooperation with Turkey, the opening of the river Dniester as a commercial trade route, and the development of the rich resources of the southeastern provinces of the Commonwealth.

The first political treaty between Poland and France had been concluded by Jan Olbracht, following which, various matrimonial and other deals between the two nations were often suggested. The Polish gentry viewed with respect a dynasty which had held the Paris throne continuously since the tenth century. Such perceptions may appear today as mere snobbery, but they carried much weight in the sixteenth century. One of the potent arguments against the election of a native Polish monarch was that he would enjoy little respect among the kings of the neighboring nations, being not of royal blood. The Vasa kings of Sweden, for example, were considered upstarts by the monarchs of Europe. Ivan the Terrible sneered at Zygmunt August for having given his sister in marriage to a wretched commoner from Stockholm. He regarded himself as superior to all, since he claimed to be the lawful heir of Julius Caesar and Octavian Augustus. Henry de Valois, a descendant of Hugo Capet, was thought capable of enhancing the prestige of the Polish crown. His accession to the throne of Wawel would mean an alliance with France, which could offer to Poland two tangible foreign policy benefits: peace with Turkey and the outflanking of the emperor, who still failed to recognize Poland's legitimate rights in Gdansk, Malbork, Torun, and Elblag. The Order of the Cross still existed as a part of the German empire.

The French claim to the Polish throne was actively promoted by the bishop of Valentia, Jean de Montluc, who resided in Konin in central Poland. He arrived in the fall, following an unofficial mission that had prepared the ground for him. As a result he enjoyed the support of the chancellor, Valentine Dembinski, and the former courtiers of Zygmunt August, now backing his sister.

Montluc had already displayed earlier in France his outstanding talents as a diplomat and politician, which he used to the full in Poland. He knew that it was a country in which much could be achieved by skillful persuasion and good public relations. He accepted meekly all the rulings of the senate and carefully avoided giving offense to anyone. Quick to appreciate the freedom of expression prevailing in Poland, he sponsored political publications appealing to the gentry, using the services of Jan Dymitr Solkowski, a talented writer.

The French ambassador had to cope with some factors damaging to his cause. His arrival coincided with the news of Saint Bartholomew's Night, which was received in Poland with horror and disgust. Montluc managed to convince the gentry that Henry de Valois was innocent of any involvement in the massacre and, despite his status of a bishop, he distanced himself from the papal legate and even avoided any display of Catholic religious practices or undue zeal.

The Catholics were obviously inclined to side with the Valois prince, but many Protestants also supported him on purely political grounds. Some of them used arguments reminiscent of those advanced by supporters of Ivan the Terrible: Whether guilty or not of the Paris massacre, he could not repeat it here, for we would not let him. If he should break or bend the law, the nation was capable of turning against him in force.

In April about fifty thousand authorized voters appeared on the election field, all of them armed. Their aides and servants constituted another throng at least as numerous. The nonvoting attendants devised an unusual entertainment: While their masters were engaged in the real election, they held a mock one, burning in effigy the candidates they disliked. There is no record of anyone being punished for such playful tricks—the example of the "Babin Republic" was by then evidently part of Polish custom.

Foreigners were amazed by two phenomena. The debates lasted several weeks and during that time the vast assembly of men and horses, next to a town of ten thousand inhabitants, never lacked for provisions or fodder and feasted freely. Another surprise was the fact that in that crowd of thousands of well-armed men assembled for a political purpose not a shot was fired nor a sword drawn in anger. Debate was confined to an exchange of views and verbal threats at most. "The Polish nation is peaceful and far removed from domestic strife," reported an eyewitness, Antonio Maria Graziani.

The gentry of Masovia was the most vocal group at the electoral camp. It demanded to a man the immediate election of the Frenchman. Asked for the reason for such unanimity, the Masovians replied candidly that they were simply following the wish of the late king's sister, the royal princess, Anne Jagiello.

The envoys of Bishop de Montluc contacted the princess at her Warsaw castle and convinced her that the young Prince Henry longed for her hand and the crown was only a means to that end. A fairytale came to life in a real political contest. The French candidacy had good chances even before, but the loud voice of tens of thousands of Masovians tilted the balance in its favor.

The gentry of Masovia has been sometimes characterized unfairly as anarchic. Actually it was quite the opposite, perhaps too disciplined. The poorly educated petty squires were inclined to accept the advice of their pastor, bishop, or governor, following it as a crowd rather than as individuals.

Since the death of King Zygmunt the Old, his widow, Queen Bona (of the Italian house of Sforza), resided in Masovia. Three of her daughters married kings: Isabel, that of Hungary; Sofia, the duke of Brunswick; and Catherine, the king of Sweden. Only Princess Anna remained single and lived in Warsaw, where over twenty five years she built a strong following. By urging the Masovians to vote for Henry de Valois, she fell unwittingly into a trap.

The French prince received an overwhelming majority of votes and the primate Uchanski, long influenced by Montluc, immediately proclaimed him king. Summoned to Warsaw, the French ambassador started by wriggling out of his earlier promises, notably that concerning the marriage with the royal princess of Poland—a matter he left to Henry's personal decision. This did not unduly worry the senators, who saw their political position enhanced.

At the last moment the election assumed an aspect that alarmed the foreigners unfamiliar with the local conditions. Marshal Jan Firlej assembled the Protestants and headed them in a demonstration against the attempt to delete from the list of conditions to which Henry had to swear, the article dealing with freedom of religion. The Polish bishops were not upset by the sight of Firlej's forces. Though opposed to the Warsaw confederacy, they had no intention of starting a civil war. Finally the article on freedom of religious faith remained among the "Pacta Conventa," prompting the papal legate to observe that "a law has no value, unless adopted unanimously." This early statement in favor of the "liberum veto" was offered to the crowd by the leader of the faction opposed to freedom of conscience.

The conditions set for Henry were comprised in two documents. One, later known as the "Henrician Covenant," was to remain binding in perpetuity. The other, given the neutral name of "Pacta Conventa," contained only the specific conditions set for the candidate. In future elections new "Pacta Conventa" would be enacted.

Both documents as a whole presented Europe with an astounding phenomenon that aroused the interest of the leading political theorists at the time. It was no less than a freely contracted agreement between the king and his subjects, setting the limits of his power. Such a constitutional method of regulating governmental authority won the encomiums of western thinkers who might be regarded as the forerunners of the Enlightment.

Viewing the situation from a perspective of centuries, we are struck by the enormity of the task faced by the gentry assembled at the election field. Without any guidelines, acting in haste and amidst conditions of chaos and unrest, it had to compose and enact what was in effect a constitution. No one had even thought at the time of setting down in a single document the framework of the state and its functions. The scholars of the west questioned the name of "Republic" or "Commonwealth" given to the Jagiellonian monarchy, claiming that in accordance with the tradition of antiquity that term could describe only a single city. The Republic of Venice could not serve as an example to the contrary, for its political structure applied to the metropolis but not to its other possessions.

The earliest formal constitutions of major nations were those of the United States and France, both enacted toward the end of the eighteenth century. The first formal constitution in Europe was that of May 3, 1791, in Poland, which remained in force for only one year. Yet the Commonwealth of Both Nations did promulgate a basic law two centuries earlier, even though it was not called a constitution. Before that act the laws defending the functions of the state were an accumulation of legal acts enacted over a long period of time. That system still prevails in Great Britain, whose constitution is not a book but a library.

The "Henrician Covenant," however, went only halfway, for it defined the king's obligations but not his rights. This was due to the fact that little time was available for codifying the basic laws of the state. The champions of reform were planning to complete that task after the election. In the meantime, granting the crown to a foreigner, they had to protect the country against his arbitrary behavior and induce him to cooperate with the citizenry, leaving other reforms to their future collaboration with him.

The study of expediency is the best guide to the labyrinths of history—meaning both political and personal self interest. People seldom act with a view to winning the approval of posterity; instead, they are mostly concerned with the interests of their own generation. That is why reform is a never-ending process.

The Polish gentry assembled at Kamien considered the candidacies of Ivan the Terrible, a Habsburg, or Henry de Valois.

The tsar was well aware of his reputation and even thought it necessary to apologize to the Polish ambassador for his cruelties. France impressed the Poles, but Henry came to Poland from a massacre of his Protestant countrymen. The rule of the Habsburgs in Bohemia was well known and the methods of that dynasty were best exemplified by Philip II, of whom it was said:

> He hardly ever appears in public and though he used to be seen by the people once or twice a year in the corridor connecting his palace with the church, he now remains secluded in his apartments.

It was there, in the closed chambers of a foreign monarch, that the fate of the Commonwealth would be decided. No one doubted that a Habsburg on the throne, if unrestricted, would mean war with Turkey. Domestically, it would be a triumph for the "Office of the Inquisition," which received from Philip II "protection and full support of its activities."

In the year of the election—1573—some armed units of the Polish crown went to Valachia to assist its ruler, the *hospodar*. The story of that expedition was written by Jan Lasicki, one of the many forgotten Polish writers of that era. He was a Protestant from western Poland, who had known Calvin and was a friend of his successor, Theodore Beza. He traveled widely and was the author of many works, some of them translated into foreign languages. They dealt with Gdansk, the customs of Moscow and the Tartars, the deities of Lithuania, the religion of the Armenians, the Baltic wars, and the reign of Stefan I, *hospodar* of Valachia. His *History of the Invasion of Valachia by the Poles*, later translated from Latin by the nineteenth-century writer Wladyslaw Syrokomla, contains information which may startle us, but not the Polish readers of the period, quite familiar with the conditions in what is today Rumania.

Lasicki reports that the hospodar:

> sentenced people to death for the slightest offence, had them skinned alive, impaled, their eyes gouged out (a common form of punishment in Valachia), their noses and ears cut off. Anyone found selling even a single branch from his vineyard, or anything subject to taxation, would be killed or mutilated by drawing a hook through his nostrils, or tied and taken to the torture. If not tortured, he could be chased through the streets by Gypsies and mercilessly flogged. What was most horrible was that the corpses of the victims were not buried, but left in streets

to provide fodder for the dogs and spread terror among the population.

Political control of authority was needed in the Commonwealth, as it was brutally abused in all the surrounding countries. In Poland, too, common-law criminals were tortured or publicly beheaded, while witches were burnt, but such atrocities were not common. The nation became accustomed during two centuries to Jagiellonian benevolence and had to build dikes to hold at bay the flood of tyranny.

Candidates to the throne had to be kept in check and that was the reason for the Henrician Covenant. It was also inspired by the recent memory of the bloodless but often arbitrary actions of the recently deceased native monarch, whose body was still waiting in Tykocin for burial. Tradition dictated that a king not be buried until his successor was crowned.

The Henrician Covenant provided that a free election should be held every time the throne became vacant. Interference with that procedure, or the designation of a successor during a king's lifetime, was prohibited. Two other articles outlined the basic principles of government recognized by the overwhelming majority of voting citizens. They confirmed the articles of the Warsaw Confederacy, that is, freedom of religion and pacifism as the guiding policy of the Commonwealth. The king was not allowed to declare war, call for a general levy of the gentry, or hire mercenaries without the consent of the Seym (parliament). That consent was also required for the imposition of taxes. The royal treasury was to provide for the protection of the borders and the maintenance of a small standing army. Except for an "urgent emergency," the Seym was to assemble every two years for a session not exceeding six weeks. It would then elect sixteen senators, who would serve successively at the royal court, supervising foreign policy and assisting at the reception of foreign ambassadors. They would, however, be acting in an advisory and not a decision-making capacity. If he could not secure their consent, the king could make his own decisions, thus retaining executive authority.

The memory of the last of the Jagiellonians inspired Article 16, which provided that the monarch could not "make any matrimonial decisions" without the advice and consent of the senators, nor seek separation or divorce.

The key article of the Covenant, known by its Latin wording as the article *de non praestanda oboedientia*, stated that "If, God forbid, we should violate or fail to abide by the laws, freedoms, articles and conditions herewith, the citizens of both nations shall be released from their oath of allegiance and obedience."

It was that article which gave to the Covenant the character of a contract rather than a mere promise.

The Pacta Conventa, applicable only to the candidate currently seeking the crown, required him to conclude a treaty of alliance with France, guaranteeing its diplomatic and military support in case of war. Paris would be required to send in case of need infantry troops to assist Poland, while the Commonwealth would reciprocate by sending, if required, Polish cavalry, which would have to be paid by the French.

The Pacta Conventa further stated that Henry should bring to Poland four thousand Gascon infantrymen (thought to be particularly brave) "for use against the Moscow prince." He was also expected to build for Poland a naval force, promote trade with France, pay the debts of Zygmunt August, bring in annually four hundred fifty thousand *zlotys* from his French revenues, educate at his cost a hundred sons of noblemen, and not promote or bring from abroad foreigners (with an exception, of which more later).

The Pacta Conventa were generally considered to bring little credit to their authors, too eager to shift to others the burdens of the state and emphasize financial matters. It was a well-founded criticism, but there were circumstances—not mitigating, but certainly explanatory—of such clauses.

Between Lesko and Sanok we can see to this day the ruins of a castle called Sobien, now hard to find, for the steep, picturesque hill is overgrown by trees and bushes. At its peak we find the ruins of a tower and a magnificent building of stone. The fortress built by Casimir the Great was destroyed in 1474 by the Hungarian forces of Matthew Corvin, which at that time had ravaged large areas of southern Poland. They were engaged in a war for the succession of the Polish crown prince, Casimir, to the throne of Hungary. The succession was its only motive, as there was no conflict of interest between Poland and Hungary.

The Commonwealth had a long experience of paying dearly in lives and money for the dynastic ambitions of its rulers. Inviting a foreigner to the Polish throne, it tried to reverse the trend by making others pay for the crown.

The constitutional consequences of the first election are often described by historians as deplorable, for they weakened the royal authority and thereby the state itself. That judgment is understandable for those viewing the situation from a perspective of centuries and aware of the subsequent course of Poland's history. It is, however, interesting to note what the contemporary political writers of Europe had to say about the Henrician Covenant and the Pacta Conventa.

The crown was awarded to Henry de Valois, a militant Catholic. It would seem that a political writer such as Anthony Maria Graziani would have deplored the restrictions of his freedom of action. Yet this is what he wrote at the time:

> The Poles are boasting that the authority of the king of the Commonwealth was circumscribed, with power remaining in the hands of the senate and the gentry. This is not true! Although they submitted themselves in correct proportion to the king and him to the rule of law, they were aiming not at subordinating the monarch to other authority, but at preventing unlimited power from being left at the mercy of the passions of an individual.

The papal nuncio Malaspina wrote much later, in 1598, with the benefit of the experience of a quarter of a century:

> Great is the power of the king, as well as that of the senate and the gentry, for no law can be binding without their consent, but the king's power is particularly great, for he holds in his hands the bread which he can give to whom he chooses.

Others argued that the power of the king of Poland was absolute in many areas, greater than that of other monarchs, for he remained the sole dispenser of offices and land grants. In skillful hands this was the most potent instrument.

The difference between our view and that of the politicians of four centuries ago is that they perceived the potential, the means at the disposal of the first elected monarch. We, on the other hand, know how these means were used, or not used.

41

The matter was best summed up by the Italian writer, John Botero, who said in 1592, "Finally, the king has as much power as his wisdom and skill will provide."

The constitutional structure of the state was not at fault. Its only shortcoming was the dangerous personalization of government, which made the nation's fate dependent on the personal qualities of the monarchs it would successively elect, particularly prior to the landmark date of 1648.

One of the conditions included in the Pacta Conventa stated: "His Majesty the King-elect shall improve the scholarly standards of the Cracow Academy, by bringing from all parts the most learned men, professors of all branches of knowledge, whom he will keep and maintain at the Cracow university in perpetuity."

It was one of the last attempts to revive the university in decline. The next—successful one—came two centuries later. The gentry assembled at the election field of Kamien showed concern for the university shamefully neglected by the previous monarchs.

KING HENRY

As soon as the result of the election was proclaimed, the bridge across the Vistula suffered a severe test as scores of thousands of hooves thundered over its wooden boards. The first election was held on the right bank of the river, unlike the subsequent ones. When the primate pronounced the name of Henry de Valois, Joachim Bielski reported:

> Pandemonium broke out amidst cries, as the sound of drums and trumpets was drowned by heavy gunfire, which continued for an hour. Then everyone rushed to the city on horseback, to sing "Te Deum" in St.John's cathedral. There was great joy and jubilation.

The news was greeted in France with relief. The queen mother, Catherine Medici, was triumphant. It was under her orders that Jean de Montluc performed miracles of diplomatic skill on the banks of the Vistula. The brilliant Italian with a viper's eyes, known in the West as "Madame la Serpente," was a veteran of the international power game. She evaluated the benefits of having the Commonwealth as an ally outflanking the Habsburgs from the east. It was

42

FORTIFIED COUNTRY HOUSE IN SZYMBARK

COURTYARD OF THE RADZIWILL PALACE OF NIESWIEZ

WOODEN ORTHODOX CHURCH, ULUCZ

TOWNHALL OF CHELMNO

J.M. PADOVANO. FRAGMENT OF SARCOPHAGUS OF ZOFIA OSTROGSKA

STANISLAW HOZJUSZ

ZYGMUNT III AS A CHILD, 1568

FRANCOIS QUESNEL.
PORTRAIT OF HENRI
DE VALOIS

DOORWAY OF THE COLLEGIATE OF ZAMOSC

STEFAN BATORY

PRINCE JANUSZ OSTROGSKI

CATHERINE RADZIWILL

STEFAN BATORY

COURTYARD OF THE CASTLE OF THE SZAFRANIEC CLAN IN PIESKOWA SKALA

ANNE JAGIELLO
IN WIDOW'S ATTIRE

H. WIERIX. PORTRAIT OF
HENRI DE VALOIS

ZUZANNA
OSTROGSKA

TOWNHALL OF TARNOW

FRAGMENT OF VALACHIAN CHURCH IN LWOW

CHURCH OF SAINTS PETER AND PAUL IN CRACOW

COURTYARD OF BARANOW CASTLE

said at the time in diplomatic circles, rather naively, that Poland could put in the field eighty thousand mounted men.

The king-elect received the good news at the walls of La Rochelle, which he had been besieging in vain for several months.

Two days after St.Bartholomew's Night, as the slaughter was still proceeding in the streets of Paris, Henry declared that the good work should be continued in the provinces. As a result, he was personally engaged in forcing the French to accept a single church.

Many cities resisted him. La Rochelle, an important port on the Atlantic coast, was filled with refugees from the region around it. Women and children, with such goods as they could save, sought asylum in the British Isles.

Before the arrival of Prince Henry and his forces, the garrison ravaged the country with religious fervor within a radius of twenty-five miles from the fortress, clearing the approaches.

La Rochelle was only theoretically under the sovereignty of the king of France. It negotiated independently with England and the Netherlands. Elisabeth of England received from the citizens of La Rochelle a letter in which they reminded her that the Atlantic coast of France had belonged at one time to the predecessors of Her Britannic Majesty. A naval force was being prepared on Guernsay (these details, reported in the work of Philip Erlanger, will be relevant to the Gdansk rebellion, of which more later).

The fire of the British ships offshore was ineffectual and the defenders, plagued by hunger and disease, valiantly repulsed the assaults, while plots proliferated among the attacking forces. Though united by common faith, the Catholic camp was consumed by mutual hatreds. A message was secretly passed to the Protestants within the walls to make a sortie and the youngest of the Valois, the duke of Alencon, would then attack the tents of his brother Henry. The Huguenots did not give credence to that outrageous proposal and remained in the fortress, but after they repelled the eighth assault, the situation changed dramatically.

Already in January 1573 Montluc wrote to Charles IX:

> If at any time between now and the election day any
> news of atrocities against the people of La Rochelle
> reaches Poland, believe me that even if [I] had ten million
> in gold to buy supporters, nothing would come of it.

Marcin Lesniowolski, the future castellan of Podlasie, a figure who was to play an important role in the third royal election but was then still only gathering experience and making a name for himself, appeared at La Rochelle in March. He was sent to France by two *voievodes* (provincial governors), Piotr Zborowski of Sandomierz and Mikolaj Maciejowski of Lublin. They were both Calvinists, but nevertheless supported Henry. Lesniowolski, who signed himself "of Obory," was called by the French "le sieur Martin de Obory." He reported the "amazing courage" of Prince Henry and also the fact that the city leaders were conferring with the enemies of the king of France. The latter news was an important argument in the eyes of the gentry assembled for the election. They were not accustomed to plotting with foreigners against one's own king.

On June 17 salvos of gunfire were heard in Henry's camp, but it was not another assault. They were greeting the "Polish Ambassador," Conrad Krupka-Przeclawski, who could not actually claim that title. He came with a retinue of seven armed men, but was only the unofficial envoy of Piotr Zborowski and other Polish Calvinists. He brought to Henry the news of his election and a request for maintenance of religious peace.

The guns at La Rochelle grew silent and the siege was lifted on July 6. Charles IX promptly proclaimed an edict allowing La Rochelle, Montauban, and Nimes to practice publicly their religion, as the Huguenots described their faith. Private services were permitted throughout the kingdom. Charles also hastily sent envoys to greet halfway the real embassy of the Commonwealth and advise it of these decisions, thus preempting their reproaches.

On August 19, 1573, the embassy arrived in Paris. It comprised eleven dignitaries, headed by Adam Konarski, bishop of Poznan, and accompanied by a hundred and fifty noblemen. The embassy was sumptuously welcomed by the royal prince, Francis de Bourbon, members of the French aristocracy, and the city council of Paris. After two days the Polish envoys were received at the Louvre by King Charles IX. Communication was mainly by sign language; all the Poles spoke Latin fluently, many of them also German, Italian, or French, but the courtiers and noblemen of Paris knew only their own language, subscribing to the notion that "a knight needs to know no more than to sign his name."

Foreign visitors in Poland were astounded by the linguistic versatility of its people. Latin was known not only by the clergy and nobility, but even by some artisans. German and Italian were widely known, while French—then considered a provincial language—somewhat less, though Zamoyski, for example, spoke it very well. The official address on behalf of the embassy was, however, delivered not by him but by Jan Tomicki, castellan of Gniezno and a Protestant.

Jacob Auguste du Thou reports that the embassy of the Commonwealth impressed the Parisians and even created a sensation. The Frenchmen were fascinated by the Polish noblemen's exotic and rich attire: sables, swords encrusted with jewels, silver-tipped boots, elaborately decorated bows and quivers. They also appreciated their education and bearing. Polish noblemen, extremely attentive when foreigners were their guests, were inclined to be haughty when abroad.

On September 10 a throng filled the cathedral of Notre Dame, where Henry was to swear his oath of acceptance of the Polish conditions. None of the Frenchmen present, who remembered vividly the recent St.Bartholomew's Night, expected what was about to happen.

Paris had just celebrated solemnly the first anniversary of the massacre. The ceremony was organized by the dukes de Guise, the most fervent Catholic leaders. They wanted to show to the Polish visitors how things stood in France. Much could also be read in the gesture of the pope, who sent to Henry on his return from La Rochelle the Order of the Golden Rose, far more prestigious than the swords of honor that he had given him earlier.

Acting under the pressure of the Polish envoys, the king lifted the siege of the Huguenot stronghold of Sancerre, which was barely holding out because of the desperate hunger in the besieged city. Despite the agreement with the defenders, the city had to pay a contribution and the royal troops committed acts of violence, including some murders. "The ministers of that city were quartered and the commander of the defense drawn by horses," reported one of the Poles to his friends at home.

He wrote his letter on August 31. Ten days later Henry was to swear to abide by a compact, one article of which guaranteed freedom of religion, conscience, and expression to the citizens of Poland. The prince tried to omit that article, evading the issue.

However, the envoys of the Commonwealth displayed a firmness that became less common among the Poles of later periods. They did not buckle under the pressure of their hosts. Jan Zborowski was the spokesman of the majority, not only of the Polish delegation in Paris, but also of the gentry at home. *"Si non iurabis, non regnabis,"* he told Henry bluntly in the presence of the French crowd filling the cathedral. "If you do not swear, you will not reign."

The prince yielded and the clause of religious tolerance was confirmed by oath.

Henry's resistance was not inspired by his French advisers alone. They were helped also by two Poles and one Lithuanian: Bishop Adam Konarski, Olbracht Laski, and Mikolaj Krzysztof Radziwill (The Orphan) had conferred earlier in Warsaw with the papal legate Commendone and hoped to nullify in Paris the Warsaw Confederacy with his blessings.

The Polish delegation was predominantly Catholic: out of its eleven members only four were Protestants. Nevertheless it carried out faithfully the will of the Polish people, who wanted religious tolerance. Jan Zamoyski, a Catholic himself, insisted sternly on respect for the instructions of Poland's parliament, the Seym.

But it was clear that the acceptance of the principles of the Warsaw Confederacy would not be won easily.

The Polish-Lithuanian mission brought to Paris the text of the Henrician Covenant, the Pacta Conventa and yet another document. It was called the "Postulata Polonica" and requested Charles IX to soften his policy toward the French protestants.

Paris had been forewarned, for Conrad Krupka-Przeclawski had mentioned the Postulata earlier. They were also known in other European countries. On their journey to Paris the envoys of the Commonwealth had conferred with French emigrés and with Protestant electors of the German empire. They heard their advice, but also their thanks to the "most devout, noble and brave Polish nation."

There are all kinds of political realism. The valid one, which requires no quotation marks, dictates that every move in favor of freedom brings a great benefit: public approval—for the simple reason that in the minds of most people "freedom" and "justice" mean the same thing.

The Postulata Polonica won wide acclaim for the Polish-Lithuanian Commonwealth. It was argued in Europe: Why cannot they get along peacefully in Paris, when people of different faiths live in harmony in Cracow? The example of a state in which the Catholic and Orthodox faiths have been peacefully coexisting for centuries was convincing. The Poles began to acquire at that time the reputation, not entirely deserved, of mild peacelovers.

Charles IX had been advised in advance of the Polish message. Anticipating its intervention and anxious to see his detested brother established far away on the Vistula, he lifted the siege of La Rochelle and issued the moderate edict.

The historian Waclaw Sobieski described in his book *Poland and the Huguenots After St.Bartholomew's Night* one of the copies of the Postulata Polonica kept at the British Museum. It carries marginal annotations by an anonymous Frenchman. One can understand the feelings of an embittered dissident, probably an emigré, who thought that the Poles were asking for too little. But the edict of Charles IX offered to the Huguenots even less, far less, though it outraged Spain and other militant Catholics.

It would be an exaggeration to claim that the Polish intervention was decisive in moderating, though temporarily, French policy in the area of religion. Catherine Medici and the Valois were far from the bloodthirsty fanaticism of some of their subjects. In the political climate of that time the tyrannical dynasty was rather on the side of moderation, contrary to popular legend and fiction. It wanted domestic peace and the Polish advice of tolerance suited to some extent that purpose.

All these factors do not detract in the least from the merit of the Polish demands. The Polish Protestants and other advocates of tolerance realized that to ensure freedom in one's own country, it is necessary to defend it also in others. They seemed to understand the inflexible law of connected vessels. That is why the authors of the Warsaw Confederacy ventured far afield and even dared to interfere in the domestic affairs of other nations. The Polish laws on freedom of thought, belief, and expression enriched European culture. Up to that time they were only an example, causing interest, envy, or flattering indignation. Now they manifested themselves in diplomatic action, which took the form of an unexpected and rather daring political intervention.

The Protestant members of the Polish delegation and their French co-religionists edited the text of the Postulata to make it more relevant to local conditions. The document was presented to Prince Henry with the request that it be passed on to King Charles IX. The text, set out in separate articles, was the result of international cooperation, but the lengthy introduction in French was surely written by one of the members of the delegation, expressing his own views as well as those of his colleagues. It spoke about the interdependence of nations, the plight of the emigrés abroad, and the Protestant princes of the Reich, friendly toward France. It also set the Commonwealth as a model worthy of imitation in the area of religious freedom and defined the basic principles of its system. It was founded on the idea of equality, applied consistently. According to the author of the introduction, the legislation of the Commonwealth followed in that respect that of ancient Rome, which, it claimed, granted equality of rights even to conquered nations.

The famous memorandum had little practical effect. Charles IX lavished compliments on its authors and promised to send his reply to Metz, on the return route of the delegation. He was eager to get the free thinkers out of France.

Bishop Jean de Montluc had resided during the royal election in nearby Plock, the stronghold of Polish counter-reformation. It was there that he received the original text of the Postulata Polonica. One of the ironies of history.

Henry made his way to Poland by land, thus disappointing Ivan the Terrible, who had hoped that the Danes might stop at sea the king-elect. The Polish adversaries of the Frenchman were disappointed by the Germans, who let him pass through, though an attempt against him was prepared in Frankfurt on the Main. Others hoped that Prince Henry might be put off by the prospect of getting for a bride the royal princess of Poland, Anna Jagiello. She was only four years younger than Henry's mother, Catherine Medici, and besides the prince seemed more responsive to male than female charms.

The Poles were as yet unaware of the peculiar aspects of the prince's personality. Later historians wrote about them with outraged horror, as though personal morals were the decisive criteria in evaluating statesmanship. The Frenchman's debauch was supposed to have shocked the Commonwealth to the core. Actually, at the time of the prince's arrival in Poland, the clan of the princes Zbaraski, which had some chances of reaching for the crown at the beginning of the sixteenth century, was already threatened with extinction by the similar proclivities of its male members, heedless of the preachers' admonitions. Several magnates of that period were addicted to what was known in Poland as "the French disease" and in Moscow as the Polish one.

Prince Henry was a man of wild contradictions. An excellent swordsman, he liked to wear women's clothes. Courageous in battle and an outstanding commander, he had an entourage of painted pretty boys for courtiers and sometimes talked about entering a monastery. The French candidacy was politically the best of those available in 1573, but it stumbled on personality. Nor was it possible to predict the fate of the house of Valois. In 1573 it had three representatives: King Charles IX, age 23; Prince Henry, 22; and Prince Francis, 18. Who could have guessed that they were the last generation of the Valois? No such conclusion could be drawn from the fact that the eldest brother, the husband of Mary Stuart, died at twenty.

The Commonwealth elected a prince who was not heir to the throne in his own country. The king and queen of France had a daughter born a year earlier, but they were still young and could expect more offspring.

Leaving for Poland, Prince Henry looked back. Others' eyes followed him from Paris. He was considered the most talented of the Valois, far surpassing in every respect the king, a fact which exacerbated the hatred between the brothers. St.Bartholomew's Night raised the esteem in which Charles IX was held at the courts of Europe. The weakling had acted decisively at last. Henry was relegated momentarily to the background, wandering about the palace in silent gloom. But the stress of St.Bartholomew's undermined the health of the tuberculous king. He enjoyed the sight of people being killed and shot some from his balcony as they fled—he was a fully fledged sadist and France knew it well. It was not the suffering of others, but his own nervous exhaustion that brought him down.

Henry adopted a certain style of his own in dealing with the Poles. Already in Paris he lavished costly gifts on the members of the Polish embassy. Jan Zamoyski received a gold chain of one hundred and seventy links. In Poland the future chancellor was given something even more valuable—the office of *starosta* (sheriff) of Knyszyn. The new king was wildly extravagant and, though generous also to his French retinue, even more so with the Poles. The ambassador of Venice observed that the Frenchman was buying the Polish lords as he hoped to reign from two thrones and wanted to keep them both. His generosity was actually cold calculation.

Princess Anna Jagiello received many compliments and more humiliations. Henry treated her with elaborate courtesy, but without any thought of marriage. The French had started very early to withdraw the promises made by Montluc before the election. The Polish senators were understanding, which may not have been very fair on their part, but showed good judgment. It was a matter of establishing at Wawel castle a French dynasty; a solitary Frenchman and the aged princess were hardly likely to provide heirs. Even the Nuncio did not support the royal princess, though she was a devout Catholic.

Some began urging the departure of the princess from Cracow and her exile to some provincial castle, not even Warsaw. But the treasury of Zygmunt August, belonging to the only surviving member of the house of Jagiello, though female, was still under lock and key at Tykocin. This was perhaps the only reason that gave Princess Anna some standing. The senators were planning to seize the treasure for the crown, while the lesser gentry remained loyal to the heiress of a great tradition and thought a marriage could stabilize the situation.

In the meantime, chaos continued. At the coronation the scene from the Notre Dame cathedral was reenacted. Henry tried again to omit the article dealing with religious tolerance, but the grand marshal, Firlej, put his hand on the crown, indicating that he would not allow the primate to place it on the king elect's head until he swore to abide by all the conditions. He won and the Duke of Anjou became King Henry I. The coronation Seym, however, questioned his right to that title.

In accordance with custom, the coronation was followed by feasting and tournaments, while new knights were dubbed by the king. The feast was all the more tumultuous as the coronation was held on Shrove Sunday, February 21, 1574. The carnival swept the city. The jousting in the tournament often had a fatal ending, but this was normal. What happened outside the tournament lists, however, was a different matter. Samuel Zborowski, "a brisk and frivolous youth, with no other qualities than his skill on a horse and with a lance," planted it in the castle courtyard, challenging all comers to a joust in honor of the king. Unfortunately the challenge was picked up by a man of low condition, by the name of Karwat, a member of the retinue of Jan Teczynski. Zborowski took it as an insult and pandemonium broke out in the royal courtyard.

The Polish courtiers rushed out to calm down the commotion or help their friends, leaving Henry alone with only his French entourage. A shot was fired and the yelling crowd approached the castle.

Used to Paris conditions, the monarch thought that the local Protestants were coming to kill him. As the door opened, the king was waiting, sword in hand, surrounded by his armed countrymen.

None in the turbulent mob had any intention of harming the king. They only wanted to complain to him, bringing with them the bleeding castellan of Przemysl, slashed by Samuel Zborowski. He had tried to mediate the quarrel and suffered the consequences.

Wapowski died soon afterward. A homicide committed in the proximity of the king or during the Seym session was punishable by death. If the offender fled, he was proclaimed banished and his property confiscated. Anyone had the right, even the duty, to kill him if he tried to return.

Zborowski was sentenced to banishment, his lands were seized or passed on to his relatives. The verdict caused dissatisfaction. It was said that Henry went too far in protecting a member of a powerful clan that had promoted his election and was now cashing in their services.

Zborowski did not wait for the royal court's sentence, but went to Hungary, to join the ruler of Transylvania, Stefan Batory.

Even without the Zborowski affair, the Seym had plenty to worry about. The reform party wanted to use the parliamentary session for further constitutional legislation, initiated by the Henrician Covenant. It requested its confirmation article by article. The oath sworn by the king included, under Firlej's pressure, the words "to maintain peace between the denominations." It was now a matter of reaffirming all the rulings of the Warsaw Confederacy, among them one which required a Catholic to defend with arms a Protestant persecuted on account of his faith.

The bishops unanimously opposed that clause and they were joined this time by Franciszek Krasinski and most of the secular senators. The entire Henrician Covenant was questioned and the Seym closed its session without reaching any conclusions. The disenchanted gentry began to grumble and hint that Henry was not rightfully king, since he failed to keep the conditions of his election. In some cases verdicts rendered by the courts in his name were disregarded.

The moderates, led by Zamoyski, managed only to establish the conditions under which the oath of allegiance to the king could be declared null and void. The monarch deviating from the law had to be cautioned first and if he mended his ways, the matter was to be closed. This blunted the sharp edge of the article *de non praestanda oboedientia*.

Zamoyski's other proposals were not adopted. The only Seym held under Henry's reign failed to make any decisions and the country was sinking into chaos. Or, perhaps, it could be said that it was going through the birth pangs of a new political order.

The king did not confirm the Henrician Covenant but, once crowned, he appeared to be the heir to the vast power of the Jagiellonians. Many of the gentry queried the validity of the coronation, but the bishops supported Henry, as did most of the secular senators. The monarch found a solid base of support. If a new order was to emerge, it would certainly bear little resemblance to the democracy of the gentry, but it could be viable. The Frenchman's person itself turned the lords away from what could have been the most dangerous foreign policy trend: pro-Habsburg leanings.

Francis Commendone had already left Poland. The Polish clergy now had a spokesman in Rome; he was Cardinal Stanislaw Hozjusz, a fervent champion of King Henry. The tide of counter-reformation was rising and lapping at the ramparts of the enemy camp. Mikolaj Radziwill (The Orphan) sided strongly with the church, though he was a Catholic of recent date. He had converted after the death of his father, Mikolaj the Black.

Henry I had received sound political schooling in Paris, where he was taught how to exploit alliances with the Vatican. The Valois collaborated with it, but only in domestic affairs and at a price. They exacted lavish rewards. Henry's grandfather, Francis I, concluded in Bologna a concordate with the Holy See which was ratified in February 1517, a few months before the appearance of Martin Luther on the public stage, and became France's sure guideline in the tumult of the Reformation. It granted to the king the right to make ecclesiastic appointments in France, subject to the pope's canonical confirmation. This placed in the monarch's hands a very useful weapon: the distribution of "bread," which was also the privilege of the king of Poland. Frenchmen eager to become bishops or abbots had to submit to the dispenser of these offices. They also had to share with the treasury the revenue of the estates belonging to the diocese or the abbey. This was one of the pillars of the power of the arch-Catholic kings.

Nor should the element of chance be overlooked. It was a piece of luck to sign a concordate at the beginning of the very year that passed into history as the birth date of the Reformation. No one could foresee in February what an obscure abbot of a provincial monastery would do in November.

A tempestuous coronation, the fatal brawl of Samuel Zborowski, and a fruitless parliamentary session were all that happened in Poland under the reign of Henry I. This does not mean, however, that the Frenchman's election was a blunder or that his rule would have brought disaster. His reign had great potential, or rather would have had, except for the personal situation of a monarch who had never seen Poland or Lithuania before.

Charles IX died on March 30, 1574, a year and two weeks after the election of his younger brother to the Polish throne. He left a daughter, but the ancient Salic law of France ruled out female succession. The crown of the heirs of Capet fell to the man who had just ascended the throne of the Piasts and Jagiellonians. Again a development that no one could have anticipated, the more so as Charles IX died at the age of twenty-four.

Henry spent four months in Poland, during which time he shocked with his behavior the future generations rather than his contemporaries, while adopting a passive political posture, as if waiting for something. He was aware, of course, of the situation in Paris and expected his succession.

Upon receiving the news of his brother's death, he announced to the Poles that he would visit France in the fall. In the meantime he sent there some courtiers, charged with the confidential mission of preparing for him relays of horses on the route to Paris. He fled Cracow secretly in the night of June 18. He had no intention of relinquishing either one of his crowns, but wanted to guard personally the French one. Actually he did not have it yet and could receive it only at Rheims. Anyone else in his place would have acted as he did. The dignitaries of the Commonwealth might have restrained his flight, so they had to be deceived. "What sense would it have made to abandon the richest and most powerful kingdom?" wrote a Polish contemporary.

The senior living scion of the house of Capet, he had to place France first. It was a duty from which no Polish election could excuse him. It is not easy for Poles to admit that fact and abstain the king from blame. Neither was any blame due to those who elected him. Thus no one was really responsible for a very damaging event at the pinnacle of state power, which was bound to disrupt its structure and shake the nation's morale. Events beyond human control exacerbated the atmosphere of distrust and suspicion. The first elected king left a burdensome inheritance to his successor.

"King Henry played a trick on the Poles," was said at the time. The monarch's flight was indeed an embarrassing episode, destructive of the moral order. Yet it opened the doors of Wawel castle to the next king, who fulfilled his promise. It did result in much confusion, some slashed heads, and bad feelings. It was fate that had played the trick and not on Poland alone, but also on other interested parties.

Castellan Jan Teczynski caught up with the fugitive near Pszczyna, already outside the boundaries of the Commonwealth. Seeing the royal retinue from afar, he laid down his arms, left at the border his escort of five-hundred mounted men and rode up to Henry, accompanied by only a few aides. He implored him to return and assured him that no one would object to his second crown. He even appealed to a sense of gratitude. He received an "indescribably gracious" reply and the assurance that the Valois king intended to remain on the Polish throne.

In Vienna, Emperor Maximilian II received the royal traveler lavishly, perceiving a chance of seeking the Wawel throne for himself or one of his sons. He ignored his advisers, who wanted the Frenchman held prisoner. He preferred to see another interregnum in Poland rather than seize her lawful king.

After Vienna, Henry turned southward to Italy, bypassing the Protestant states of Germany. In Venice he was met by an emissary of Cardinal Hozjusz, who already knew what had happened. Alarmed by the possibility of a new election that might give the crown to a less devout Catholic, he begged the king to appoint a viceroy and return as soon as possible.

Though he left Poland surreptitiously, Henry did not intend to abdicate. He wanted to keep both crowns and the dukedom of Lithuania. It was an impossible dream. As the royal convoy approached France, the far-ranging plans of greatness of Catherine Medici began to fade away.

The rivalry between her and the "House of Austria" had been going on for generations. The Habsburgs held Spain with its colonies and the Netherlands, encircling their French adversary. The election of Henry in Poland threatened a counter-encirclement by France. Only a year had elapsed from Henry's election and plans were already brewing for the eviction of the Habsburgs from the imperial throne, to be replaced by the Valois. It was also an elective throne and Paris was a staunch ally of the Protestant princes of Germany.

Henry entered his native country from the south, to resume the role of protagonist in one of the darkest chapters of its history. He left behind him in Poland much bitterness, which later colored the views of Polish historians. One of them referred to Henry, writing in the nineteenth century, as "expert in debauch, plunged in indolent sloth, skillful in deception and crime, the notorious Henry I."

Yet modern history counts Henry III among the outstanding kings of France.

CHAPTER 3

THE RIGHT MAN

The senators dispatched to all parts of the country letters advising the gentry of the political developments and left for their respective provinces. Princess Anna Jagiello returned to Warsaw, which she thought the best place for her in view of the impending new election.

The Commonwealth went through a major upheaval, responding with sorrow, anger, puzzlement, and shame. An amateur poet translated some French satirical couplets, far different from the paeans to Poland published by Frenchmen before the election:

> Farewell noisome Poland, land to be sorely missed
> Forests, bushes and deserts are thy glory
> Frozen into eternity as they are
> Under snow and thick ice.
>
> Farewell, strange country with weird buildings
> Where one lives in a hot bakehouse
> Shared with beasts by people
> Who gladly lie down with pigs.

Jan Kochanowski responded with a far superior poem, but this was little help. The enraged gentry fought duels and skirmishes at the county council sessions. In Masovia alone six were killed and forty wounded. Everyone was trying to find those guilty of the fiasco. Zamoyski was blamed by some, but since the election was held *viritim* (by unanimous vote), if anyone was to blame, everyone was.

In the prevailing atmosphere of tension and confusion, it was necessary first of all to determine whether Poland had a king. In the fall Henry received two letters from the country of which he was still nominally the ruler. The first, from the Poles, was courteous but reserved. It did not address the Frenchman as "his majesty" and was actually an ultimatum, setting a deadline for his return by May 12, 1575, failing which a new election was to be held.

The letter from the Lithuanians was different in tone. The gentry of Lithuania had resolved at a convention held in Wilno to continue to recognize Henry Valois as the monarch. Addressing him as the Grand Duke of Lithuania, it set no conditions but begged for the monarch's return.

Aside from the main issue, the Lithuanians objected to the reference to the "traditional loyalty of the Poles" toward their kings, in the letter of the Polish gentry. The Lithuanians were irked by such language, considering themselves citizens of the Commonwealth, but not Poles.

At a time of crisis the dual character of the Commonwealth came to the fore. The Grand Duchy did not want to break up the Union, on the contrary, it insisted that its terms be strictly observed.

Even in Poland proper there were regional differences of views. Royal Prussia shared the Lithuanian position and was reluctant to give up Henry I. But the gentry of "Great Poland" (northwest), "Lesser Poland" (southwest), and Red Ruthenia (southeast)—that is all the lands ruled by Casimir the Great and politically consolidated ever since—took a different line. They felt that any provisional arrangements could breed anarchy, wanted to abandon the French experiment, and proceed to a new election. That was the policy which prevailed. The core of Poland, the realm of Casimir the Great, assumed the leadership of the multinational state. These were the provinces that had the longest tradition of political unity. Thus the state gave birth to the nation, contrary to theories claiming the opposite.

But the episcopate continued to support Henry I, as did the

primate of Poland, Uchanski, acting as the *interrex* or regent. Cardinal Hozjusz also refused to recognize the throne as vacant.

Henry wrote letters from Paris, insisting that he intended to keep the Commonwealth "within the orbit of the House of France." Since the appointment of a viceroy was ruled out, the idea of a crowned proxy of the Valois was launched. The first candidate suggested for that position was Francis d'Alencon, the king's brother. The second was Alphonse, duke of Ferrara, immensely rich and with a white eagle in his crest. Each of them was supposed to marry Anna Jagiello as a condition of ascending the throne. But Francis could have been her grandson and the duke of Ferrara was her junior by a dozen years at least.

Bishop Piotr Myszkowski, an old hand at the political game, was the first to realize the frivolous character of the French plans and turned toward the Habsburgs. He was soon followed by the other bishops, all the Lithuanian senators and most of the Polish ones. Emperor Maximilian had shown good judgment in not barring Henry's way to France.

But in May 1575, at the parliamentary session of Siennica, the gentry rallied under the slogan "A German sticks in our throats" and another, "We could take a Fyodor like Jagiello," meaning a prince from the east. Oddly enough, it was repeated by those who were officially in favor of a "Piast," that is an ethnic Pole.

The idea of a native-born monarch gained popularity and its supporters staunchly resisted at Stezyca the senators who were by then Vienna-oriented. Among the leaders of the "Piast" faction was Mikolaj Siennicki, who had distinguished himself earlier in parliamentary debates under Zygmunt August. All that was lacking was a candidate.

When the emissary of Ivan the Terrible spoke at Stezyca, the "Piast" champions listened attentively.

The "Piast" campaign was a typical political maneuver, not to be taken too literally. It was the expression of disappointment with foreigners and a desire to rely on national resources. The utopian dream of a bond with France failed and the pendulum swung to the other extreme. The "Piast" program was also a good weapon against the Habsburg candidacy. The Sultan of Turkey tried to urge the gentry of Poland to elect one of their own, so the "Piast" movement was likely to placate him, which was a shrewd move for national security.

Yet all the reasons which prevented the election of a Polish candidate still remained valid. In the course of a senate debate Piotr Myszkowski said bluntly that no province could claim primacy over others. The principle of equality, which the authors of the Postulata Polonica had extolled in Paris, argued against a native candidate.

The senate realized that the call for a "Piast" was actually a political metaphor. The castellan of Szrem, Jakub Rokossowski, declared that the only genuine "Piast" was Anna Jagiello, suggesting that she should marry Archduke Ernest Habsburg, thus bringing together that dynasty with the national tradition.

The Jagiellonian dynasty, extinct in its male line, was the keystone of the state which it had built and brought to the status of a major power. The Jagiellonians were recognized and accepted by both Poland and Lithuania; their name alone was a symbol of the Commonwealth's unity. The passionate attachment of the people to the Jagiellonian tradition was an expression of respect for the unity which it gave to the multinational state.

It had seemed that the arrival of Prince Henry in Cracow put an end to the career of the elderly and plain royal princess. The two nations of the Commonwealth accepted the Frenchman, foreign to both of them, thus resolving the problem of equality. But with Henry off the stage, Anna became again the center of attention and enjoyed wide popularity. The parliamentary session of Stezyca resolved to award to the princess the revenues of the province of Podlasie and she was also granted three counties in Masovia. Yet she was a private person under the law, since the Commonwealth did not recognize the position of crown prince, much less princess.

The deep loyalty of the people of the Commonwealth to the Jagiellonian tradition was not mere sentiment, but also evidence of sound political instincts.

Princess Anna played her cards with consummate skill. Wise after the French misadventure, she refrained from casting her vote for anyone. Her objective was to secure a husband and the throne at the same time. She did not care who might lead her to the marital bedchamber, provided that it was at Wawel castle. To keep her options open, she humbly declared that she left her fate in the hands of God and the estates of the Commonwealth. Her seemingly naive, but actually artful moves did not deceive the agent of the Habsburgs, Andrew Dudycz, but they were misunderstood by future historians, who described the last of the Jagiellonians as a simple, emotional, and not overly bright woman.

It seems that Anna would have personally preferred one of the Habsburgs. The family of her grandmother was second in antiquity only to the House of Capet, which had been reigning for six centuries. It had seized the crown a century ahead of the Jagiellonians and regarded the Habsburgs as equals.

The Polish Habsburg supporters decided to elect Maximilian II, who was already married, while Anna would marry his son Ernest and eventually ascend the throne with him after Maximilian's abdication. In the meantime, Anna would be the crown princess, according to a plan devised by the primate, the bishops, and the senators. Jan Kochanowski was one of the few members of the gentry to support it, but he was respected only as a poet, not as a statesman. The person most concerned, Anna, showed caution and did not take any firm position—a fact which subsequently played an important role.

The electoral convention was held this time on the left bank of the Vistula, near the village of Wola. It looked ominous at first. The retinues of the magnates were strong, but they were outnumbered by the mass of the armed gentry. The first to arrive were the knights of Red Ruthenia, from the regions of Lwow, Sanok, and Halicz. This was unexpected, as that part of the country had been recently ravaged by the Tartars. It was perhaps that misfortune that incited the gentry of Ruthenia to seek a solution that could bring peace with the Sultan and his dangerous vassals.

The Habsburg supporters, called Cesarians, left the election field and set up their own well-armed camp at Nowe Miasto. On December 12 the primate, Jakub Uchanski, backed by Jan Chodkiewicz, marshal of Lithuania, seized an appropriate moment and proclaimed Maximilian II king. A "Te Deum" was sung immediately in the cathedral, though with tremulous voices, while infantry detachments guarded Anna's residence at Warsaw castle. It seemed at first that the coup had succeeded, but the overwhelming majority of the gentry regarded it as an outrage. On the following day, as the primate was walking from the castle to the market square, someone fired a shot that missed him by inches. No great efforts were made to find the culprit.

The electors assembled at the Wola field were taken by surprise, but they continued their debates on the next day, firm in their opposition to "the German." Already prior to the primate's coup, Jan Zamoyski had aroused the gentry with a magnificent address in which he took a position contrary to the one he had advocated at the previous election. He called for a "Piast" without naming any candidate. He probably had in mind the Russian prince and perhaps also himself. The thrust of his speech was that the Habsburg candidacy threatened Poland with German domination. As the faint cheers for Maximilian were heard in Warsaw, Zamoyski recognized Anna Jagiella as a "Piast," while she remained in the castle guarded by the "Cesarians," still trusting her destiny to the Lord.

The highhanded action of the primate backfired by polarizing public opinion. Illegality and threats of violence were not tolerated in the Commonwealth.

The nomination of Princess Anna was easily adopted. She was given as guardians the *voievodes* (governors) Kostka and Teczynski, who had been themselves potential "Piasts" a few days earlier. Finally the castellan of Biecz, Stanislaw Szafraniec, put up the name of Stefan Batory, duke of Transylvania, who was to become the husband of the royal princess. The debate soon won over the few supporters of Theodore Ivanovich, the son of the tsar. As to the Habsburgs, the example of Bohemia and a part of Hungary served as a warning against accepting any German ruler. The memory of the lands of Silesia and Pomerania, lost to the Germans, was still fresh. Faced with an attempted coup, the "Piast" camp was stirred to action. Princess Anna barely fitted the Slavic aspirations of the "Piast" faction. Her ancestry was Lithuanian, Italian, and German, with a touch of the Ruthenian from her grandmother Sonka. The candidate for her hand and the crown was pure Hungarian, son of Stefan Batory of Somlyo and Catherine Telegdi.

On December 14, 1575, the Speaker of the Seym, Mikolaj Siennicki, proclaimed Stefan Batory king of Poland and grand duke of Lithuania "provided that he joins in matrimony the royal princess." Thus the coup of the magnates was countered by one of the majority of the gentry of Poland, Lithuania, and Ruthenia. The proclamation of the king-elect, normally the prerogative of the Archbishop of Gniezno, was made by a layman, furthermore an Arian, a heretic in the eyes of the church.

The royal princess evaded any commitment when Mikolaj Radziwill told her "Your Highness can take no other than Archduke Ernest." But after the proclamation of Stefan Batory's election, she changed course and even gave money to his supporters. After all it was better to become a queen than a crown princess with distant prospects of the crown. The hand that led the minor Hungarian prince to the throne might seize the rudder of the state. The ambitious lady preferred the Magyar because he was politically weaker (she could hardly have hoped to manipulate the Habsburgs) and less ridiculous as a husband, since he was only ten years her junior, not thirty as was Ernest Habsburg.

Advised of his election, Stefan sprang into action without losing a moment. He expressed his thanks for the honor of the Polish crown. He swore to observe the Pacta Conventa and married the princess per procuram (by proxy). He also told the Polish gentry that he had sent to the Sultan and the Tartar khan envoys to urge them to respect the boundaries of the Commonwealth. He promised to come to Cracow as soon as he settled matters in Transylvania. He assigned his position as ruler of Transylvania to his brother Christopher and proceeded to the border river Prut as a man free of the dubious privilege of being Turkey's vassal.

Immediately after the election, the gentry called a general levy with assembly in mid-January near Jedrzejow. Those failing to report would risk being stripped of their rank of noblemen. Only the three southeastern provinces were exempted from the draft and charged with guarding the border against the Tartars.

At the appointed time the villages in the vicinity of Jedrzejow were filled with an armed throng. The few magnates siding with the "Piast" faction brought with them mercenary troops, others mortgaged their property to raise funds for the cause. Beyond debates and declarations of loyalty toward Anna and Stefan, they did what was most urgent: seize Cracow, which played in Poland the same role as Rheims in France. The coronation had to be held only there.

Summoned by her loyalists, the princess left Warsaw and arrived in Cracow in February 1576 with her court, greeted as the lawful queen of Poland.

The energy displayed by the Batory supporters was in contrast to the ineptness of the Habsburgs. Maximilian held in Vienna a ceremony of acceptance of the election, he swore the Pacta Conventa and announced throughout Europe his accession to the Polish throne. But these were mere gestures rather than deeds.

Nevertheless, the emperor still had reason for hope. The primate and most of the bishops were on his side, as well as many of the secular senators. Most important of all, none of the Lithuanians had voted for Batory. Stefan I, one of the most outstanding of the elected kings of Poland, was chosen by the gentry of Poland proper and Ruthenia.

The princess—almost queen—no doubt found some satisfaction in residing in the same apartments at Wawel castle that had been occupied a few months earlier by Henry I. She had to wait, but was sure of achieving her goal. Whoever became king could not ignore her. To be on the safe side, however, she refused to take part in a ceremony of marriage by proxy. She preferred to see a live groom.

Anything could happen. The distance, enhanced by the barrier of the Carpathian mountains and the still primitive transportation, was a serious obstacle. Stefan failed to appear on the date he had first promised, but even with the best of will the problems in Transylvania could not be dealt with overnight. The gentry waited together with the princess, while rumors about the little-known Hungarian prince circulated in the country.

At the first election Batory's candidacy was dismissed with a shrug, but at the second he was the winner. This was no accident and his supporters knew what they were doing. Since July 10, 1575, the image of the candidate had undergone a major change. It was on that day that he won a decisive victory on the River Maros in his country. He defeated the superior forces of rebels inspired by the emperor, precisely in order to neutralize a rival contestant for the Polish crown. Maximilian offered to Stefan an opportunity to prove his talents as a commander and the news of the victory reached the election field at Wola.

Long before the election the astute ambassador of Venice, Lippomano, asserted that Batory had a good chance among the Poles. They knew of him as a politician and a soldier. Batory was a Catholic and was strongly promoted in Poland by his special envoy, a former physician of Queen Bona, George Blandrata, himself an Arian. Playing both sides of the board often pays off in politics.

Samuel Zborowski was a guest of the court of Transylvania, while his four brothers were active in Poland. Their powerful clan contributed significantly to the election. The magnates backing Batory expected, as did Princess Anna, that they could rule on behalf of a foreigner, a minor Hungarian prince who did not speak Polish. After his victory on the Maros, Batory confiscated the estates of many of the rebels, so that his electoral campaign was not without means.

Batory had previously many contacts in Hungary and Austria

with Poles and Polish problems. As a young courtier he was a member of the retinue of Catherine Habsburg, who married the duke of Mantua and later Zygmunt August, king of Poland. He also knew personally the king's sister, Isabelle Jagiello, the wife of the rather theoretical king of Hungary, Jan Zapolyi. He witnessed her sad departure for Poland, a consequence of a pact between the Habsburgs and the Jagiellonian monarch, protecting his marriage with Barbara Radziwill. A few years later Batory greeted Isabelle with a speech on her return to Transylvania. He became the duke after the death of her son, Jan Zygmunt. He was formally elected by the Hungarian parliament, but actually appointed by the sultan. In addition to that servitude, he had to endure, secretly for the time being, the dominance of the emperor. He was imprisoned for a time at Maximilian's order and used that opportunity for completing his education, started at the University of Padua and then interrupted. He sought the Polish throne because a Commonwealth under the Habsburgs would have meant the total encirclement of Hungary and the end of its struggle for independence. Conversely, a Hungarian at Wawel castle could find ways of saving his native country.

He came from a country long plunged in such disasters that the situation of the Commonwealth could appear by comparison idyllic and its domestic affairs calm and orderly. The Polish and Lithuanian magnates were sometimes unruly and could occasionally raid Valachia, but their license did not change the boundaries of the state. The Hungarian ones could decide one day that their estates belonged to Transylvania and the next to the empire, or even the sultan.

Stefan was still a young man when a prominent Hungarian politician, George Martinuzzi, of Croat descent and the former abbot of the Pauline monastery of Czestochowa, was murdered at the order of an Austrian general. His body was left at the scene for two years and the ears, cut off the corpse, were sent to Vienna as a present for Emperor Ferdinand I.

Batory came from an area ruled by methods against which the Commonwealth was quite consciously defending itself by means of constitutional laws and Henrician Covenants.

In April 1576 he arrived at Mogila and immediately went hunting with a handful of courtiers, acting as if no one could threaten him and the country was unanimously at peace. A shrewd judge of men, he knew that such behavior would speak louder than a whole batch of manifestos. By trusting his subjects, he invited them to trust him. He took a risk, knowing that he had to win or lose all.

He entered the capital on Easter Monday, April 23. Tall, dark, impressive in bearing, he was a soldierly figure in his scarlet attire. He greeted the senators with simple dignity, dismounting and shaking the hand of each in turn. He was followed by his personal retinue—the purple guard, in which many Poles served, the red Hungarian infantry and the armored heavy cavalry—an escort worthy of a king. Everything about him bespoke a man at arms.

The wedding, followed by the coronation of the royal couple, was held on May 1. The Lithuanian envoy, Prince Massalski, protested in the cathedral on behalf of the Grand Duchy. The ceremony was performed by the bishop of Kujawy, Stanislaw Karnkowski, the only member of the episcopate to join Stefan's party early, at the Jedrzejow convention. The primate Uchanski still maintained that Maximilian was the lawful king, as did the nuncio Vincent Laureo. The coronation was assisted by only a minority of the senators and none from Lithuania.

The outlook was rather grim. The diplomacy of Vienna was frantically busy. An agreement concluded between Vienna and Moscow outlined a plan for the partition of the Commonwealth: Lithuania for Ivan the Terrible and the rest of the country for the Habsburgs. The imperial emissary who had engineered the plan was also inciting Gdansk to resistance. Those who called the December move of primate Uchanski, the election of Maximilian, a crime were not far wrong. The proclamation of the emperor as king of Poland handed a weapon to all of the foreign enemies of the Commonwealth and also to all the disruptive elements within the country. Poland's main port, Gdansk, had a predominantly German population and resented the "Karnkowski Statutes," enacted in the last years of the reign of Zygmunt August, which limited its autonomy. The city seized the opportunity and declared its allegiance to the German emperor rather than to the man elected by the Polish gentry. This was all the more alarming as both Royal and Ducal Prussia also opposed Stefan.

The new king did not yield to pressure. No one secured any concessions from the king seated on a shaky throne. The first person to discover the strength of his character was his wife. "I see that she will not be able to dominate him, for he is a real man," wrote the castellan of Minsk, Jan Hlebowicz, from Cracow to Lithuania. The papal nuncio reported to Rome that members of the queen's entourage, former courtiers of Zygmunt August, were brushed aside. The Zborowski clan also met with disappointment: only one of the five brothers was given an office of the crown—he was Jan, clearly the most outstanding member of the family, appointed to be castellan of Gniezno. In the spring of the following year he was to display his talent as a commander, proving that the king had made the right choice. Stefan's remarkable intuition and judgment were evident also in another instance. The venerable old chancellor Wincenty Debinski was retired and appointed castellan of Cracow, the highest senatorial office under the crown. Disregarding the claims of the Zborowskis, the king appointed Piotr Wolski chancellor and Jan Zamoyski, the best political mind in Poland at that time, vice chancellor.

"He knew people and he knew his subjects," a contemporary wrote about Stefan. At the very beginning of the reign a lifelong alliance was formed between two brilliantly able men. It was later said of Batory and Zamoyski that the former should never go into council without the other and the latter not go into war without him. It was something of an exaggeration, as Zamoyski proved later, after the king's demise, who was no laggard at war.

The Commonwealth called to power a ruler who knew how to spot and attract the best talent. A powerful personality himself, he did not seek mediocrities among which he could shine. That type of courage is rare at the political summit and when it does occur it is vastly appreciated below.

The king's qualities of mind and character were matched with a harsh manner. No one experienced it in a more humiliating way than the queen. It is true that Stefan, as was recorded at the time, did "perform his matrimonial duty," but after a couple of nights he stayed away from his wife. He let her wait in vain in his bedchamber, yet he never heeded the senators' suggestions of divorce. He was brutally candid and totally honest.

Soon after the wedding and coronation, the king undertook a triumphant journey northward. First he secured the surrender of the primate Uchanski. He invited him to Warsaw and when the archbishop excused himself on grounds of ill health, the king announced his visit to Lowicz and sent ahead some Hungarian infantry. Uchanski then had no choice but to recover and come to Warsaw. The nuncio, who had hitherto maneuvered so as not to meet Stefan, left for Wroclaw.

Batory's envoy to Rome had an unusual diplomatic experience. The French ambassador strongly opposed his request for an audience with the pope, since Henry III of France still considered himself Henry I of Poland. Then Emperor Maximilian, who claimed the same title himself, had the Polish embassy staff arrested.

In the meantime Stefan behaved in Poland as though no one was challenging his rule. He soon won over the representatives of Lithuania, headed by the Chodkiewicz clan. Royal Prussia's turn was next. Stefan confirmed the rights of both parts of Prussia, swore to respect them, and was recognized as the sovereign. Only Gdansk remained loyal to Maximilian and demanded more privileges under its status of autonomy.

The king called a parliamentary session in Torun for October 19. A week before that date Emperor Maximilian II died in Ratisbon. Fate removed Stefan's dangerous rival and cancelled the Austrian agreements with Ivan the Terrible, while it confirmed the view of those who preferred to negotiate rather than fight with Gdansk.

The royal message announcing the convocation of the Seym makes strange reading. It states that the treasury is empty and throughout the country "license erodes sound ancient customs, replaced by vicious crime, homicide, violence, robbery, shootings, debauch, usury, perjury, extravagance, and many other vile deeds. There is also much wrongdoing in the military, whereby any armed action is rendered difficult. May the Lord grant that these abuses be curbed and the Commonwealth may flourish, second to none in splendor."

All these wrongs had been denounced by Andrzej Frycz Modrzewski a quarter of a century earlier. The Seym had urged reform and a national revival. Then, under a Jagiellonian monarch, heir to a great dynasty, such a reform would have been much easier than under a stranger restricted by electoral covenants. And the gentry had changed too, even more accustomed to privilege and grown somewhat cynical after Zygmunt August's capricious behavior and two elections separated by the French interlude. It is hard to say whether history repeats itself, but missed opportunities very seldom come back.

The king outlawed the city of Gdansk, but the Seym did not vote funds for military action against it. An urban mob started looting the properties in Gdansk of the bishop of Kujawy, who had ecclesiastic jurisdiction over all of Pomerania. It was then that the abbey of Oliwa near Gdansk was sacked and demolished and the priceless library of the Cistertian order lost. Gdansk defied the royal authority over the city, the port, and the sea.

Stefan issued another decree of interdiction against Gdansk, pawned the crown jewels, made loans, and appealed to the clergy and the county councils for funds—this time successfully.

In April 1577 the Gdansk burghers took offensive action against the small Polish and Hungarian garrison of two thousand men near Tczew, commanded by Jan Zborowski. The attacking force, six times more numerous, was led by Hans Winkelbruch, well known in Germany. In Poland he was called Hans of Cologne. He devised a complicated amphibious operation, sending four ships with troops and artillery up the Vistula to Tczew, while he mounted an outflanking move near the lake of Lubieszow. The reports of his death in the battle of April 17 proved inaccurate, for Winkelbruch escaped, only to be killed on August 23 at the Gdansk Lighthouse fortress. Though Winkelbruch saved his life at Tczew, he lost more men than the entire Polish force. The road to Pruszcz was reported lined with bodies.

The outcome of the battle was thought at first to be a foregone conclusion, in view of the wide disparity between the opposing forces. But the contest was decided by a single charge of the Polish heavy cavalry, the hussars. One used to read with condescension about the cavalry charges of time gone by, but World War II proved the tactical value of an armored strike.

Some reservations, however, might be permitted regarding the efficacy of the firearms of the period. Bartlomiej Paprocki, writing about the battle at the Lubieszow lake, reports, "A cannon ball hit under the commander's horse, so that it swung around; Zborowski immediately rode away, shouting orders to his troops." He had among his soldiers a man by the name of Zarczycki, so confident in the strength of his armor that he invited his comrades to shoot at him. Unfortunately, on April 17 "God called him, the armor failed," perhaps weakened by earlier experimentation.

Among the officers who distinguished themselves in battle was young Lieutenant Stanislaw Zolkiewski. He was destined to decide years later the outcome of the battle of Kluszyn by another massive cavalry charge, opening the way to Moscow.

Winkelbruch lost all his cannon and eight standards, on one of which the words *Aurea Libertas* (Golden Freedom) were embroidered. The German burghers of Gdansk had evidently borrowed the favorite slogan of the Polish gentry.

In September a Gdansk river fleet appeared at Elblag, which was still loyal to the crown. The Hungarian force, rushed by night to the rescue, thought at first that the city was lost as it seemed to be on fire. As it turned out, only some lumber yards and almost-empty granaries were burning. The Magyars drove away the Gdansk raiders, who fled with heavy casualties. Elblag addressed to the king a message of thanks, praising to the skies the commander of the relief force, Caspar Bekesh, "known for his virtue, moderation, humanity, and military skills." He was no other than the loser in the battle on the river Maros, in which he had been defeated two years earlier by Batory. Once his rival for the dukedom of Transylvania, he now served Stefan faithfully and became his lifelong friend. He died in Grodno, as did Stefan himself, and was buried in Wilno at the summit of a hill known to this day as Mount Bekesh.

The Elblag incident highlights an important aspect of Stefan's character. He was one of the few men totally free of any desire for revenge, a priceless asset in a statesman. It was possessed later by Talleyrand and to some extent by Napoleon.

The defeats at Tczew and Elblag, a bombardment, and the diversion of the Radunia branch of the Vistula delta somewhat softened Gdansk, but did not force it to surrender. The royal army failed to take the city and its fortress, known as the Lighthouse. It was defended by Scottish mercenaries hired by Gdansk, which also received some assistance from the king of Denmark.

In December 1577 a compromise was reached. Gdansk apologized for its actions and swore allegiance to the king, promising to pay reparations in the amount of two hundred thousand *zlotys*, plus another twenty thousand for the restoration of the abbey of Oliwa. The customs duties paid to the crown remained in force, while the king confirmed the city charter granting it a degree of autonomy.

Stefan complained that Gdansk responded to his iron bullets with golden ones, meaning that it bribed some of the Polish lords. This was true, but it was not the main reason for the compromise.

70

We will deal presently with the real cause. At any rate it was clear that only a compromise solution was possible in a conflict with a major port, which had twice the population of Cracow, Poland's capital. Let us recall the trouble the Valois had with the port of La Rochelle and the fact that until the late eighteenth century some French ports denied entry to ships of the royal navy, invoking ancient laws. The unification of state territories proceeded slowly in Latin Europe and this no doubt helped to enrich European culture.

Gdansk was too strong to be simply crushed and subdued, as was Jaroslaw, where a fair famous throughout Europe and the borders of Asia was held every year. Poland allowed the patricians of its largest port to accumulate wealth, but it could rely on Gdansk later, when the very existence of the Commonwealth was at stake. Tolerance may be costly but it pays off in the long run.

Another less favorable compromise was struck in the north. Ducal Prussia, with its capital in Krolewiec (Konigsberg) was nominally ruled by Albrecht Frederick Hohenzollern. His right to reign was legally unimpeachable, impaired only by the young prince's insanity. The actual administration of the province was in the hands of a Governing Council, which sided with Maximilian and secretly supported Gdansk in its conflict with the Polish crown. Already at the time of the first interregnum there was some interference in Prussian affairs by the Margrave George Frederick Hohenzollern of the Brandenburg branch of the family, the one allowed by Zygmunt August to be the heirs of their Konigsberg cousins. As a relative of the mad prince, George Frederic sought the position of his curator, which would amount to being the ruler of Ducal Prussia. He maneuvered adroitly, adopted a neutral posture in the contest for the Polish throne and finally secured the favor of Stefan I by lending him two hundred thousand *zlotys* for his war chest. The decision taken in Malbork made him the guardian of Albrecht Frederick and the Brandenburg Hohenzollerns began to settle down in Konigsberg.

It was said that the king sold the duchy of Prussia to the detriment of the Commonwealth. Stefan's situation was very difficult at the time but it improved later. The Prussian estates, fearful of the Hohenzollern expansionism, begged for the appointment by the crown of a Polish governor and promised to pay more tribute than George Frederick. Yet the king did not turn back from the path he had taken, nor did his successor. In the meantime Albrecht Frederick lived for forty years in madness and survived two curators.

The decisions concerning Gdansk and Ducal Prussia were made in 1577, in the spring of which the Tartars invaded the southeastern borderlands of the Commonwealth. Radziwill "the Orphan" wrote: "In the seventy-seventh year I was mostly playing with my doctors, until the time of our Lithuanian expedition to Inflanty, when that province was ravaged by the Moscow prince; King Stefan had then set his camp near Gdansk."

Ivan the Terrible attacked without any declaration of war. The Polish frontier garrisons had received earlier instructions to avoid any provocation. In the fall of the preceding year Moscow had granted letters of free passage to the "great embassy" of the Commonwealth.

The tsar seized the Inflanty as far as the river Dvina. He did not dare to challenge the well-fortified city of Riga and its Dyament castle, but did take Dyneburg. Wilno, the capital of the Grand Duchy of Lithuania, was threatened as never before.

Everyone knew what Ivan was capable of doing. Michael Halaburda, who had served as envoy to Russia during the first interregnum, was received in Great Novgorod, which still bore the scars of the "pacification" by massacre carried out by Ivan three years earlier, in 1570. It seems that the news of the Lublin Union had revived in Novgorod an ancient sympathy for the Jagiellonians, whose rule respected the law and ethnic identities other than their own. The tsar punished the city in a way that relegated to oblivion the atrocities committed there a century earlier by Ivan the Cruel. His namesake surpassed him. He ordered hundreds of monks beaten to death with clubs, others were tortured, hanged, or beheaded. Thousands were drowned in the river Wolchow. The "Oprychniki," the tsar's personal guard, lashed children to their mothers with ropes before throwing them into the river. Others, armed with spikes, cruised around in boats to make sure that all went under.

One can only wonder at the strong nerves and pro-Slav leanings of those of the Polish gentry who considered Ivan's candidacy in two elections, notwithstanding the reports from Novgorod. But this came to an end when Inflanty offered a repeat of the Novgorod performance. The small garrison of Wenden deliberately blew itself up rather than be captured by the tsar's troops. It was reported that fire was set to the gunpowder by the women in the castle. Death by explosion is quicker than by being raped by battalions of soldiers.

Those who surrendered immediately were left alone, but anyone who attempted the slightest resistance had no alternative but to die in battle. The Russian guns and supply trains crossed marshes over dikes made of the bodies of still-living prisoners tied together in bundles. Burning on a slow fire was also a common practice.

By going too far in terror, Ivan lost German support. For the time being the German princes preferred to side with the Commonwealth, even though they did not love it. Ivan in Inflanty and Stefan near Gdansk were both fighting against the Germans. But Stefan's behavior was very different from Ivan's. Here are excerpts from the "articles of war," enforced both in the Gdansk campaign and the later one against Moscow:

> Anyone taking by force or secretly any goods other than food shall be hanged.

> The looting of a church shall be punished by death, even if it is in enemy territory. . . . Whoever dishonors a girl or a woman shall be punished by death, even in enemy territory. . . . It is forbidden to kill virgins, women, children, and elders in enemy territory. . . .

Ivan the Terrible was a very shrewd politician, but his actions made him, in the eyes of both close and distant neighbors to the west "a beast in human guise." His cruelty went beyond anything that could be tolerated for political expediency. National policies are sometimes inspired by fear or revulsion against what happens beyond the border.

As he invaded Inflanty, the tsar declared that he was fighting there only the Germans. The Lithuanians and Poles captured by him were well treated and released, sometimes even with gifts, but this did not help him much. It was known that he claimed all the lands east of the "White Water," as he called the Vistula. Later he also produced spurious arguments, in the fabrication of which he was a master, justifying his claims to Prussia. It was obvious that Grodno, Halicz, or Wilno might share the fate of Novgorod. The Inflanty had joined the Commonwealth under Zygmunt August and its inhabitants were its citizens.

The tsar's invasion of Lithuania and Poland spurred them to an effort not seen since Grunwald in 1410.

The Polish historian Jan Natanson-Leski's comment is all the more significant as he was writing in 1930, when there was a tendency to glorify all of King Stefan's victories:

> The thought occurs that if Batory . . . instead of conquering Polock and Wielkie Luki, besieging Pskov, ravaging Muscovy and even instead of liberating the Inflanty and pushing Russia away from the Baltic, had subdued Gdansk and placed in Konigsberg a royal governor and royal *starostas* (sheriffs) in the forts of Pregola and the Masurian lakes, history might have taken a different turn. Was not the Polish coast from Oliwa to Memel, with the estuaries of the Vistula and Niemen, more worthy of sacrifice than the Latvian and Estonian coasts? If King Stefan had turned his forces and his remarkable talents to the protection of these vital interests of Poland, if he had secured the support of the people in that enterprise and managed to wrest from Moscow even only Lithuania, events might have taken a different course both in the east and west.

Speculation of what might have been is, of course, a marginal exercise at best. We may note, however, that Stefan could not have accepted a humiliating defeat at the hands of Moscow. Ailing Radziwill "the Orphan" had to mount his horse "when King Stefan set his camp at Gdansk." In 1577 we witnessed another replay of the syndrome that existed already before the Union, under Olgierd, and which we referred to often in "Jagiellonian Poland": desperate swings of Polish policy between Moscow and Malbork or Konigsberg. The hereditary enemy of the Grand Duchy turned Poland's forces against the east. It was an alternative of either winning a decisive victory or abandoning Lithuania and losing the heritage of centuries.

Let us indulge in another speculative hypothesis: if Poland under Casimir Jagiello, during the Thirteen Year War, which gave Poland Malbork, had gone a step further and took also Memel with Konigsberg. It was a feat quite feasible at the time.

Gdansk caused Poland some trouble, but never threatened its existence. The same was true for a long time of Konigsberg. But Ivan had placed a knife at Lithuania's throat and Stefan was the monarch of Both Nations.

Living as we do in the twentieth century, we value highly the often-violated principle of national self determination. From that point of view, the powers contesting Inflanty could be considered as having equal rights, except for the fact that the Latvians—the native population of the province—are the kinsmen of Lithuanians, but not of Poles or Russians. When a guerrilla warfare started against Ivan, it enlisted not only citizens of the Commonwealth and Germans, but also the Latvian natives. If a referendum were to be held, which of the powers fighting over their country would they have chosen? As far as the German burghers were concerned, it would have probably been Sweden. Zygmunt August complained in a letter to his sister that the people of Revel had ousted a Commonwealth garrison and invited into their walls "King Eric's motley men."

Moscow needed a gateway to the world more convenient than that of Archangel, and Lithuania wanted the mouth of the Dvina. In the last analysis the claims of all parties were based mainly on force.

Through 1577 and the whole of the following year war preparations continued under the cover of apparent peace. The Swedes still held Revel. King Stefan entrusted the command to two dynamic Radziwills: the *voievode* Mikolaj and his son Christopher, with the suggestive nickname of "Piorun" (Lightning).

The Russian garrisons felt secure and underrated their adversary, thus allowing him to regain some forts. One of them, Dyneburg, was taken by a simple subterfuge. Wilhelm Plater and Boris Sawa sent to the fortress, as a token of good will, some food and a considerable quantity of vodka. After the garrison had consumed the liquor, it failed to notice the ladders at the ramparts or the Polish soldiers climbing them. The castle of Kies was also captured by ruse: Maciej Debinski ordered his men to simulate an attack on one side, while he opened the gate on the other with keys secured from a compliant locksmith. In the fall of 1578 the town was besieged by Russian forces. What happened then was an exception, though perhaps it should have been the rule in the interest of the Commonwealth and its northern neighbor. The Polish-Lithuanian garrison entered a provisional understanding with the Swedes and joined forces with them. The Russians were defeated and twenty-four heavy cannon taken from them were sent to Wilno by way of Riga.

As the multinational victors took the Russian positions, they saw dead men sheltering the guns with their bodies and the remains of others draped over gun barrels, choosing suicide over surrender. Most of the subjects of the Terrible tsar remained loyal to him.

At the king's request, the county councils of Lithuania raised taxes after Ivan's invasion. In 1578 the Seym proclaimed a special levy, scheduled for two years. Stefan was in no hurry to open his campaign and made meticulous preparations. He enlisted Hungarians openly and Germans covertly to fill the gaps in his infantry units. He ordered new equipment and weapons for the Polish cavalry. He was the first king of Poland to enlist six hundred Zaporozhe Cossacks. Artillery from the whole country was moved to the northeast, mostly by waterways, as inland water transportation was then used much more widely than in the twentieth century. Elaborate movable bridges suitable for land transport were also prepared.

King Stefan took with him maps and skilled cartographers ready to draw new and more up-to-date ones. He also had a field printing plant and what amounted to a press bureau, which had functioned already in the Gdansk campaign. In 1577 a small book about the Gdansk rebellion was published in Malbork. It was written under the direct supervision of the king by Andrew Patrycy Nidecki, a philologist enlisted as a political publicist. Stefan I gave to psychological warfare more attention than anyone before him and few after.

He went too far, however, in enacting in 1580 a preventive censorship of all publications or pictures relating to politics or history. Printers publishing without approval risked the death penalty. The field printing shop was managed by Walenty Lypczynski. The cartographer, Stanislaw Pachlowiecki, and the historian Reinhold Heidenstein were later raised to noble rank in recognition of their services.

The army was concentrated at the crossroads of Swir, northeast of Wilno, so that the direction of its thrust could not easily be guessed. The solemn act of declaration of war, dated June 26, 1579, was delivered in Moscow by Waclaw Lopacinski, who was imprisoned there after performing his mission. He returned later when Ivan decided to change his attitude toward Stefan and the tone of his messages. Until then he addressed him condescendingly as "neighbor," instead of "brother" as was customary among monarchs.

The army of twenty odd thousand was ready and in perfect trim. The proclamation of war goals was printed on the spot in Polish, Latin, German, and Hungarian. The king was commander in chief, with Jan Zamoyski, recently appointed chancellor, at his side. The Polish contingent was under the command of the old *voievode* of Podole, Mikolaj Mielecki, who had gained fame already under Zygmunt August. The Lithuanians were commanded by Mikolaj Radziwill and the Hungarians by Caspar Bekesh, ailing but insisting that he had never felt better. The Germans were led by Ernest Weyher and Christopher Rozraszewski, a Germanized Pole.

Speaking of ethnic groups, a number of offensive raids, mostly by Ruthenian citizens of the Commonwealth, took place later in the same year. The *starosta* (sheriff) of Orsza, Kmita-Czarnobylski, reached as far as Smolensk; his colleague from Mscislaw, Jan Solomerecki, attacked Roslaw. Further south the Princes Constantine and Janusz Ostrogski, as well as Michal Wisniowiecki, raided Czernihow and Starodub at the head of their private armies of Cossacks and volunteers.

In the main war theatre, the *voievode* of Braclaw, Prince Janusz Zbaraski, distinguished himself in action. He was a native Ukrainian, recently converted to Catholicism. King Stefan was reported saying that Zbaraski was fit for the crown.

The Poles constituted the bulk of their Hungarian king's forces, they made the greatest contribution, and fought well. Yet it would be a major error to give credit for Stefan's victories only to the Poles. The multinational character of the army caused much comment in Poland and Lithuania, while the king was charged with favoring his countrymen and also the Germans. In the course of operations there was friction between hetman Mielecki and Bekesh, between Mielecki and Radziwill, and so on. Marching against Sokol after taking Polock, the stern old hetman stopped the column and told all the Hungarians to stay behind. He wanted to prove that the Poles could take enemy castles without Magyar help.

It would not have been surprising if Stefan did indeed favor his kinsmen. It seems probable though that the masterful commander deliberately encouraged a competitive spirit among his men. It came to a point where there was keen rivalry between national groups to be in the forefront of an assault. When trial cavalry charges were made near Pskov, volunteers from the Polish gentry, wearing white shrouds over their armor, appeared among the troops.

They might have met among the infantry peasants from their own villages. Legislation enacted by the Seym in 1578 created a new type of infantry, called "select infantry." One volunteer could be accepted for every twenty *lans* (unit of land, similar to the acre) of royal estates. He had to report quarterly for training and be ready to join his unit at any time. When in active service he received pay and when out of service he was relieved for life from the obligations of servitude and taxes. The law stated that, to avoid loss to the treasury, the other nineteen peasants had to make up for the soldier.

The "select infantry" acquired a character of its own. It used no armor, was light and mobile, and was trained also in sappers' duties. In addition to a sword and hatchet, every soldier had a firearm, mostly muskets. The uniforms varied according to the preference of local commanders. In the sixteenth century the "select infantry" wore caps with upturned rims, in the seventeenth century they wore hats. A broad cloak was a feature of most uniforms.

The "select infantry" soon gained the reputation of excellent soldiers. The royal decree setting it up explains the reason. The nobleman commanding the unit had to select personally those among the volunteers he judged most fit for service. Only one man was accepted for every twenty *lans* of land, but more volunteered and only the best were chosen.

The landed gentry did not like war, for they had more to lose than to gain. For the peasants, on the other hand, every campaign opened the opportunities for advancement, in some cases even decoration by the king or a grant of patents of nobility. There was also the chance of rich booty. The Commonwealth was vast, the class divisions fluid, and identity documents had not yet been invented. Even in the cavalry, which we tend to visualize as composed wholly of noblemen, there were many plebeians and some of them reached officer rank. Hundreds of men, enriched in war and polished by the experience, never returned to the plough but made careers that sometimes reached high. The infantryman had plenty of incentive to fight well.

In the beginning of the seventeenth century a malicious neighbor charged a certain Walenty Duracz with using unlawfully the crest of the Odrowaz clan. The suspicion was unfounded, for Duracz had been legally ennobled by the Seym in 1578. The informer only reported that Duracz, the owner of forges, "made cannon balls for King Stefan against Moscow . . . also hoes and spades," that he bought with the proceeds of that trade the village of Sadek near Sandomierz and became a squire. And before making artillery ammunition, he had supplied iron for the famous Vistula bridge near Warsaw. Not only war, but any major state enterprise offered opportunities for upward mobility to many people. This was well understood by the gentry, before it acquired later habits of passive apathy. Under Stefan Batory the country was on the move as it had not been since Casimir the Great.

The bullets made by Duracz and others were commemorated not only in the jealous informer's complaint, but also in documents of state at the highest level. The two monarchs at war had time for a correspondence in which they generally accused each other of all kinds of villainies. Ivan the Terrible wrote to Stefan more or less in these terms: "You send people's souls to perdition with devices out of hell and you call yourself a Christian monarch?"

He was referring to the so-called fireballs or incendiary missiles. King Stefan was regarded by some as their inventor, but that was obviously not the case, as he replied to the tsar caustically that he was evidently out of touch with modern technology if he raved about a type of ammunition well known in civilized countries.

In Russian tradition infantry is not the "queen of battles." That honor is reserved for artillery. It seems that Moscow's respect for gunnery was enhanced by its wars with Stefan I.

The Hungarian's missives were matter of fact and sharp witted. When Ivan offered to him in one of his letters the dignity of "brother," Stefan replied that he would gladly relinquish that title in exchange for the Inflanty. He attached to another letter a German book describing at length Ivan's atrocities.

They were not a matter of the past. As the advance guard approached Polock, they saw logs of wood floating down the river with the bodies of slaughtered prisoners attached to them.

The summer of 1579 was exceptionally wet and the autumn chill set in early. The wooden walls of the two Polock castles would not catch fire and the garrison offered stiff resistance, helped by the town residents. The former population had been deported by Ivan and replaced by settlers from Moscow and its environs.

The neighboring smaller forts were still held by Russians, as the king did not want to disperse his forces and only some minor castles were taken or burned down. Food supplies for the army besieging Polock were scarce and the roads made impassable by rain. The Commonwealth army suffered hardship and hunger, felt more keenly by the Germans, unused to waging war in such conditions.

The Hungarian and Polish infantry coped best with the situation. The Magyars even displayed excessive zeal and endurance: they killed a ten-person delegation sent by the defenders to negotiate. They preferred a successful assault to a capitulation, which would have deprived them of the right to booty.

On August 29 the walls of Polock finally caught fire. It was set by a boilermaker's apprentice from Lwow, by the name of Was. His courage was rewarded by a grant of nobility under the name of Polotynski (of Polock).

The terms of surrender were very generous. The military and the inhabitants were offered a free choice: they could either rejoin Ivan or stay as subjects of King Stefan. Most chose the former and went east. Contrary to their stoic expectation, Ivan did not treat them as was his custom and they were not tortured or executed. Evidently he admitted that they did their best and could do no more.

The capture of Polock rendered a signal service to a remarkable man and to European culture. Radziwill "the Orphan" felt that it would have been inappropriate for a man "of knightly calling" to go on a prilgrimage to the Holy Land while his fellow citizens were fighting. He accordingly joined the army and was wounded in the head by a musket shot, but recovered. Encouraged by this "new proof of the Lord's grace," he departed on his journey, about which he wrote later one of the finest works of literature of the century.

As the garrison was leaving Polock after the capitulation, special guards ensured its safety. The king himself struck with a mace a soldier who surreptitiously tried to rob some of the defeated. Quite different ways prevailed after the castle of Sokol was taken.

Mikolaj Mielecki commanded the Polish and German troops who took the fort. They were incensed by what they saw in Polock after entering it. They found in the castle dungeons the bodies of cruelly murdered prisoners. Some had been boiled alive, others' bodies were covered with a mass of cuts indicating torture.

When the first German detachment forced the walls of Sokol, the defenders lowered the gate and butchered all the invaders. The gate was broken down by others and a massacre began. The veteran colonel Ernest Weyher said that he had never seen such piles of corpses. The Germans were particularly fierce in their revenge for countrymen slain in Polock, but the Poles were not idle either. The Russian cavalry which escaped the fortress had more luck, for it encountered the force of Prince Janusz Zbaraski, who spared the lives of the prisoners.

Torowla was seized by the Cossacks without a struggle. The 1579 campaign won for Poland eight forts and recaptured the Polock region lost under Zygmunt August. The Grand Duchy of Lithuania held again the middle course of the Dvina, thus immensely improving its security and trading potential. King Stefan even took a boat ride on the river to inspect its banks.

Immediately after concluding the northern campaign he had to start together with Zamoyski a new one—in the Seym. The lands lost earlier were recovered, with the exception of Inflanty, and article 4 of the *Henrician Covenant* stated clearly that: "We and our heirs, the kings of Poland, pledge with our royal word never to take the armed forces of Both Nations outside the borders of the Commonwealth."

In the war of 1579 it was Ivan who seemed to be following the Jagiellonian tradition of passive defense. Stefan attacked and won. The gentry treasured the ancient principle of fighting wars in the east only within the historic borders of Lithuania. There had been no attempts at conquest since the times of Olgierd.

Jan Zamoyski was familiar with that outlook and the reluctance of his fellow noblemen to pay taxes. He turned them skillfully to his advantage by arguing that since all the provinces of the Commonwealth had equal rights, they would all profit by the acquisition of new territory, the income from which would reduce their tax load.

The colonial program was never carried out, but the chancellor's argument merits attention, for it illustrates the basic equality of all the components of the Commonwealth, as well as Zamoyski's forensic skills.

Moaning and grumbling, the Seym did vote taxes at the same level as before and in July 1580 an even greater army of over thirty thousand was stationed further east, at Czasniki on the river Ula. It was again a crossroads and strikes could be made in several directions. Stefan chose to cut the Inflanty off from Muscovy and marched on Wielkie Luki, a city that had never belonged to Lithuania. The war reached beyond the boundaries of the Grand Duchy.

It was the first campaign in which the "select infantry" took part and Jan Zamoyski was commander in his own right. Both performed very well. The king ordered the chancellor to take Wieliz, which had been lost under Alexander Jagiello, and flanked on the east the route of the main army. It was a part of the country that had not been crossed by any army since the days of Witold, protected by old forests, marshes, and abatis.

The Russians had not forgotten the lessons of the previous year. They remembered that only three "fireballs" sufficed to set on fire the palisades of Sokol. The ramparts of Wieliz were covered with turf, which was supposed to shield the underlying wood. But the layer of turf was too thin and the incendiary bullets worked even better; instead of piercing the wood, they ignited its surface. The guns of Mikolaj Urowiecki set the walls on fire and after two days the garrison surrendered, to be released free, though disarmed. A week later Mikolaj Radziwill took Uswiat without encountering any resistance. The sight of the assault preparations was enough.

Stefan's army earned the enemy's growing respect, but its victories did not inspire the citizens of the Commonwealth with any ambitions of conquest. At Wielkie Luki the king negotiated in vain with Ivan's envoys and struggled at the same time with the opposition of some of the Lithuanian senators, who advised the siege to be lifted and the army withdrawn. They did not want to assume additional burdens and argued that even if the fortress should be taken, Moscow would sooner or later try to recapture it, leaving the embers of war smouldering. The article of the *Henrician Covenant* quoted above reflected the sentiments of the majority.

Nevertheless, the king and Zamoyski prevailed. The siege was not lifted and it lasted only ten days.

The fortifications of Wielkie Luki were protected by a layer of turf five or six feet thick, against which artillery was ineffective. Another method, requiring great courage, was adopted: a volunteer carrying incendiary equipment would run up to the ramparts under cover of musket and gunfire, to dig a hole in the turf with a spade and reach the combustible wood underneath. The "select infantry" supplied many volunteers for this type of work and some of them were later granted patents of nobility for their feat.

On September 4 the fortifications caught fire and on the following day the castle was for the taking, but the king never seized it.

The Hungarian troops sent ahead to put out the fire were followed by an unruly mob of auxiliaries and camp followers greedy for booty. Looting and a massacre started amidst chaos. As the chronicler reports, "captains, colonels and the hetman himself tried

82

to stop them, but it was impossible." In the meantime the fire reached the arsenal with its gunpowder stores and the castle was blown up with all its military equipment and the loss of several hundred Poles and Hungarians.

Stefan was dejected, but he did not give up. He drove his men to work and the fort was soon rebuilt. The capture of the castles of Newel and Ozieryszcz by two Nicholases, Drohostajski and Radziwill, secured its rear and communication with Polock.

The campaign was concluded by the man who had started it, Jan Zamoyski. He was assigned the task of taking Zawolocz, a powerful fort, almost impregnable because it was situated on an island in the lake of Podsosz. "It sits on the water like a duck, with no access on any side," wrote the chronicler.

In cold October weather the chancellor's men had to assume the unfamiliar role of sailors, fighting from boats. When they finally built a pontoon bridge, a strong counterattack was launched from the fortress. Too many Poles rushed to the help of the attacking Hungarians, causing the bridge to collapse in the middle and more than two hundred men drowned. Then two separate bridges were erected to avoid rivalry and congestion, one for each of the two national groups. But no assault was needed, for the garrison surrendered when it saw the scale of the preparations. Zamoyski let the defenders go free and held only their officers, but offered them a banquet.

The victorious king returned to Warsaw late in the year and drove up to St.John's cathedral in a sledge, greeted by enthusiastic crowds. But ovations did not influence a Seym longing for peace.

After long deliberations and brilliant speeches by Zamoyski and the king himself ("The enemy will keep the peace only as long as it suits him," said the first; "Time is running out, we have three hundred miles ahead of us and we quibble about expenses," raged the second) the Seym voted taxes, but only for two years instead of the three requested by Stefan.

Some thought the war might not continue at all. There were rumors of conciliatory moves by Ivan. His embassy, which came to Warsaw together with King Stefan, behaved correctly and hinted at concessions. It rejected, however, the key Polish condition: yielding the Inflanty to Poland. In the spring of 1581 the Jesuit Antonio Possevino, envoy of Pope Gregory XIII, arrived in Warsaw. He was on his way to Moscow to discuss a reconciliation of the churches and a league against the Turks. His mission was the result of Ivan's initiative conveyed to Rome by the *boyar* Shchevrigin.

Later historians presented Possevino as a sinister figure, a man who deprived Poland of the fruit of her victories. His likeness in the well-known painting by Matejko is grim and menacing. But in 1581 Father Anthony was greeted by many as a harbinger of peace and a welcome mediator. He was particularly well liked in Lithuania.

The tax revenues were slow in coming and on the appointed date only the Hungarian mercenaries were ready. Even late in June it was not at all certain whether a campaign would be launched.

A decision was forced by a sudden turn in the tsar's position. His new envoys brought to Wilno a writ "as large as a sheet of Cologne cloth" and their language was tough, even insulting. They called their master "ruler by the will of God, not by rebellious human desires." They furthermore backed away from earlier promises and concessions. At the end of June a Russian army, breaking the truce, crossed the Dnieper and reached Mohilev. It was repulsed, but the war was started again.

"Jesus, this is something big, like another Paris," cried the king's secretary, Father Piotrowski, when he first saw Pskov. "A vast city," he wrote in his diary, "such as we do not have in Poland, churches thick like trees in a forest, all of them of stone. Walls so high that one cannot see the houses behind them."

The king came to Pskov with an army greater than any the Commonwealth had ever raised. He had about forty thousand soldiers, not counting the auxiliaries. The forces of the garrison of Pskov, commanded by the Princes Ivan and Wasyl Szuyski, were reportedly even larger. Stefan blocked the Wielika river with logs linked by chains, thus cutting Pskov off from the lake Peipus, and opened the siege.

The double or even quadruple walls were soon broken down by artillery fire. A more serious obstacle was offered by the additional wood and earth fortifications inside the fortress. The first rather spontaneous assault was resisted, though the attacking force took two towers and flew their colors from them. The people of Pskov rushed to the defense and the archbishop ordered the holy relics removed from the cathedral, urging the faithful to defend it.

This happened on September 8, 1581. Temperate weather continued only until the end of that month, but by late October the waters were frozen. The besieging army found itself in a situation similar to that endured later by the French in 1812. Some soldiers yearned for Moscow in the belief that its climate was milder than that of Pskov. Food was scarce and expeditions in search of it were threatened by enemy units roaming the countryside.

On October 22 the triumphant cavalry regiments arrived from the east, led by Christopher Radziwill ("Lightning") and Kmita Czarnobylski. They had crossed the Dnieper in August, made the famous raid to the sources of the Volga, and returned to Pskov via Cholm and Stara Russa. Their action relieved the pressure on the army besieging Pskov and also very nearly changed the course of the war and that of history.

The raiders found themselves at night very near Staryca on the Volga, where Ivan the Terrible was staying, accompanied by Possevino and guarded by only a few hundred men. The tsar saw from his windows the glare of the fires set by the Polish cavalry. He owed his life to a devoted servant, Daniel Mura, who managed to infiltrate the nearby Commonwealth camp and told its soldiers about the allegedly enormous forces guarding Staryca. They believed him and as a result Radziwill and Kmita passed Staryca, which they could have easily taken together with the tsar, and moved northward.

Possevino went directly from Staryca to Pskov to mediate the negotiations there. The psychological effect of the grim night spent with Ivan may have influenced him. The Jesuit was on the whole well received in the Commonwealth camp. Zamoyski was infuriated by premature peace demonstrations, the news of which reached the Pskov defenders. Cold, hungry, and generally lacking enthusiasm for the war, the gentry and soldiers did not conceal their desire for peace. About that time a letter from Szuyski to the tsar was intercepted and additional information secured from the messenger under torture. Pskov was starving, there was no fuel, and the people were rebellious. The chancellor concluded that the fortress could not hold out until spring.

On November 30 a delegation sent to negotiate with the tsar's plenipotentiaries left the camp. A Russian messenger came to ask for a safe conduct for them just when the ring around Pskov was about to be loosened, so that the troops could find better quarters. That plan was then abandoned and the army remained at Pskov, but in much reduced strength. On December 1 the king left for Poland, accompanied by the Lithuanian hetmans, most of the volunteers, and the Germans, whose endurance was at its end. Zamoyski had seven thousand cavalry left, with some infantry, the mercenaries, and only six hundred Lithuanians.

The negotiations were to be conducted in the village of Jam Zapolski, on territory held by the royal troops. That was why the tsar's envoys required a safe conduct.

The delegation of the Commonwealth comprised Janusz Zbaraski, Albrecht Radziwill, and Michal Halaburda. They would be described at the time as two Ruthenians and one Lithuanian, while today they would be called a Ukrainian, a Lithuanian, and a Bielorussian.

The ethnic origin of the Commonwealth's negotiators speaks volumes about its character. Later historians, using a modern perspective, sometimes speak about "Polish expansionism," "Polish acquisitiveness," or even "Polish colonialism." But the role of the ethnic Poles in the multinational Commonwealth bore no resemblance to the role of the French in Algeria or the British in India.

There was, however, one native Pole in the delegation. He was Christopher Warszewicki, an outstanding political writer, also known in western Europe for his translations from Italian to Latin. He was charged with watching the interests of . . . the king of Sweden, who was supposed to be included among the parties to the agreement. Such service by Warszewicki was in line with the statement he had made in his writing to the effect that we are all citizens of the world and should help one another.

The negotiations progressed sluggishly, while the troops at Pskov suffered hunger and were literally freezing to death. Every morning sledges brought back to the camp the numb men of the night watch, or their frozen bodies. There were sorties from the fortress and one of them almost brought disaster. Zamoyski's farsighted caution saved the day. Knowing that the half-frozen guards could offer little resistance, he kept a cavalry reserve in readiness.

The army held on, sustained by its commander's inflexible character. A certain Italian was to call him soon the damned, diabolic chancellor whose tenacity was hardened every day by adversities. Camp discipline was harsh. Even an officer of noble birth was hanged, while stocks and fetters were commonly used.

Zamoyski was rescued by Janusz Zbaraski, one of the negotiators in Jam Zapolski. Knowing that the choice was between peace and disaster, he threatened an immediate break in negotiations. It was the right move, for Moscow was also desperate. He was helped by Possevino's nervous breakdown, which caused him to abandon Jesuit affability and turn to invective.

The truce signed on January 15, 1582 left to the Commonwealth the regions of Polock, Wieliz, Ozieryszcze, Uswiat, and the Inflanty. Wielkie Luki and other territories occupied by the king's forces reverted to Russia.

On February 6 Zamoyski departed from Pskov. The haggard troops shaped up and marched "in an orderly and dignified fashion, so as to give the enemy a fine spectacle." They were going to the Inflanty to occupy without contest the castles that had to be vacated by the Muscovite garrisons under the terms of the truce. On March 13 Stefan met his soldiers in Riga.

He could not reward Zamoyski with high office, since he already held the highest. On the way to Pskov he appointed the chancellor the great hetman of the crown (commander-in-chief), bypassing Jan Zborowski, who had distinguished himself at Tczew. The choice was well made, as Zamoyski had the talents and character of a leader. What was a terrible error, however, was to give the hetman lifetime tenure. An official appointed for life often becomes uncontrollable and therefore above the law. The very existence of high officers of the state with life tenure is a sure recipe for disaster. In this instance that privilege was granted to military commanders, which meant that the standing army slipped outside the king's control. The monarch was left with only the general levy, which could be called to service only with Seym consent and could not be divided into operational units. The office of "great hetman of the crown" did not carry with it senate membership, but it was generally held by members of the families of magnates.

Stefan's personnel policy was consistent. He was right in promoting Zamoyski and his followers, but he went too far by making him hetman for life and allowing personal favor to disrupt the structure of the state. It was, as Talleyrand said, "worse than a crime, a blunder."

The evil consequences of that decision were not immediate. Zamoyski served the country well, as did his successors Stanislaw Zolkiewski and Stanislaw Koniecpolski. But the principle of placing the military power in the hands of one man appointed for life took a heavy toll. That principle was modified, but not until 1776, after the first partition. It was by then too late to correct the errors of the past.

In 1578, when he was trying to induce the Seym to vote taxes for the war, Stefan agreed to relinquish the royal prerogative of civil jurisdiction, in favor of citizens' courts with elected jurors. It was not only a matter of political expediency, for the pressing need for judicial reform was discussed already during the interregnums, and provincial tribunals of last resort were established. Now the problem was resolved by a compromise between the king and the gentry. The royal Seym tribunal retained jurisdiction in urban matters, the criminal cases of the nobility, cases of high treason, and fiscal matters. The provincial tribunals were the courts of appeal in all other matters.

Such a tribunal in Piotrkow served Wielkopolska (western Poland) and another in Lublin dealt with cases from Malopolska (southwest). Three years after the judiciary reform in Poland it was also adopted by Lithuania, and tribunals were established in Wilno and Minsk. A few years later Royal Prussia joined the other provinces. As we see, the autonomy of the component parts of the Commonwealth was not a fiction. A separate tribunal was also established in Luck for Ruthenia, but it did not gain popularity and Ruthenians continued to file in Lublin.

The weak spot of the tribunals was that their judges were elected by the gentry for a single session and could not be elected again until four years later. As a result, the laymen jurors could not acquire experience or legal training. The Polish gentry were neither the first nor the last to commit the error of placing their trust in democratically elected amateurs rather than in professional jurists.

In March 1579, after he arrived in Wilno a few months before starting military operations, the king performed a historic act by raising the local Jesuit college to the rank of an academy, thus establishing the first university in eastern Europe.

It had three faculties: theology, philosophy and liberal arts—as law and medicine were of less interest to the Jesuit order. It had from the first the right to grant degrees and enjoyed the autonomy and privileges customary for universities at the time. The language of instruction was first Latin, then Polish, and more recently Lithuanian. The Stefan Batory University, as it was called after its founder, reached its apogee in the early years of the nineteenth century, under the direction of the Sniadecki brothers, both distinguished scholars. It owed its fame to eminent professors and even more famous poets who were its alumni. Discontinued after the rising of 1830, the university was revived in 1919 when Poland regained independence.

The establishment of the university at Wilno was a major contribution of the Polish-Lithuanian union to the cultural development of eastern Europe.

The character of the university was well defined by its first rector, Piotr Skarga, on whose political activity we will have occasion to comment. He was an outstanding writer and orator, a man of strong character. Skarga Paweski was born in Grojec near Warsaw and the mission he assumed in the east was inspired by the obligations undertaken by Poland at the time of the union in 1386.

Poland's first university, that of Cracow, did not fare well under Stefan Batory. During the first interregnum it almost acquired a scholar of international standing. Bishop de Montluc had planned to take with him to Poland, and to safety, a French Protestant philosopher and grammarian, Pierre Ramus, regarded as a forerunner of Descartes.

The scholar refused and was killed two weeks later during St. Bartholomew's Night. Another eminent French humanist, Francis Balduin, also died as he was about to leave for Poland, invited by Jan Zamoyski to a chair of law in Cracow.

The promise of a revival of Cracow University included in the *Pacta Conventa* was not carried out. King Stefan had considered various plans in this respect, but finally took the easiest course: He started to support the educational activities of the Jesuits, who became the ruthless rivals of the Jagiellonian Academy of Cracow.

About that time the old Polish tradition of seeking instruction in the west began to undergo a change. The journeys in search of knowledge continued, but their compass now pointed more to the north. Italy used to be the goal and now the trend shifted to those of the German universities which were dominated by the counter-reformation. Under Stefan I and later there were many Polish students in Vienna, Gratz, in the Bavarian Ingolstadt and Dillingen, in Freiburg, Wurtzburg, and Mainz. They were the alumni of Jesuit schools in Poland, encouraged by their teachers to attend universities with a similar orientation. They returned with a different set of mind than did the Polish students of earlier generations, who sought during the Golden Age the guidance of the leading progressive thinkers of Europe in the homeland of the Renaissance. An evil seed was sown and the harvest was reaped in the next century—the seventeenth.

Jesuit colleges proliferated in Poland. One was even founded in the recently conquered Polock. King Stefan allegedly had promised Father Skarga at the very beginning of the siege that if it was successful such a college would be established.

It happened that the *starosta* (sheriff) of Lwow refused to consider a lawsuit filed by an Israelite but he was compelled by royal order to appear in court. "Both the Jew and the *starosta* are subjects of the crown," said King Stefan. On another occasion he outlined the monarch's role thus: "I rule the people and God rules their consciences. There are three things that the Lord alone can do: create something out of nothing, foresee the future, and guide the consciences of men."

Both those who suspected the Hungarian at first of Protestant leanings and those who feared that he might be influenced by a fanatical clergy were proved wrong. The harsh Magyar resembled in this one, but most important, respect the effete Zygmunt August, who had also said that he was not the master of people's hearts. Stefan was a Catholic and helped the church as much as he could, but he never encroached upon the law of religious tolerance. He was in this respect, as in many others, in total harmony with Zamoyski. The great chancellor, who had been a Protestant in his youth, avoided the excessive zeal of the convert. He declared that he would give half of his life for Catholic unity and all of it to prevent religious persecution. He strayed from that path only in his old age.

The Jagiellonian tradition of freedom of thought and expression was still alive, though in decline. There were some incidents of interference with non-Catholics, cases of profanation of churches and cemeteries. The king punished severely such excesses, but Cardinal Jerzy Radziwill ordered the books of "heretics" burned publicly in front of his patron's church. Princess Anna Jagiello, a Catholic bigot, strayed from the traditions of her dynasty and declared with pride that there were no dissidents in her province of Masovia.

Zamoyski brought some Jews to his city of Zamosc and granted them a special charter. He assigned to them land outside the city walls for a cemetery and a street within the city; the Jews were not compelled to wear any special attire and could carry arms as did all the other citizens. The sword was not a monopoly of the gentry at that time.

The establishment of Zamosc was hailed throughout Europe and even in Turkey. Witness the settlement there of merchants and artisans from many countries, ranging from England and Portugal to the Middle East. The chancellor promised to the settlers many benefits and full security and he kept his promise. Built on the site of the village of Skokowka, Zamosc became one of the few cities planned by architects and its fortifications were the last word in military engineering. Some decades later it resisted a Cossack army and during the Swedish invasion it was one of the few Polish towns never occupied by the enemy. It served as a sad example of what could have been done elsewhere, but was not.

Jan Zamoyski was a good administrator and he knew how to get the most income from his estates, which spread as far as the river Dniester and were mostly royal grants. The peasants' charges were rather higher than average and the city council and guilds of Zamosc had to swear allegiance to the chancellor "as good vassals should."

Some of the gentry were critical of the methods Zamoyski used to develop his holdings:

> . . . he filled his lands with fugitives and rabble, granting them all kinds of liberties. Even the worst villain, who may have killed his father and mother, brother or master, could count on welcome and protection, so long as the villages were settled. . . .

The chancellor's practices were normal at the time, though far removed from the extreme liberalism of the Polish Brethren, or our present notions of democratic government. One can either condemn or try to justify them, but it was an organizational achievement creating viable communities. The basic condition of their success was their defense potential. Zamoyski guaranteed his subjects security against outside invaders, setting an example for the whole nation, which was not followed by its rulers.

Zamosc received its foundation charter in 1580, the year of King Stefan's expedition against Muscovy. Later, after the king's death, Zamoyski founded in Zamosc a college, which became in 1594 the third university in Poland. It existed for a hundred eighty years and was revived after Poland regained its independence in 1918.

The Zamosc college was headed by Sebastian Klonowicz, the author of poetic works such as "Flis" ('The Boatman') and "Roxanne"; he was assisted by Szymon Szymonowicz, who wrote "The Idylls."

Zamoyski's second marriage, to Christine Radziwill, was also an event of Polish literature. The wedding, held in Ujazdow, featured the premiere of "The Farewell of the Greek Envoys," the classic by Jan Kochanowski.

The martial reign of King Stefan seemed to promise a welcome change in the relationship between the royal court and the arts. Polish literature had flourished during the Jagiellonian Golden Age, but it was not particularly favored by the kings. The writers did share to some extent in the Jagiellonian generosity, but it has been observed that their patronage could not match that of the Renaissance popes, the Italian princes, or the Valois of France.

Under Stefan I the royal court and that of his second in command, Chancellor Zamoyski, were wide open to a galaxy of scholars and writers. The king himself, an assiduous reader of Julius Caesar, particularly favored historians. He followed closely the work of Reinhold Heidenstein and even corrected it personally. He funded the studies of Stanislaw Sarnicki and sought access to the Vatican archives for Polish historians. He granted to Lukasz Gornicki, an outstanding writer, the office of *starosta* (sheriff) of Wasilkow, even though he had already received from his predecessor the *starosta* of Tykocin. At the very beginning of his reign, Stefan took from his wife's court Andrzej Patrycy Nidecki and kept him in his immediate entourage, finally appointing him a bishop.

Zamoyski surpassed the king as a patron of the arts. Alexander Bruckner writes: "His court attracted the writers of the time: jurists, historians, linguists, poets, even more than the courts of Tomicki or Maciejowski, while the chancellor also had contacts with Italian and French intellectuals."

Zamoyski, fluent in several languages, kept in touch with the west, where he had been educated. Among the western thinkers whom he helped, only one was a German—Jan Casselius, a classical scholar. That fact reflected the chancellor's political leanings.

The troops that Zamoyski commanded in his second campaign against Muscovy were in mourning, for Christine Radziwill died early. The chancellor's third marriage had political overtones. His bride at the altar of the Cracow cathedral was Griselda Batory, a niece of King Stefan and a Protestant. Did this mean that the groom hoped to inherit the crown of his wife's uncle? If so, it was an excellent idea, though very difficult to carry out.

This time, in 1593, the wedding was not immortalized by any literary event. Cracow was humming with feasts, entertainments, and tournaments, while models of the fortresses taken from Tsar Ivan were on display. Zamoyski came to the capital for a short time and his domestic staff had to make sure that their master lacked for nothing. Inventories of the chancellor's wardrobe on that occasion were described in a book by Jan Tarnawski. We can now peer under the festive attire of Jan Zamoyski and examine even his underwear. He brought with him to Cracow fourteen "Italian" shirts and thirty-five "hussar" ones, including nine threaded with gold and three with silver; twenty five pairs of underpants; forty-two handkerchiefs; nineteen towels, including one large bath towel; ten bedsheets; and eighteen pillow cases.

This was the groom's equipment. It may be that the lesser members of the wedding were not as well supplied, but even so they were lavishly dressed in the Polish sixteenth-century style. Let us recall that it was a time when the stairs of the Louvre palace in Paris served as the courtiers' toilets and the cemeteries in the center of the French capital emanated an unbearable stench. Stefan surprised the senators early in his reign when he took off one of his boots during a session of the royal council, displaying a none-too-clean sock. Zamoyski was ahead of his king in personal grooming, for he came to the wedding with six pairs of silk stockings, two cotton and several linen ones.

Immediately after the chancellor's wedding, King Stefan went hunting in Niepolomice. (He was an avid hunter. When working hard in Dzisna preparing the Pskov expedition, he nevertheless rode every day at sunrise into the woods to hunt). It was rumored that men with designs on the king's life were lurking in the Niepolomice forest. There was also an assassination plot during his proposed journey to Lublin and the attempt was to be made at Zborow, by the three Zborowski brothers—Christopher, Andrzej, and Samuel. The latter reportedly withdrew from the plot and advised against it.

His marriage to a Batory princess confirmed Zamoyski's position as second only to the monarch, but it also hastened domestic strife. The events of the following year—1584—barred the chancellor's path to the throne, if he had indeed contemplated it.

The conflicts that shook the nation after the Muscovy wars stemmed from the king's personnel policy. Stefan was consistent in rewarding his supporters with the "bread," of which he was the dispenser. Graziani and other foreign theoreticians considered the prerogative of granting lands and offices as a valuable instrument of government.

As is always the case, the favors received by some embittered others. The magnates envied Zamoyski and the peaceloving gentry complained about the benefits of the military. The Zborowski clan was particularly incensed by the "injustice" it suffered. They had expected great things when helping the duke of Transylvania to become Stefan I and were bitterly disappointed, for power had already seemed within their grasp.

The Hungarian was an elective king and faced a problem that is as familiar in today's politics as it was in the sixteenth century. People are convinced that if they vote for someone, they merit a reward and make no bones about demanding it. Stefan was well aware of that fact and he rewarded generously those of his supporters whom he judged to be of value to the state. He left the others in the cold, a feat that few politicians manage to perform.

The best of the Zborowskis, Jan, behaved with some restraint, at any rate by the standards of the period. But Christopher plotted with Vienna and Moscow, even took money from Ivan the Terrible during his war with the Commonwealth, while Andrzej assisted him. Samuel, an adventurer banished ten years earlier, was stirring up trouble in the Ukraine and in Poland. All three were inciting opposition and contributed to the failure of the Seym session of 1582.

The government knew about their contacts with foreign powers and had intercepted certain letters, as well as information about actual or alleged designs on the king's life.

In May 1584 Zamoyski learned on his way to Cracow that Samuel Zborowski and his men were following him. The chancellor waited deliberately until both groups were within the area of his jurisdiction as *starosta* of Cracow and then ordered Samuel arrested in Piekary. Little resistance was offered and only one man was killed. The hetman's order was carried out by officers who had distinguished themselves in the field and were rightly rewarded by Stefan: Stanislaw Zolkiewski, Jan Drohojowski, Mikolaj Urowiecki, Wojciech Wybranowski.

After consulting the king, Zamoyski ordered Samuel Zborowski executed and he was beheaded on May 26, 1584, at the Lubranka tower on Wawel hill, where criminals were hanged. His body was immediately delivered to the family, which placed it on public display.

The execution was carried out by virtue of a verdict ten years old, for the homicide of castellan Wapowski. No new trial was held. This was an error of the king and the chancellor, which had far-reaching consequences. Everyone knew that Zborowski had returned from banishment unlawfully, but he did so with Stefan and later remained in the country unmolested for several years, with the knowledge of the king and the hetman-chancellor.

Public opinion was outraged. The county councils went berserk. That of Proszowice held its meeting in the church in which the coffin of Samuel was guarded by his young son.

Political agitation was not the only reason of the unrest. The way in which the Samuel Zborowski case was handled offended the sense of legality of the gentry.

Despite the outcry of the county councils, at which the king's supporters, however, also spoke openly and boldly, the senate decided to call the Seym to session in Warsaw in January 1585 and put Christopher and Andrzej Zborowski on trial.

It was a spectacular event. The castle was under heavy royal guard, the opposition was vocal, some well-intentioned people tried conciliation, and the king with his chancellor stonewalled the issue.

Christopher Zborowski was sentenced to banishment and the confiscation of his estates, while the case against Andrzej was postponed. Zamoyski, charged by both brothers with planning to poison them, was the winner. The opposition failed to influence the policies of King Stefan, which was the real goal of the contest.

The subsequent tragic course of Poland's history caused Samuel Zborowski to become a gruesome symbol, the subject of many literary works. Some of them referred to the "boundlessly free Polish soul," that "flagellates itself in madness, understood by no one, not even by itself." But a contemporary witness of the events, the papal nuncio Laureo, wrote that the Poles' blood was thinned by their inordinate love of beer and made it impossible for them to engage in real political battle.

Magnates plotting against their own monarch were very common in Europe at the time. Those we would not describe as guilty of treason were the exception rather than the rule. The three

Zborowski brothers were actually political small fry and owed their prominence only to their vast estates. As to Samuel, he was merely a junior cavalry officer and an adventurer. To clean his escutcheon he took part in the Moscow campaign but, unlike many others, he failed to distinguish himself, though he was not lacking in courage. In the countries of western Europe, more advanced than Poland, treason was practiced at that time and much later by personalities of the highest rank. The Great Condé, worshipped in France much more than all the hetmans put together were in Poland, had fought against France for years in league with the king of Spain. That was in the seventeenth century. But at the time of the Zborowski affair, in 1588, Henry III of France ordered two dukes of Guise, one a cardinal and the other a layman, murdered without any trial. He could not even dream of charging them in a court of law, but he protected the integrity of France. The Sorbonne university condemned him, and most of the cities formed a coalition against him (even though the article of *non praestanda oboedientia* existed in Polish, but not French constitutional law). The Spanish ambassador started recruiting troops against the king in France, his own country. In the following year Henry III was stabbed and killed by a monk, Jacob Clement. France was saved, but by what means and at what a price!

At the beginning of Stefan's reign, Prince Janusz Zbaraski roamed freely in the Ukraine, quite needlessly provoking the Turks, with the assistance of the Cossacks. The king warned him several times and finally sent him a letter phrased in language which the magnates did not take seriously under Zygmunt August: "Know that you will not be able to easily excuse this away. . . ." The prince understood the message and immediately turned around. Eager to appease the king, he acted despicably when he deceived and delivered to the royal authority his Cossack associate, Ivan Podkova, who was later executed in Lwow.

The case of Samuel Zborowski and other conflicts with the powerful lords were evidence not of decay, but rather of the Commonwealth's sound health. The government brought the Zborowskis to heel, though it erred by doing so outside the law. The tumultuous outcries of the county councils calmed down and within two years after Samuel's execution the king was again popular among the gentry, so much so that he could plan again major foreign campaigns.

No one could foresee that by the time the ill feeling was fully dissipated, a new election would have to be called.

The Seym session of 1585 failed, not because of the much-publicized Zborowski affair, but by reason of another, less-known event. In the last day of the session a small group of deputies, headed by Mikolaj Kazimierski, protested the resolutions. The protest was recorded and the session closed without enacting any legislation. It was the second time this happened, the first being three years earlier, immediately after the wars with Muscovy. It was becoming clear that the Seym of the Commonwealth was on its way to being the instrument of the minority rather than the majority.

There was as yet no *liberum veto*, which could allow an individual to nullify a parliamentary resolution. This was to come seventy years later. Mikolaj Kazimierski and his associates created the worst of precedents, but they actually had not invented anything and merely acted in accordance with the spirit of the system. Their action was possible in the absence of a majority-vote rule and another that would determine that the members of parliament were the representatives of the entire nation—even if only its gentry—and not those of a particular county council. In the absence of any such rules, the Seym became a "federation of counties" and as such could not ignore the voice of any one of them.

Under Zygmunt August, in the heroic era of the great Seyms of the Polish crown, the feat of reaching unanimity was regularly performed over several decades and the majority decided. The Seym of the Commonwealth of Both Nations failed to do so. The mechanism had not been properly set up in time, though this could have been done easily. It was still functioning to some extent but not as a whole. Some gears turned loose, uncoupled from the rest.

With the Seym impotent, the transaction of any business required an appeal to the county councils, thus confirming them in their conceits of omnipotence and running a vicious circle. It was still rotating rather slowly and there was time for breaking out. The old neighborly method of persuasion and winning the opposition to the majority side was no longer enough, indeed it amounted to a trap tempting with easy solutions.

The organism of the Commonwealth was sound but it needed a clear-cut constitutional base and a leadership with definite goals. Any government must rely on popular support and seek it, but it has to set its programs first. Political parties aiming at a constitutional or other reform usually start by trying to assume power. Political power is an indispensable instrument in the life of any human community.

Under Stefan I foreign affairs were the primary concern of the administration. Ivan's invasion of the Inflanty brought the security of that province and Lithuania to the forefront. But there was also the judiciary reform—the governmental structure was consolidated, and the gentry induced to make a major effort in the national interest. The king then placed on the Seym agenda the matter of the legislation setting the rules of the next election.

One can well understand why the king and Zamoyski were anxious to finish quickly the Samuel Zborowski imbroglio instead of starting a long-drawn judicial process. The year was 1584. In early spring Lew Sapieha was sent to Moscow as the Commonwealth's ambassador, but was met halfway by momentous news. Ivan the Terrible died on March 18 and was succeeded by an incompetent minor.

The tsar was married six times (or perhaps even eight), in violation of all the canons of his church and had eight children. At the time of his death only two sons survived. The 27-year-old Theodore—the one whom the Polish gentry had favored in the last election—was well fitted to be a hermit, a monk, or ascete, but not even an abbot. Extremely devout, he was called by his countrymen "Simple Fyodor" and was furthermore in poor health. His half-brother, Dymitr, the offspring of the tsar's last marriage, was an unknown, since he was aged two.

The original heir to the throne—Ivan—died on November 19, 1582. He was killed by his father with the sharp spike with which the tsar used to stab members of his entourage. There were rumors to the effect that the tsar had removed Ivan from succession and wanted to keep it for Dymitr, but this seems unlikely, as at the time of the tragedy at the Kremlin Dymitr was exactly one month of age, while the Crown Prince Ivan was nearly thirty. The well-known painting by Elias Riepin, an old man with fear and madness in his eyes, grasping the blood-soaked body of his son, probably reflects the truth.

Soon after the return of Sapieha another ambassador was sent eastward. He was old Michal Haraburda, "a man of ready wit and well versed in Muscovite matter," recently appointed castellan of Minsk and senator. He carried proposals inspired by the almost habitual and addictive fantastic dreams of union. In the event of the death of one of their rulers, the Commonwealth and the Grand Duchy of Moscow were to be united under a single monarch. In the meantime Haraburda proposed a perpetual peace, conditional upon Smolensk, Novgorod, and Pskov reverting to the Commonwealth. The Russian side responded with equally ambitious territorial claims.

It was quite permissible to discuss in the Polish Seym the eventuality of the monarch's demise, without causing any offense. But the *boyars* refused to hear any mention of the tsar's death and the metropolite threatened with excommunication anyone mentioning the subject.

Stefan I was of the opinion that the death of Ivan the Terrible invalidated the ten-year truce concluded at Jam Zapolski. The provisional agreement stated that the truce would be terminated in June of 1587. Haraburda refused an extension and left Moscow for Grodno, where he reported to the king and soon afterward died himself.

King Stefan already had at that time the promise of the first installment of the papal subsidy, twenty-five thousand gold ducats. When the military operations started, that sum was to be paid monthly. Pope Sixtus V, persuaded by his legate Anthony Possevino, decided to give to the Hungarian king of Poland financial support. The recently deceased Gregory XIII—who had reformed the calendar—also supported Stefan I, but preferred to spend his funds on Catholic schools throughout Europe.

Only five years had elapsed since the parliamentary session at which the gentry reluctantly voted the funds for the Pskov expedition and listened with little enthusiasm to the king's words: "God is my witness that if the good of the Commonwealth required it, I would think of conquering not only Muscovy, but all of the north. . . ." In 1586, as Jan Solikowski noted, "there was a change of mind and funds for the war were voted gladly." Other evidence also shows that the next parliament would not be in opposition to the king.

Niccolo Machiavelli recommended to rulers great deeds as the surest way to the hearts of their subjects. Batory humiliated Gdansk only formally, he dealt with the problem of Prussia superficially but he won three campaigns in the east and recovered lost territories, he showed thoughness by breaking down the Zborowski clan and secured the support of Rome. The Commonwealth had not seen such a string of successes in generations.

The pope funded his endeavors because the king convinced him that the road to Istanbul led through Moscow. It was a matter of defeating Muscovy, seizing its throne, achieving a union, and then attacking the Sultan with united Slav forces.

Rome aimed at a fusion of the churches and a general Christian crusade against Islam. Many of Stefan's statements prove that his ultimate goal was the liberation of Hungary. Nevertheless, many scholars regard such ambitious plans as a feint. They believe that the proposed expedition had one goal: the Commonwealth's victory over Moscow. This interpretation is consistent with the fact that the gentry had elected Batory precisely to avoid a war with Turkey.

As far as is known, Niccolo Machiavelli was the first to describe Poland as the "Bastion of Christendom." The Polish political writers of the sixteenth century were inclined to yield that glorious title to Moscow, without attenuating the conflict over the Ruthenian provinces, started under Gedymin and Olgierd.

The county councils were on the whole pro-government and the Seym session scheduled for February promised to be successful. The truce with Moscow was due to terminate in June.

Stefan I died in Grodno on December 12, 1586, after a five-day illness. His death was so sudden that the king, though a practicing Catholic, did not have time for confession. His death gave precedence to the next election over the planned war, as a headless state could hardly undertake military initiatives.

Wawel housed for ten years a real ruler, but he passed by rather than reigned. He fell victim to an old complaint and not to poison, contrary to rumors. According to medical experts it was probably a case of uremia or arterosclerosis, from which he had suffered already in Transylvania. A stressful life, the wars, and a love of liquor and hunting contributed to an early death. Fifty-three was not considered old age even then.

Zeromski, a great writer of the early twentieth century, made Stefan I the protagonist of "The Hetman's Saga," which said:

> "You stamped my corpse into the ground and pierced my
> breast with an aspen stake, so that the ghost could never
> rise and bring great designs into your midst."

Bishop Pawel Piasecki, who had known the king, wrote: "His remains, brought in solemn procession from Grodno to Cracow, were buried there in the cathedral; the entire funeral service was at public cost—this is only done for kings that earned a special affection among the people; the expense of the burial of others is charged to their personal treasury, usually well filled.

The subsequent loss of independence caused certain deformations in the Poles' way of thinking. Any opposition to the monarch is cited as evidence of anarchy. A disobedient community is judged depraved, decadent. Such a view contributes to many complications in the life of the nation and also to erroneous historical judgments.

Conflict can be eliminated from political life no more than from nature. The overcoming of obstacles is life's rule, not an exception. The example of the Valois prince who fled from Poland shows that the opposition encountered by Stefan Batory was less than par for the Europe of his time. One can rather marvel how so much could have been achieved in ten years. The monarch was not alone, all the best elements of the gentry were on his side. "After the death of King Stefan, Poland was left orphaned," but the next election was won by his men, those who had collaborated with him; and those sharpening the aspen stake lost out.

The harsh verdicts of some historians are all the more misplaced as they are contradicted by many of the leading European thinkers and political writers of the period. The Commonwealth was at the time the object of keen interest in the West, which perceived the value of the political experiment it was witnessing. The continent was then in the throes of a contest between the advocates of royal absolutism and those proclaiming the national community superior to the monarch. The opinions of both factions were collected in the major work of professor Stanislaw Kot, *The Polish Commonwealth in the Political Literature of the West*. Reading it, we may deplore the decline of later centuries, when even a minor article about Poland published abroad was greeted as a political event. In the sixteenth century, political developments in Poland were followed with keen attention by the leading authorities of Europe. Their opinions varied, but none displayed indifference.

The nation that restricted the authority of its monarchs by law and entrusted them with power only on the basis of a written contract not only prospered and won military victories, but grew and developed. There were no massacres or mass persecutions, citizens lived in conditions of freedom that were the envy of other nations. That was the feature of the Polish-Lithuanian experience which aroused keen interest throughout the continent. The Commonwealth, democratic by comparison with its contemporaries, functioned well and had good prospects, despite the difficulties encountered by its leaders. The European thinkers of the time, the forerunners of the Enlightenment, found in that fact a convincing argument in support of their theories.

King Stefan's ambitious plans in the east, including the conquest of Muscovy and its ultimate union with Poland, were no doubt visionary. Istanbul remains Turkish to this day and even the emperors of Great Russia never managed to seize it. The expedition funded with papal ducats probably would have brought victories and the capture of Smolensk at least. The king, strong in the glow of success, would have had an excellent chance of carrying out constitutional reforms. Jan Zamoyski had advocated majority vote in the Seym already at the time of the first interregnum, while the king was certainly not a man inclined to tolerate anarchy and chaos.

It must be emphasized that Poland's and Europe's interest did not require at all the conversion of the Commonwealth into an absolute monarchy. All that was needed was a strengthening of its constitutional system, which might then have served the continent as a valuable model.

Some of the writers commenting on the Polish-Lithuanian state viewed it from a denominational point of view. The Catholics naturally criticized the Warsaw Confederacy and the freedom it granted to heretics. The latter, however, were not unanimous in their approval of a constitutional system that extended religious freedom also to the Arians, whom they detested. The Commonwealth was blamed on that ground also by Calvin's successor, Theodore de Beze, who was himself sentenced in absentia to the stake by the king of France.

CHAPTER 4

SERVANT OF DOCTRINE

A small group of advisers may easily arouse the hatred of citizens and inflict on the body politic a protracted and malignant disease. Such an illness is more easily prevented than cured.

I

The county councils, convoked in December in support of King Stefan's military plans, proved very helpful after his death. Taken by surprise by the news, they promptly adopted resolutions ensuring peace and order throughout the country. It was for the third time in a brief fourteen years that the Commonwealth was faced by an interregnum. This time, however, the majority of the electorate took a firm position from the very onset of the crisis. Political storms raged in Warsaw, but did not reach the provinces until after the election. The great lords feuded, but the mass of the gentry failed to follow them, wary of a civil war.

Nevertheless, some troubling events risked nullifying the resolutions of the county councils. Precedent and national interest dictated a confirmation of the religious peace. All the secular senators and most of the deputies urged it at the March parliamentary session, but the episcopate resisted the motion. Stanislaw Karnkowski, the primate, left Warsaw, followed by the bishops—some of them making dramatic gestures. Fortunately one of the bishops was persuaded to turn back. He was Wawrzyniec Goslicki, bishop of Kamieniec, a writer and intellectual, author of the *De Optimo Senatore*, a work acclaimed throughout Europe. His signature on the covenant of religious tolerance, with the cautious annotation "for the sake of peace," did not enhance his career, for Rome never forgot it.

The papal nuncio, Hannibal of Capua, had just entered Poland and was stopped at Oswiecim. Polish customs prohibited foreign diplomats from traveling in the country during an interregnum. Hannibal flouted the law and left town at dawn. The few guards on duty did not stop him, perhaps impressed by the size of his retinue and its ecclesiastic character. He was held up in Cracow for a time before finally reaching Warsaw, where he hastened to the royal castle and the dowager queen, who had just been awarded by the pope the Order of the Golden Rose. Anne Jagiello greeted the envoy of Rome with reverence and the record of their conversation was one of total accord. The nuncio and the queen assured each other of their sincere desire to see the election of a Catholic candidate.

The nuncio, however, had been instructed to support the Habsburgs, while the dowager queen was determined to seat on the throne her nephew, Zygmunt Vasa, the crown prince of Sweden.

Both candidates had flawless Catholic credentials, but Rome put its money on the German prince, as did Vienna, Madrid, the Catholic princes of the Reich, and even the largely Protestant Zborowski faction. Philip II sent to Prague ample funds for bribing the Poles. Suddenly a quantity of *thalers* with the likeness of Rudolph II turned up in circulation. Even the vast fortunes of the queen and Jan Zamoyski could hardly match such competition, but human talents, characters, and passions proved more powerful than gold.

The election of 1587 was the only chapter of Polish history shaped by a woman. It is true that Jadwiga was part of an even far greater event, but the girl queen—though she played the leading part—was neither the author nor the director of a play staged by the Polish and Lithuanian lords, not forgetting Jagiello himself. This time his great granddaughter was in control. It was she who check-mated the Habsburgs, put up a counter-candidate and overcame his reluctance to assume the crown.

Anne Jagiello was forty-nine when, after her brother's death, she first appeared on center stage. She was sixty-three when she reached the apogee of her bitter life. The tomb prepared by her order had been awaiting her for three years in the Zygmunt chapel of the Wawel cathedral.

Throughout the reign of Stefan I, his neglected and lonely spouse was working on her own secret plan. She was preparing the election that would follow the death of a husband ten years her junior. Her scheme was well designed, but it could never work without her presence. When Anne first conceived her plan for young Zygmunt, his father welcomed the glory that the crown of Poland would bring to his dynasty. But by 1587 John III no longer wanted it for his son. Catherine Jagiello, Zygmunt's mother, was dead and the court of Stockholm had changed its orientation.

Anne wanted to see at Wawel Castle one of the children of the king of Sweden, whose mother had been a Jagiello. She remained loyal to her clan's greatness and tradition. Last of the dynasty, she was the bearer of its historic policy. Yet she did not share the anti-Habsburg bias of the Polish gentry, who cried, "A German sticks in our throats." She had perceived long ago that Maximilian was the one of the emperor's brothers who would have the best chance and decided that, if Zygmunt should fail to become king, at least his sister could be queen of Poland and Lithuania. To do so, she would have to marry the Habsburg archduke and the queen managed to convince Vienna that Stockholm was agreeable to the plan. The old queen knew how to bend the truth to suit her designs.

They fitted perfectly the mood of the Polish gentry, enamoured of the Jagiellonian tradition and eager to see the next chapter of the Commonwealth's history as a continuation of the earlier ones. Already under King Stefan a secretary of the papal mission in Poland wrote to Rome that it was hard to see the election of a native "Piast" in a country whose greatest magnates were Ruthenians. That was why, the Italian diplomat argued dispassionately, the candidate with the best chance would be one related to the Jagiellonians, though himself a foreigner.

Such considerations ruled out the election of a native Pole, even though one of them was eminently qualified. The future history of

105

the Commonwealth might have taken a very different course if Zamoyski was elected instead of Vasa. The chancellor and great hetman still had eighteen years of life ahead of him. He had proved his talent and his character; he was a first rate administrator, though somewhat ruthless, which may be an asset in a political leader. One can assume that he would have fortified the Commonwealth as he did his own domain of Zamosc and that he would not be a wastrel. His descendants live to this day and the future was to prove that the Polish gentry, though guarding jealously the principle of elective monarchy, was inclined to call to the throne the king's son, if he had any. The case of the Sobieskis, in a different era, does not invalidate that argument.

It seems that Zamoyski contemplated his own candidacy, but could not promote it himself. The fury of the Zborowski opposition was turned against him and only three years had passed since Samuel's execution. The storm raised by that affair did not dislodge the king, but it barred the chancellor's path to the throne, though it did not prevent him being the leader of an important section of the electorate.

Lithuania stepped aside. Its delegates even set up their tents on the right bank of the Vistula, far from the Polish tents. The Lithuanians wanted to keep for themselves the Inflanty, won for the Commonwealth by common effort. They also concluded with Moscow a ten-year truce, without consulting Poland. An independent foreign policy is one of the main attributes of a sovereign state. No one could deny that the Grand Duchy kept its separate identity within the Union of Lublin which associated it with Poland.

In all three elections of the sixteenth century Lithuania adopted delaying tactics, which actually prolonged the crisis. It was the price paid by the Commonwealth for being a multinational state.

Queen Anne remained in Warsaw, witnessing the convocation that seemed to favor the Zborowski clan. She dealt with them and did not burn her bridges to Vienna. She helped the nuncio in his correspondence, sending his letters to Rome under her own seal, while she constantly pressured Stockholm at the same time. With an unending stream of envoys and messages, she demanded no less than a union of Poland and Sweden, with Estonia assigned to the Commonwealth. The queen held up her sleeve a card of which John III was well aware. Gustav Eriksson Vasa, the son of the poisoned King Erik XIX, was traveling in Europe, temporarily outside Poland. Anne had brought him up at her court, thus clearing the way to the Swedish throne for her brother-in-law, but she was prepared to advance Gustav's claim if necessary. The aging lady included blackmail among her weapons.

She won her first point when she persuaded King John III to send his ambassadors to Poland. They were representatives of the Swedish aristocracy, who welcomed the departure of their crown prince to Poland, likely to leave them in effective control of Sweden.

The convocation, largely dominated by the Zborowski clan, set the opening of the election Seym for June 30, a date chosen to discourage the attendance of many of the gentry, absorbed at that time with harvest preparations. Contrary to that expectation, the electorate turned up in droves, eager to decide the country's fate and attracted by the great show that the elections had become. Thanks to the tireless efforts of Queen Anne, the three Habsburgs competing against one another—Ernest, Matthew, and Maximilian—were faced by the Swedish Crown Prince Zygmunt. The Swedish envoys arrived in Warsaw on June 22 and held two days later a lengthy secret conference with the queen. A week later the chancellor arrived at the head of three thousand cavalry, whom he deployed by the royal castle as he conferred with the queen.

The Moscow candidacy, which Zamoyski considered, won support in Lithuania after Ivan's death. The incompetence of Theodore was already known in Poland. The attempted candidacy of the Tartar khan was greeted with laughter.

Two acts of violence, attempted by the Zborowski clan and the Stanislaw Gorka faction, backfired, proving that the Commonwealth did not tolerate such methods. Zamoyski frustrated the attempted kidnapping of the primate; his soldiers surrounded the Bernardine abbey and the archbishop was moved with honors to the royal castle. The appearance of the armed troops of the opposition at the election field also failed to produce the desired result. The forces under hetman Zamoyski, still in mourning, held their positions, backed by the regiments of one of the most powerful magnates of the Commonwealth, Prince Constantine Ostrogski, a pillar of the Orthodox church.

An armed clash was avoided, though the burghers had needlessly closed the city gates. In the evening the nuncio observed the election field near Warsaw from the belfry of St.John's Cathedral. At sunset both sides left their positions, but the chancellor was politically the winner as he was not the one who had threatened violence. The undecided among the gentry began to lean toward Zamoyski.

He took action when the interrex (regent), the primate Stanislaw Karnkowski, offended by the behavior of the Zborowskis, joined his side. On August 19, 1587, the majority of the senators and gentry elected the Swedish prince as King Zygmunt III. As the "Te Deum Laudamus" was sung in the cathedral, Queen Anne listened, invisible in a gallery. She preferred to witness the moment of her greatest triumph alone. She pledged her entire fortune as a guarantee of the conditions sworn upon by the Swedish envoys, which included the transfer of Estonia.

Zamoyski seized the opportunity and won. On the following day the primate apologized to the nuncio, explaining that he was under heavy pressure from the gentry. Two days later, on August 22, the Habsburg supporters declared the election of Archduke Maximilian. The role of the primate was enacted in that illegal election by the bishop of Kiev, Woroniecki, although he had no authority to perform that function. His king-elect, Maximilian, had troops just across the border, as well as the support of the emperor and in Poland that of the Zborowskis, Gorka, and their friends, among them the notorious Stanislaw "the Devil" Stadnicki of Lancut, the Polish version of a robber baron.

The Swedish naval squadron carrying the king-elect and his sister, Princess Anne Vasa, was driven into Gdansk harbor by a storm. Following parental guidance, Zygmunt had planned to receive the officials of the Commonwealth first aboard a Swedish ship, but weather conditions compelled him to go on land. He demanded a safe conduct from the city of Gdansk and was proclaimed king in the cathedral of Oliwa. A week later, without undue haste and though urged by his father to turn back, he proceeded southward via Malbork, into parts of the country where the Zborowskis' and Maximilians' forces were loose.

Zamoyski defeated them in the Garbary suburb of Cracow, leading personally an attack by his "black" infantry. Andrzej Zborowski, commanding on the Austrian side, fled at the sight of the hetman, fearing that he might share his brother Samuel's fate if captured.

Zygmunt received news of the victory at Korczyn, where he was crossing the Vistula. Another messenger brought him at the same time a letter from his father, ordering him to return to Sweden.

Zygmunt reportedly replied that he would enter the capital, be crowned, give his sister in marriage to Archduke Ernest and yield to him the crown before returning home.

Gabriel Holubek, commander of the garrison of the castle of Rabsztyn, distinguished himself in the military operations of the period. He was a Cossack from the Zaporozhe region of the Ukraine, known for a sharp tongue as well as for valor in battle. When Maximilian tried to entice him with promises of favors, he replied, "There are no more traitors in Poland, they are all on your side." Holubek was envied by other officers when he defeated by a sudden attack an Austrian cavalry unit escorting a large supply train. His Cossacks took rich booty, as did also the local miners enlisted by Holubek.

Cracow greeted the new king in festive attire. Triumphal arches were adorned with portraits of his ancestors, all the seven Jagiellonian monarchs' likenesses based by Zamoyski's order on "the oldest statues." The coat of arms of the dynasty of Vasa "the Sheaf" was also on display and can be seen to this day on many Polish monuments. Zygmunt was welcomed by the elite of the nobility and addressed by Wawrzyniec Goslicki and by Swietoslaw Orzelski, also a writer, author of famous memoirs and activist of the reform party under Stefan I. Both speakers emphasized the ties of Zygmunt with Poland and greeted him as "one of our own."

The crowd was delighted when the king responded in Polish, the language of his mother. He treated Zamoyski with some reserve and coolness in an otherwise bombastic and self-congratulatory address. Some people had already tried to turn the new monarch against the chancellor. Zygmunt was of a suspicious nature, easily prejudiced and very reluctant to change his ideas.

Yet no one tried to replace Zamoyski, and the army under his command pursued Maximilian as he retreated toward Silesia. The chancellor's adversaries hoped for his failure, but on January 24 he defeated the archduke's forces at Byczyna, while Maximilian sought refuge in the town with the remnant of his entourage. On the following day Zamoyski compelled them to surrender, taking prisoner Maximilian and his Polish supporters. The huge booty was shared by the soldiers, except for Habsburg's personal belongings, which were immediately returned to him.

Gabriel Holubek fell at Byczyna and Stanislaw Zolkiewski was seriously wounded. About eighteen hundred Poles and almost as many Germans were left on the battlefield. The month-old coronation of Zygmunt III was sanctioned by victory.

In the night before the battle, Zamoyski hastily wrote a letter to the king, dated from the village of Zadluby. He reported a successful skirmish at Parzymiechy, in which the troops of "the Devil" Stadnicki were wiped out and the main enemy force compelled to leave Wielun and retreat toward Silesia in the direction of Byczyna. Some units were already in pursuit; others would move "as soon as the moon rises." As to Maximilian:

> He flees in haste with little dignity, followed by his cavalry, many of them discarding their weapons on the way. I shall report to Your Majesty what happens next. In the meantime, Your Majesty may thank God Almighty that your rival, the heir of many emperors and the emperor's brother, fled from your realm in shame by night.

The reign of Zygmunt III started under favorable auspices, better than those of Stefan, his predecessor. The majority of his subjects welcomed the young monarch affectionately because of the memory of his Jagiellonian ancestors. His coronation was sealed by a victory over famous German regiments, some Polish dissidents, and Hungarian mercenaries. King Stefan had fought successfully in the east, but these were victories at the walls of Cracow and in Silesia. A foreign observer then in Poland wrote that the Poles do not long for a war with Austria, but almost no one is afraid of it.

II

Some months later another foreign observer noted with glee that the Polish adversaries of Austria were incensed by the development of events. They were engaged by the splendor of the reception offered by the king to the mission of Hipolite Cardinal Aldobrandini (the future Pope Clement VIII), who was known to be acting as a mediator between Poland and the Habsburgs. Zygmunt treated him with special honors and held with him secret conferences.

Emperor Rudolph II wanted peace and the release of his brother, but he insisted on negotiating only with the senators, as he did not recognize Zygmunt III as king.

After prolonged talks conducted in Bedzin and Bytom, an agreement was reached. The Habsburgs withdrew their claims to

110

the Polish crown and concluded with the Commonwealth a treaty of perpetual peace, which actually did prove durable: in the seventeenth century Austria helped Poland to recover Cracow from the Swedes, while the Poles reciprocated with Sobieski's relief of Vienna threatened by the Turks. A radical change did not occur until the participation of Austria in the partitions of Poland in the eighteenth century.

The treaty alone would have been acceptable to the gentry, always anxious to keep peace, but its circumstances were peculiar.

Archduke Maximilian was kept in Krasnystaw in gilded captivity under the supervision of Zamoyski, who treated the prisoner courteously, but only within certain limits. Finally the king paid a visit to Maximilian. The senators barely managed to convince the king that it would have been inappropriate for him to dismount his horse until the archduke, who had refused at first to leave his chambers, reached the bottom of the steps. Zygmunt III was noted by history as the "most royal of kings." He was that to his subjects, but not to a Habsburg.

Maximilian received lavish gifts. He was particularly delighted by a dozen fine horses, among them eight "tinted beautiful yellow."

Under the agreement he was supposed to swear an oath confirming the Bedzin-Bytom treaty. He declared haughtily that he would do so only after crossing the Polish border, but afterwards he refused to swear, simply breaking his promise. The persuasions of Bishop Goslicki and other senators failed to move him and all they could do was to decline any gifts and refuse participation in a farewell banquet. "So children will jeer us when we return to Poland," said Mikolaj Firlej, *voievode* of Cracow.

One of the members of the Polish group went into rage and drew his sword, but the others managed to contain his fury. The name of the hothead, who was ready to risk his life to avenge an insult to his king, is worth remembering. He was Mikolaj Zebrzydowski. Rudolph II eventually compelled Maximilian to swear the oath required under the agreement, but the archduke continued for some time to style himself "von Gottes Gnaden Erwalter Konig in Polen" (by the grace of God elected king of Poland).

When Zygmunt was proclaimed king in the cathedral of Oliwa, the vice-chancellor of Sweden, Erik Sparre, told the Polish senators:

> He is young, aged twenty-two; he is like a blank book and whatever the Poles write in it will be like an imprint on

wax. Whether you make him a good or bad master will be your own responsibility, for his father and Sweden vouch for his good native character.

Volumes would be needed to record all the nonsense solemnly dispensed by various statesmen, but this one would be near the top of the list. The vice-chancellor was a believer in the myth, widely held then as it is now, of the "blank book" in which educators can write what they wish.

Zygmunt was, unwittingly of course, an example of the psychological phenomenon discovered later: the major role of early experiences, engraved in the subconscious if not in actual memory. The young man who came to Poland as its ruler brought with him the heavy burden of his past. Twenty years later the great preacher Piotr Skarga seemed to sense that secret when he alluded in a sermon to the "inclinations which had formed the youthful Swedish prince."

Zygmunt was born in a prison. He was just over a year old when his barely sane uncle, Erik XIV, released his parents amidst weird scenes of begging forgiveness from them and the baby. He grew up as crown prince at a court constantly held at bay by a series of domestic and foreign plots. His despotic father hated the Poles and wanted his son to become their king. The Swedish aristocrats wanted to get rid of him by sending him to Poland. The situation was skillfully exploited by his uncle, later a successful rival, Prince Charles of Suderman. The king of Sweden could not trust his foreign mercenaries or the diplomats, also hired abroad. The man who was the first to suggest Zygmunt for the Polish throne after Henry's flight was later cruelly executed in Stockholm.

The prison guards, however, were native Swedes. It was from them that Catherine Jagiello bought the ragged shirts she used as diapers for her children. The Swedes demanded that she should renounce her faith. The only people the boy could trust were foreigners from distant parts, fervent apostles of their faith. The Jesuits gained such influence over him that they dissuaded him from escaping to Poland. It was a childhood that left many scars.

When on the Wawel throne, Zygmunt III listened mainly to foreigners, Germans and Swedes, and chose them for his aides. During his brief visits to Sweden he changed his entourage, but not the principle of its choice. He then favored Poles and Lithuanians.

He applied in each country the instinctive reflex of distrusting the local natives.

His subconscious was well prepared for conflict with the Commonwealth, which had become used to an open public life over generations, was not xenophobic, but guarded jealously the right of the citizens to decide their own destiny. Nor was this all: Zygmunt could not accept the religious tolerance of the post-Jagiellonian Commonwealth. The young monarch loathed it more than anything else, attested a contemporary Frenchman.

In Sweden independence and Lutheranism were almost synonyms. The nation was emancipated during the Reformation and remembered that the higher clergy did not favor independence, siding with Denmark and Rome. Already in 1529 the Swedish Synod organized its own church, while the vast estates of the Catholic clergy passed to the state and the nobility. The attitude of John III, Zygmunt's father, was not in line with that of the majority of his subjects, but inspired some hope among the members of the recently founded Society of Jesus. Not all the colleges founded by the Jesuits in the Commonwealth were intended for training its future leaders. That of Braniewo aimed at Scandinavia. John III, with a Catholic wife, knew such personalities as Stanislaw Hozjusz and Anthony Possevino. The king closed the Protestant university of Uppsala and favored some form of agreement with Rome, coupled with autonomy for the Swedish church, recognizing marriage of clergy, communion with bread and wine, but rejecting the cult of the saints. He insisted on a program that was bound to repel both the Vatican and the majority of Swedes. Arbitrary, brutal, and deaf to others' arguments, he was dragging his son into a moral and intellectual wasteland. He once slapped him for trying to avoid a Lutheran service, but he also attacked with a sword a Protestant teacher who discouraged the young prince from attending a Catholic mass. Zygmunt's father wanted his son to be religiously ambivalent, openly professing two faiths that were at the time mutually exclusive. He was, after all, to be the ruler of Lutheran Sweden, with the possible prospect of the throne of predominantly Catholic Poland. Such an educational program amounted to a course in duplicity and deception, but it actually triggered a clear-cut choice.

Erik Sparre was right when he assured the Poles that the young prince was basically honest. He was in error, however, in giving credit to the father, whose influence could only twist the boy's moral sense. Later, when Zygmunt received at Wawel Castle reports of anti-Protestant rioting in the city, he calmly continued his game of ball. His choice had been made and he viewed the world in black and white, without any compromise.

Soon after the death of Stefan I, Rome ordered Anthony Possevino to leave Warsaw and return to Italy. The papal diplomacy had decided to back the Habsburgs and was removing from the scene an advocate of the crown prince of Sweden. It was a major blunder. The brilliant Jesuit had plans that could achieve more for the counter-reformation than the Vatican imagined. He knew Zygmunt well and had already gained influence over him ten years earlier, while his keen political instinct suggested to him how to put it to best use. Anne Jagiello corrected the error of the Vatican and was sincere in assuring Hannibal of Capua that she wanted the Catholic candidate's victory. She meant a candidate more likely to serve the interests of the Commonwealth and more acceptable to the gentry as a scion of the Jagiellonian dynasty, but she was not aware at the time of his personal orientation.

The contest between the state and the champions of religious tolerance will be a recurring theme in our narrative. Let us try to define the nature of their conflict.

Many historians and writers justified the counter-reformation and even praised it on the ground that a state needs an ideological bond uniting all its citizens. Other dismissed the Polish and Lithuanian tolerance as merely a symptom of indifference and lack of commitment to principle.

Yet the freedom of thought, expression, and cult that developed in the Commonwealth in the sixteenth century was a major phenomenon of vital importance. It was far more than mere accommodation. That freedom amounted to a declaration of faith, which recognized religion as the foundation of public order while granting equal rights to all its manifestations.

The ideological bond had existed in the Commonwealth long before the reformation and was well tested by time. It was unique in Europe and original in concept, matching the dual character of the Commonwealth and recognized by all its citizens regardless of their denomination. It was not founded on any imported doctrine, but on the experience of centuries. Religious tolerance was born in Poland at the time of the friendly coexistence of the Catholic Piasts with the Orthodox princes of the House of Rurik, especially since the time when Casimir the Great annexed Red Ruthenia and did so in a statesmanlike manner, respecting the religious belief of the local population. Lithuania went through the same experience on an even broader scale. It created an empire in which eighty percent of the population spoke Ruthenian and belonged to the Orthodox church while its rulers still remained pagan, which did not prevent the Grand Duke of Wilno from seeking a Christian metropolitan see for Kiev.

The champions of the counter-reformation were set on destroying an already existing ideological bond overriding difference of faith and discarding the accumulated wisdom of centuries.

The fusion was still far from perfect. Only Catholic bishops sat in the senate, while neither Orthodox nor Protestant clergy were admitted. Yet, to repeat it, the bond did exist. Without engaging in any ideological excesses, it set the country apart from others, to its advantage, and proved its viability during the two interregnums and the wars of King Stefan.

Experience was now to suffer the assault of doctrine. Anthony Possevino had visited Sweden in an endeavor to win it back for Rome and form a political linkage with the Habsburgs. This was the goal of his mission, in which he was joined by two Polish Jesuits, Bartholomew Tomaszewicz and Pakosz Bernard Golynski. They sailed to Sweden in 1585, when King Stefan still seemed to be in robust health, and no one could foresee the far-reaching consequences of their expedition. Golynski, graduate of the college of Braniewo and the German Jesuit college of Rome, became Zygmunt's confessor, his lifelong friend and counsellor. Golynski, known as Father Pakosz, was hated by the Polish Protestants and by many Catholics. His intrigues contributed to many personal feuds and promoted dissent. Zygmunt III trusted no one except a few hand-picked men, but he lacked Stefan's genius in judging people. He was also inclined to be easily prejudiced against the best.

Golynski did not leave any writings, but he was skillful in political backstage plotting. When, toward the end of his life, he was ill and wanted to convalesce on the Adriatic coast, Catholic Venice denied entry to that archcatholic activist. The shrewd merchants were not deceived by appearances. Father Pakosz had to take his cure in lands ruled by the Habsburgs, whom he served well.

The astounding obsequiousness of Zgymunt in his dealings with the imperial court was not accidental. The king-elect had brought with him to Poland an orientation totally at variance with what was perhaps the best founded of the political biases of the Polish gentry. Some years later, Elizabeth I of England pointed out derisively to the Polish ambassador this strange weakness of Zygmunt for a dynasty that had tried to deny him his crown.

The Vasa monarchs of Sweden were treated as parvenus by the European royalty of both west and east, with good reason. Even in Scandinavia itself there were several families of higher standing and greater antiquity. In 1616 the chancery of the Polish crown suddenly requested the Cracow Academy to confiscate the book *De rebus Sigismundi I . . . gestis*, dedicated to King John Casimir. The work of Szymon Starowolski contained nothing but praise for the Vasa king, but was banned because of a brief passage mentioning the modest origins of Zygmunt's grandfather, Gustav I.

The cherished ambition of the Vasa was a family alliance with the house of Habsburg, but Vienna rather rudely ignored letters from Stockholm. Zygmunt did have a drop of Habsburg blood through his great grandmother, the "mother of kings" and spouse of Casimir Jagiello. By ascending the Cracow throne, the young Swede drew closer to his goal, for the Habsburgs had given their daughters in marriage to several of his predecessors.

Zygmunt's fascination with the imperial court and his attempts at social climbing continued until the end of his long life. Let us examine the sculpted cartouches with the royal coat of arms of that period. The white eagle of Poland bears on its breast the "sheaf" crest of the Vasa, surrounded by the chain of the Habsburg Golden Fleece. No symbol could better express the king's aspirations.

A family alliance with the Habsburgs, Zygmunt thought, would both legitimize his royal standing and appease his conscience, as the Habsburgs headed the camp of militant Catholicism.

The multinational and multidenominational Commonwealth needed a leader of another caliber than a man riddled with complexes, moderately gifted, and governed by ideological fanaticism. He placed religious bigotry ahead of national interest.

The theoreticians of the Protestant movement in Europe, when enumerating the forces sent by Providence to bring down dissolute Rome, never omitted the archcatholic king of France, the "eldest daughter of the church." The Valois and Bourbon kings did not oppose the pope, but fought bitterly the Habsburgs, which was quite enough for the Protestant political writers. Ideological platitudes could convince the students of Jesuit colleges, but not Henry IV, who knew that religion was an instrument of the expansionist designs of the house of Austria. There were also in Poland those who understood it well, but Zygmunt was turned against them by Father Pakosz.

The Protestant camp never formed the supranational council recommended by the theoreticians. Nations such as the Netherlands or Sweden did not relish the prospect of an English hegemony. The Protestants, though united in their opposition to the pope, were careful not to become puppets in the hands of a Protestant power.

At the turn of the sixteenth and seventeenth century a curious metamorphosis occurred in the Commonwealth.

In August 1573, soon after the first election, a certain Father Izdbienski protested at the Proszowice county council against the law of religious tolerance. The gentry of the council were outraged, but Chancellor Walenty Debinski soothed them by saying, "their (the clergy) protests do not amount to much." Sixty years later, in 1633, Jerzy Ossolinski, was telling Pope Urban VII:

> Even in that sad moment when we were mourning King Zygmunt, that model of piety taken from this earth to heaven, you could see, Holy Father, the Seym, the Senate, the whole Polish nation, more concerned with fighting the heresy of their co-citizens than with guarding the security and integrity of their country, or the election of its next monarch.

Even if Ossolinski did exaggerate somewhat, he discerned the trend that was to bring Poland to ultimate disaster in the eighteenth century. And this was the nation that had kept its common sense when the rest of Europe was waging wars of religion and which instructed France in the merits of tolerance!

The reign of Henry Valois was but a flash, Stefan observed in a statesmanlike manner the law of tolerance. It was under Zygmunt I, advised by religious fanatics, that the tiller of the state swung to a course headed for catastrophe and disgrace. The personalities of the rulers do count in history.

Zygmunt received with reverence Hannibal of Capua, who had worked so eagerly for the election of Maximilian Habsburg. But the nuncio knew what to do, regardless of the result of the election.

Here is an excerpt of a letter he sent from Warsaw on June 9, 1587, to the papal secretary of state, Cardinal Montalto, a nephew of the pope:

> Your Grace ordered me to make the utmost efforts to persuade both the prelates of this realm and its most influential senators to revoke and annul the religious freedom secured deceitfully by the heretics during the interregnum after the death of Zygmunt August, under the false pretext of a confederacy for the protection of public peace and order. Or at least to prevent its endorsement by the senate, the estates of the realm or the new king. The order of Your Grace shall be faithfully carried out.

A concerted action was started against the Warsaw Confederacy, which was the institutionalized expression of Poland's national philosophy in the area of religious faith. The king, the nuncio, and other lords were backing the anti-Protestant charges of the Masovian gentry, referring to goat thieves, evil spirits, and the Psalms of David.

Sweden was at the time even more bigoted than Masovia. It had proposed legislation to deport every non-Lutheran and to punish with death persons giving shelter to Jesuits. Zygmunt may have borrowed such methods from his countrymen, but he wanted to apply them in the opposite direction. The attempt failed, for the Commonwealth never adopted religious repression on the Swedish or English model.

A year after the letter just quoted, the nuncio was writing another, reporting on a lengthy private audience with King Zygmunt, six months after his accession. Hannibal of Capua demanded that ecclesiastic offices be granted to worthy candidates, but he also went further by insisting that the higher secular offices should be reserved for Catholics only.

It was the third time in fourteen years that a king was instructed by a prelate on how to rule the Commonwealth. Hannibal's requests were strikingly similar to those presented by Graziani to Henry Valois. Bishop Jan Solikowski, when he greeted Batory in Sniatyn, spoke about the role of the church in the state, but stopped short of recommending religious bias in government.

Symptoms of the new policy could be observed in Cracow, where the daily visits of Father Pakosz at Wawel Castle irritated the champions of the traditional even-handed treatment of all faiths by the state. On the occasion of a church jubilee the king, accompanied by his aunt, Queen Anne, solemnly took communion at the cathedral, joined by many prominent magnates, some of whom, as the nuncio noted, "did not have time to prepare properly for the sacrament." Favors were granted to those who displayed zeal in turning back from the path of error. Mikolaj Firlej, who did not even wait for the death of his father, a fervent Calvinist, to convert to Catholicism, was appointed *voievode* of Cracow. Another favorite was Lew Sapieha, who had been previously Orthodox and then "Helvetian" (Calvinist). He boasted to the nuncio that he had managed to win for the church of Rome his wife, Dorota Firlej, and begged for permission to have mass celebrated in his home so that they could attend it daily.

These sudden conversions coincided with the royal distribution of "bread." When Zygmunt was elected, the senate of the Commonwealth was already predominantly Catholic, which was a major change since the time of the Union of Lublin, when, according to the historian Adam Kersten, the upper chamber comprised 55 Catholics, 53 Protestants and 2 members of the Orthodox church. In the first years of his reign the king had to reward those who won for him the throne and appoint Protestants. But already from the very beginning of the seventeenth century the senate acquired a strong Catholic majority, with only a few Protestant and Orthodox members. Ideological conformism was dominant and the *dissidentes de religione* and supporters of Chancellor Zamoyski were losing ground. Among those set aside as the "main obstacle to friendship with Austria" was the castellan of Podlasie Marcin Lesnowolski, "le sieur Dobory," who had opened Zygmunt's path to the throne as ambassador to Sweden and brought him to Poland. He was a " man equal to his calling, serene in bearing and manner, skilled in politics and, what is rare among those of his rank, modest and equally courteous to all." Removed from the court, he placed on his house in Kanonicza street in Cracow the Latin inscription "Virtue suffices unto itself." The men who had guarded freedom in their own country and tried to implant it in France were disappearing from the political stage. The role that the Commonwealth had played as a champion of tolerance was soon to be forgotten and Poland began to acquire the reputation of a country of religious fanatics, which became later a millstone at her neck in times of political weakness and disaster.

The strategy of the counter-reformation aimed at securing influence at the centers of power and then using them as instruments for the advancement of its goals. It was a trend that continued until our times and the pontificate of John XXIII. The church of Rome was busy building walls separating it from the other Christians, who were then not thought of as "brothers." Any openings in such walls were used to launch ruthless attacks. For a federal Commonwealth uniting people of several faiths, cultures, and traditions, such a policy could only mean a permanent state of crisis. The doctrine of the counter-reformation was in contradiction to the very essence of the Commonwealth, threatening the harmony that gave it its strength.

Even before it had time to arouse the resentment of the citizens of other denominations, the counter-reformation exerted a significant influence on state policies. The first Seym sessions under Zygmunt III were uneventful and fairly calm, perhaps because the most disruptive elements of Poland were first in Maximilian's camp and after the battle of Byczyna in prison or abroad. The coronation Seym, held while the war with the Habsburgs was still in progress, enacted taxes, placing the burden, of course, on the burghers, peasants, and Jews; prohibited duels; and confirmed the peace with Moscow that Lithuania had concluded separately earlier. The next Seym, in 1589, decided to clear the beds of the rivers Warta, Bug, Wislok, and Wieprz, but failed to address effectively some far more important problems.

Yet two issues of vital importance were on the agenda: the confirmation of the Warsaw Confederacy and the reform of the system of royal elections.

Prior to the opening of the session, the nuncio held in St.John's Cathedral in Warsaw a conference of all the bishops, urging them to "defend the cause of the holy faith, the dignity of the church and its rights." He received assurances of unanimous support, which was so effective that he could report in his letter to Rome, dated March 27, 1589, the defeat of a bill on public peace, which included a confirmation of the Warsaw Confederacy, or what we would have called today the executive order for its implementation.

Nor was that all. Jan Zamoyski submitted the draft of a law regulating future royal elections. The nuncio reported that the chancellor's proposal restricted the candidates to "only the offspring of His Majesty and, if they should be lacking, those of Slav nationality." It was a return to the Jagiellonian tradition, which managed to combine the elements of an elective monarchy with the hereditary principle. If the king should have no male heirs, the path to the throne would be open to native candidates. The term "Slav" was interpreted rather broadly at the time and could include a Lithuanian, perhaps even a Hungarian.

Zamoyski proposed that the election should be held within eight weeks of a king's demise and not last more than a month. All those convicted of infamy, receiving money from foreign sources, owning no land (this meant the personal staffs of the magnates), or coming with too large retinues would be barred from the vote. The convocation was to be abolished. The gentry of each province would hold its own election and send delegates to the national electoral convention, the Seym. This method combined the principle of the general "viritim" election and representation, with the latter playing a decisive role. The balloting on all levels would be by stages: seeking a three-quarters majority first, then one of two-thirds and if that failed, simple majority.

The primate Karnkowski opposed the chancellor's proposal and requested a rule requiring the king to be a Catholic. This was not welcomed by the Protestants, but they were ready to agree, subject to a formal confirmation of the terms of the Warsaw Confederacy. The bishops refused to consent and when agreement on a Catholic king was almost reached, the primate stiffened his position and demanded a resolution allowing only a Roman Catholic on the throne.

This objection caused the resolution to be abandoned. Both sides were aware that the dispute was not over religion. Zamoyski wanted to institutionalize the election and bar the way to Habsburgs, while the primate's amendment aimed at promoting them. The House of Austria had been related in the past to the Piasts of Masovia and the Jagiellonians, so it might qualify as "Slavic," especially if backed by sufficient force. The success of Karnkowski, supported by the nuncio, would have been a stinging defeat for the adversaries of the Habsburgs.

"Thus, despite the devious efforts of the heretics, they failed to achieve anything and the entire business of election law was left in abeyance . . .," the nuncio reported jubilantly to Rome.

The "business of the election" was not the only thing left in abeyance, for the principle of majority vote in the royal election was also not affirmed. Had it been, the practice would surely have been passed on to the Seym debates.

With the memory of three increasingly alarming elections still fresh in everyone's mind, the Seym assembled to deal with the plan of reform. Many of those present were still mourning relatives lost in the battle of Cracow and Byczyna. Yet the reform was deliberately torpedoed, mostly by purple-clad dignitaries. The opportunity was not taken. Later, time healed the scars and other matters came to the fore. The next election was held forty-three years later by another generation. It turned out to be calm and harmonious, elevating to the throne the eldest son of the deceased King Zygmunt, even though Zamoyski's resolution suggesting that course of action was never voted into law. There was no sense of urgency and time went by, until in 1648 when a king had to be elected after a disastrous defeat, in the midst of a civil war. The turmoil of catastrophe overwhelmed and ravaged the nation, its citizens by then indoctrinated by the counter-reformation, but the "business of the election" still remained unresolved, in a state of vague traditionalism. It was then too late to reform the Commonwealth. The opportunity for restructuring the system never occurred again.

In the debate of 1589 the contest was between Zamoyski and Karnkowski. Zygmunt III stood aside, remaining neutral. A head of state who fails to support reform in such a situation is a political criminal.

The indifference of the rulers to the efforts of those trying to bring about a reform of the system became a habit. The decade of Stefan Batory's reign was the exception and it did produce results.

Recognizing the merit of King Stefan, the Seym granted patents of Polish nobility to his nephews. It also agreed to King Zygmunt's visit to Rewel on the north Baltic for a meeting with his father. No one knew what the two Swedes talked about and the custom of holding secret conferences about matters concerning the Commonwealth was spreading. It was rumored that they discussed a plan to yield the Polish crown to Archduke Ernest Habsburg in return for a major concessions to Sweden. They were supposed to include the inheritance of Queen Bona's fortune, the customs revenues of Prussia, and the province of Inflanty—with a promise by Poland to defend it thrown in. It would have meant Poland and Lithuania giving up a province for which they had both fought hard, and undertaking its defense against Moscow on behalf of its new master.

At one point King John of Sweden ordered his son's personal luggage loaded on a Swedish ship, as he did not want him to return to Warsaw. The Swedish aristocracy protested, as did the Jesuits. The vice-chancellor of the Commonwealth, Bishop Wojciech Baranowski, pleaded emotionally for the king's return.

Zygmunt did not yield his crown and was back in Warsaw in the fall of the same year, while Baranowski heard the reproaches of Zamoyski and others, who had realized by then that the Swede was ill suited for the Polish throne. "His mind," wrote a contemporary who knew him well, "is obstinate, inclined to favor Germans and out of tune with Polish thinking." Soon afterward Baranowski, despite his devotion to the king, was removed from the position of vice-chancellor, but rewarded with promotion to the large and rich diocese of Plock. Zygmunt's personnel policy was as consistent as that of his predecessor, but it worked in exactly the opposite direction.

Wojciech Baranowski had a brilliant career and in 1608 became primate of Poland, his rank gained at the cost of greater subservience to the king. He built the first primate's palace in Warsaw, but was not popular among the gentry, critical of his greed for advancement and his allegedly plebeian origin. The latter charge seemed ill founded, as Baranowski was descended from the petty nobility of western Poland. His ability was first recognized by King Stefan and Zamoyski, to whom he owed his earlier promotions. Zygmunt III did not like him, but they did share a hatred of heresy and opposition to religious tolerance.

"King Stefan was good for soldiers and this one will be good for the clergy," said Hannibal of Capua at the time of the election.

Without Zygmunt's eager assistance, the counter-reformation could not have been as successful, for his favors offered powerful weapons to its champions. In the same year, 1589, Henry IV became king of France and accepted the Catholic faith, but also curbed the excesses of religious fanatics. Before enacting nine years later the famous Nantes Edict of religious tolerance, he banished provisionally the Jesuits as "corrupters of youth, disturbers of public peace, enemies of the king and the state." On December 27, 1594, a pupil of the Jesuits, Jean de Chatel, made an attempt on Henry's life and confessed under interrogation, no doubt assisted by torture, that he had learned the principles of "tyrannocide" from a Jesuit by the name of Gueret. He was torn apart by horses, his teacher banished, and the monk Guinard, charged with keeping writings directed against the king, was sent to the gallows. Henry did not hesitate to use harsh means to ensure domestic peace and a chicken in every Frenchman's pot. In Poland no cruelty was needed to attain the same objectives. The principle of religious peace and tolerance was already recognized by the majority of the gentry, which had enacted the Confederacy of Warsaw. In France the king had to use all of his executive power to support the more moderate elements among his subjects, while in Poland the monarch sided with an ideologically extreme faction and invited it to participate in the government, while shunning the moderates. The Commonwealth was sinking into a pit from which other nations were emerging. The widely hailed Edict of Nantes granted to the Huguenots only a fraction of the rights that religious dissidents had enjoyed earlier in the Commonwealth. It became a historic landmark, for it was surely a great step forward. But the Commonwealth was going backwards at the same time and that is why its former role of pioneer of tolerance was soon forgotten.

That tragic retreat was to become evident soon, but in the meantime Poland still basked in the reputation it had acquired in its Golden Age. In 1594 the Paris lawyer Anthony Arnaud delivered a fervent speech against the Jesuits, demanding their expulsion from France. He had it printed with a dedication "To the senate and people of the city of Wilno."

Under Zygmunt August the state displayed excessive laxity by leaving unpunished the outrageous act of Erasm Otwinowski, who trampled publicly the Holy Host in the course of a religious observance in Lublin. But under Zygmunt III, in June of 1611, a ghastly execution took place in the market square of Wilno. The executioner tore out the victim's tongue and hung on the pillory parts of his body. This was the punishment of a young Italian, Francus de Franco, who dared to make critical comments about the cult of the Host, addressing the crowd during the Corpus Cristi procession.

Only forty years separate the trial that acquitted Otwinowski from the torture death of Francus de Franco. The speed of the change was frightening.

Prince Jerzy Zbaraski, a Catholic free of fanaticism, complained that "the Poles are not as bright and wise as the Frenchmen and Italians, or rather not as perceptive." This judgment was contradicted by the personal conduct of this first generation Pole of Ukrainian descent. Wanda Dobrowolska, the author of a book about him and his family, reports that Prince Zbaraski founded in Cracow in the early years of the sixteenth century "a secret and effective anti-Jesuit center," which produced a stream of publications and conducted speaking campaigns. The prince himself was the author of pamphlets in which he argued that the Jesuits "care more for foreign princes than for their own king and strive to overthrow monarchs and establish a fictitious Spanish empire."

John Milton regarded the catholicism of the counter-reformation era as a champion of the "state of Rome," a view paralleling the earlier arguments of Zbaraski. The Catholic reaction aimed at reviving the medieval idea of a papal authority dominating all nations. It was a concept unacceptable for the national states, but it suited very well the Habsburgs, by sanctioning their plan of a new Roman Empire under their rule. The patriarch of the dynasty, Philip II of Spain, who died on September 13, 1598, had only one regret on his deathbed: not having killed enough heretics and Jews. Incidentally, Zygmunt III had tried to help bring the Protestant Netherlands under the sovereignty of Spain, an attempt which caused a regrettable incident, the verbal sparring between Queen Elizabeth and the Polish ambassador to England, the presumptuous Paul Dzialynski.

When counter-reformation had gained the upper hand, the posthumous works of the great poet Jan Kochanowski were censured, while the first *Dictionary of Polish Writers*, published by Szymon Starowolski, made no mention of the outstanding writer Mikolaj Rey, because he was a Protestant. Waclaw Potocki destined his best work in advance "for the drawer," as he knew that it would not be tolerated by the censors. In such conditions it is not surprising that few records remain of the stubborn resistance of the more reasonable members of the gentry against the encroachments of religious bigotry. Voices of protest were raised even at coronation ceremonies, including that of Zygmunt III himself.

The parliamentary system collapsed because of sabotage by the executive, which frustrated an almost ready legislative act of tolerance—of which more later. Some of the Polish Protestant publications of that period were known throughout Europe, translated into foreign languages and circulated in many editions. The best known of them was the *Monita privata Societatis Jesu*, written by the ex-Jesuit Hieronim Zahorowski and funded by Prince Zbaraski. It was published three years after the execution of Francus de Franco and it was far from being the swan song of the religious dissidents in Poland. The version according to which the religious tolerance movement was not deeply rooted in Poland is superficial itself. The counter-reformation encountered stubborn resistance.

It was, however, unwittingly assisted by certain historic trends and developments.

Already in the fifteenth century the western part of the Jagiellonian Commonwealth, that is Poland proper, began to catch up with the rest of Europe in cultural creativity. In the sixteenth century it was almost drawing even with the West, though the intellectual exchange still showed more eastward than westward traffic. Poland did produce works of the highest quality, but not in the same volume as France, the Netherlands, Italy, Germany, or England. In areas such as academic education or art, Poland was still lagging. Poland owed its best architecture to Italians, who were also its leading painters and sculptors. Poland's contribution in literature and the arts, though not negligible, was in its early stages. In the Middle Ages Polish culture was under strong influence from the West and that tradition persisted, while a national culture was developing. Since the later sixteenth century the well-worn channels from the West began to bring in new trends, alien and uncongenial to the Commonwealth's tradition, but nevertheless interesting, sometimes even fascinating.

The ideologues of the counter-reformation could not accept works of art such as the picture by young Tintoretto, in which Hephaistos sought on the naked, spread body of his wife the traces of Aries' virility. But the Jesuits were too intelligent to fight depravity by covering the naked Aphrodite with a gothic cloak. They knew that the society in which they were active was far removed from mediaeval standards and would not respond to archaism. The Catholic reaction sought more modern weapons.

One of the few Polish friends of Zygmunt III was Mikolaj Wolski, a man of wide culture and learning, a graduate of western universities. He was thought cold and reserved, but was nevertheless capable of occasional outbursts of Sarmatian panache. Wolski left as his monument the Camadolite church and hermitage of Bielany near Cracow, considered to be the finest of all the monasteries of that order in Europe. Castellan Wolski was an active supporter of the counter-reformation, as was King Zygmunt, but the church he built was different from the Renaissance Zygmunt chapel in the Wawel cathedral. Its style was what is known as mannerism; if the religious emblems were removed from its facade, it could have been a palace.

Such innovation was enough for the mossbacked Camadolites, who shunned the outside world and even pastoral work, but not for the Jesuits. They started building churches, in Lublin and elsewhere, from plans brought from Italy and modelled on the Del Gesu church of Rome. They implanted in Poland a new style—the baroque. It left its mark on Poland until this day, at any rate in the provinces in which Catholicism became dominant again. Splendid baroque churches are to be found in central Poland, in Lithuania and the Ukraine, also in Silesia, but not in Pomerania, where the counter-reformation did not make much headway. The last princes of Pomerania remained loyal to the teachings of Martin Luther.

Baroque made an early appearance in Nieswiez, the seat of Mikolaj Krzysztof Radziwill "the Orphan," a devout Catholic. The baroque church of Saints Peter and Paul was built in Grodzka Street in Cracow, funded by the king himself. The second capital of the Commonwealth, Wilno, was quick to adopt the new style and later acquired some of its masterpieces.

Promoted by the Jesuits, baroque was the visible symbol of the counter-reformation. They understood well the psychological impact of that style on minds formed by the turbulent events of the era, the wars of religion, the conflicts of conscience, St.Bartholomew's nights. The sober austerity of the Renaissance was not enough. The dynamic, imaginative new style bordering on hysteria matched the mood of the period in which the sword was the preferred instrument of persuasion. The exuberant, opulent interior of a baroque church offered a perfect setting for the fervent, inflammatory rhetoric of the preachers. A Jesuit church was designed to focus all attention on the ornate altar and the pulpit, without the privacy of somber side aisles and secluded chapels.

The novelty of the style and its colorful, joyous effervescence exerted a powerful appeal, drawing people to the Jesuit churches. The wise friars did not expect instant conversions, offering their blessings also to those who intended to die in the faith of their fathers. The Society of Jesus was content to win the next generation and mostly did so. Prince Adam Wisniowiecki, heir to vast estates beyond the Dnieper, a firebrand and drunkard, attended Jesuit

127

schools in Wilno. He and his cousin Michael founded many Orthodox churches and monasteries; both were firmly opposed to "popery" and remained members of the Orthodox faith to the end of their lives. But Prince Michael's son Jeremy, a Catholic by free choice, was very active in propagating the church of Rome in the Ukraine. The Jesuits cast their nets wide and if they could not get the father, waited for the son.

An anonymous seventeenth-century writer said that Catholics of recent vintage could be easily recognized "for they have a rosary dangling on their belt next to the sword, pictures and crosses in their rooms, all kinds of secret conspiracies." He deplored the departure of the generation of "old Catholics" who knew how to combine attachment to their church with respect of other faiths, for they "never mixed religion with police work."

The ability to distinguish and separate these two areas was in decline. Pathos and bombastic rhetoric in word and deed were used to win the young, a method never used before in free schools, open to all.

"They did not invent anything new," wrote the historian Alexander Bruckner about the Jesuit pedagogues. The Council of Trident, the starting point of the counter-reformation, also did not invent anything new insofar as it did not proclaim any new dogma. Yet it strengthened immensely the church organization, carrying out a reform of its "head" as it was then called. That operation formed a system of action intended to restore the obedience of the "members," recover earlier losses, and make new conquests. The system itself was an innovation, even if its content was not.

The strategists of the counter-reformation may not have invented any new truths, but they realized that a replay of boring clichés was not likely to win the hearts of the masses. Condemning the heathen Renaissance, they did not propose to revive the dead Gothic. While reverting to the theocracy of the Middle Ages, they steered clear of its medieval forms of expression. They dared to bring in a new style in art and rhetoric, which swept many countries and poured into Poland through the old channels of cultural influence from the West.

Counter-reformation was bound to reach Poland and contribute to its miseries. In France, Louis XIV revoked the edict of tolerance of Henry IV and by doing so helped not only his Protestant neighbors, but also distant Prussia.

It could be argued that the counter-reformation profited the dissident nations, while it was damaging to Poland's national interest. The shift to a new direction, burdening the nation with serving unattainable, utopian goals, was made possible by a ruler who followed blindly the guidance of Rome. As the master and dispenser of "bread," he found many willing followers.

III

On his way to Rewel the king received news of a Tartar incursion, which reached in August 1589 the cities of Tarnopol and Lwow in the southeast. An even more alarming message followed: The Turks had attacked and burned down the border town of Sniatyn.

Zygmunt did not turn back. Later he sent a messenger to Warsaw, asking for additional funds for his travels. Neither of these moves enhanced his standing among the gentry. The treasury was bare, every penny spent on mercenaries. In Rewel Peter Skarga delivered a great and tragic homily. He put the king to shame, urging his return and graphically describing the plight of tens of thousands of his subjects taken into slavery by the Tartars.

The Tartars had been provoked by a daring raid of the Cossacks, who reached Eupatoria in the Crimea and burned it down. The Crimea was ruled at the time by the khan, Ghasi Girey, subordinate to the sultan, Amurat III. The sultan of Turkey said that he "sleeps well though many princes in Istanbul conspire against him, but fears only the Cossacks, that evil Polish spawn threatening many monarchs." The Istanbul court was in a belligerent mood and the grand vizier declared that the Commonwealth had to pay immediately a tribute of three hundred thousand *thalers* or be trampled into dust. He demanded the money or prompt conversion to Islam as the only alternatives.

As it turned out, the war was averted by a man of an entirely different level of political sophistication. He was Edward Burton, the British ambassador, who tried to restrain the grand vizier by pointing out to him that an attack against Poland would not be to his advantage. He explained that England depended on Poland for lumber and other supplies for its shipyards. Deprived of these raw materials, the English could not continue to give support to the rebels fighting in the Netherlands against Philip II, the archenemy of the Turks, who would then be free to wage war against Turkey.

When the vizier did not accept that argument, the English diplomat managed to overthrow him in a minor palace coup. His successors adopted a more moderate stand after receiving from the Commonwealth a gift of a hundred *soroks* (*sorok* means forty in Russian) of ermine pelts.

Poland was not alone in buying peace from the Turks and Tartars. Emperor Rudolph II also found it cheaper to pay off their leaders than to fight them.

Later Zygmunt III interfered with the English in the Netherlands, acting for purely ideological reasons. He was guided by a political philosophy more akin to that of Istanbul than of London.

The king did not turn back from Rewel, but merely sent to Zamoyski and other lords letters urging them to cope with the emergency. Hetman Zamoyski went to Lwow and raised troops, largely with his own funds, while reinforcing the defenses of the fortress of Kamieniec. He was personally lucky, for the forces of Jacob Strus, the Potockis, and Podlodowski defeated the Tartars besieging the castle of Baworow, in which the chancellor's sister had sought refuge. It was still possible to set free the people seized by the Tartars, as the *voievodes* Konstanty Ostrogski and Janusz Zbaraski had ample troops at their disposal. But the old feud between the two magnates prevented their joint action and allowed the Tartars to escape with their human booty, which was estimated, with probable exaggeration, at sixty thousand.

The magnates of Ruthenia were the most powerful lords of the Commonwealth. They had vast estates of hundreds of thousands of acres, opulent castles, and private armies, but seemed unable to protect their own territory of the Ukraine. On the contrary, they sometimes brought upon it disaster, by provoking, directly or through their Cossack proxies, the khans of the Crimea and the sultan of Istanbul.

Their conduct revealed a lack of mental discipline, sometimes called political instinct. Sound statesmanship was still unknown in these parts. The Ukraine was the European equivalent of the Wild West, where life was lived from day to day and each man was his own master. Janusz Zbaraski was capable of doing good work, but only under the direction of Stefan I, a man of higher level of sophistication and political judgment.

Under Zygmunt the Old, the squabbles of the Lithuanian magnates had allowed the Muscovites almost to reach Wilno. The same thing happened on a smaller scale in the Ukraine in 1589. The Commonwealth paid dearly for the primitive thinking of the citizens of its eastern part. Europe did not yet reach beyond the river Bug.

Jan Zamoyski was not intimidated by Tartar raids or repeated Turkish threats and he conceived bold, even daring plans. King Stefan's friend did not believe in adopting a purely defensive posture. He proposed first to place Moldavia under Polish influence and then, having secured a base of action there, drive the Tartars out of the Crimea and the Turks beyond the Danube, liberating the southern Slavs. The hetman had conceived a preventive strategy on a grand scale, perhaps visionary except for the part concerning Moldavia and the Crimea. These two goals were quite realistic. Zamoyski based his plan on the resources of the Commonwealth alone, discarding the dream of a Christian League. He also knew that he could not count on any help from the emperor.

Father Stanislaw Zaleski, author of *The Jesuits in Poland*, wrote approvingly that Zygmunt III planned a war against Turkey, whether within a coalition or singlehanded, considering it his sacred duty. He was converted to that view by the Jesuits, first Possevino, then Golynski, Skarga, and Stanislaw Warszewicki. "They and the king," wrote the historian, "were guided solely by the Holy See, which demanded help for the emperor."

Nevertheless, the obsessive ideas of the king coincided to some extent with the chancellor's plans for the security of the state. Unfortunately, another royal delusion was soon about to engage the forces needed for the protection of the southeastern borders. Later still these armies were to thrust in the same direction and suffer defeat on the very site of Zamoyski's earlier victory.

The Seym of 1590 performed well. Since Archduke Maximilian had not yet ratified the Bedzin and Bytom agreements by his oath, the Seym voted a special "resolution of insurance," by which Maximilian was barred forever from the Polish throne. Responding to the Turkish threat, the Seym voted taxes four times greater than those levied for Stefan's war with Muscovy. They were to pay for an army of a hundred thousand, enough to carry out Zamoyski's design.

As at the previous session of the Seym, the primate Karnkowski prevented again the enactment of laws governing royal elections. He campaigned without scruple against the chancellor, his rival for the position of the most powerful man in Poland, second only to the king. He called in the town of Kolo a convention of the gentry of Wielkopolska (western Poland), for the purpose of debating and then approving or disallowing the resolutions of the Seym. He charged Zamoyski with exaggerating the danger from the East with a view to strengthening his position as hetman (commander-in-chief). The Kolo convention resolved, of course, to reduce the taxes and passed various other resolutions.

Most of the gentry were outraged by "a disgraceful attempt to undermine the authority of the legitimate Seym," while the dislike of Karnkowski, according to a contemporary cleric, "spread to all the bishops to such an extent that even many of the Catholic magnates thought that they should be replaced by monks subsisting on alms." The authority of both legislative chambers was impaired and some historians perceived the primate's act as a step in the direction of the *liberum veto*, for it was nothing less than the annulment of parliamentary resolutions by a minority, opening the way to such action even by individuals.

Diplomacy averted war with Turkey, but the unrest triggered by Karnkowski's dissidence required calming down. Zamoyski himself announced that the taxes voted for the army would not be collected, but the unpaid mercenaries began looting the countryside, more particularly the royal estates, so that a general levy had to be called to subdue them.

A head tax on the Jews was imposed to raise funds for the gifts promised to sultan's *viziers*. At any rate, the ermine pelts cost a great deal less than an army. The anarchy that threatened the country did not originate spontaneously among the mass of the lesser gentry. It was inspired and provoked at the very summit.

The matter of the king's marriage was the current concern of the country. Zygmunt came to Poland single, but not entirely free, for he was engaged to Christina, princess of Holstein. The engagement was a major success for the Swedish Protestants, so all the Catholic activists in the young monarch's entourage began an assault on his pledge to the Protestant princess. Despite direct orders from Rome, the king resisted for more than two years. If obstinacy is typical of the Lithuanian character, Zygmunt was a true scion of Jagiello and even his ancestor Gedymin. Zygmunt August was also known for his tenacity, but he at least responded to persuasion by hitting the table with his fist and with the words "I want it." His none-too-bright nephew drove people to distraction simply by remaining silent.

Dowager Queen Anne had conceived already prior to the election a plan to marry her nephew to her namesake, Anne, the eldest of the fifteen children of Archduke Charles of Styria. The queen arranged the matter through the intermediary of the Jewish merchant Mandel, whom she often used for confidential missions. When Zygmunt had consolidated his position on the throne, the circles favoring an alliance with Austria recalled the plan and thought the queen's idea excellent. The Styrian branch of the Habsburgs was noted for its Catholic zeal and hatred of heretics.

There was among the gentry some apprehension of a "Paris wedding," as the memory of St.Bartholomew's Night was still fresh.

In 1591 a mob attacked and burned down two recently built Protestant churches in Cracow. There was also some rioting in Wilno.

A Protestant convention held in Chmielnik sent to the king a delegation of twenty five, one of whom addressed Zygmunt:

> Lest anyone should place a wrong interpretation upon our mission, we declare before God, the throne and the nation that we are sent to Your Majesty not to disturb public peace, but on the contrary to protect the Commonwealth and the person of Your Majesty from harm. Your Majesty's subjects expect, after you swore on oath to uphold their liberties and rights, that they will be respected. Liberty and public order were violated in the capital cities of Cracow and Wilno, also in other parts of the realm, by assaults against temples of the God whom we all—though in a different rite—worship and praise. The danger that such disturbances can bring to our country can be seen by the example of France. . . .

The Protestants had displayed no disloyalty to the crown and had sought no foreign support, observing the old order of national solidarity overriding differences of religion.

Those responsible for the riots in Cracow and Wilno were not punished. The king did not allow the reconstruction of the destroyed Protestant temples and declared illegal the proposed convention to be held in Radom.

In the next year both Catholic and Protestant gentry assembled in large numbers in Lublin and Jedrzejow. Zamoyski was also there, by then at odds with the king and with evidence of his secret plotting in his hands. The massed gentry protested violently against the clandestine negotiations for the king's marriage with Anne Habsburg. Nevertheless it took place on June 1, 1592, and Anne became the queen. While wedding festivities were held in Cracow, storm was brewing in nearby Jedrzejow.

The example set by Primate Karnkowski found followers and conventions outside the Seym were becoming a habit. But there were significant differences: the meeting called by Karnkowski in Kolo opposed lawful Seym resolutions; the Protestants in Chmielnik demanded observance of the law; while the conventions of Lublin and Jedrzejow defended the sovereignty of the state.

The harshest charges of the speakers at these conventions paled into insignificance when the gentry heard the revelations of Archduke Maximilian's agent, Ducker. Maximilian, pretender to the Polish throne, who still considered himself its lawful monarch, disclosed the secret agreements between Zygmunt III and Ernest Habsburg. They involved no less than trading away the crown of the Commonwealth. Zygmunt was to abdicate in favor of Ernest Habsburg, who promised that as king of Poland he would enter an alliance with Sweden and yield Estonia to the Swedes, while Zygmunt would receive the inheritance of Queen Anne's fortune as well as four hundred thousand *thalers*.

Zamoyski barely managed to restrain the gentry assembled in Jedrzejow from taking armed action. He was in opposition to the king himself, but he understood well the line dividing dissent from rebellion and did not want to see it crossed. The aging statesman's greatness was recognized even by his bitterest foreign adversaries. They said openly that it was not his office or power that intimidated them, but his mind and character.

The Seym of the fall of 1592 was held under the pressure of an armed mass of gentry, which marched on Warsaw to watch the development of events there. The session was later known to history as "inquisitorial." The deputies, some of the senators, and the armed crowd of the lesser nobility were conducting an investigation of their monarch, charged with attempting to sell the crown to the Habsburgs. Five years earlier the nation had fought a war to prevent precisely what Zygmunt III was now trying to bring about. The king had betrayed his subjects and was to be paid for it in cash.

Conspiring with foreigners and accepting money from them were common at the time among European nobility and the Poles were no worse in that respect than others. But such plots and corruption were always directed against the monarch. This time it was the king himself that was charged with treason.

Five years of the new reign were enough to produce a crisis of confidence without precedent in the history of the Commonwealth. Zamoyski pacified the crisis, as he did not want another royal election, while the new nuncio, Germano Malaspina, acted as a skillful mediator. Zygmunt partly admitted guilt, showed some contrition, and promised never to leave Poland for Sweden without the consent of the Estates of the Commonwealth. The storm subsided, but not without leaving in people's minds a heavy negative charge. Royal treason and its investigation by the subjects opened a new chapter in the history of the relations between the monarch and the nations of the Commonwealth. Following this period every move of the king was greeted with suspicion, which became an instinctive reflex bred into the genes of generations to come. The events of the fall of 1592 were etched in the communal subconscious.

Zygmunt was elected king because the majority of the nobility had trusted his sincerity and good will, extended moral credit to him. To squander such a capital of trust is political suicide—worse than that of an individual, for it affects the entire society.

The opposition of the majority of the Poles to the Habsburgs was not directed personally against any of them, nor motivated by chauvinism. The Germans of Gdansk or Krolewiec (Konigsberg) were not disliked. The country was simply defending its independence, which it would lose by becoming a province of the Habsburg empire. Zygmunt conspired against that independence, though he had been called to the throne to defend it. Poland had fought on his behalf a war against the Habsburgs. All this was bound to leave deep psychological scars.

Soon after the Seym session the nuncio arranged an ostensible reconciliation between the king and the chancellor, which Zygmunt III needed badly. His father, John III, died in November and Zygmunt was heir to his crown. A personal union of Sweden and Poland was impending, but it required the king's presence in Stockholm to assume the crown. In the meantime he addressed to his prospective subjects a message expressing his regret for having had to leave Sweden some years earlier. He explained that he did so in the interest of Sweden, to prevent the tsar of Russia taking the Polish throne. He also said that he had sought Polish-Lithuanian help in securing peace with Moscow on terms favorable to Sweden.

The Seym session of May 1593 gave its consent to the king's departure, but demanded his solemn promise of return within a year. For further assurance, the recently born Princess Anne was to remain in Warsaw as a token of her parents' loyalty to Poland, placed in the care of the queen dowager, her aunt. Relations between the monarch and the citizens entered a new phase when the king's word alone was not thought to be enough and a baby had to be kept as hostage.

The royal couple sailed along the Vistula to Gdansk and remained there for a month. Zygmunt sent to Torun and Elblag orders restoring to the Catholics one church in each of these cities, while the bishop of Kujawy, Rozrazewski, initiated steps for taking away from the Protestants the Church of Virgin Mary in Gdansk, the largest in the country. Fighting broke out as a result of the mounting tension, with some twenty people killed on the Polish side and half a dozen on the Gdansk. Bullets smashed the windows of the royal apartments above the Green Gate.

In Sweden Zygmunt immediately found himself in trouble, for the same reasons as in Gdansk and in Poland. He took with him wherever he went his religious bigotry and his exceptional talent for antagonizing the natives. A recent synod in Uppsala had ruled Lutheranism the only legal religion in Sweden, but the king demanded the coronation ceremony to be performed by the papal nuncio, Malaspina, who had accompanied him on the voyage from Poland. The pope's envoy became Zygmunt's chief adviser in Scandinavia, the others being Poles. They justified the king's confidence and frustrated an attempted coup against him in Uppsala when a small group of Poles confronted the Swedes in their own country. In the spring of 1594 three thousand Polish troops were brought across the Baltic to protect Zygmunt against his countrymen.

The king ceased to insist on a Catholic coronation when his ecclesiastic advisers told him that he would not be morally bound by any provisional concessions he might have to make to the Protestants. They represented a philosophy against which the rector of the

Cracow Academy, Paul Wlodkowic, had argued at the Council of Constance almost two hundred years earlier. There were always those, in the Middle Ages, in the era of the counter-reformation, and also in our time, who consider any agreement contracted with people of a different faith as null and void by its very nature.

The royal couple accepted the crown from the hands of a Protestant minister. Sweden and the Commonwealth now shared the same monarch, but the technology of the period made it impossible to rule across the sea. Zygmunt had to return to Poland, leaving as regent in Sweden his uncle, rival, and adversary, Charles of Suderman. It was he who had mounted in Uppsala a coup against his nephew, frustrated when Zygmunt's Polish guard seized Charles. After that experience, Charles of Suderman told his supporters: "Remain quiet until the king's departure."

While in Sweden, Zygmunt must have met his former fiancée, Christina of Holstein. He had married the Austrian princess in May 1592 and Christine became the wife of Charles of Suderman three months later. Some historians perceive in Christine's conduct motives of personal vengeance. When Zygmunt was leaving Sweden after the coronation, she was pregnant. On December 19, 1594, she gave birth to a son whose name left a mark on the history of the seventeenth century—Gustav Adolph. Thanks to his military genius, Uppsala, the scene of the bold intervention of Zygmunt's Polish retinue, was to acquire soon the library of Nicholas Copernicus. It has been claimed that a child may inherit the passions that possessed the mother carrying it. A great commander must bring into the world a rage driving him to offensive action and that was surely the case of Gustav Adolph.

The ships of the royal party entered the port of Puck, near Gdansk, and Zygmunt hastened to Cracow, where he received Zamoyski's letter advising him of plans reaching as far as the Crimea. The situation in the southeast had become very complex: the emperor was at war with the sultan and he incited the Cossacks to provoke a Turkish attack against Poland, an objective pursued also by the secret diplomacy of the Vatican.

The next session of the Seym was to be held in Cracow, to the displeasure of both Wielkopolska (western Poland) and Lithuania, which preferred the more centrally located Warsaw. The proposals for a Christian League failed to materialize, as everyone was concerned solely with his own interest. In view of the clear danger, the

137

Seym voted adequate taxes and the formation of new military units. The aged primate Karnkowski continued to cross the hetman, continuing his consistent policy of opposing all those greater than himself. The spiteful, capricious old man penned a pamphlet entitled *"Festina lente"* (Make haste slowly), addressed to taxpayers, which did result in the loss of much revenue by the treasury. The dignity of primate made him responsible to no one and oblivious of the laws.

Even though the treasury was bare again, the Commonwealth staged one of its boldest offensive initiatives. The Crimean plans had to be postponed, as they might have triggered a war with Turkey. A small, elite force crossed the river Dniester and moved, under Zamoyski's command, into what is today Rumania.

It was a move motivated by the same kind of political thinking as that which compelled France to cross the Alps and become involved in Italian wars. One cannot allow a radical and detrimental change of the balance of power in neighboring countries. It is true that Zamoyski owned vast estates along the river Dniester and founded there the town of Szarogrod. But he did not have to go as far as Moldavia to enlarge his holdings and his action was surely not inspired by personal greed. The Lithuanian lords held fast Kiejdany or Nieswiez, but were not interested in Wielkie Luki and withdrew from Pskov at a crucial moment. Owners of huge estates on the border avoided wars, likely to result in devastation on both sides of the frontier. This was particularly true when dealing with an adversary as agile and aggressive as the Tartars. In this instance class interest dictated inaction, but national interest called for action.

The lands which now constitute Rumania were about to be united under the protectorate of either the emperor Rudolph or the sultan Amurat. The Commonwealth intervened in order to either take under its protectorate the entire region, or at least annex some of its parts. Three men were active in the area on behalf of the Habsburgs, who had granted them titles of princes of the Empire: Zygmunt Batory, nephew of King Stefan, prince of Transylvania; the Hospodar Michael the Brave; and Aron of Moldavia (soon succeeded by Stefan Rozwan). The Polish army brought to the ravaged city of Jassy another pretender: Jeremy Mohila, who was related to the Potocki family and was a member of the Polish nobility. He had escaped from Moldavia to Poland and was now returning to his native land with Polish backing. If the proposed Christian coalition should defeat the Turks, Moldavia was to become a province of

Poland. If, on the other hand, the peace should continue, Mohila would remain Hospodar of Moldavia, but as a vassal of the king of Poland rather than the sultan's. Zamoyski's initiative was intended to protect Poland against both Vienna and Istanbul, a risky but potentially profitable project.

A large Tartar force commanded by the khan Ghasi Giray himself and supported by the Turks was approaching from the east. The seven-thousand-strong Polish corps set up a fortified camp on a plateau surrounded by hills and awaited the battle. The hetman ordered his troops to hold their positions and refuse to be drawn outside, which was the Tartar objective. Fighting continued for two days; a janissary shot dead a horse under hetman Zamoyski and the attacking Tartars suffered considerable casualties. Then negotiations were started and resulted in a major success for Zamoyski. The khan agreed to leave Moldavia within three days, recognized Mohila as Hospodar, and promised to secure his recognition by the sultan of Turkey.

The site of Zamoyski's mostly political victory was called Cecora. Among his senior officers was Stanislaw Zolkiewski, field hetman of the crown, who personally helped his men to build fortifications.

A few months later, in 1595, Jeremy Mohila, Poland's new vassal, scored another success. With minor assistance from Polish troops under Wojciech Chanski and Jan Potocki, he defeated, seized, and impaled according to local custom his rival, Stefan Rozwan, backed by Zygmunt Batory and his patron, the emperor.

The intervention of the Commonwealth in Moldavia was not well received in Vienna and in Rome, which even charged Poland with helping Moslems. The Habsburgs were skilled in using ideology as a cover for their dynastic designs.

In the same year, 1595, Polish forces under Zolkiewski defeated in the Ukraine the rebellion of the Cossacks of Szymon Nalewajko. The Poles found in his camp weapons and standards sent by Rudolph II, who incited the Cossacks against Poland in revenge for his setback in Moldavia.

IV

In the last decade of the sixteenth century the Ukraine took the center stage of Poland's foreign policy problems.

The slogan "Poland from coast to coast," expressing the nationalist ambitions of an empire between the Baltic and the Black Sea, made its appearance much later. In the sixteenth century the Catholic bishop of Kiev, Joseph Wereszczynski, who died in 1599, wrote about a Ukraine "longer and wider than Wielkopolska and Malopolska together" and his book was printed without any objection by Master Piotrkowczyk of Cracow.

The fertile soil of the Ukraine brought wealth to some Polish aristocratic families, but only trouble to the Commonwealth, mainly because the duchy of Ruthenia was recognized too late as a member of the federation, coequal with Poland and Lithuania.

The development of southern Ruthenia, as that of other countries, was interrupted and delayed by an Asian invasion of Mongolians, ironically called Tartars after a tribe they had exterminated. The splendor of the city of Kiev before the invasion was admired by German merchants, who reported it to the bishop and chronicler Thietmar. He recorded these impressions before his death in A.D. 1018. But in the second half of the thirteenth century it was said that those still alive in the Ukraine envied the peace of the dead.

A huge territory obviously well fitted to be a sovereign state, as it had been in the past, was ruled first by Lithuania and after the Lublin Union by Poland. The Commonwealth took over a country ravaged by repeated invasions and injected new blood into its drained arteries, but could not resolve all its problems.

The stereotypes of literature often deal with the civilizing role of Poland in the Ukraine and later with Ukrainian serfs working for Polish lords. Actually, Polish peasants worked just as often for Ruthenian lords.

Under Lithuanian sovereignty only the provinces of Wolyn and Podole were settled and enjoyed a fairly normal life, while in the rest of the Ukraine people handled the lasso better than the plough. Under Zygmunt August travelers brought back reports about fertile lands stretching all the way to the Black Sea, described as wilderness. After the Lublin Union the entire province of Kiev was incorporated to Poland, but its management was not the same as in lands around Poznan, Sandomierz, or Cracow. The lord of the manor granted to settlers rent-free possession for twenty years, sometimes more, recruiting them through special agents sent west for

140

that purpose. The Ukrainian lords were powerful enough to ignore the laws controlling fugitive peasants.

Flight is sometimes an act of courage. Only the boldest take the risk of moving to unknown and threatening lands, and this was true both of the Mayflower Pilgrims and the Polish settlers in the Ukraine. Many smaller towns and villages in Poland lost some of their most dynamic and enterprising citizens. Queen Anne was worrying about the depopulation of her estates in Masovia. The alleged colonial exploitation of the Ukraine by Poland was a fiction, since Poland invested in Ruthenia what it needed most—people. Thousands were lost to Poland, which had in the sixteenth century a population of barely eight million.

The lord of the manor theoretically had the right of pursuing his subjects who left the land without his consent, but the enforcement of that rule was difficult. A Polish peasant who escaped to the Ukraine changed his name and joined the Orthodox church, assuming a new personality. He was Poland's loss and Ruthenia's gain, the more so as the country was very sparsely populated. Bohdan Chmielnicki, who later led a Ukrainian rebellion, spoke on behalf of "all the Ruthenian people," including new converts, when he promised expansion "as far as Lublin and Cracow." The Commonwealth never attempted to make Poles of all its citizens, while the freedom it offered stimulated the development of other cultures. The advocates of straight nationalism could not understand the immense value of the heritage of a multinational state formed by voluntary association, not conquest. The historian Michael Bobrowski described narrow nationalism as "a denial of centuries of our history and labor."

The assimilation of many Poles in the Ukraine was not always a matter of expediency. There was also the remarkable attraction of the Ukrainian folk culture. It is working even today: many Polish immigrants in Canada change their ethnic allegiance, not to British or French, but to Ukrainian.

The metropolite of Kiev Piotr Mohila (nephew of the *hospodar* Jeremy) started his educational activity late in the seventeenth century, founding the Kiev College, which was later elevated to the rank of an Academy. Ruthenian culture and literature at the level of the Kochanowskis, Orzechowskis, or Modrzewskis in contemporary Poland, multilingual graduates of western European universities, was quite meager. But the Poles who came to settle in the Ukraine were not those who read these authors or listened to the homilies of Piotr Skarga. The most learned treatises in the church Slavic language would not have appealed to the Polish peasant, but the bewitching Ukrainian folk songs did. They even influenced much of Polish poetry and such works as Sienkiewicz's *Trilogy*, with the Ukraine the scene of much of its action.

People can be assimilated by another culture not only through venality, fear, or ambition. Esthetic and other psychological attractions can also accomplish the same end without a sense of humiliation.

Among the Ruthenian lords adopting the Polish language and faith, some requested in their testaments to be laid to rest in an Orthodox church after receiving the last sacraments from a Catholic priest. There are intangibles difficult to define and yet very real. The Dnieper country with its cemeteries fragrant with cherry trees in bloom, its deep ravines, incredibly rich soil, and old icons can cast a magic spell. In 1590 the Seym granted to the princes Wisniowiecki vast "desert" lands beyond the Dnieper, on both banks of the river Sula, allowing them to include in the grant some ill-defined adjoining territories. The aggressive Prince Adam took this to mean a wide belt of steppes along the vague frontier of the grand duchy of Moscow. Janusz Ostrogski, a recent Catholic convert, owner of a hundred towns and castles, as well as over a thousand villages in the province of Wolyn, since 1593 castellan of Cracow, received from the generous king and Seym the rich heart of the Ukraine: the counties of Biala Cerkiew, Bohuslav, Braclaw, Czerkasy, Korsun, and Perejaslav. He became the greatest magnate of the Commonwealth, until he was overtaken by the Wisniowiecki clan. The grand duke of Lithuania could have awarded these lands earlier, but no one sought them, for vacant territory without population was of little value. The Polish peasants were the factor that enhanced the value of the fertile Ukrainian soil.

Ruthenia was supposed to pay taxes to the Polish crown. Prince Konstanty Ostrogski, Janusz's father, a magnificent old man with a white beard to his knees, owed the government millions, but never paid a penny. The modern concept of exploitation does not fit the relationship between Poland and the Ukraine. Even the modest garrisons guarding the southeast against the Tartars were paid by the revenue of royal estates in central Poland. Taxes collected in the

Cracow region were often spent in the Ukraine. Rather than deriving profits from Ruthenia, Poland spread its forces thin over an immense territory in great need of investment and development. This was also the story of Poland's union with Lithuania, a country with much land and little population.

Some native Poles; the Zamoyski, Koniecpolski, Potocki clans, and many lesser ones made fortunes in the Ukraine, but the ploughmen on their estates were also Polish. Actually it was easier for them than for Ruthenian lords to attract settlers from Poland.

Chancellor Zamoyski did much to develop the left bank of the Dniester and founded there some towns. If as much investment and effort had gone into central Poland, perhaps all of it might have looked like the model city of Zamosc.

But the Ukrainian wilderness held more appeal for men such as Stanislaw Golski, *voievode* of Ruthenia, born in the Kujawy region of western Poland. He fought at Cecora under Zamoyski and then served as envoy to Turkey, where he negotiated the agreement won by the victory. Married to a Buczacka and after her death to a Potocka, Golski became a man of wealth. He visited England, France, Spain, Italy and wrote about his travels a "very interesting diary," which perished in the fires of the Warsaw Rising in 1944, never having seen print in three hundred years. Golski was a typical example of a nobleman of his era, a man of the world and an astute politician. He supported the king against the rebels, then against Wisniowiecki and his own brother-in-law, who became involved in Moldavian intrigues.

In the meantime little was done to consolidate or develop northern Poland, especially Pomerania.

The emigration of Polish peasants to the Ukraine actually contributed to strengthening anti-Polish forces, for Bohdan Chmielnicki could not have raised as many regiments if Poles had not been pouring into Ruthenia for three quarters of a century. He would not have had to raise any army at all if the problem of the Ukraine had received a sensible political solution.

Paradoxically, that failure was largely due to the pull of Polish high culture, which attracted most of the potential leaders of the Ukraine, the Ruthenian gentry. They became Polish and later played a role similar to that of the Lithuanian Radziwill, Sapieha, and Chodkiewicz clans.

A look at the mausoleum of the last generation of the Princes

Zbaraski, in the Dominican church in Cracow, tells the story. Born in Krzemieniec in Ruthenia, but baptized in the Catholic faith, the young Princes Jerzy and Jeremy Zbaraski left the land of their fathers. They were immune to the charms of the Ukraine, for they had already glimpsed wider horizons. Poland served them only as a bridge to the West, which they came to know intimately. While in France, they developed a dislike of the Jesuits, exacerbated by the intrigues of Father Pakosz. Though in opposition to Father Skarga, they heard his great homilies, masterpieces of rhetoric and scholarship. The Orthodox church could hardly offer competition, for it had only just introduced sermons. Until then the faithful had to listen every Sunday to the same stereotyped phrases written on a card "so that people would not question the mysteries of the faith, but believe blindly."

The Zbaraski brothers left the Ukraine and acquired a splendid town house in Cracow at the corner of the Market Square and Bracka street (now number 20). They also built in Solec, Pilica, and Konska Wola Renaissance palaces with Italian gardens. The sarcophagus of the brothers was designed by Anthony and Andreo Castelli.

At the time of the Chmielnicki uprising only one of the Ukrainian magnates was in residence in that country. He was Jerzy Wisniowiecki, but he was a Catholic, member of a church characterized by the patriarch of Moscow as "the worst of heresies."

Two migration streams crossed the Commonwealth in opposite directions: the Ruthenian lords moving to the west and the Polish peasants to the east. The latter was a mass movement and the former involved only a small elite, but it was very comprehensive, as it cleared out almost the entire upper class of Ruthenia.

For a century and a half the Orthodox church did not lose any ground in the Commonwealth, although until 1563 only Catholics enjoyed full political rights in Lithuania. One would have expected the equality of rights granted by Zygmunt August at that time to freeze the Orthodox share of the population at its current level. Yet, oddly enough, it started shrinking precisely at that time.

The expansion of Poland's cultural influence in the eastern provinces of the Commonwealth should not be interpreted in terms of present-day nationalism. It owed its penetration not so much to native Polish genius as to the great intellectual movements of the time: the Renaissance and the Reformation. They reached that part of the continent under Polish guise and that explains the mystery. The increase in the numbers of Polish gentry owed much to Martin Luther and John Calvin, for the Orthodox church started first to lose its aristocratic members to the Protestant denominations. A change of faith opened the way to a change of ethnic and cultural allegiance and that was how it was perceived by the people.

Joseph Wereszczynski became a Catholic almost by accident. He had two uncles, both clergymen—one Orthodox, the other Catholic. The latter proved more enterprising and baptized his nephew immediately after his birth as a Catholic, despite the opposition of his Orthodox parents. The future bishop of Kiev had a difficult childhood, as his relatives shunned the "Devil's own Pole."

The Ruthenian people cherished the memory of the victor of Orsza, hetman Konstanty Ostrogski, buried at the Orthodox monastery of Lavra Pecherska near Kiev. Loyal to the king of Cracow, the Ruthenians were unforgiving of apostates. The recognition of that fact by the Commonwealth could only strengthen it by gaining the support of the Orthodox church, as it had those of the other denominations.

Latin Poland and with it Lithuania were ebullient with innovation, while Orthodox Ruthenia slumbered in lethargy. When the impact of the Renaissance subsided, its place was taken by baroque, which soon reached Jaroslaw, Przemysl, Ostrog, and Lwow, exerting an even more powerful attraction. Its exuberant bombast was well suited to the tempestuous atmosphere of the Ukrainian steppes—saints who assumed fighting postures on the altar were more appealing than the hieratic icons unchanged for many centuries.

The Roman faith not only opened to Joseph Wereszczynski the doors of the senate of the Commonwealth, but also offered to him opportunities which he could not have found in Orthodoxy. The bishop became an original and prolific writer. His principal work remained in print for three centuries. The last edition of the *Sermons or Christian Exercises for Eighteen Sundays* was published in 1854. To his dissolute fellow citizens he addressed *The Sure Path to the Moderation of Their Excesses for Tosspots, Rakes and Libertines*. His other works ranged from a book on the education of youth to a memorandum on a war against Turkey, submitted to Pope Sixtus V, in which the bishop recommended Zamoyski as commander-in-chief.

Polish Catholicism was the carrier of the culture of the West and that was the secret of its appeal to the Ruthenian upper class. The Ruthenian magnates could have kept their seats in the senate as members of the Orthodox faith, but they did not want to represent a plebeian, stagnant, and archaic constituency.

The political fate of the Ukraine was the outcome of trends over which no one had control. A country geopolitically capable of forming a sovereign state was losing its leadership class, which had members with enough wealth and power to secure for Ruthenia the rank of the third co-equal member of the federation, placing the Archangel coat of arms of Kiev on the seals and standards of the Commonwealth alongside the emblems of Poland and Lithuania.

Just prior to the Lublin Union, the Princes Ostrogski, Wisniowiecki and Zbaraski moved the boundary of the grand duchy of Lithuania several miles westward into Red Ruthenia, a province of the Polish crown. Without asking anyone's permission, they enlarged their holdings by twenty-seven towns and villages, as well as fifty-three ponds stocked with fish. At the turn of the sixteenth and seventeenth centuries the Zbaraski estates covered several hundred square miles, more than the area of some of the sovereign dukedoms of the German Reich. Prince Adam Wisniowiecki built his private castles on land claimed by the tsar of Moscow.

The Ukrainian magnates surpassed in wealth and power the lords of Poland. Yet they ignored the call of history and pursued quite ruthlessly their narrow interest, incapable of a broader political vision. The chasm between them and a statesman such as Jan Zamoyski was immense, nor did they even match the Radziwills.

Lithuania joined Poland as a fully formed state and offered it a dynasty. The Lithuanian leaders maintained a national identity after the union and never denied their past, though they sometimes failed to grasp the wider problems of the Commonwealth as a whole.

The Ukrainian lords' position in their country was the same as that of their Lithuanian equivalent in theirs, with considerably more wealth and military capability—but their actions were very different.

In 1587 Lithuania did not participate in the war against Maximilian. Some of its senators came to Cracow and sent some of their men after Zamoyski's army, ordering them to set up a chain of relays of horses, which enabled the Lithuanian lords to receive news of the victory of Byczyna three days ahead of the king. They took advantage of this intelligence and concluded with the crown an agreement in their favor. They recognized the coronation of Zygmunt, received his promise of ratification of the treaty they had concluded on their own with Moscow, and consent to an equal division of public offices in the province of Inflanty between Poland and Lithuania. Zamoyski had refused such a split before, on the ground that the Lithuanians had retreated from Pskov, while the Poles held on and were therefore entitled to the spoils.

Contrary to the allegations of some historians claiming that the Lublin Union abolished the separate identity of Lithuania, Wilno continued to conduct its own policy within the Commonwealth. Unfortunately that was not the case of Ruthenia, which lacked qualified spokesmen. Cracow made many compromises with the Lithuanians and would have done so with the Ruthenians if their leaders had demanded it.

Eventually the Cossacks of the Zaporozhe became the self-appointed representatives of the Ukrainians, but they could not be accepted as such by a monarchy with the structure of the Commonwealth. The Cossacks, thought little better than brigands, were not acceptable partners for any negotiation.

Tsarist Russia, which controlled the entire basin of the Dnieper, had eleven Cossack military formations, which existed until the October Revolution. They were the Cossack troops of the Don, Astrakhan, Orenburg, Ural, Kuban, Tersk, Siberia, Ussur, Trans-Baykal, Amur and Seven Rivers. But there were no Zaporozhe Cossacks, even though they had been the first of all and had the richest history. In 1709 the regiments of Peter I captured the Sich of Zaporozhe by a ruse and executed most of the Cossacks taken prisoner, while the rest were sent to Siberia. In 1775 Catherine II ordered the Nova Sich totally destroyed and its inhabitants resettled far away, while forbidding the very use of the name of Zaporozhe. Poland was not alone in its inability to negotiate with the Cossacks, unless executions and deportation are a form of negotiations.

To understand the roots of the tragedy we should stop looking at the Cossacks as the misguided, lost offspring of either Poland or Russia. The Sich of Zaporozhe was the embryo of a state. It could not become a fully-fledged member of the Commonwealth federation because the appropriate constitutional measures were enacted too late. Then the tsarist empire destroyed the embryo, as it could not tolerate its existence.

The main attributes of sovereignty are the freedom to determine the domestic system of government and to conduct an independent foreign policy. The Sich of Zaporozhe exercised both of them. It recognized the suzerainty of the king, but refused to accept rules enacted by the Seym, in which it was not represented. The Cossacks formed a hierarchical society, contrary to the opinion of a Polish seventeenth-century writer who said, "That sturdy nation consists of peasants more skilled with arms than with the plough." The Sich refused to respect legislation that characterized the Cossacks as fugitive serfs.

The political zigzags of the Cossack chiefs, submitting to Turkey, then to Moscow or the Commonwealth, are difficult to understand or remember in their complexity. They could be charged with inconsistency or primitivism, but there is no doubt that these transient alliances with neighboring powers constituted a sort of foreign policy, qualitatively different from even the most ambitious intrigues of the individual magnates.

There was on the lower Dnieper an element of state authority derived from the will of the Sich brotherhood, acting as Ukraine's voice and her hope, not as the personal appendage of the hetman. This was the seed of a sovereign state.

The first "Sich" (the name given to the Cossack community) was founded by Dymitr Wisniowiecki. The Cossacks won early renown, since Jean de Montluc used them in his courting of the Polish gentry. Henry of Anjou will give you ships, he argued, and with Cossack crews they will perform wonders in the Baltic. In the sixteenth century the Ukrainian magnates often walked hand in hand with the Cossacks, who had among their protectors the Zbaraski and Ostrogski clans. After the Cossack attack on Oczakow, King Stefan I sent there a courtier by the name of Glebocki to investigate. The mission cost him his life, as he was drowned in the Dnieper. Prince Michael Rozynski, who was at the time the hetman of the Zaporozhe Cosscks, managed to settle the matter. In its early phase the development of the Cossack community seemed to be making good progress. If the Orthodox magnates of the Ukraine had remained the leaders of a movement which was political by its very nature, the problem would have been debated at the level of the Commonwealth senate, but the great lords mostly turned Polish and distanced themselves from their Ruthenian origins.

The outstanding Cossack leaders were Piotr Sahajdaczny, a minor squire or perhaps a burgher from Sambor, and Bohdan Chmielnicki, also a member of the petty gentry.

In the sixteenth century the numerous, well-educated nobility of Poland, with full representation in the Seym, managed to push through only a part of its political agenda after a long and strenuous struggle. In the seventeenth century the equality of all "persons of gentle birth" became a fiction, no more than a slogan. Men such as Chmielnicki, heading a mob of commoners, could only hope for a miracle or resort to rebellion.

The Commonwealth could no doubt have resolved the Ukrainian problem if its government and parliament comprised only rational thinkers of the caliber of Modrzewski or even only Rey. But toward the end of the sixteenth century these supreme organs of state power, motivated by fanatical ideology, acted in a manner bordering on insanity. They imposed a union of the Catholic and Orthodox churches within the boundaries of the Commonwealth and abolished at one stroke the Orthodox hierarchy in that territory. Slightly earlier Boris Godunov had granted the title of Patriarch to the Orthodox bishop of Moscow.

In all fairness we should note that the decision of King Zygmunt and his advisers was greeted with amazement and dismay by many of the county councils of the gentry. The nobility of the provinces of Poznan, Kalisz, and Cracow, far removed from the Ukraine, spoke in defense of the Orthodox faith. Their action was probably inspired by the Protestants, but the speakers were mainly Catholics. Most of them were simply confused: "We hear that there is some split among people of the Greek rite. Anxious to avoid any discord which might spread further, we advise. . . ."

Piotr Piasecki, a Catholic bishop and a mature witness of the events, wrote:

> They struck in Rome medals to commemorate this act, with the likeness of the pope on one side and Ruthenians submitting to the Holy See on the other. But when these delegates returned home, they found the minds of their co-religionists, both clergy and laymen, as well as their own, turned against the fusion with the Catholic church, called the Union.

The laymen, more particularly the most prominent ones who have a leading role in the religious life of that nation, were displeased to see a decision of such importance taken arrogantly by a small group of people acting on their own. Especially Prince Constantine Ostrogski, the *voievode* of Kiev, who stands high among his people by his wealth, military power and senatorial rank, was deeply offended by not being consulted in the matter of the union of churches. Hence others, who had disliked the union but did not dare to speak against it, opposed it now more boldly with such backing and so denigrated it among their people that its very mention triggers violent opposition. Nothing could harm the Commonwealth more than the rebellious unrest and constant complaints about the union provoked by that action.

Casimir Chodynicki, an expert on the period, affirmed that the authors of the act of the Warsaw Confederacy of 1573 were concerned only with peace between the Catholics and the Protestant denominations. No one had heard at that time of any conflict between the churches of the Roman and Greek rites, which had coexisted peacefully for centuries, requiring no special legislation to regulate their relations. Yet a quarter of a century later a misguided move caused "rebellious unrest" and disruptive friction. Such are the results of doctrinaire policies violating long established traditions.

Zygmunt III disagreed with Chancellor Zamoyski on many matters, but they joined forces on the union. The aging statesman was getting very devout and even dreamed of the peace of a monastery. His support for the union of churches, however, was politically motivated. In 1588 he had conceived a bold and brilliant plan for transferring the seat of the Orthodox Patriarch of eastern Europe from Moscow to Kiev. He was ahead of Boris Godunov in his thinking, but no one supported his plan and he eventually backed instead King Zygmunt's misguided idea.

Later, many martyrs paid with their lives for the union and its right to exist. The courage of the Uniates was immortalized by the great writers Stanislaw Reymont (Nobel laureate) and Stefan Zeromski. The present author's critical view of the political act of 1596 does not imply any disrespect for the members of the Uniate church.

The worst possible strategy was used in carrying out the unfortunate plan, for a matter concerning the religious beliefs of millions was decided upon by a small coterie. The initiative was taken by the Catholic clergy, with Piotr Skarga, the eminent preacher, foremost among them. A few Orthodox bishops participated in the initial discussions and when the king was approached he approved the project, but did not submit it to the Seym. Consequently he could not guarantee that the Uniate bishops would become members of the senate and that basic condition was never fulfilled, resulting in incalculable damage. The king prohibited an Orthodox conference. Two Ruthenian lords went to Rome: Hipacy Pociej and Cyril Terlecki. They swore there the oath of the union, but interpreters had to be used as neither of them knew any foreign language.

Constantine Ostrogski, the main enemy of the union, used quite different tactics, by starting to incite the masses against an elitary decision. He demanded the convocation of an Orthodox Council and immediately communicated with the synod held in Torun by the Protestant denominations. He threatened the king with civil war and had on his side the influential Orthodox fraternities of Lwow and Wilno. In October 1596 a synod held in Brest Litovsk solemnly proclaimed the union, but the Ostrogski faction assembled in the same city to protest it and declare loyalty to the old Orthodox church. At the last moment two bishops, Gideon Ballab of Lwow and Michael Kopystynski of Wilno, broke away from the union. No one dared to strip them of their ecclesiastic rank and they remained prelates without dioceses or legal means of action.

Soon afterwards Zygmunt III went as far as cancelling judgments favorable to the Orthodox rendered by the courts, submitted all the Orthodox clergy to the authority of the Uniate metropolite, and even wanted to place him in charge of the Lavra Pecherska monastery in Kiev. The Seym had to moderate the king's excesses and prevent state intrusions in the area of religion. The union was making progress and winning numerous adherents, especially in Bielorussia, but those who remained Orthodox started looking to Constantinople under the Turks and particularly toward Moscow, where the Orthodox faith was dominant and served the interests of the state. The historian Felix Koneczny wrote that "the union built a bridge not between Poland and Ruthenia, but between Ruthenia and Moscow."

The Orthodox hierarchy, abolished in 1596, was revived twenty-four years later in a clandestine and illegal ceremony conducted by the Patriarch of Jerusalem, Theophanes, returning from the Kremlin. The service was held at night in an Orthodox church with shielded windows and the singing was muffled. The patriarch was escorted by Cossacks as he left the Commonwealth on his way to Moldavia. In the main square of Busha, Theophanes blessed the kneeling crowd of Zaporozhe cossacks and absolved them of the sin of having served recently in the Polish king's war against Moscow, on the condition that they would never again raise the sword against Russia.

The ceremony at Busha took place twenty-seven years before the Chmielnicki rebellion, so that the passions aroused by religious fanaticism had plenty of time to grow and fester.

Zygmunt III, hereditary Christian for many generations, had less sympathy for the Christian Orthodox church than the heathen Olgierd and Witold, born pagans. These dukes of Lithuania endeavored eagerly to establish a Greek Orthodox hierarchy in their country, while Zygmunt ruthlessly abolished it. Casimir the Great, a pre-Renaissance Catholic, also wanted Ruthenia to have its own metropolite. Counter-reformation tended in some cases to push people back into the darkest Middle Ages, at any rate in Poland.

The religious conflicts in Poland and Lithuania were disturbing, but in the Ukraine they posed a mortal danger. In the west and north Poles feuded with other Poles and Lithuanians with other Lithuanians, but in the Ukraine the religious confrontation coincided with the class conflict between the Polish gentry and the Ruthenian plebeians. Besides, everyone was fighting everyone in the Ukraine even without bringing in any religious differences, which were fuel poured on an already lively fire.

The Cossacks staged expeditions against the Tartars by sea and by land, while the Tartars responded with raids into Commonwealth territory. When not fighting and robbing the infidels, the Cossacks could seek glory and profit in Moldavia, Hungary, or elsewhere, looting on their own account or in the service of the magnates. The attitude toward the Cossacks of the Princes Zbaraski and Ostrogski was highly equivocal. Prince Janusz Ostrogski promised them wages as mercenaries, pretending to be acting on behalf of the emperor. In the course of the Nalevayko rebellion towns in Lithuania were mercilessly sacked, though they could hardly be held responsible for Poland's actions in the Ukraine. Squires compelled by Nalevayko to supply provisions for his men threatened the government that unless it protected them they might be forced to "join the Cossacks." At that, Kiev supplied the Polish commander Zolkiewski with boats and other means of crossing the Dnieper, as it feared the Cossacks more than the crown of Poland.

The fighting in the Ukraine had social overtones, but class was by no means the only motivation involved.

Court records provide a glimpse of the conditions that prevailed in the Ukraine in the sixteenth and seventeenth centuries. The clan of the Princes Zbaraski was sued by their neighbors on the following grounds: Stealing cattle, destruction and robbery of beehives, chasing beaver from the river, sending servants on a raid against a neighbor, stealing serfs, invasion of property, killing and robbing people, taking lumber from the forest and fish from ponds, destruction of dam and water mill, and so on. About sixty lawsuits were filed against Prince Janusz by neighboring landowners. His private wars against local squires were not exceptional or unusual in the Ukraine.

The historian Jablonowski wrote: "It was a time of unbridled economic expansion; everyone grabbed what he could: the prince, a feudal lord, the burghers, the Cossacks, and the clergy.

The Princes Wisniowiecki enlarged their holdings in the province of Kiev alone with remarkable speed. In fifteen years their domain jumped from about 600 to 38,000 farmsteads, inhabited by 230,000 subjects. The population of the kingdom of Sweden was at that time about one million. The joining of the fertile and under-populated Ukraine with long-settled Poland unleashed forces over which no one had control. Russia, despite its power and having no rival since the downfall of the Commonwealth, did not manage to pacify its southern province until the late eighteenth century and did so by using methods of the utmost brutality.

The Ukraine was then the scene of the same social phenomena that we witnessed much later in the American Far West. Major migrations and the sudden arrival of large numbers of people uprooted from their former environment invariably result in wild, uncontrolled behavior. In such circumstances the social restraints of the former society are lost and new ones are not yet in place. The most ruthless individuals thrive in such conditions, imposing their pattern of conduct on others. The lawlessness and turbulence of the Ukraine of that period was not exceptional, but typical of countries in that situation.

153

Outside interference only served to aggravate the turmoil. In the summer of 1594, just prior to Zamoyski's expedition into Moldavia, the Cossack Sich was visited by two foreign envoys. Vasili Nikiforovich represented the tsar of Russia and Eric Lassota von Steblau the Emperor Rudolph II. Both tried to induce the Cossacks to support Russia, while Simon Nalevayko did so on his own, independently of the Sich of Zaporozhe.

The Orthodox clergy could have exerted a stabilizing influence in a country undergoing a sudden transition, but toward the end of the sixteenth century religious discord contributed instead to further disruption.

Prince Janusz Zbaraski attacked the Orthodox church of Pinsk and robbed it of liturgical vessels, books, even candles. Yet this was a man who had been himself Orthodox not long before. Bishop Hipacy Pociej had barely returned from Rome when he raided the monastery of St. Elias in Wlodzimierz. Later he fought in the same town for the Orthodox church of St. Vasili and ordered the arrest of a priest who rejected the union.

In February 1620 a Cossack delegation arrived in Moscow, seeking service under the tsar. The Orthodox priests asked the visitors about religious persecution in their country and were told that there was none. Until that time the Cossacks had displayed little interest in religion and did not pretend to be its defenders, but Moscow evidently changed their minds, since they escorted soon afterwards the patriarch Theophan and knelt before him in Busha.

The counter-reformation, helped by Zygmunt III and his advisers, made the Cossacks standard bearers of an Orthodox ideology supplied to them by Moscow and the patriarchates functioning under the Turks.

V

Lithuania also saw change in the late sixteenth century, but it was very different in character from that in the Ukraine.

Zygmunt III decided to move the bishop of Wilno, Cardinal Jerzy Radziwill, to the diocese of Cracow. It would be a promotion, carrying with it a higher rank in the senate. The Polish gentry protested, citing earlier royal pledges granting preference to native Poles for appointment in Poland. The opposition soon subsided, even though the county councils demanded that reciprocity be observed by admitting Poles to all the public offices in the grand duchy of Lithuania.

The king wanted to send to Wilno Bernard Maciejowski, the bishop of Luck and future cardinal and primate. Lithuania opposed his appointment and won after a dispute that lasted eight years.

Maciejowski was a prominent personality and one of the authors of the union of churches, so that he could be expected to promote it among the Orthodox population of Lithuania. He was backed by the king, the pope, the nuncio Malaspina, the cardinal legate Gaetano, and the Jesuits. Lithuanians, however, were unanimous in rejecting him. The *voievode* Krzysztof Radziwill, himself a fervent Calvinist, took an active part in the debate, which was only ostensibly ecclesiastic. Father Ambrose Beynart, of the Habdank crest, was sent by the chapter of Wilno to Rome, where he was to explain to the pope that even his will could not override the laws enacted under the Statutes of Lithuania. Though a native Lithuanian, the canon wrote from Rome letters in Polish, which was also the language used by Procop Bartlomiejowicz, the author of a pamphlet warning against concessions to the Poles. He wrote: "It is easy to stray from the straight path, but difficult to find it again. If lost, you will have only yourselves to blame." This champion of Lithuanian autonomy used impeccable Polish.

The rights of the "noble Lithuanian nation" were fully respected. Ignoring the pressure applied by the king and the pope, the Polish gentry accepted the Lithuanians' argument and declared at the Seym of 1597 that they no longer requested the appointment of Maciejowski to the see of Wilno. It was another example of the spirit of compromise that characterized the relations between Poland and Lithuania within the Commonwealth. Benedict Woyna, recognized by the chapter as a "Lithuanian born and bred," was appointed bishop of Wilno. He was a native of Minsk and a member of the Orthodox church in his youth.

Such facts contradict the view of some modern writers, who imply that after the Lublin Union the Poles grabbed all the land and power in Lithuania.

The prolonged debate over the bishop's appointment merits attention. This method of settling differences consolidated the Commonwealth and strengthened the bonds of the federation. Genuine solutions were sought instead of cosmetic ones, which often leave unresolved hidden tensions likely to surface later.

The issue was debated openly, in a manner that was amazingly democratic for its time. The powerful Calvinist lord had his say, as did the petty squire or the humble graduate of a Jesuit school. Decisions reached after such a free public debate are usually durable as they reflect the relative influence of various trends of public opinion. After two centuries of experience the association of Poland and Lithuania was reaching full maturity. It was understood in Poland that concessions by the stronger partner, freely made, may be to his advantage in the long run.

Such political sophistication was lacking in the Ukraine, a young country still at a primitive stage of development. Only thirty years had elapsed since the decisions of 1569.

The first confrontation with the Cossacks could hardly be described as an uprising or even a rebellion. It was led by Christopher Kosinski, a member of the Polish petty nobility, who was awarded by the Seym the estate of Rokitno in the Ukraine and feuded over it with Prince Janusz Ostrogski. The contest between the Ruthenian magnate and the Polish squire ended by the latter's capitulation at Piatek on February 2, 1593. Later Kosinski attacked at Czerkasy another Ukrainian lord, Prince Wisniowiecki, but lost his life in the battle. Simon Nalevayko, an authentic Cossack leader, fought on the magnate's side against Kosinski, but three years later started a rebellion himself, though not with the Sich, but with the colors of Emperor Rudolph in his camp. When the Polish hetman Zolkiewski besieged Nalevayko at Solonica, Prince Rozynski—whose cousin had been recently commander of the Zaporozhe Cossacks—terrorized the rebels by impaling Cossack prisoners in sight of their ramparts.

Zolkiewski defeated the rebels and could have anticipated by a century the act of Peter I taking the strongholds of the Sich. He did not do so because he thought that the Zaporozhe Cossacks could be used as a shield against the Tartars of the Crimea. He sent Nalevayko to Warsaw, where he was beheaded, but released fifteen hundred Cossack horsemen.

The Ukraine has been called "the Balkans of Poland," a congeries of diverse forces constantly at odds with one another. Catherine II of Russia pacified it in 1775 by taking three drastic actions: the first partition of the Commonwealth, the leveling of the Cossack Sich and the conquest of the Crimea.

The year 1596, which saw the Nalevayko incident and the union of the churches, was also the date of Warsaw's inauguration as the national capital. We are fortunate in having a vivid description of the city at that time, by Giovanni Paulo Mucante. He was master of ceremony of the retinue of Cardinal Gaetano, the papal legate, who took residence at the Ujazdow palace and then paid his respects at the royal castle to queen dowager Anne Jagiello, who died on September 9.

The new capital impressed the Italians favorably, except for the mud in the poorly paved streets after a rainy day. Held within a tight double ring of walls, the compact city could not provide the legate with a spacious residence. His staff was quartered in the narrow townhouses bordering the main square. The New City section outside the walls was thought by the visitors more attractive, even though its streets were also muddy and most of the buildings wooden. Giocanni Mucante praised the bridge on the Vistula and the royal castle, but he did not write about Warsaw with the rapture he reserved for the rich city of Cracow, where the finest goods of Europe were on display.

Lithuania could no longer complain about the too-distant capital. The boundary between the grand duchy and Poland ran between Bielsk Podlaski and the Bialowieza forest. Wielkopolska was also pleased, for Masovia and Warsaw were part of its administrative area. The waterway traffic, very active at the time, brought Warsaw close to Gdansk and Torun. But the new capital had to look also toward the northeast, Inflanty, and the southeast, the Ukraine. The forces that could have been nipped in the bud then were destined to draw closer to Warsaw and finally invade it.

Soon after the transfer of the capital, the king ordered major alterations of the castle, the former seat of the dukes of Masovia and then of the dowager queens Bona and Anne Jagiello. Mucante saw the castle before the alterations and judged it "magnificent and commodious." The king's example was followed by numerous magnates, who built their residences outside the city walls, the most sumptuous among them the Kazanowski palace. The senators visiting the capital no longer had to stay in burghers' townhouses, but the deputies to the Seym continued to do so. They conducted their debates in a new two-story-high chamber in the royal castle, adjoining another columned hall intended as a theatre.

The castle was majestic and somber, with walls "like a fortress" facing the river at the rear and a clock tower with copper roof and two corner towers in front. There was nothing frivolous in the life of the still youthful monarch, about whom Mucante wrote approvingly:

> He is a lord of the greatest dedication and piety. He recites prayers daily, like a priest, attends every day first a regular mass and then a sung one with a sermon. He observes strictly all fasting days, abstains from the matrimonial bed every Wednesday and Friday, as well as two days before and after confession. He spares no effort in spreading the Catholic faith and if he had his way there would not be in this great kingdom a single schismatic, Calvinist or Lutheran.

Zygmunt rose every morning at the same time and started the day by attending mass. He then worked industriously, reading and signing papers, conferring with his aides. After dinner he relaxed by playing ball or engaging in his hobbies of alchemy and jewelry making. They were rather more refined than those of his French contemporary, Louis XIII, an expert blacksmith who could fix a broken coach axle or cast a small cannon. Perhaps such crafts might have been more acceptable to the Poles, who distrusted attempts at making gold.

Before visiting him at the royal castle, Cardinal Gaetano sent to the king from the Ujazdow palace "several excellent paintings by famous masters, much loved by the king," who actually copied them with his own hand, another one of his hobbies. He appreciated the company of painters, poets, and musicians, among the latter the famous Thomas Delabella and his countryman Luca Muranto, who conducted the royal orchestra. Polish artists were also welcome at the court: the royal secretaries were the writers and poets Andrzej Zbylitowski, Stanislaw Niegoszewski, and Thomas Treter, who also painted. Among the lords close to the monarch were Zygmunt Myszkowski and Mikolaj Wolski, both art connoisseurs. Adam Jarzebski, the talented son of a burgher from Warka, was engaged in 1615 as a violinist in the royal orchestra. His work as a composer made a significant contribution to Polish chamber music. He was also active in designing the decoration of the Ujazdow palace and wrote a valuable description of the city of Warsaw. The gifted plebeian prospered at the court, witness the fact that he was owed sixteen thousand *zlotys* by King Zygmunt's son and heir, Crown

Prince Wladyslaw. The road to advancement was wide open to qualified commoners, not only in the area of the arts.

In the early years of his reign the king was constantly accompanied by about a dozen young Swedes and two "old adventurers" from that country. The court was also full of Germans, Italians, and Hungarians, with an occasional native thrown in, not always one of the best. The king's factotum and confidant, the chamberlain Andrew Bobola, was not popular among the gentry. An inveterate bachelor and bigot, he had the king's ear, though also getting occasionally a royal slap. He dealt with both political and lesser matters, indulging in intrigue and spreading capriciously his favor or disfavor.

Queen Anne brought with her as chief lady in waiting Ursula Gienger, a German woman heartily disliked by everyone in Poland. Even the nuncio noted with surprise that, contrary to law and custom, Ursula always attended the king's private audiences with foreign diplomats. She was generally thought to be an official agent in the service of Vienna. At the same time Zygmunt discontinued his predecessor's practice of consulting the senators before taking decisions of importance. The queen's mother, the archduchess of Styria, visited Poland from time to time and always tried to exert a pro-Habsburg influence on her son-in-law through her daughter. She played an important role in Poland's political life.

The two chief Jesuits at the court formed a team working together under strict instructions, though their personalities differed widely. Even his superior in the order did not hold Father Golynski in high esteem: "A courtier, knows little, choleric disposition, good at taking confessions—especially of women." His colleague was Piotr Skarga, whose great work *The Parliamentary Homilies* was first published in 1597. The brilliant preacher never delivered them from the pulpit, but wrote them for publication. On the other hand, many of the sermons he had actually preached were never printed—among them that of October 1587, announcing to Cracovians that the lawfully elected king had landed in Gdansk, also another celebrating the victory of Byczyna, in which he castigated the Habsburgs for "trying to force a yoke on the neck of free people, to rule us by force and treat us as their servants." Earlier, Skarga had handed to Chancellor Zamoyski, unopened, a letter he had received from Maximilian Habsburg. The archduke was asking the Cracow Jesuits for help in seeking the crown of Poland. Skarga did

159

not yield to pressure then, but the monastic discipline eventually curbed the spirit of the great writer and orator. It was helped in doing so by the Catholic fervor inspired by the counter-reformation fanaticism of his native province of Masovia. He had fought heresy bitterly even before joining the Society of Jesus.

The Austrian queen did learn Polish, but her court remained purely German. Zygmunt's sister, Princess Anne Vasa, a dedicated champion of the Protestants, also had mostly foreigners in her entourage. Ever since the death of the last of the Jagiellonians, Polish faces and customs were seldom seen at the court of the Commonwealth's monarchs.

Queen Anne, a model of wifely virtue, gave birth to four children, only one of whom, Prince Wladyslaw, had a long life. Three daughters died in early childhood. The queen herself died just before her fifth delivery. She seemed to be in good health and a slight cold did not prevent her from joining her husband at the dinner table. Then a sudden attack of a mysterious illness, rapid heartbeat with moderate fever, killed her within twenty-four hours. She was nine months pregnant, so the physicians kept her mouth open after she died "to help the baby to breathe." A surgeon cut open her abdomen and removed a male child, christened Christopher, who gave signs of life only for an hour.

On the same day of February 10, 1598, Samuel Laski addressed the Estates of Sweden at Uppsala as the envoy of the king, reproaching the regent, Charles of Suderman, for disorders and plotting, while announcing the prompt arrival of the king.

The situation in Sweden did not bode well for Zygmunt. Charles of Suderman ruled the country by brutal and cruel methods, but he nevertheless secured the support of the more numerous classes: the peasants and burghers, as well as the rank and file of the clergy. His adversary had only one class left to back him, the aristocracy.

In July the ships carrying Zygmunt and his retinue, as well as small detachments of German and Hungarian troops, sailed from Gdansk. The ships were chartered from Danish and English owners by the Polish treasury, as Sweden did not send a fleet for her king. The Polish lords traveling with him paid their own expenses.

The Seym had approved the expedition unanimously, though with reluctance. The decisive argument was concern for the king's prestige, tarnished when Charles of Suderman almost evicted him from his hereditary throne. Zygmunt ignored Zamoyski's advice and did not mobilize an adequate armed force, particularly not a Polish one. "I am going to my subjects," he said, "against whom I do not need any soldiers, for I will bring them back by words of reason." He was not a violent man and believed in persuasion. Political expediency suggested that if force were to be used, it should not be Polish, so as to avoid any appearance of domination of Sweden by the much larger Commonwealth. Trying to play simultaneously on two instruments of different tune, separated by the sea, was a hopeless task.

Zygmunt traveled from Kalmar to the capital in a carriage drawn by peasants' horses. Sweden did not offer a royal welcome to her hereditary monarch.

Samuel Laski seized without opposition Stockholm, which Charles of Suderman had abandoned, but an armed confrontation followed soon. Zygmunt won at Stegeborg and if he had acted more decisively, if he had displayed any leadership qualities, he could have captured his adversary. But he failed to do so and did not have long to wait for a reversal of fortune. On September 25 he was defeated at Linkoping and taken prisoner by his uncle. He was later released, but he had to deliver to the enemy his principal supporters, among them the chancellor Eric Sparre. It was by then useless to keep the other terms of the agreement and risk a visit to Stockholm. Zygmunt left in Kalmar a small garrison, which was forced to surrender a year later. He addressed a solemn protest to the monarchs of Europe and boarded a sailing ship, casting a last glance at his native land. He landed in Gdansk on October 30, far ahead of the August 24 deadline set by the Seym for his return. Four months sufficed for crossing the Baltic twice and suffering a defeat that soon triggered a series of far worse disasters. Zygmunt did not want to relinquish the resounding title of king of the Swedes, Goths and Vandals, nor his plan of winning Scandinavia back for the church of Rome.

The parliament of Stockholm dethroned him in July of 1599, but recognized Crown Prince Wladyslaw as heir to the throne on the condition that he return to Sweden within six months and be raised there in the Lutheran faith.

Chancellor Eric Sparre and four other Swedish noblemen whom Zygmunt had delivered to Charles after his defeat were beheaded. Charles of Suderman remained regent for the next five years before being crowned as Charles IX.

In the meantime important changes were also taking place in

another country, in which the emblem of power was a sceptre headed by a cross. The tsar of Muscovy, Theodore Ivanovich, died in January 1598. His younger brother Dymitr had been stabbed to death in Uglich on May 15, 1591, probably at the order of the powerful "great boyar" Boris Godunov. This meant the extinction of the House of Rurik, which had been ruling Russia since pre-Christian times and Moscow since its very foundation.

The Council called to the throne Boris, whose succession was vividly described by Nicholas Kostomarov, a Ukrainian writing in Russian. The patriarch Hiob, at the head of a crowd of Muscovites, went several times to the monastery in which Godunov was hiding, begging him to accept the crown, under pain of divine wrath and chastisement. It was all carefully planned and orchestrated, for the passing of the throne of Moscow to an upstart boyar of Tartar descent from Kostroma, whose ancestors had never held any office, required very good stage management.

Godunov had been long planning his patient, ruthless ascent to power. He married the daughter of Maluta Skuratov, the chief of the notorious *Oprichina* of Ivan the Terrible, as sinister a figure as his master; then he had his sister marry Theodore, the last of the House of Rurik to sit at the Kremlin. He won power and with it a set of mortal enemies. The great princely families could not forgive the rise of the talented climber. Boris dealt with them harshly: he deported them north and south, sent some to monasteries, and executed others. Prince Ivan Shuyski, the hero of the defense of Pskov, died in faraway Bialozier, probably murdered. His brother Vasili was astute and pliable enough to survive. He headed the commission that investigated the death of the crown prince Dymitr and found that he accidentally stabbed himself in an epileptic fit.

Some years later, at the tsar's order, the same Dymitr was proclaimed a saint and a martyr, his body allegedly found in its tomb intact and not decomposed. By that time Godunov was openly charged with Dymitr's murder and his body in turn was removed from the church of the Archangels, the burial place of the tsars.

Some time before these miraculous happenings an extraordinary project was conceived by the chancellor of Lithuania and immediately backed by that of Poland, but failed to be carried out. Leo Sapieha devised an original plan for a union between the Commonwealth and the grand duchy of Moscow. Zygmunt III and Tsar Boris were to keep their thrones and a common monarch was to be elected only after the death of one of them, but even prior to that the two countries were to establish close ties of trade, currency, and navigation.

In 1600 the Seym authorized a mission to Moscow, headed by Leo Sapieha, chancellor of Lithuania, and Stanislaw Warszewicki, *castellan* of Warsaw. The plan they proposed to the boyars was staggering in its scope. The two states were to have a joint foreign policy, with a common treasure for military purposes kept in Kiev. The subjects of both states would have the free choice of residence in either of them and could enter mixed marriages, while the Catholic and Orthodox churches would enjoy equal rights. The delegates of the Commonwealth also wanted to help Russian youth to learn Latin, the international language of Europe.

The mission bringing such sensational proposals was carefully isolated by the hosts, who viewed it with hostility and suspicion. Tsar Boris had no love for his western neighbor and plotted against the Commonwealth with the sultan, the emperor, Sweden, and anyone else willing, though he avoided war. The boyars negotiating with Sapieha and Warszewicki were willing to conclude a "perpetual" peace, which of course would only be one in name, but rejected all the innovative ideas. The talks, intended by one party to bring about a fraternal union, ended in sharp recriminations.

The union was sponsored by Leo Sapieha, Christopher Radziwill, and Jan Zamoyski, a trio fully representing the multinational character of the Commonwealth and its historic heritage. Their initiative aimed at establishing an even broader federation than the existing one. It was also an expression of the vague yearnings that had manifested themselves occasionally in Moscow candidacies proposed for the throne of Wawel.

The real author of the concept of union between central and eastern Europe was the experience of two centuries of the Polish-Lithuanian federation. Such an idea could only be born in a society used to a pluralistic culture and one that had outgrown parochial definitions of statehood. It could be advocated only by men who inherited the knowledge that mortal enemies can become partners and the patient work of generations can build unity out of enmity.

The union between Poland and Lithuania had begun with cautious probings, long-drawn diplomatic soundings starting from a point of mutual distrust. Yet their initial agreements created facts that eventually changed the basic attitudes of both partners.

163

In 1600 only one of the parties negotiating at the Kremlin had the benefit of that experience, which encouraged bold planning for the future. The other party clung desperately to the old ways of tribal chauvinism and the tradition of many "perpetual" treaties of peace, broken on battlefields.

Eventually a peace treaty was concluded, but it did not even pretend to be perpetual, for its term was to elapse on August 15, 1622.

There was in Leo Sapieha's entourage a young man destined to attain soon a durable though not honorable fame.

The moves of the chancellor of Lithuania were largely inspired by personal motives, for a tightly closed border denied to the Sapiehas access to their estates in the territories lost to Russia by Zygmunt the Old. Personal interest may motivate either good or bad policies. When the union plan misfired, Leo Sapieha sought other, less commendable means of finding an opening to the east.

The negotiations at the Kremlin coincided with a crisis threatening the Commonwealth. Tsar Boris knew it well, for he was among those invited to participate in the spoils. The events, however, took an unexpected turn.

A considerable role in them was played by a man whose name can still be seen on the wall of the great hall of the bishop's palace in Lidzbark in the province of Warmia by the Baltic coast. Cardinal Andrew Batory left his almost princely seat there, in an endeavor to recover Transylvania. His adversaries were the emperor and his vassal, Michael, with the flattering nickname of "Valiant." But he did not expect the betrayal of the mediator, the nuncio Germanic Malaspina, who had moved from Warsaw to Vienna and entered the service of Emperor Rudolph II, enticed by promises of a cardinal's hat. Batory's fortunes varied until the time when, deceived by false promises, he dismissed his Polish mercenaries. He was captured in lonely flight and met a tragic end.

The nations within the sphere of Turkish influence acquired the odd habit of shortening people by a head. In the course of the operations in Sweden, the commander of the Hungarian regiment, Bekesh, galloped joyfully from the scene of the first skirmish, bringing to the king proudly a trophy, a head on his lance. "You have not yet chopped off all the heads in Sweden," snapped Zygmunt, who did not have a headsman's tastes.

It is not known whether the head of Cardinal Andrew Batory

was presented to the emperor or to nuncio Malaspina. At any rate, his execution was cause for celebration in Vienna.

In the same fall of 1599 Michael the Valiant drove Jeremy Mohila out of Jassy, seized Moldavia and in the spring started marauding in the foothills of the eastern Carpathians. He had vast plans for the dismemberment of the Commonwealth and urged Sweden and Moscow to take their shares. He had secured in Istanbul a gold-lettered charter appointing him king of Poland. It sounded fantastic, but on the Bosphorus even fairytales sometimes come true.

In the summer of 1600 a Polish-Lithuanian army of twenty thousand men crossed the river Dniester. Money was scarce, as usual, but the private regiments of the magnates filled the gap. Zamoyski himself was in command, wise and cautious as his age dictated. He declined Tartar offers of help and lent his ear to the advice of his younger aides, Stanislaw Zolkiewski, and the *voievode* of Lublin Mark Sobieski. They attacked the well-fortified positions of the enemy, held by double their number, the infantry leading the assault.

Ninety banners taken in the battle were stored in the Gniezno cathedral. Many more were used by the soldiers as material for sumptuous attire. When Julian Ursyn Niemcewicz, the writer and friend of Thaddeus Kosciuszko, visited Gniezno in 1812 he did not find a trace of these trophies, probably taken by the Swedes or other invaders.

About a thousand of Michael's men perished in the battle fought on October 20 at the village of Bucova near Ploesti, in what is today Rumania. On the following day the remnants of the defeated force turned up at the Polish camp, eager to enlist. Political allegiances in Valachia were rather fluid and people gravitated toward a center of force.

Zamoyski installed Jeremy Mohila in Jassy again and his brother Simeon in Bucharest. They were both vassals of the Commonwealth, thus extending its influence to the Danube. Jan Potocki, *starosta* of Kamieniec, sealed the success by defeating Michael once again.

The sultan's gold-lettered charter did not help the Valiant much. The unfortunate prince lost the emperor's favor, but soon regained it when another Batory, Zygmunt, made his appearance in Transylvania. Michael helped to drive him out but then became a nuisance himself. He was killed by the order of George Basta, an Austrian general. The bearded head was not sent to anyone, but tossed on a heap of manure, while the trunk was left in the open without burial.

Was meddling by the Commonwealth in these barbaric feuds mere adventurism, as some claimed? It would not seem so. Maintaining an armed presence in the southeast was a necessary security precaution. Zamoyski said that allowing a powerful enemy, the sultan or the emperor, into Moldavia would be like having them in one's backyard. A strong position on the river Prut provided a base against the Tartar Horde of the Crimea, which sometimes sent raids as far as Sanok. The most dangerous Tartar horde, that of Budziak, camped in the steppes between the mouths of the Dniester and the Danube, the way to which led through Jassy and Bucharest.

In the spring of 1601 Zygmunt III sent to the Crimea Lawryn Piaseczynski, a skillful diplomat and the author of a valuable work on the duties of an envoy. He was instructed to demand the recognition of Commonwealth sovereignty as far as the Black Sea, without making any promises concerning the Cossacks.

An active policy in the southeast could have opened opportunities for using the Cossacks of the Zaporozhe. They fought well at Telezyna and took five enemy cannon, spreading panic among Michael's troops. If the Commonwealth had developed that relationship, it could have assumed the aspect of political cooperation rather than the use of mercenaries. The instructions given to Piaseczynski meant that the king did not want to dispense with the potential of the Sich of Zaporozhe as a future political weapon.

The positions won in the southeast were not kept long. The new *hospodar* of Moldavia, Radul Szczerban, was a vassal of the sultan and Transylvania also came again under Turkish sovereignty.

This happened mainly because the Polish forces had to leave hastily the theatre of their victories in Moldavia and rush north. Stanislaw Zolkiewski could spend only one day with his family between one campaign and another. A new war was starting and no one could foresee the string of reverses it would bring about. The day when Zygmunt August offered his sister in marriage to a Swedish prince was one of evil omen for Poland.

Zygmunt III did not accept the Stockholm resolution removing him from the throne of Sweden. He reacted by carrying out the clause of the "Pacta Conventa" that required him, as king of Sweden, to yield to the Commonwealth the territory now known as Estonia, which was actually of little value for Lithuania or Poland. He did so on March 26, 1600, and the Seym responded by witholding taxes, for it feared that the money would be spent on defending the king's gift against the Swedes, rather than in Moldavia, where Zamoyski was just opening his offensive.

These events are usually described in current literature as "repulsing the Swedish invasion." But Bishop Pawel Piasecki, their witness and a writer candid almost to the point of cynicism, took a different view. He said that the Seym and Senate wanted to avoid war, but ". . . they were entangled in it by individuals who, eager to win royal favor, broke the ancient peace between the Commonwealth and the kingdom of Sweden. When Charles entered Estonia, taking Rewel with all the lands that had been until then considered Swedish possessions, Jerzy Fersenbach (*starosta* of Wenden) instead of only defending against Charles the Polish Inflanty, crossed the border into Estonia and harassed Charles' forces."

Asked to explain this action, he failed to reply and sent the Swedish envoy to Warsaw. In such a situation Charles preferred to move his operations into poorly defended enemy territory. Fersenbach had only about six hundred soldiers, while Zamoyski was campaigning in faraway Moldavia. The Swedes soon occupied most of the Inflanty as far as the river Dvina. Riga held out, but Parnawa, Kies, Wolmar, and Dorpat were taken by the Swedish army and all the acquisitions of Stefan I were lost.

It was the beginning of the Swedish wars, which lasted sixty years in the seventeenth century and, after an interval, some more in the eighteenth.

The hetmans Christopher Radziwill and Jan Karol Chodkiewicz scored some successes in the spring, aided by Fernsenbach. The operations were impeded by the fact that the two Lithuanian commanders were "like a couple of tomcats" constantly feuding with each other. The Seym in Warsaw honored Zamoyski for his victories in Moldavia and he was again in favor at the court, for the time being anyway. The Seym voted double taxes, though the deputies had started by debating ways of terminating the unpopular war. But while it could do very well without Estonia, the Commonwealth had to defend the Inflanty.

In October 1601, a year after the campaign in Rumania, Jan Zamoyski started another, his last. He was fighting in Latvia against a new enemy. Sweden joined the list of adversaries inherited from the Jagiellonians and the burden was becoming unbearable.

The conflict between the Commonwealth and Sweden was absurd, for common sense would have dictated their alliance. But the famous Swedish chancellor Axel Oxenstierna was right when he said later: "Quantilla sapientia regitur mundus" (A particle of wisdom rules the world).

Zamoyski started hasty negotiations with Gdansk and Prussia, urging them to build a navy. It was of course impossible, as a navy cannot be improvised, but requires long preparations and training. We may note at this point that its past and the character of the Commonwealth inclined it to choose the route taken successfully by Russia: from land power to sea power. Peter the Great opened his "window to Europe" with massive forces of infantry, cavalry, and artillery. Moscow became a power in the sixteenth century but its navy was not significant until the eighteenth. The achievements of the Russian fleets at sea were historically far behind those of the Russian armies on land, in the air, and lately in space. The assertion that the Commonwealth was doomed because it lacked a navy is a myth, as is the theory blaming everything on national character. Zamoyski did well in his campaign without any ships. The real problem was a bare treasury and an incompetent crowned commander-in-chief. "King Zygmunt only turned up in September, delayed by the vast baggage train of the throng of useless courtiers." The camp followers stripped the countryside of provisions before finally turning back toward the Vistula. The price of grain in Lithuania rose, shortages developed, and then epidemics. The army in the field was hard pressed. The mercenaries had not yet been paid for the Moldavian campaign, some regiments refused to fight unless they received their wages.

Yet the forts taken earlier by the Swedes were recaptured one after another, recalling the string of victories of King Stefan in the same region. Charles retreated from Riga and then, during a winter campaign extremely onerous for the attacking side, he lost Wolmar, Kirempe, Helmet, Neuhausen, Ansen, Marienburg, Adsel. In April 1602 only four thousand exhausted, mutinous men stood before the fortress of Fellin. The rest of the twenty-thousand-strong army was either lost in battle or through desertion when the money for their pay ran out.

During one of the assaults Jerzy Fersenbach, mortally wounded, fell into a moat. Stanislaw Zolkiewski carried out the dying officer. Next to him a musket bullet pierced Zamoyski's belt buckle. The commanders set an example for the demoralized soldiers by facing the fire in the front line of assault. Dismounted cavalry climbed the ramparts alongside the infantry. The old hetman caught a cold in the winter, had frostbitten feet, and suffered insomnia, but he carried on. He pawned his own valuables to pay the troops.

Fellin surrendered on May 17 and in June siege was laid to Weissenstein (Bialy Kamien), a fortress surrounded by deep marshes. The siege guns bombarded the fortification from a distance, but did so in vain until Zamoyski ordered the execution of major earthworks. It was said that he wanted to prove to the Frenchmen and Germans in his camp that the Poles knew how to take fortresses, not only to fight in the field, as Stanislaw Zolkiewski had just done again when he defeated with his cavalry an enemy force that tried to relieve the besieged fortress. "Iron will and endurance overcame all obstacles, causeways were built of lumber, earth, and firewood collected in the vicinity, so that they reached the bottom of the marsh." Heavy guns approached the walls over the new dikes and the garrison surrendered in August on honorable terms, allowed to leave with arms.

The successful siege of Weissenstein was Jan Zamoyski's last feat of arms. He waited for the fifty thousand *zlotys* sent from Warsaw, added to them nineteen thousand of his own, and left for his seat of Zamosc. Jan Karol Chodkiewicz took over the command.

The country lost two great commanders: age removed Zamoyski from active service and death took Radziwill "The Lightning," but other outstanding military leaders succeeded them: Stanislaw Zolkiewski in Poland and Jan Karol Chodkiewicz in Lithuania. Other great talents were waiting in the wings: at the time of the siege of Bialy Kamien, Stanislaw Koniecpolski was a boy, Stefan Czarnecki was three or perhaps not yet born (the date of his birth is not known accurately), while John Sobieski was to be born a quarter of a century later.

How did the pacific Commonwealth, hating war and with only a small standing army, produce so many brilliant soldiers? And in all the three nations of the federation too. For Piotr Sahaydaczny and Bohdan Chmielnicki, both Ukraininans, were also born and raised within that community and absorbed its characteristics.

Some mysteries have to be approached with humility. No one knows how and why a genius is born, but we can detect certain

169

conditions favorable to the development of talent. We cannot lightly reject the theory of those who claim that there is an abundance of talents in the world, but only a few of them encounter currents that bring them to the surface. Nature and history both seem to be wildly wasteful, picking at random a few from the millions and giving them a chance to survive and flourish.

The Commonwealth was at that time wide open to the influence of Europe and the adjacent countries of the Middle East. This was evident even in the attire of the gentry and the burghers, who wore Italian, French, Hungarian, Turkish, Spanish, German clothes, following any fashion they liked. The same pluralism in the field of military science meant familiarity with the arts of war of many nations. This was particularly true of the neighboring countries, but some Poles also served in the forces of the French Huguenots, in the Netherlands, and in other countries, even as distant as Brasil, where Arciszewski helped the Portuguese conquest. Christopher Zbaraski studied for three years under Galileo to acquire the scientific knowledge needed in war. Seeking knowledge wherever it may be found, profiting by the experience of others, sharing in a pool of information drawn from many sources—all are invaluable assets. Citizens of the Commonwealth did not have to travel far to learn from others, for they had plenty of foreigners at home. Many books of foreign origin were published in Poland, either in Latin or in Polish translation.

A Frenchman who came to Poland immediately after the death of Zygmunt III, to assist in the negotiations with Sweden, wrote: ". . . there were in the royal antechamber (in Torun) many noblemen and eminent people, both clergy and others, who talked a great deal with us and among themselves. It was a pleasure to hear them speak Polish, Italian, English, German, French and finally Latin, which was the local *lingua franca*. There were even some who spoke Danish and Swedish."

It seems that Spanish was the only major language not heard in the antechamber of the king of Poland.

That free intercourse with people of many nations, in a country open to all, may have contributed to the development of native talents. The classical education and general knowledge of Latin may have also helped to train future leaders, including military ones.

Jan Karol Chodkiewicz was a worthy successor of Zamoyski. In August of 1605 a twelve-thousand-strong Swedish army landed on

170

the Inflanty coast, commanded by Charles IX himself. It laid siege to Riga, after taking its coastal castle of Dyament. On September 27 Chodkiewicz challenged King Charles to battle at the village of Kircholm. The Polish-Lithuanian force comprised only four thousand men, including a thousand of regular infantry. The Swedish army, triple in number, left on the battlefield nine thousand dead, sixty banners, and eleven guns. Charles IX managed to escape by sea. This "most memorable of all battles" lasted only three hours.

The chronicler reports that the news of the victory encouraged the royal court of Warsaw to accelerate its preparations for the wedding, but the forthcoming marriage carried the seed of great dangers for the country. The Commonwealth was entering a period of continuing crisis.

VI

Thirty years had elapsed since the demise of the last of the Jagiellonians and the reign of Stefan I Batory was also receding into the past. The theoretical structure of the Commonwealth remained unchanged, but its reality was no longer the same.

In 1563 the Seym, which won a partial victory in its long struggle for the "execution of the laws," also resolved that one quarter of the revenues of the crown should be assigned for the upkeep of a standing army, accordingly known as the "quarter troops." But thirty years later, Father Wereszczynski, advocating plans for the defense of the Ukraine, urged the provincial officials to "contribute fairly one quarter of the revenues of their county, as they now give barely a tithe."

The power of the state was being sapped by the very people whom King Zygmunt III favored as the pillars of his authority. He was about to observe the twentieth anniversary of his reign when the news of the battle of Kircholm reached Warsaw.

The democracy of the gentry was gradually becoming an empty phrase, as the oligarchy of the magnates gained influence. Its power was immensely enhanced by the development of the land grants in the "deserts" of the Ukraine. The holdings of the Ruthenian, Polish, and Lithuanian lords in the Dnieper country were expanding rapidly. In the relatively densely populated Poland proper some of the lesser gentry lost their homesteads, while the estates of families such as the Lubomirski or Ossolinski grew in size, while next to them eastern potentates such as the Radziwill, Zbaraski, Ostrogski, Chodkiewicz clans acquired vast holdings. All three nations of the federation participated in that evolution. Central Poland was characterized by a prevalence of church properties. In some provinces the church owned more land than the crown. Under Zygmunt August one of his favorites, Mikolaj Polkozic Wolski, sequestered by force the parchment deeds of the lesser gentry and transferred title to their land to his subjects. In 1598 the rector of Bnin, Opalinski, started collecting private taxes from these smallholders and proclaimed himself a prince, but his claim did not hold.

The county councils fell under the influence of the magnates and according to some historians only three such councils in the whole country—those of Opatow, Proszowice, and Sroda—kept their independence. Yet the role of the county councils was becoming decisive, as deputies had to abide by their instructions and there was still no rule of majority vote in the Seym.

We have noted earlier that under the reign of Zygmunt August the Lithuanian gentry complained that their county councils, unlike those of Poland, were dominated by the magnates, who sometimes resorted to threats of violence. Ever since its inception, the internal evolution of the Commonwealth consisted in the penetration to the east of the more advanced and democratic practices of the west. Toward the end of the sixteenth century that process was reversed and the brutal supremacy of the powerful lords, traditional in the east, began to spread into the western sections of the federation. It brought with it assassinations that were not always punished and common assaults.

Jarema Maciszewski, a modern historian, carried out a study of the origins of the wealth of a family which was to play a key role in the period under review, the Ossolinski.

Sebastian Lubomirski, founder of his clan's fortune, had in 1581 only four villages and shared in two others. In 1629 his son, Stanislaw, was the owner of ninety-one villages, shared in sixteen, and the town of Wisnicz. He also enjoyed the usufruct of royal estates in the province of Cracow, including eighteen villages, two towns, and the county of Dobczyce with five villages. Zbigniew Ossolinski, a nobleman in the adjoining province of Sandomierz, owned before his first marriage a share of seven villages, but none outright. Yet when he divided his holdings among his sons in 1620, thirty-six years later, he had sixteen villages, the large estate of

Zgory, a share in two more villages, and the usufruct of several royal estates.

These rapidly growing fortunes were based on royal grants. Zygmunt III distributed them both among the old nobility and those he elevated himself to noble rank. He even gave them money from the Gdansk customs, toll revenues, the salt monopoly, and lumber from the royal forests.

He made his choice and counted on the wealthy lords, not the mass of the middle and lesser gentry. A descendant of the Jagiellonians, he abandoned one of the finest political traditions of the dynasty, its alliance with the entire class of landed gentry, which allowed the monarchy to resist the pressures of the magnates. The royal largesse was not confined to the Poles, for many foreigners also received generous grants, the recipients of which were called the so-called "regalists" faction. Their ideology was militant Catholicism and counter-reformation. Royal appointments and promotions were largely influenced by the Jesuits.

If the favorites of Zygmunt III had lived in France, they would have provided rich material for its literature, for many of them were colorful personalities. Felix Kryski, called the "Polish Demosthenes," was a brilliant orator and diplomat, so enamored of the classics that he used to bring a volume of Tacitus into the senate chamber. He promoted with great skill the eastern expeditions of Zygmunt III and started his career under the patronage of one of the leaders of the royalist faction, a powerful lord.

Zygmunt Myszkowski, grand marshal of the crown since 1601, had an impressive start. Well educated abroad, he inherited together with his brother Piotr the fortune of his uncle, the bishop of Cracow and a noted humanist and patron of the arts. It comprised vast estates and eight million *zlotys* in gold specie. The bishop had once rendered a service to King Stefan by lending him sixty thousand *zlotys* for the Gdansk expedition.

Zygmunt Myszkowski served as a royal ambassador on five political missions to foreign countries. It was he who acted as proxy for his monarch in marrying *per procuram* Constance Habsburg and escorted her to Poland, where the marriage was greeted with dismay. A dozen years earlier he had returned from Rome with the title of margrave, awarded to him by Pope Clement VIII. In the following year he also acquired a new name when Vincent Gonzaga, duke of Mantua, adopted him as his son.

The Margrave Gonzaga Myszkowski was not popular in Poland, for he looked down on the rank and file squirarchy, while displaying excessive devotion to the house of Habsburg. He used crown troops for settling his personal disputes—if even a magnate such as Firlej could not resist him, the simple squire had no chance at all. Modern historians praise the margrave as a collector and patron of the arts, though he could hardly match in this area his uncle, the bishop.

The year 1601, in which Myszkowski became grand marshal, brought him another blessing. The Seym sanctioned the entailment of the estates of Pinczow, the property of the marshal's brother Piotr, who had just died. They comprised the towns of Pinczow, Chroberz, Mir, and Ksiaz in Malopolska (southwestern Poland), Wieprz in Silesia, Onyszow and Szymanow in Masovia. Under the terms of the entailment these holdings could be neither sold nor divided.

The marshal's sons died without issue. Later, his great grand-daughter Krystyna Komorowska brought the entailed estates as her dowry into the Wielopolski family, which also adopted the name and title attached to the entailment.

There is reason to believe that Alexander Count Wielopolski, Margrave Gonzaga Myszkowski, the political figure of the nine-teenth century largely responsible for the 1862 uprising, regarded the grand marshal Zygmunt as his model. They both shared the same arrogant pride and conviction of the basic stupidity of the common people.

On April 4, 1589, the Seym witnessed an unusual event, typical of the trend prevailing at the time. A week earlier the nuncio, Hannibal of Capua, had held in the Warsaw cathedral a bishops' conference, which mounted an attack against religious tolerance.

On April 4 Hieronim Gostomski, castellan of Naklo, made in the Seym chamber a solemn profession of Catholic faith, renouncing heresy. Only a little earlier he had advocated a national church, funded a Protestant parish in Poznan, deplored his son's conversion to "papism," and had his tutor jailed for permitting it. Now he started giving money to the Jesuits, built for them a church and convent in Sandomierz, and funded other monasteries. Within three years of his conversion he was appointed the *voievode* of Poznan, on the nuncio's advice.

Gostomski was King Zygmunt's loyalist and confidant. He knew the king's plan of relinquishing the crown to Archduke Ernest and he promoted all of his master's projects, including those in Sweden. He was a bitter adversary of Jan Zamoyski, whom he called the "vizier pasha." While supporting royal absolutism, he was at the same time praising the "golden freedom" of the gentry. He hated and persecuted whenever possible the Protestants, Jews, and burghers.

None of the political endeavors of Hieronim Gostomski bore fruit. Though a skillful parliamentary orator, he failed as a diplomat, but performed without fail in delivering the vote in his province of Poznan, for the gentry knew the consequences of electing candidates not of his choice. Then as now, a provincial political boss and a statesman are far apart.

Gostomski had six brothers, so he inherited only a seventh of the estate of their father, Anselm, *voievode* of Rawa and a sound administrator. Yet when he died in 1609 he left a vast fortune, which included revenues from the counties of Gabin, Grojec, Warka, and Strzelce. A few years before his death he was awarded by the king a hundred-year lease of the county of Sannik.

The king elevated his favorites and supporters to positions of power and eventually became dependent on them, for not only constitutional monarchs but even autocrats have to recognize the status quo they have themselves created. Privilege, once granted, cannot be easily taken away. King Zygmunt's entourage knew how to enrich their families and practiced nepotism worthy of the Borgia popes. Yet the vast entailed estates of the Pinczow domain supplied to the crown only fifty cavalrymen and one hundred infantry as their contribution to national defense.

Krzysztof Warszewicki, whom we have quoted earlier, wrote in his *De optimo statu libertatis*:

> A monarch eager to do good and mindful of his conscience should remember that he must overcome any obstacles by all the means at his disposal. No one will later query or judge the means by which he attained his goal, only how soon and how surely he reached it.

It was a philosophy not far removed from that which Hitler offered to his generals on the eve of the attack against Poland in 1939. But there was a difference, for Warszewicki at least recognized tacitly the existence of inadmissible means.

175

Zygmunt III managed to create an instrument of action. At the beginning of the seventeenth century the party of the "regalists" was dominant. Less than a quarter of the senate were the opposition, the "chancellor's men," whose leader was Jan Zamoyski.

Coming years were to show how promptly and surely the king and his party were to reach their goals and what they were.

* * * *

In Brahin, at the court of Prince Adam Wisniowiecki, one of the young members of his retinue suddenly declared himself Dymitr, the last of the sons of Ivan the Terrible. He said that, warned by a German physician, he went into hiding while another boy was killed in his place in Uglicz. He revealed the secret and placed himself in the hands of the powerful prince.

The year was 1603 and if the tsarevich had lived, he would be in his early twenties, so at least the chronology was plausible. The youth passed into history as the First False Dymitr, but in the Commonwealth he was called an impostor, adventurer, and liar, or "the little tsar."

Even Boris Godunov himself could not attest to the truth of the story, for no witnesses of the events of May 15, 1591, in Uglicz had survived. The incensed people stoned to death the true or alleged assassins. Even if Godunov had sent them he could not have received their report. Immediately afterwards all the inhabitants of Uglicz were also brutally punished. Those closest to the scene were summarily executed and the others had their tongues torn out. Every inhabitant of Uglicz, regardless of age or sex, was deported to Siberia. The bell which had tolled over the boy's body was also sent there. No witnesses could survive.

Alexander Hirschberg, a patient student of the mystery, discovered a sensational statement by the *starosta* of Orsza, Andrew Sapieha, according to which it was Godunov himself who had resurrected Dymitr. Still insecure on the throne, the "great boyar" spread the news of the tsarevich's reappearance and found someone to play the role, in the hope of using him as his pawn. The boyars disclosed the hoax and tempestuous disputes shook the Kremlin, but the declaration of Boris reached Smolensk.

The technique of using self-styled pretenders was popular in Europe at the time. Especially the Cossacks and the Ukrainian lords were in the habit of invading Moldavia as champions of the restoration to the Hospodar's throne of its "rightful heirs." Godunov had brought to Moscow Gustav Ericsson Vasa, to be used as an instrument of blackmail against Sweden. Now the same weapon was about to be turned against him. For several years all of Muscovy was the scene of a huge ongoing investigation, with informers and executioners busily at work. They extorted by torture confessions of sinister plots, without ever mentioning the real object of the manhunt. The mass arrests and reprisals were supposed to lead to the track of Dymitr or his proxies. No one dared even to whisper the true object of the search.

When news of the appearance of new pretenders came almost simultaneously from the Ukraine, the Volga region, and Inflanty, Boris called the dignitaries to the Kremlin and told them, "It is your work, traitors, princes, and boyars."

He was right. The opposition wanted to overthrow the usurper at any price. After disposing of Godunov, some way would be found to deal with the pretender.

Boris fought against the great families, but promoted the class from which he rose himself—the middle boyars. He did so at the cost of the peasants, forced into serfdom and attached to the land. Fate did not favor the able tsar, who tried during his brief reign to achieve the same objectives that Peter the Great realized later on a far larger scale. Godunov secured access to the sea in Karelia, founded new cities, intensely colonized Siberia, sponsored schools, and brought from the west scientists, artisans, and various experts. About three thousand Poles settled in Moscow under his reign and they were certainly not noblemen.

In the year 1601 not a single grain was harvested in the central provinces of Russia. Incessant rains through the spring and summer were followed by frost in late August. The result was a famine. Dutchmen, Englishmen, and Germans brought from the west by Boris left appalling accounts of widespread cannibalism. There was unrest in the harshly oppressed countryside. Rebels headed by a peasant by the name of Kosolapy marched on Moscow and were barely defeated at its gates, though the commander of the tsar's troops was killed.

It was a situation in which any diversionary attempt, especially one with foreign support, could have a good chance of success. The opposition, comprising the leading Moscow boyars, acting in concert with some Lithuanian and Ruthenian lords, among them no doubt

Leo Sapieha, found a suitable actor to impersonate Dymitr. They staged a performance designed to revive the attachment of the rebellious people to the old dynasty.

Who was the young man who told his confessor, on a spurious deathbed, and to Prince Wisniowiecki in a bathhouse encounter that he was Dymitr Ivanovich? Linguists who examined his letter to the pope determined that he could not have been a native Pole, as his command of the language was very poor. Nor was he the illegitimate son of Stefan I. Such a son existed, but he lived in Grodno and his only connection with Moscow was that he took part in the war against it and found in Russia a bride whom he brought back with him. The naive nuncio, Claudio Rangoni, thought that the false Dymitr's fine hands were proof of his royal origin, but there is no reason to think that a scion of Ivan the Terrible would have the physical characteristics of a high-bred aristocrat.

Godunov ordered his diplomats to proclaim that the pretender was a fugitive monk, a squire's son, Gregory Otriepiev. He even dispatched to Poland his uncle, Smirnoy Otriepiev, to identify the impostor. The tsar's theory was endorsed by some senators and also by the eminent historian Waclaw Sobieski (deceased in 1935), who assembled substantial evidence in support of his claim.

It seems almost certain that the future false Dymitr was a member of the entourage of Leo Sapieha on his mission to Moscow in 1600. He remained in Russia, then surfaced in the Ukraine, at first in the monastery of Lavra Pecherska, then at the court of Prince Konstanty Ostrogski. He met there the prince's chamberlain, Gabriel Hoyski, a member of the Arian Protestant sect, in whose mansion in Hoszcza he took part in "Anabaptist ceremonies." The young man displayed an adventurous bend before entering the political front stage. He managed to get involved with the Cossacks and joined them in plunder in the Kiev region. Pursued for these misdeeds by the princes Ostrogski, he sought asylum with the Wisniowiecki, their sworn enemies.

On October 7 Prince Adam Wisniowiecki wrote about Dymitr to Chancellor Zamoyski, soliciting his support. He said that he had pondered the problem long, but was convinced when nearly twenty people from Moscow "recognized" the tsarevich. The old statesman replied cautiously and advised that the pretender should be handed over to the king, or to himself as chancellor and hetman of the crown. Such a suggestion meant that he intended to snuff out the affair and perhaps also its protagonist.

Boris Godunov also tried to restrain Wisniowiecki. He demanded that the impostor be delivered to Moscow, in return for which he promised territorial concessions. When amicable proposals failed, the tsar's army attacked Przyluki and Sniatyn, forts built by the Wisniowiecki on disputed territory, and burned them down, slaughtering the population. Hostilities between the tsar of Moscow and the Wisniowiecki clan did not necessarily involve the Commonwealth, which never recognized the pretender. The Seym disbelieved his claim, but the king was secretly contacted by the promoters of the self-styled tsarevich.

The Wisniowieckis were passing him from hand to hand. Prince Adam took him to the family seat, Wisniowiec, ruled by Prince Michael (Jeremy's father). Then the oldest of the clan, Konstanty, took the false Dymitr to his father-in-law, Jerzy Mniszech, lord of Sambor. For a man who started out as a page at the court of Zygmunt August and then robbed his treasury of Knyszyn at his death, he had made a dazzling career. He won the favor of Zygmunt III and shared in the royal largesse, helped by his cousin, Bernard Maciejowski, a bishop, future cardinal and primate. The king appointed Jerzy Mniszech *starosta* of Lwow and *voievode* of Sandomierz, granted to him the estates of Sambor for life, and a lease on the Ruthenian salt mines. A princely style of living was costly—five young Mniszechs were studying abroad in western Europe and debts, especially for taxes, were mounting up. The youth brought by Wisniowiecki promised to share with his supporters the legendary wealth of the tsars of Moscow and in the meantime asked for the hand of the fourth of Mniszech's daughters, Maryna, a woman of cold but repellent beauty, driven by ruthless ambition.

The young couple were well matched. Whether his real name was Otriepiev or not, whether he was a fugitive monk or a robber, the false Dymitr was an adventurer of remarkable caliber. Of rather small stature, reddish hair, two warts on his face, and one shoulder slightly higher than the other (distinctive features supposed to prove his identity as tsarevich), he was undoubtedly a man of courage, uncommon ability, and extraordinary audacity. He had no scruples whatsoever and was quite ready to stab yesterday's benefactor without any qualms. He enjoyed over his royal protector the advantage of total indifference to faiths and ideologies. He could easily worship at many altars.

His most rewarding display of devotion was that which he staged in Cracow during Lent of 1604. The pretender found in the former capital a new protector in the *voievode* Mikolaj Zebrzydowski, "a hunter of heretics' souls." It was in his home that he heard for the first time a Catholic sermon. An old custom observed in Cracow at the time was a street collection for the poor, carried out by prominent personalities concealing their identity under hoods of coarse canvas. Masked in this manner, the false Dymitr and Zebrzydowski left the house of the Fraternity of Mercy, circulated for a while in the city and then dived into the gate of the Jesuit house of St. Barbara, where a confessor, Father Sawicki, was waiting. They took precautions not to be seen by Dymitr's countrymen in Cracow.

An important role was played by the Jesuits and the nuncio Rangoni, who embraced and kissed the pretender on their first meeting and then led him personally to Wawel castle.

> His Majesty was standing with his usual dignity, leaning against a table and with a smile extended his hand to be kissed. After doing so, the tsarevich told him about the injustices he had suffered and asked for help.

At the chamberlain's signal the visitor left the room. Zygmunt wanted to be left alone with the nuncio. The king's response was so gracious that the pretender was left speechless and Rangoni had to speak for him. The king granted the "tsarevich" an annual pension and permitted him to seek the support of "our lords." On the same day, in Mniszech's house, the nuncio urged his protégé to propagate the Catholic faith and promote the Jesuits throughout the state of Muscovy.

After Dymitr and the Mniszechs returned to Sambor, a prenuptial contract was drawn up. The pretender to the throne of Moscow promised his bride, in addition to silver and jewelry, the cities of Pskov and Novy Novgorod. He also promised his future father-in-law a million *zlotys* and the provinces of Smolensk and Siewierz, perhaps forgetting that he had promised them earlier to the king.

The story of Dymitr and Maryna was a sensational crime thriller, far stranger than any fiction.

Zygmunt III asked Zamoyski for his support of the enterprise.

He had great hopes connected with Dymitr, mainly in his dynastic conflict with Sweden, as well as a planned future action against Turkey. He decided not to consult the Seym. The chancellor firmly rejected that condition and refused to cooperate, as did the hetman Stanislaw Zolkiewski. Jan Karol Chodkiewicz, a great military commander and a fearless soldier, responded to the king in a memorable letter, published recently in Hanna Malewska's *Letters of the Vasa Era.* The hetman wrote: "An appetizing opportunity, but the outcome is uncertain, matters are not settled at home and, what is more, we have a treaty which, once disturbed, will never be effective." The letter was dated March 19, 1604. A twenty-year peace treaty with Moscow was concluded only two years earlier.

Encouraging Zamoyski to support a private war of the Mniszech and Wisniowiecki clans against Moscow, the king argued: "Our countries can barely contain swarms of restless and ebullient youth. What better field can they find for their knightly jousts?"

Oddly enough, the seasoned soldier Jan Karol Chodkiewicz spurned military adventurism and wanted to "settle matters at home," while a king used to playing ball and making jewelry indulged in bellicose fantasies.

In September 1604 the private regiments of the magnates, joined by a motley crowd of volunteers, Cossacks, and others eager for plunder, formed the pretender's army on its way to the Moscow border. Prince Janusz Ostrogski, opposed to the whole project and particularly to the Wisniowiecki faction, tried to impede the crossing of the Dnieper by that force.

The throne of Tsar Boris was indeed shaky. One Russian town after another surrendered to Dymitr's small army, only about three and a half thousand strong: Morawsk, Chernihow, Purywl, Rylsk, Kromy. The impostor won the battle of Novgorod Siewierski, but he lost at Dobrynicze not only the battle but almost his life as well. His lance, taken on the battlefield, was delivered to Boris at the Kremlin. The *voievode* Mniszech had to return home for new recruits, as the original force was almost nonexistent.

The battle of Dobrynicze was fought on January 31, 1605, while Warsaw was witnessing one of the parliamentary sessions that history characterizes as watershed events.

Yet a matter that had been causing concern for some years was not the subject of official debate. After the death of Queen Anne, rumors began to circulate about the king's new matrimonial plans.

These plans were reportedly discussed at a conference in Niepolomice, but none of the Commonwealth citizens knew the truth, as Zygmunt had invited only Germans to the conference. The chancellor was absent at Niepolomice, but Miss Ursula Gienger, the Habsburg agent, was there. Let us not suspect him of hypocrisy. He firmly believed that he had discovered a truth others had not yet perceived.

Hardly more than half a century had elapsed since the wedding of Zygmunt August with Catherine Habsburg, sister of the Jagiellonian monarch's first bride, Elizabeth. His marriages did cause considerable political concern, but little metaphysical anguish.

Nicholas Christopher Radziwill ("The Lightning") died in 1603 after surviving four wives. The second and the fourth, Catherine and Elizabeth Ostrogski, were sisters. The powerful hetman overrode opposition and married Elizabeth, but none of the Protestant denominations sanctioned the union.

Fanaticism flourished on both sides of the barricade. Half a century later many Polish Protestants continued to hold on to their Swedish or Hungarian co-religionists as in a suicidal spasm, even after they had been defeated. The best time for a revival of the Commonwealth had passed away. Under Zygmunt August the Commonwealth's public opinion favored a posture reminiscent of the French "politicians," whose pragmatic philosophy inspired Henry IV. But the last Jagiellonian's coldly fanatical nephew ruled bigoted people incapable of rational political thinking, as he was himself.

The royal party proposed in 1605 a program designed to establish an absolute monarchy, an efficient instrument in a ruler's hands. These plans were never fully revealed, but historians have traced them and there is no doubt that they included some positive measures. The introduction of permanent taxation and a stronger standing army were ideas for which credit is due to Zygmunt and his advisers. However, the attempt to liquidate the Seym and reduce the senate to the role of an advisory council of aristocratic officials was less commendable. Experience has demonstrated over and over again that advocating unrealistic projects is the best way of losing what is feasible.

The worst of it was that the reform would have made the Commonwealth an instrument of political action, but not its independent author. The plan of change became absorbed in much broader projects unrelated to Polish or Lithuanian interests.

Zygmunt proposed to return to Sweden and stay there, leaving in Poland the crown prince Wladyslaw, crowned in his father's lifetime but leaving the administration of the country during his minority to an Austrian archduke acting as governor. Sweden was, of course, to be reconquered and returned to the fold of Rome. This was to be accomplished with the help of Moscow under the pretender, also converted to the Catholic faith. The resulting great northern league could then act decisively against Turkey.

It was a grandiose but chimerical design. Its ideological character required converting the Commonwealth to a nation with a single religion, at the cost of crushing the Orthodox and Protestant churches, by force if necessary.

The Seym closed its session without achieving anything, as the king refused to sign a resolution of thirty-five articles, among them the confirmation of the Warsaw Confederacy, which supported religious tolerance. A French writer reported that the Confederacy aroused Zygmunt's violent revulsion. The monarch had lost his senses, while his subjects retained a measure of sanity. No reform, however wise and beneficial, was ever carried out without the participation of competent and effective leaders.

Already before the parliamentary session, the royal party, powerful and confident, had seized most of the key offices of the state. Except for Leo Sapieha, a capable man though given to devious intrigues, it lacked personalities of ability and character. The opposition, on the other hand, was headed by Jan Zamoyski, seconded by hetman Stanislaw Zolkiewski, Marek Sobieski, and the bishop of Kujawy, Piotr Tylicki, respected for his brain and integrity. A pamphlet published at the time revealed the bishop's origins: "In his youth he was the vice-chancellor's errand boy, called Tyla; he took tips from the burghers when he wrote up their charters, wore shabby clothes and squirrelled away his money. . . ." It seems that Piotr Tylicki was born in the small town of Kowal in a humble family, but his talents enabled him to rise to the rank of senator.

The caliber of the members of the opposition said much about the quality of the ruling party.

There was also an independent center group, favoring moderate reform and trying to reconcile the other parties. It was headed by Jan Ostrorog, castellan of Poznan, assisted by Goslicki, a political thinker and writer of European renown. That faction desired neither adventurism in foreign relations, nor religious persecution at home.

Zygmunt III created at great expense a numerous and powerful party, which proved adept only at grabbing lucrative offices and squabbling over them. It failed to steer the ship of state into clear waters, though opportunities for doing so existed.

The Seym heard Jan Zamoyski's swan song. The text of the last political speech of the great chancellor was later falsified to bolster the claims of a rebellious section of the opposition. Actually Zamoyski kept his rhetoric well under control and abstained from attacking the king, stepping beyond constitutional legality, or rejecting any thought of reform. He did not, however, spare the instigators of the Dymitr escapade. Here is the conclusion of the old hetman's last address, which he delivered standing and with tears in his eyes: "I love, so help me God, Your Majesty and serve him faithfully—and I will repeat again—in loyal service; may Your Majesty also love us, his subjects. Then money will come in easily, as will greatness for the state; all will come from the subjects' love. You can make, Your Majesty, a Pole into an Alexander and a Lithuanian into a Hercules, only love is needed and little can be done without it."

The great leader of the opposition did not exaggerate when he spoke of his faithful service, inspired by love of country. After all, it was Zamoyski who had secured the throne for Zygmunt and then, not counting many other services, extended his influence as far as the Danube and won the Inflanty campaign. Now he complained of the monarch's lack of confidence and benevolence toward the citizens.

The chancellor died in Zamosc on June 3 of the same year, 1605. A few months later the author of an anonymous political pamphlet hit the bull's-eye by asking the citizenry to enforce "what our constitution had long secured, that his majesty the king should be content with our nation alone."

The informed public opinion clearly understood and the rest of the people sensed that the Commonwealth was for Zygmunt only an instrument or a stage for the accomplishment of his dynastic or ideological goals inspired by the counter-reformation.

The pamphlet's title was "Matters Requiring Correction by the Seym or by Rebellion in the Commonwealth." The death of Jan Zamoyski removed from the scene a man who wanted to act only through the Seym and had enough authority and talent to restrain his fellow citizens from rebellion.

On March 11, 1605, immediately after the closing of the parliamentary session and without consulting the deputies, the king and his senatorial advisers decided the fate of Krolewiec (Konigsberg) and Ducal Prussia. Its mad prince was still living and the curator appointed by King Stefan Batory had died two years earlier. King Zygmunt appointed as his successor Joachim Frederick Hohenzollern, the elector of Brandenburg, counting on his support in the impending war for the throne of Sweden. The prospects of the incorporation of Ducal Prussia to Poland, of which it was a vassal, were receding. The diplomats of Brandenburg had tried before to bribe Zamoyski but the chancellor rejected their offer and made it public.

It has been sometimes asserted that the free royal elections, the Henrician Covenant, and the Pacta Conventa had diluted the king's authority and left him a mere puppet. Yet Zygmunt III had enough power left to accomplish the following: change the social structure of the country (by endorsing the primacy of the magnates), abolish the hierarchy of the Orthodox church, support the affair of Dymitr the Pretender, and place a coastal province in fief to the Polish crown under the administration of the elector of Brandenburg. The problem was clearly not the alleged curtailment of royal power, but the manner in which it was wielded.

The Seym and the county councils made it clear that the overwhelming majority of the gentry condemned the endorsement of the Dymitr adventure. They demanded the punishment of his protectors, while the council of Belz tactlessly recalled that "Your Majesty had just solemnly sworn in Wilno an alliance with the present tsar of Moscow, Boris."

The tsar's time was running out. The pretender recovered after his defeat of Dobrynicze and had many backers who hoped to profit by his accession.

There were many versions of the cause of Godunov's sudden death, that of suicide being the most plausible. On April 23 Boris took a walk after dinner on the walls of the Kremlin, from which he could see all of Red Square, the Lobnoye quarter, and the Vasili Blazenny church, still new at the time, as it commemorated the conquest of Kazan by Ivan the Terrible. There, on a spot well chosen for a last farewell to the city, the tsar was seized by a paroxysm that could have been caused by poison. He was succeeded by his young son Theodore. In June, Dymitr the Pretender took Moscow without encountering any resistance, while his supporters strangled the sixteen-year-old new tsar and his mother. Boris's body was removed from the Archangels' church and buried on the site of his former private house. The victorious False Dymitr opened his reign and sent messengers to Poland for Maryna Mniszech.

On November 22 she was married to Dymitr by proxy in Carcow, amidst elaborate and sumptuous ceremonies. Immediately afterward she left for Proszowice in order not to witness the wedding of Constance Habsburg, whom King Zygmunt was marrying despite opposition. Maryna signed herself in the commemorative book of the Cracow Academy: "Maryna, tsaritsa of Moscow, by her own hand." It was a political provocation, as the Commonwealth did not recognize the title of tsar. A retinue of more than three thousand accompanied the pretender's wife on her journey to Moscow, about as many as Chodkiewicz had cavalrymen at Kircholm.

His dazzling victory over the Swedes and the Habsburg marriage encouraged Zygmunt to call a new session of the Seym in the spring, with the intention of pushing his plans through by force if necessary. A detachment of German mercenaries was brought to Warsaw, as well as two thousand of Chodkiewicz's gallant cavalrymen, but Zygmunt was mistaken in thinking that Zamoyski's death made his task easier. Some people fail to understand the potential power of a legal opposition acting within the boundaries of constitutional law.

Its emerging leader was the *voievode* of Cracow, Mikolaj Zebrzydowski, a supporter—even a disciple—of the late chancellor, but totally devoid of his master's political judgment. Popular among the Cracow gentry, he initiated the convocation of a conference in Stezyca, scheduled for April 9, a few days before the final session of the Seym. It meant that while the legal parliament was assembled in Warsaw, a self-styled and armed group was conferring in Stezyca.

It was clear that if the Seym should achieve its objectives, Zebrzydowski's followers at Stezyca would become irrelevant. By the same token the Seym's failure to enact viable legislation could make of Stezyca a bastion of the opposition or even a bridgehead for an assault against the government.

The royal program was enriched this time by a positive proposal, that of introducing majority vote in the Seym. The conflict between the king's party and the rest of the gentry focused on the problem of religious tolerance. The opposition demanded guarantees of the confirmation of the Warsaw Confederacy. Cardinal Macie-jowski, who was opposed to that idea, argued that the confederacy was never in force, as it was not resolved unanimously. It is not clear how one could take such a stand while advocating at the same time majority vote in the Seym. Father Piotr Skarga denounced that anti-Jesuit resolution on the ground that one negative vote was not taken into account. It would seem that Zygmunt's henchmen wanted majority vote only when it was in their favor.

The parliamentary debates concentrated on a vital issue, that of the freedom of thought and conscience. The opposition stubbornly demanded freedom, indispensable in a multinational state. It was well understood that in the absence of such freedom the Commonwealth might be torn apart by its religious and ethnic diversity. It was obvious that the adoption of a state religion would imply the presence of censors and guardians of ideological purity, likely to become a privileged ruling class.

On April 17, 1606, on the eve of the conclusion of the debate, the relevant legislation on which the approval of taxes was conditioned, was ready for adoption. It was phrased in moderate language and merely required state authorities and courts to punish those responsible for religiously motivated disturbances of public order. The bishop raised no objection to the proposal and the day of April 18 promised to be politically a sunny one. The deputies were to take back to their county councils an assurance of domestic peace and the government was to secure taxes for defense and, more importantly, significant domestic political gains. The endorsement of the guarantees of the Warsaw Confederacy could bring over to the king's side many Protestants, whose support would have eased the adoption of the other points in the king's program.

The deputies adjourned the session and peacefully went to sleep, expecting to put the final touches on the bill of the following day. Others, however, never slept a wink. It was the "night of the Jesuits." The official historian of the Jesuit order and witness of the events reported that:

"The most devout monarch thought the matter suspect, so he sent to us secretly at night a draft of the proposed legislation, to make sure whether it contained anything that could be a stain on his conscience."

The ideological commission checking the doctrinal purity of the bill consisted of two watchful members: the royal confessor Bartch and Piotr Skarga. They were both horrified to discover that the proposed law not only granted to heretics freedom of belief and worship, but also required them to be defended against any infringement of that freedom. One could not expose innocent souls to such iniquity.

Both holy fathers promptly summoned some of the more pious deputies and visited with them the rooms of the bishops before dawn, in a passionate outburst of lobbying. One can easily imagine the situation of the pastors accused of reprehensible softness in matters of church doctrine by the leading representatives of the all-powerful order directed from Rome, the king's confessor and his preacher.

On April 18, after long debate, the deputies appeared in the senate chamber, declaring their support for the proposed law on religious tolerance and the taxes. Even those who a few hours earlier had helped Skarga and Bartch to drag the bishops out of their beds had evidently changed their minds. All the secular senators joined in the opinion of the junior chamber. The primate Maciejowski responded on behalf of the clergy. He raised the often-discussed issue of the right to appeal to the pope by priests convicted of offenses against the law. The dissidents bristled, but finally agreed to a compromise formula, leaving the matter largely open. They did retreat and adopted a conciliatory attitude, even though their spokesman was Stanislaw Stadnicki "the Devil," not noted for moderation.

The bishops, out of arguments, did not reply to the lord of Lancut castle, but resisted in stubborn silence. Janusz Radziwill then entered a veto and the Seym was accordingly dissolved.

The king tried to use military pressure to create a fiction of a unanimous vote on the fiscal legislation, but he failed.

Some provinces contributed funds to Zebrzydowski, the champion of "golden freedom," rather than to the royal treasury. The failure of the Seym to enact adequate legislation revived the movement toward rebellion, which would have otherwise died a natural death.

The king, had he tried, might have won for his plan many of the Protestants. Now, frustrated and furious, they gave to the Stezyca group so much support that it became suspected of being wholly inspired by the "heretics." Yet the initiator and leader of the rebellion was a former pupil of the Jesuits, a friend of Skarga and the founder of the "Zebrzydowski Calvary," a Catholic shrine with the stations of the cross. He was a devout Catholic and was buried in a monk's habit.

It was all sheer madness. Piotr Skarga explained in his sermon of September 17 of the same year, 1606, in Wislica, the principles that governed the staging of the tragic charade. He defended his homilies, saying that they "do not interfere in politics, but bring policy closer to theology by warning people and steering them away from national disaster." These were his words, but his deed was to prevent the enactment of a law authorizing the courts to punish violence for religious motives.

The king submitted a piece of parliamentary legislation, in draft form, to the scrutiny of two persons outside the Seym who then destroyed the result of its labors. It was total anarchy, imported together with the totalitarian features of the counter-reformation. It was obvious regression from progressive positions achieved earlier. Already under Zygmunt August a decree granting equal rights to the Orthodox church was signed by three Catholic bishops as well as by the king. The destruction of the evolutionary achievements of a society constitutes cultural and political vandalism.

The historian Waclaw Sobieski wrote about the "memorable session of the Seym":

> By concentrating excessively on one of his goals: the prompt re-conversion of Poland to Catholicism, he forfeited the other, the strengthening of royal power.
>
> Zygmunt proved himself absolutely consistent on one point: obeying at every step the church and the clergy. Such conduct earned him the pope's appreciation and gratitude. When he heard about the fate of the proposed legislation on religious tolerance, the pope wrote a letter to Zygmunt in which he thanked God for granting him such wisdom and eulogized his virtue, piety, and determination in the defense of Catholic faith.

Zygmunt III wanted to impose on Poland an ideological bond, the authors and champions of which cared little for the welfare of the Commonwealth. In the following year, 1607, Rome divided it into two Jesuit provinces: one for Poland and the other for Lithuania. The latter included Masovia with Warsaw, which had never belonged to Lithuania. All protests were in vain, as the local tradition, the ethnic structure of the country and the wishes of its people were of no concern to the authors of the plan.

* * * *

In the grim spring of 1608 fate smiled on the Commonwealth while playing a gruesome jest. On May 27 a revolt against the already crowned pretender broke out in Moscow. The boyars who initiated it told the people that the Poles and Lithuanians wanted to kill the tsar and they encouraged a massacre of foreigners, while in the meantime they attacked the Kremlin and killed the False Dymitr. This done, they calmed down the rioting rabble, as they did not wish any conflict with the Commonwealth. "That thief cheated you as well as us," one of the boyars said later at an official conference. They wanted the people to be their confederates in the coup and that explains their conduct.

It cost dearly the Polish and Lithuanians brought to Moscow by the Dymitr affair. The only ones among them to survive were those who barricaded themselves in their houses and fought to the last. Hundreds were killed, many of them innocent servants. The fate of the women, seized in their shirts only, or without them, was grim. They were imprisoned after their captors "had their fun with them." The *voievode* Mniszech found himself prisoner, as did Maryna, just crowned as tsaritsa, now stripped of all her jewels and costly attire.

These two, as well as others who volunteered for the Moscow expedition, had only themselves to blame. But what about their retinues and even the merchants who came to the tsar's wedding with their wares? The news of the Moscow massacre caused outrage in the Commonwealth and calls for revenge were heard. The Dymitr escapade poisoned the relations between the two nations, bringing them down to a criminal level.

No one was convinced by the arguments of the boyars, who blamed the Poles and Lithuanians for supporting Dymitr, though they had hailed him as their lord themselves, after having murdered Godunov and his family. One of the Polish envoys openly told a turncoat dignitary: "Shame on you, Mihailo, you are speaking against yourself!"

The members of the Commonwealth mission were held in Moscow, actually under house arrest.

Yet the immediate outcome of the bloody Moscow coup was on the whole favorable to Warsaw. The historian Waclaw Sobieski has unearthed evidence showing that Dymitr was planning a westward march to take Zygmunt's throne by force. The large entourage of Maryna Mniszech was supposed to serve as cover and remove from the enterprise the stain of a foreign invasion. The pretender was in league with his earlier protector Zebrzydowski, as well as Stadnicki and Janusz Radziwill.

He ostentatiously favored the Orthodox population of Lwow and showered it with gifts, was on the best of terms with the Protestants, and in his final days urged desperately the Provincial of the Jesuits to come to Moscow to discuss "matters concerning the entire Holy Church." He ordered massive armaments and was reportedly preparing supplies for an army of three hundred thousand. The sum of a hundred thousand *rubles* earmarked for the support of the Zebrzydowski rebellion in Poland was already loaded on carts that were seized by the Moscow coup. Dymitr Szuyski, who was to head the westward expedition, brought secretly into the city at night some of his troops and used them in carrying out the coup against Dymitr.

It is quite possible that Polish politicians also played a part in it. Already in January some of the senators spoke about the overthrow of Dymitr, who was becoming a menace. His agents had been active in the Commonwealth since the fall. In the beginning of 1606 the Szuyski clan in Russia launched the idea of calling Poland's Crown Prince Wladyslaw to the Moscow throne.

Zygmunt III knew that the impostor was scheming and looking for excuses for aggression, abusing the embassy of his recent protector. With most of the gentry antagonized by the failure of the Seym to enact the legislation endorsed by the majority, the Zebrzydowski convention in Stezyca, and Dymitr plotting in Moscow, Zygmunt's situation was precarious.

The Stezyca faction called a convention in Lublin for June 4, where it was resolved that the gentry would meet in Sandomierz for a "rokosh," a term that did not mean at that time an armed uprising, but only a general assembly of the entire knightly estate—the gentry, the senators, and the king—conducted outside the Seym. Zygmunt, of course, did not contemplate attending the Sandomierz convention. He was feverishly busy consolidating his own party, handing out grants, promotions, and appointments. The old and the new magnates were showered with favors and each of them was sod thrown on the coffin of the king's reform plans. A state cannot be reformed by leaning on the class that does not desire a strong government.

The country was swept by a wave of political agitation, the county councils were in constant debate, and there was a flood of publications in verse and prose, some of high quality, even brilliant, and the rest mediocre.

Before the confrontation state was reached, the army took the king's side, including even those who had left the Inflanty front when their wages were unpaid and started looting. Though hardly model soldiers, they remained loyal to their commander, Stanislaw Zolkiewski. The hetman, the most outstanding of the disciples of Zamoyski and a firm opponent of the king's plans, left Lublin in a somber mood. He went to Ruthenia to join his regular troops. When the "rokosh" forces were assembling in Sandomierz, he was already approaching the Vistula at the head of his regiments, bringing rescue to the king.

The standing army has been the mainstay of all the modern centralized monarchies. (The French royal regiments behaved in their country just as lawlessly as did the Polish, but they did fulfil their role as guardians of the throne. They were numerous enough.) The private detachments of the secular and ecclesiastic magnates assembled in Cracow by the king were twice the number of Zolkiewski's cavalry, the strong arm of the Commonwealth. Zygmunt distributed land grants, the revenues of customs and tolls, even tax revenues to his royal party's Polish, Lithuanian, and Ruthenian magnates, but he had little money left for his own army, that of the crown.

He lagged in passing on to Zolkiewski the hetman's baton of Zamoyski. He preferred to reward the field hetman's loyalty with some mills in Gdansk.

The rebellious gentry became disappointed in Zolkiewski and pamphleteers began to take an interest in him. One of them wrote (in verse):

> The calf is said to be stupid
> Others think the ox is even more so.
> You have the choice, take the name you want
> Or even both of them.
> For inconstancy, our mother Eve
> Was driven from paradise for eternity.

> You, though a man not a wife
> Do not keep your word either.

Not all the political dissidents would agree with this doggerel, for there was discord in their camp. In Stezyca as well as Sandomierz, Zebrzydowski played a dominant role while Janusz Radziwill was elected marshal of the confederacy. Thus both the royal party and that of the opposition were headed by magnates, who could hardly be expected to fight against the hegemony of their class.

There were squabbles at Sandomierz, even conflicts between the leaders and the mass of the gentry, which emphasized that it opposed not the king himself but only some of his bad advisers and senators. Finally it failed to produce any cohesive program and in the key parliamentary area advanced retrogressive ideas, for example demanding that the instructions given to the deputies by the county councils should be absolutely binding.

Already before the "memorable session" of the Seym, the gentry were horrified by the king's proposals of majority vote. Now, at Sandomierz, they adopted the principle that majority vote was acceptable when debates were conducted under the seal of confederacy. Thus the flood brought with it unwittingly a lifeboat. In the future, Seym sessions conducted under the seal of confederacy ignored the "liberum veto" and the minority could not invalidate the resolutions voted by the majority. Such was the case of the Great Seym of the eighteenth century, which voted the Constitution of May 3.

It would appear that the rebellious gentry, Father Piotr Skarga, and Cardinal Bernard Maciejowski were all operating at the same level of political thinking and that was the root of the evil. They all favored majority vote only when it suited their particular purpose, but did not want it adopted as a general principle. The era of counter-reformation and baroque did not inspire dispassionate, rational thinking.

Some historians characterized these events as an attempted "rebuilding of the Commonwealth," but it is questionable whether the manifestations of discontent among the gentry merited that description, borrowed from the title of the great work of Frycz Modrzewski, who had advocated a genuine basic reform.

193

Since the intellectual trends triggered by the Renaissance and the Reformation were not turned to constructive political ends, the nation had to wait for the next flow of mental tides, which was the Enlightment. We are apt to overlook the extent to which the political orientation of a society is shaped by intellectual fashion. The Commonwealth needed a thorough, fundamental reform, which could only be carried out by rational people, free of superstition and the slavery of encrusted customs.

Some sparks in the embers of the attempted rebellion did cast a little light, but they were too feeble to start a fire and no one was blowing to keep it alive.

The king called a rival convention at Wislica, came there personally and then . . . beat a retreat. He declared officially that he did not seek absolute rule, that he recognized the free royal elections now and forever, and that he submitted his actions to the scrutiny of the senators at his court. He made no further reference to parliamentary reform, nor to the confirmation of religious tolerance. Speaking from the Wislica pulpit, the leading ideologue of the royal party, Piotr Skarga, struck a similar note. The next edition of his homilies no longer included the treatise "On Monarchy." The clergy was changing its strategy, shifting to the side of the champions of the "golden freedom." It appeared that the power of the church within the state could be better enhanced in cooperation than in conflict with the gentry. Both sides, the clergy and the landed gentry, were basically conservative. They could consolidate and expand their privileges by mutual agreement but the national interest called for curbing them.

This policy turn, detrimental to the Commonwealth, was unwittingly encouraged by the bold and perceptive political literature of the period. The ruler failed to heed the citizens' voices of concern for the country at large. They responded by protecting their own special interests, becoming champions of the "golden freedom" and their class. As a result the clergy, more particularly the Jesuits, became official censors of thought and expression.

The years of the "Rokosh" opposition were a heroic era of Polish anti-clericalism in which the country matched other European nations. The Jesuits had by then secured the right of return to France, but the king curtailed their activity. On April 16, 1606, the Holy See excommunicated Venice, but the local clergy sided with the government of the Republic. Only the Jesuits refused to do so and they were banned from Venice for half a century. They were also expelled from Catholic Bavaria. Driven out of Transylvania, they moved to Poland.

The pope instructed the nuncio to communicate with the Jesuits in Poland only secretly, such was the distrust in which they were held by the people. The gentry were tired of their backstage political intrigues and their arrogance.

The opposition movement brought together not only the restless and rebellious element, but also some serious thinkers trying to save the state from clerical rule. This and the reaction against the pro-Austrian foreign policy of Zygmunt were the positive aspects of the "rokosh."

Some writers warned against political power wielded by persons under alien influence; they wanted the vast estates of the church to be taxed at the same moderate rates as those paid by lay land-owners; they demanded that the Jesuits be refused entry to Poland. The majority did not go quite as far and one of the resolutions adopted in Sandomierz suggested that the Jesuits be allowed to reside only in some cities.

The pamphleteers who sneered at the "paper gun" aimed by the pope against Venice spoke too soon. In 1606 a pamphlet entitled *Consilium de recuperanda et in posterum stabilienda pace in regni Poloniae*, probably written by Jerzy Zbaraski, insisted that Poland would never know peace until all the Jesuits were expelled. This work remained popular for a hundred years, was translated into many European languages, and saw twelve Latin editions, but none in Polish. This was understandable because under the rule of the counter-reformation, publications aimed against the all-powerful order could not be tolerated.

Zebrzydowski's dissidence defended the "golden freedom," but failed to advance any serious proposals of constitutional reform, nor did he have the means for carrying it out. Only a government wielding effective power could have prevented the clerical hegemony within the state, avoided adventurism exemplified by the Dymitr affair, curbed the waste of public funds, and the giveaway of ducal Prussia to Brandenburg. All these issues were addressed by the political literature of the period, but without a basic reform such well-founded warnings were empty verbiage incapable of initiating action.

It is significant that the boldest and wisest proposals were made by the political writers, not by the official resolutions of the "rokosh" movement. The writings of that era remain a testimony to the sound statesmanship of their authors and the freedom of expression that still existed at the time but was later restricted in the interest of the ruling class of magnates.

The Sandomierz and Wislica groups never reached agreement. The king rejected the resolutions of the opposition and requested its members to disperse and return to their homes to await the convocation of parliament. He was right in doing so, for if he failed to lead the gentry against the magnates, which would have been the best move, he had to uphold at least the authority of the crown. This could mean the imposition of absolute rule by force. Anything was better than that alternative, even an Austrian archduke as governor.

The opposition proclaimed a general levy for October 12. The royal army left Wislica on September 25 and after four days was facing its retreating adversary on the Vistula at Janowiec. Stadnicki "the Devil" had crossed to the right bank, as did many others. Zebrzydowski and Radziwill, both men of personal courage, remained on the left bank at the head of only three thousand troops. Against them, Zygmunt himself headed the royal army, in helmet and armor.

Instead of battle, the senators started conciliatory negotiations. Finally the only point that remained to be settled was whether Zebrzydowski would have to dismount before apologizing to the king. He did, but not before the royalist senators dismounted first. He approached in the glare of torches the king on his horse and kissed the extended royal hand.

"I take for witness the Lord, before whose awesome judgment I was about to stand as I was ready for battle," he said, "that all I did was done in the public interest, and I pledge loyalty in the hope that Your Majesty will deign to heed the demands of the nation."

Janusz Radziwill in turn declared, "What I was doing was not inspired by lack of respect for Your Majesty, but I followed my forebears in the defense of our freedoms and these I will, as a true nobleman, defend with my life."

Neither of the two leaders recanted or showed contrition. The crown's victory was purely theoretical. The first phase of the uprising did not bring any solution, but merely aroused people and set an example for the future.

In 1607 the rebellion erupted again, more aggressive than before. A convention called to Jedrzejow later moved to Czersk, close to Warsaw, where the Seym was in session, quiet and peaceful in the absence of most of the opposition. There was no reference to any reform increasing the king's power and only bland resolutions were voted. "Zygmunt's earlier obstinacy was turned by necessity into boundless sloth," commented a contemporary writer.

On June 24 Zebrzydowski proclaimed the dethronization of Zygmunt III and an interregnum. There was only one possible response to that move. The royal army advanced from Warsaw toward Warka in pursuit of the rebels. The relatively small force of eight thousand had eminent commanders: Jan Karol Chodkiewicz and Stanislaw Zolkiewski. When battle was given at Guzow on July 6, the former commanded the left wing, the latter the right one, and the center was under the three Potockis: John, Jacob, and Stefan. The army that defeated the rebels was only partly that of the crown; most of its units were the private regiments of the magnates. They were fighting for the king on that day but could turn against him on the next.

One of the cavalrymen seized as booty the reserve mount of Janusz Radziwill, with saddle, harness, and even stirrups studded with gold and precious stones. The soldier offered it to the king, who gave him in reward another horse and a village bringing an income of a thousand *zlotys* a year. No one could believe the claim that the Commonwealth could not afford to support a standing army. One of the opposition pamphleteers reported that the king spent forty thousand *thalers* a year on his musicians alone. Patronage of the arts is commendable, but neglect of the military brought to the Commonwealth disasters that turned it into a cultural wasteland.

Nine years before the Zebrzydowski rebellion and the battle of Guzow, Krzysztof Warszewicki, a staunch supporter of Zygmunt, published a treatise entitled "De optimo statu libertatis." It recommended that after crushing a rebellion a monarch should treat leniently the rank and file but punish severely the leaders.

The king had evidence of treason: correspondence with Gabriel Batory, prince of Transylvania, slated to become king of Poland. Yet only Jan Herburt and Procop Peczyslawski spent a couple of years in prison, while all the others went free. The conference of senators in 1608 and the Seym of 1609 proclaimed a general amnesty and the confirmation of all the clauses of "golden freedom."

The Zebrzydowski rebellion was nothing unusual in the Europe of its time, when far worse disturbances were common. The historian Bobrzynski observed that "everywhere else a king's victory in a civil war invariably brought about a strengthening of the royal power, absolute rule or even oppression. The victory of Guzow had no such consequences." What was the reason?

Zygmunt had been ruling for twenty years, making the worst possible use of the considerable powers left to him in spite of the Henrician Covenant and the Pacta Conventa. He formed a party incapable of carrying out a reform. The royal party represented the magnates, while the opposition was also led by magnates, temporarily at odds with the king. Zygmunt antagonized the ablest men and drove them into opposition. He could have launched a reform at the beginning of his reign, but not without the cooperation of Zamoyski. Hetman Zolkiewski stood by the king when the rebels challenged the crown, but after the victory he protected the offenders. He was a reasonable and humane man, though capable of harshness when the situation called for it. He witnessed the execution of Samuel Zborowski. In the course of the campaign against the "rokosh," Zolkiewski ordered gallows to be erected at Warka for the public hanging of a nobleman guilty of treason by disclosing to the enemy the camp's password. Yet after the Guzow victory, the hetman held back the pursuit.

Bobrzynski was right when he said that "Zolkiewski and his supporters feared Zygmunt more than the rebels." The hetman had served devotedly King Stefan Batory, whose policies, though not without flaws, were clearly motivated by national interest. That was not the case of his successor and that fact accounted for his political defeat after a military victory. Zygmunt III pursued goals that did not serve the best interests of the Commonwealth, such as the total hegemony of Catholicism throughout Europe, which endangered the structure of a state comprising several nationalities and faiths. He also used Poland as a stepping-stone to the throne of Sweden. Such endeavors could only harm the country.

With such outstanding military leaders as Chodkiewicz and Zolkiewski, the king could not fail to win in the field, but they also had far sounder political judgment than the monarch. It was Chodkiewicz who had turned down the Dymitr venture, saying that "matters are not yet settled at home," while Zolkiewski was the first to call the pretender "a cheat."

The Zebrzydowski rebellion broke down the opposition and with it the concept of reform, advanced first a century earlier under

Alexander Jagiello and developed under Zygmunt August. The wise plan of basic reform failed because it was not supported by the rulers, while the landed gentry—the only politically active class outside the royal court and its lords—turned inward in its frustration and abandoned ambitious projects, content with protecting its privileges.

In the years after the rebellion Zygmunt seemed to change course. He no longer surrounded himself with foreigners and did not hold any more conferences attended only by Germans, as was that of Niepolomice. The change came too late and was too halfhearted. The first twenty years of the Swedish king's reign bred a well-founded suspicion of the monarch's motives, which turned eventually into paranoia. The gentry began to suspect every initiative of the crown, perceiving it as an attempt to curtail its freedoms.

The Henrician Covenant and the Pacta Conventa did not render the monarch powerless. Though solemnly proclaimed, they remained the letter of the law but were not fully observed in practice. According to these covenants the king should have been building defensive castles and funding a strong army. Actually even the overseas expeditions he launched for his own dynastic purposes had to be financed by the Commonwealth. It was not until the formal confirmation of all the rights of the gentry by the post-rebellion Seyms that the political situation deteriorated, the power of the executive was restricted, and Seyms became merely conventions of sovereign provinces. The king's behavior at the "memorable session" of the Seym provoked a rebellion, which compelled Zygmunt to abandon his plans of absolute rule. After the king's victory over the rebels there was no retribution. This established a precedent that haunted the country ever since.

The existing laws became ossified and carved in stone, making any reform or basic change impossible. The only way out, ironically, was that used by the Sandomierz "rokosh," that is, the formation of a confederacy, which could collaborate with the king or embrace the entire Seym. It was the only way as it nullified the power of a minority to veto the resolutions of the majority. All the resolutions of a confederacy were taken by majority vote.

While this arrangement had some merit, it could be used for either good or harmful purposes, witness the later confederacy of Targowica.

After the Zebrzydowski rebellion, when all the privileges of the landed gentry were confirmed and the clergy, headed by the Jesuits, became a staunch champion of that class, any constitutional change became virtually impossible. Any critic of the status quo was declared an enemy of the knightly estate and the church. Schools glorified the "golden freedom," while writers and orators were expected to praise the existing system. It was a form of unofficial censorship that paralyzed independent political thoughts. A reform required almost a miracle: a major section of the gentry and the clergy demanding a restriction of their own rights. Yet that was what happened in the course of the intellectual upheaval of the eigthteenth century.

A book subtitled *The Silver Age* should actually end with the Zebrzydowski rebellion. The story reaches the stage of self congratulatory lethargy at this point but the conditions of everyday life have not yet changed. One could then still live well in the fertile, well-established Commonwealth, which even scored several military successes, extended its boundaries, and was counted nominally among the leading powers of Europe. We should therefore bring our narration to the moment when bills were presented for accounts as yet not settled, describing the last forty years of prosperity enjoyed by the Commonwealth of Both Nations. It was a relative prosperity, but the generations that followed never tasted even that.

VII

The battle of Kircholm brought to the Commonwealth such fame that even England began to show concern over the growth of a power whose soldiers were capable of working miracles. But the Swedish war was dragging on and the few successes did not have significant strategic or political consequences.

When Jan Karol Chodkiewicz was busy chasing Zebrzydowski in Poland, the fortress of Bialy Kamien (Whitestone) in the Inflanty, won at such a high cost by Zamoyski, was lost despite the heavy artillery brought from Wilno and Tykocin for its defense. Andrew Zborowski, the young and inexperienced garrison commander, thought that he could intercept and take by surprise the Swedish forces approaching the fortress. He was instead surrounded and captured himself, while the defenseless fort fell easily to the enemy, as did the forts of Fellin, Kokenhaus, and Dyament.

The campaign of 1609 displayed to the full the talent and tenacity of Jan Karol Chodkiewicz. The long unpaid, hungry, and ragged troops under his command threatened mutiny, but the hetman's leadership made them march across snowbound forests and along the frozen seacoast to Parnawa. The hetman himself remained on his horse for thirty-two hours in subzero weather, waiting for an opportune moment for attack. He had forbidden fires, which would have alerted the enemy, and set his men an example of endurance. When he finally drew his sword, ready to lead the assault, his soldiers tried to hold him back, knowing well that without him they would all be lost. The dismounted cavalry took the fortress of Parnawa after blowing up its gates with petards. Chodkiewicz seized in the harbor two Swedish men-of-war and some smaller craft, then purchased several English and Dutch ships. Manning this improvised fleet with his lanlubber soldiers, he won a victory at sea by aiming at the enemy boats loaded with combustible material, which set the Swedish ships on fire and forced them to flee. Later Chodkiewicz defeated at Riga not only the Swedes, but also their Scottish, Dutch, and French mercenaries. He recaptured the fortress of Dyament, but soon found himself almost without any army, as the men refused to wait for their pay any longer and simply dispersed.

Sweden, however, had troubles of its own. The Stockholm parliament was tired of the war and refused to vote taxes. This upset King Charles IX so much that "seized by fulminous rage, he lost his speech and his mind." He died on October 30, 1611, leaving the throne to his seventeen-year-old son, Gustav Adolph. Even though he was not yet of age, his guardians—among them the queen mother Christina—called the promising youth to power. Soon after his accession to the throne, Gustav Adolph appointed as his chancellor Axel Oxenstierna, a statesman who matched him in political talent and surpassed him in reflection. The young king's instinct was right—Oxenstierna was twenty-eight when he became chancellor.

Chodkiewicz received little support from Zygmunt III, but a good deal from the Radziwills of the Nieswiez branch. Old Nicholas Christopher Radziwill, "The Orphan," equipped regiments at his own expense and sent them to the Inflanty, as did his son and other relatives. Without their help, the great hetman could not have won, for though a superb commander, he was not a miracle worker.

The war with Sweden had actually started as Zygmunt's private enterprise in his endeavor to hold on to two thrones at once, with that of Sweden having first priority in his mind. It was hinted that he was not eager to see the province of Inflanty in Polish hands, as he preferred to rule it as the hereditary monarch of the Swedes, Goths and Vandals. Poland and Lithuania were weary of the war; as it dragged on, the funds voted for it were reportedly used in part for other purposes.

During a lull in operations, Jan Karol Chodkiewicz went to Wilno to plead with the king personally for money for his troops. Zygmunt was on his way to an expedition against Moscow.

The Commonwealth could expect at that time some relief from Denmark, which had declared war against Sweden, but Zygmunt managed to create a new front by initiating a war against Muscovy. It is significant that King Christian of Denmark did not act against Sweden until 1611 and did so only after he knew that Zygmunt had been engaged against Russia since 1609. Zygmunt actually tried to dissuade Christian from attacking Sweden, fearing that he might take away some of the possessions of the Swedish house of Vasa.

Dymitr the Pretender lost his life on May 27, 1606, at dawn. His massacred body was dragged to the Lobnoye section of Moscow on a rope tied to the genitals and left there in the open. Its condition made identification impossible. It became even more so when the remains were later burned and the ashes loaded into a cannon to be fired westward.

Vasili Shuyski became the tsar but his accession did not stabilize the situation. Other pretenders started popping up one after another. An adventurer called Ileyko launched an astounding career in the Lower Volga region. His fellow Cossacks designated him as pretender to the throne of Moscow because he knew that city well. He was named Pyotr, the nonexistent son of the tsar Theodore Ivanovich. The boyars, far bolder and more disruptive than Zebrzydowski in Poland, were ready to endorse him as one of their own, taking advantage of the rebellious turbulence spreading across the land. The tsar's forces did not catch Pyotr until October 1607, when they compelled the surrender of Tula by building a dam on the river Upa and threatening to flood the city.

Four months earlier another equally wild but more dangerous adventure was started when in July 1607 a coarse and totally unknown individual claimed to be the tsar Dymitr, miraculously saved from the Moscow massacre. His adviser was a Pole, Mikolaj Miechowiecki, who had been close to the first "False Dymitr" and knew his secrets. He used that knowledge in coaching his successor.

J. FALCK. PORTRAIT OF LOUIS XIII

HETMAN JAN KAROL
CHODKIEWICZ

J. FALCK. THE GREAT MOGUL

THE WISNIOWIECKI PALACE IN CRACOW

WLADYSLAW IV AS A CHILD

W. HONDIUS. PORTRAIT OF
LEO SAPIEHA

C. LAMBERT. PORTRAIT OF
ANNE OF AUSTRIA

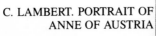

TOWNHOUSE IN GDANSK

CASTLE OF KRASICZYN

PORTRAIT OF QUEEN CONSTANCE

BOGUSZEWICZ. PORTRAIT OF MARYNA MNISZECH

CASTLE OF THE KMITA CLAN IN WISNICZ

HOUSE OF THE PRELATES OF PELPIN IN GDANSK

UNKNOWN FLEMISH ARTIST. PORTRAIT OF WLADYSLAW IV

TOWNHALL OF SZYDLOWIEC

ST. JAMES' GATE IN GDANSK

J. SUYDERHOF. PORTRAIT OF
ZYGMUNT III

W. HONDIUS. PORTRAIT OF
ADAM KAZANOWSKI

JACOB SARSZ, MAYOR
OF TORUN

DOLABELLI SCHOOL. CHANCELLOR ZADZIK AND HETMAN KONIECPOLSKI

The Poles and Lithuanians imprisoned in Moscow were sent to various remote towns where they fared poorly. The official embassy of the Commonwealth, headed by castellan Mikolaj Olesnicki, remained held in Moscow for two-and-a-half years. Its chaplain was Father Pawel Leczycki, who brought with him a copy of John Botero's work *Relazioni universali*, a book widely known in Europe and translated into many languages, which contained a whole chapter devoted to Poland. With plenty of time on his hands during his captivity, Father Leczycki translated Botero's book to Polish and published it later in Cracow. It seems that the only benefits derived by Poland from the Dymitr affair were of a literary character, as several fascinating memoirs and also some poems by Sebastian Patrycy commemorat ed the event.

Jerzy Mniszech, transported to Jaroslaw, adopted a policy of camouflage by growing a long beard and hair to his shoulders to make him look like a Muscovite. He carried on a correspondence with the enemies of the tsar Vasili, helping them to spread rumors to the effect that the first Dymitr was still alive and would soon claim his throne. The emergence of the second pretender was prepared by a barrage of propaganda, but it took some time to find someone who even remotely resembled the first Dymitr.

In July 1608 a new commonwealth mission concluded with Vasili a four-year peace treaty. Both parties undertook to abstain from hostilities or any interference in one anothers domestic affairs. The king's envoys also promised to evacuate from Muscovy all the Commonwealth citizens.

Vasili released the prisoners, though not without misgivings as to their loyalty. They were to be escorted to the border, but Mniszech and his daughter managed to break away from the rest, evidently looking for trouble. They were soon apprehended by a detachment sent by Dymitr the second pretender and taken to his camp of Tuszyn near Moscow, where he held court with his Russian, Polish, Lithuanian, and Cossack supporters. Mniszech hastily recognized him as his son-in-law, in a contract by which Dymitr promised him three hundred thousand *rubles*. Despite her initial reluctance and disgust, Maryna soon followed her father. She had learned about her husband's death on the way to Tuszyn, but now she recognized the pretender as her miraculously surviving spouse. To make sure, however, she wed him secretly in church.

The clause of the treaty that required the evacuation of the

Commonwealth citizens from Russia could not be carried out. The new pretender called Lithuanians and Poles to the service of the "great tsar Dymitr Ivanovich," as he styled himself. One of the first volunteers was a Jozef Budzillo of Mozyr, whose very interesting memoirs were published by Hanna Malewska in her *Letters of the Vasa Period*. He was also responsible, together with Miechowiecki, for Dymitr's first success in the field in October 1607 at Kozielsk.

Some of the great names of Lithuania and Ruthenia were to be found in the camp of the man who passed into history as the "Thief of Tuszyn." There was Samuel Tyszkiewicz, followed by Prince Adam Wisniowiecki and Roman Rozynski, the latter permanently drunk. They treated the "tsar" with all due respect, kissing his hand. In August 1608 Jan Piotr Sapieha, *starosta* of Uswiat and first cousin of Leo Sapieha, chancellor of Lithuania, joined their company. At this point the situation acquired international political overtones.

The *starosta*, a man with a degree from an Italian university, was a veteran of many battles, including that of Guzowo, as well a staunch supporter of Zygmunt III. He was prompted to go east by his cousin the chancellor. The Sapieha clan was still in the early stages of its ascent to power and received frequent favors from the king. Its original family seats of Opakow and Jelna were in the province of Smolensk, lost to Muscovy under Zygmunt the Old. The recovery of these estates could have enhanced greatly the wealth and standing of the clan. That family aspect of the situation inspired both the military moves and the plans of union with Russia of Chancellor Leo Sapieha. Now it also helped him to get involved with Dymitr, the second pretender of that name.

In 1608 his position improved considerably. The rebellion in Poland died down. Zebrzydowski apologized to the king, and the veterans of both sides in the conflict hastened eastward in search of fortune. Some were motivated by simple greed, others had ambitious political plans, even going as far as placing the "Thief of Tuszyn" on the Polish throne. The vast spaces of the grand duchy of Moscow became a theatre of civil war and a veritable school of robbery, brigandage, and every kind of atrocity. When that school's graduates, finding no more booty on the Volga, returned to the Commonwealth, the Seym was compelled to enact a law that stated that "an expatriate who kills a member of the Lisowski band is free of any penalty and may return home."

Alexander Joseph Lisowski was a squire from a Pomeranian

family long settled in Lithuania. He started his career as a standard bearer in a Hussar regiment, fought at Kircholm, and was on Zebrzydowski's side in the rebellion. He joined the pretender Dymitr early, commanded at first the Don Cossacks and then formed his own brotherhood of rogues, superb fighters and fearsome brigands. Lisowski's mounted pirates, who became almost an army, sacked countless cities and killed thousands. Their field of action extended from the White Sea to Moldavia, Italy, and Champagne. Hardly any country in Europe was safe from the depredations of the Lisowski bands. Their founder died early in 1616, allegedly from poison. His fame was such that large bodies of troops dispersed in panic at the mere mention of his name. Once, taken by surprise at night by a far superior force, he did not even give his men time to dress. He had them leap on their horses bareback, half naked and barefoot themselves, to launch a mad charge and win. He was a military genius on a tactical, regimental level. His talents, however, not only did not help the Commonwealth, but harmed it.

In February of 1609 the tsar Vasili entered a treaty of mutual assistance with Sweden. Zygmunt III regarded it as a breach of his treaty with Moscow and started the long-planned war, which he conceived as a Catholic crusade against the Orthodox. Pope Paul V proclaimed a jubilee and a plenary indulgence for the "victory of the glorious king over the schismatics" and blessed a gift of a sword and hat for the "knight of the church," while the nuncio ordered solemn services in all the Catholic parishes of Poland and Lithuania. The king's main objective in his expedition was the propagation of the Catholic faith in the east, stated the historian Waclaw Sobieski. Some concessions to the domestic Orthodox of the Commonwealth did not disprove that view. Zygmunt started by asking Rome to accelerate the canonization of Ignatius Loyola, whom he selected as the patron of the enterprise. The bishops, the clergy, and particularly the Jesuits had long been urging war against the infidel.

Radziwill "the Orphan," though a devout Catholic, was opposed to it. Jan Karol Chodkiewicz was not thirsting for new laurels and all of Lithuania, with the exception of the Sapiehas, wanted peace. In Poland Stanislaw Zolkiewski, still with only the rank of field hetman, remained true to the teaching of Jan Zamoyski, who wanted to take advantage of Moscow's precarious situation for an alliance or agreements, perhaps going as far as union, but was careful to avoid war, particularly one started without Seym's consent. As he went to war, he demanded from the king the assurance that "Your Majesty seeks no private goals, only the Commonwealth's good and the extension of its lands."

The decision on war was taken by a small clique of the king's advisers. It was confirmed in secret session by almost the entire senate, urged on by Queen Constance, a champion of her native Austria and an advocate of militant catholicism. The war was intended to win Moscow for the Roman church and then turn from the conquered Kremlin northwest toward Sweden. Zolkiewski was right in suspecting Zygmunt III of seeking advantage for his own dynasty rather than for the Commonwealth. It was also thought in the royal circle that success in the east would result in a change of the dominant religion in Persia.

No wonder that such adventurism encouraged smaller men to engage in their own wild enterprises. Lisowski's bands also thought of themselves as stalwart defenders of the faith.

The king's gigantic plans were out of proportion to the meager preparations for the campaign, held back by the fact that the proposed war in the east was kept secret from the Seym until the last moment. Zygmunt started out late in August, besieged Smolensk in October, and remained stuck there for two years. Already Tsar Godunov had surrounded the fortress with walls seven fathoms high (fathom = 6 feet) and two fathoms thick. There were also other defensive earthworks. The commander of the garrison, Michael Szein, burned down the city and its suburbs. He had under him some thirty thousand fighting men. "The worst of it," complained Leo Sapieha, "is not that Moscow does not want to surrender, but that we have nothing with which to compel it to do so. They thought they were going on a trip to the outskirts of Cracow."

The ineptness of the king and his "chamber council" became evident at Smolensk, when they could not reach a decision. Zolkiewski advised that Smolensk be bypassed and the outcome be decided in Moscow, not necessarily by military means alone. Sapieha insisted on clinging desperately to Smolensk. The very active Queen Constance meddled from distant Wilno, where she held court with the nuncio, Father Piotr Skarga, the crown princes Wladyslaw and the just-born John Casimir, as well as the ubiquitous Miss Ursula.

Intrigue and squabbles were thriving, while the situation on the Moscow chessboard was one of infinite complexity. The official enemy, Tsar Vasili, was in Moscow. He was challenged by the "Thief of Tuszyn" from his camp near the capital, where he was accompanied by about seven thousand Polish and Lithuanian volunteers ready to sack the Kremlin, as well as numerous boyars from the leading Russian families. There was also in Tuszyn Filaret, the metropolite of Rostiv, appointed patriarch by the pretender Dymitr (the real patriarch, Hermogenes, was in Moscow and hated the Poles, Lithuanians, and the church of Rome). Before Tsar Borys turned him into a monk, Filaret was called Theodore Nikitich Romanov and was known as the leading dandy of Moscow.

The boyars accompanying Vasili in Moscow were afraid that the city's fall would be followed by a massacre. Those in Tuszyn had reason to fear the same. The great popular rising of Ivan Bolotnikov was crushed in 1607, but neither the peasants nor the burghers were appeased and they sympathized with the pretender, who promised change. Landowners died in their country estates by the knife or a hangman's rope and the *voievode* of Wielkie Luki was impaled. The boyars simply sought survival. Some of them yearned for the freedoms enjoyed by the gentry of the Commonwealth, but their decisions can only be understood if we realize that they feared for their lives and were willing to sign any promissory notes on parchment to save them.

The negotiations with the subjects of Zygmunt III supporting the pretender resulted in the enlistment of some of them in the royal army. Their back pay was to be paid from the tsar's treasury, which had to be seized first. If that should not be the case, the king promised to pay them himself, though in a lower amount. The pretender, shocked by the defection of many of his men, fled secretly to Kaluga. Moscow breathed relief and Tsar Vasili proclaimed himself defender of the Orthodox church.

He had received from the west reports about King Zygmunt's hostility toward the Orthodox. The king's religious fanaticism was coming home to roost. The tsar, in his precarious position, could hardly recruit spies in Lithuania or Poland, but that was not necessary because the Orthodox citizens of these countries supplied him with information spontaneously. One of the volunteer informers was publicly beheaded in Wilno when Zygmunt III was passing through the Lithuanian capital on his way to Smolensk.

Jan Herburt—the first publisher of the great historian Dlugosz—himself a troublemaker but a man of high intelligence, wrote in 1611 in a pamphlet entitled "A View of the Ruthenian Nation": "What profit does His Majesty derive from the many problems he had with the Ruthenian nation? The profit is in the fact that there are eighteen Slavic nations. All of them placed their hopes for freedom in the kings of Poland, they all believed that the Polish nation could set them free of the pagan yoke. They were all ready to lay their lives at the call of the Polish king and people. But now, when harm is done to the Ruthenians, they became our chief enemies. Now they would prefer to die in battle and have their wives and children burnt, as in Smolensk, rather than join forces with us. And what is the obstacle to peace with Moscow? Nothing but their Orthodox faith."

There is here some exaggeration. The Balkans continued to look upon King Wladyslaw, Zygmunt's son and successor, as another Saint George and their savior but there was also much truth in Herburt's argument.

Reports of the character of a religious crusade assumed by Zygmunt's campaign influenced the attitude of the boyars assembled in Tuszyn. They sent to Smolensk an embassy offering the throne of Moscow to Crown Prince Wladyslaw, but only under certain conditions. The prince would have to be baptized in the Orthodox faith and accept the crown from the patriarch. He would have to abstain from any propagation of Catholicism. The negotiations lasted two weeks and Zygmunt finally gave his approval, but did so deceitfully. He wanted to secure the boyars' oath of allegiance and gain time. He promised to send his son to the Kremlin only when "this monarchy will have fully settled down." The boyars swore to uphold the agreement but the king did not.

Zygmunt III obviously wanted himself to be the ruler of a conquered Moscow. His ideas were far removed from Zolkiewski's dream of a concord of nations and a dynastic union. The nuncio, still in Wilno, was outraged by the news of the king's "concessions," but he calmed down when it was explained to him that they were merely tactical moves. Zygmunt was under constant pressure by the church and his character ruled out any attempt at emancipation from the Jesuits.

Tsar Vasili sent westward a powerful army under the command of his brother, Dymitr Szuyski. It encountered the much smaller force of Stanislaw Zolkiewski. If the king's favorite, Potocki, had been in command, the Polish contingent would have been much larger.

On July 3, 1610, the hetman learned from some fugitive German mercenaries the position of the enemy. He left some of his troops at Zaymishche, which they besieged, and departed at night at the head of only two and a half thousand cavalry and a mere two hundred infantrymen. His two small cannon became stuck in the mud and had to be left behind. On July 4 at dawn, a Sunday, Zolkiewski surprised Szuyski near the village of Kluszyn.

"They were a countless multitude, awesome to behold compared to our meager force," wrote a participant in the battle, Samuel Maskiewicz, one of the hussars of Prince Porycki. The relation of strength was even worse than at Kircholm, with the enemy holding a sixfold superiority at least.

Only one squadron remained in reserve, the others were sent eight or ten times into the battle, which lasted five hours. The decisive moment came as a surprise to the victors. The worn-out, decimated Polish troops were attacked by two fresh detachments of mercenary cavalry, who performed an artful tactical maneuver recently invented in the West. The first line advanced in well-spaced formation and after firing its pistols allowed the second line to charge through its ranks. The maneuver was well executed, but a countercharge of Polish hussars with swords in their hands—the lances had all been broken earlier in the battle—broke down the enemy ranks. "Thus the Lord turned the defeated into victors and we chased them for a mile or more," reported Maskiewicz.

The mercenary foreign regiments in Russian service ceased fighting and after negotiation some of them passed over to Zolkiewski, who accepted their oath of fealty to Prince Wladyslaw. Dimitri Szuyski fled to the capital, leaving behind his baton and the standard with the emblem of a two-headed black eagle.

The hetman turned back toward Tsarove Zaymishche. He obtained the surrender of its garrison, far stronger than the troops he had at Kluszyn. His army reinforced by the turncoat mercenaries, he marched on Moscow, proving himself not only a great commander, but also a far more perceptive politician than the king's "chamber council." He had been long advocating a political solution as the way to the Kremlin.

"We had only been gone a few miles," wrote Maskiewicz, "when messengers from Moscow reported to the hetman that Tsar Vasili Szuyski was shorn as a monk, together with his brothers Ivan and Dimitri, while the boyars are waiting for us and want our crown prince as their ruler."

The simple-minded soldier did not know that his commander used not only arms but also diplomacy. Supported by Piotr Sapieha, the Pretender was again threatening Moscow. Hetman Zolkiewski promised to the boyars, through his secret envoys, that he would defend them against the Second Pretender and that turned the scales. Negotiations were opened on August 5, while the hetman received a string of critical missives from the king, still besieging Smolensk. Zygmunt urged him to take a tough line. The crowned missionary objected to the sparing of the lives of the Szuyskis and refused to accept the main conditions of the Russian side, which included guarantees of respect for the Orthodox faith, Wladyslaw as the tsar, and no territorial concessions. The Swedish monarch recalled that since he was descended from the Jagiello dynasty on the distaff side, he was a scion of Ruthenian rulers, through Casimir, son of Sonka of Holsza. On this ground he claimed hereditary rights to the Moscow throne. "The tsar's crown on Zygmunt's head would be the best guarantee of a religious revival among the Muscovites," wrote the papal nuncio to Rome, making clear the motives of Zygmunt's policy.

On August 28 Zolkiewski concluded an agreement with the boyars. A document was drawn up attesting to the election of Crown Prince Wladyslaw to the throne of Moscow.

The Polish-Lithuanian garrison did not enter the Kremlin until October. Zolkiewski preferred to keep his troops at first in nearby villages, to avoid suspicions of a foreign occupation. He was sincere in not wishing it and expressed in his personal letters the hope that a better order might emerge from chaos. After all, the union of Poland with Lithuania took well over a century to mature.

The Kremlin garrison was commanded by Alexander Gosiewski, Referendary of the Grand Duchy of Lithuania. Moscow bid a solemn and to some extent perhaps cordial farewell to the hetman as he left for Smolensk, taking with him the overthrown Tsar Vasili and his brothers Dimitri and Ivan.

The victory of Kluszyn and the seizure of the Kremlin confirmed Zygmunt III in his plans. He considered them both his own achievements. The king received Zolkiewski with some coolness and "with anger rather than gratitude in his countenance." He said, "For good reasons I will not allow my son to become the tsar of Moscow," rejecting contemptuously the documents of his election. The victor of Kluszyn had to wait eight more years for the rank of grand hetman of the crown. "Zygmunt, intimidated and surpassed by a giant such as the late Chancellor Zamoyski, was not eager to promote the rise of another," wrote the historian Waclaw Sobieski. Rejection of men of outstanding talent was becoming a habit.

Intrigue was rampant at the walls of Smolensk and in Wilno. The fortress of Smolensk still resisted all assaults. In the spring Zolkiewski boarded a riverboat and sailed to Kiev, to keep watch on the southeastern border. He refused to return to Moscow and help its pacification.

Zygmunt III arrested the envoys of the Moscow boyars, the metropolite Filaret and Prince Vasili Golitsyn, who insisted on having Wladyslaw as their tsar. Both remained in Poland for many years.

Alexander Gosiewski, left in Moscow, conducted himself with caution. When a drunken soldier fired a shot at the icon of the Madonna in the Nikolski gate of the Kremlin, the commander ordered his arms and legs cut off and the trunk burned at the site of the crime. The offender's hands were nailed under the desecrated holy icon.

Another soldier, who slapped an Orthodox priest, was saved from death by the intervention of the patriarch, but Gosiewski ordered instead his right arm to be cut off. He also had twenty-seven Germans, mercenaries who had passed over to Zolkiewski, executed by firing squad and twenty others tortured. The intelligent but ruthless officer realized that he was sitting on a powder keg and he punished mercilessly anything that might have triggered an explosion. His methods were harsher than those current in the Commonwealth, but quite normal for the Europe of the period.

As time went by, Gosiewski relaxed his vigilance. Even before Zolkiewski's departure, the soldiers quartered in the vicinity of the capital ". . . grabbed the wives and daughters of even the greatest boyars and took with them all the liberties they wanted. Moscow was much upset about it and with good reason . . . we live among them with distrust on both sides, we drink with them, but the rock (as they say) is under the coat; we offer banquets for each other, but keep our thoughts to ourselves. We also watch very carefully our security, with guards at the gates day and night, also at the principal crossroads."

In December Piotr Urusov, "a baptized Tartar," killed the Pretender during a hunt and the boyars breathed relief. They were no longer threatened by a man capable of inciting the people to a massacre, a "Cossack tsar." The attempts of Maryna, widowed for the second time, to promote the succession of her newly born son were not a serious menace.

The Kremlin garrison redoubled precautions and searched every sleigh entering the city. Whenever the soldiers found "muskets covered with grain or produce, the drivers were delivered to Gosiewski and he ordered them pushed under the ice on the river."

In March of 1611 a rebellion broke out in Moscow. The fighting was brief, but the city was burned down, set on fire by the Kremlin garrison. The houses under the snow did not burn easily until tar was used to set them aflame.

On June 13 Smolensk was finally taken by the Commonwealth force. Bartholomew Nowodworski, a knight of Malta, placed an explosive charge in the sewer discharging waste from the fortress. Jacob Potocki was the first to mount the ramparts, winning at last the glory for which he had been long competing with Zolkiewski.

Lost ninety-seven years earlier, Smolensk reverted to the Commonwealth. All the far-reaching plans of conquest or union were abandoned, leaving behind them only the hatred fueled by the anti-Orthodox crusade and the sponsorship by Poland and Lithuania of the successive pretenders.

Some years later, in the course of the peace negotiations, the Russian envoy Theodore Sheremetiev said:

"Your licentious soldiery knew no bounds to their insults and excesses: after taking whatever gold and silver was in the house, they sought hidden treasure by torture. Husbands watched the rape of their beloved wives; mothers, the shame of their daughters. The memory of your debauched violence is still fresh in our minds. You wounded our hearts with contempt, our people were never called anything but Muscovite dogs, thieves and turncoats. Our divine temples were not safe from your hands. The capital was turned to ashes and the treasure long accumulated by the tsars looted, the whole country ravaged. Is it not enough that we have suffered these indignities so long?"

Stanislaw Zolkiewski had a different vision and other plans, but they vanished in the smoke of burning Moscow.

The Kremlin garrison fared from bad to worse. Jan Karol Chodkiewicz, whom King Zygmunt had won over to his side, tried to relieve the Polish-Lithuanian troops. He met on his way a delegation of boyars on their way to Warsaw, where they sought Crown Prince Wladyslaw, their candidate for the tsar's throne. He turned them back to Moscow, but the persistent Muscovite supporters of the Polish prince sent another mission. When it failed, they had to give up their goal of a Polish tsar.

Chodkiewicz was active in the east for a whole year, but accomplished little. He could not even bring adequate supplies to the Kremlin garrison, while the country was swept by a national uprising. It was centered in the inaccessible Nijni Novgorod and its leaders were Kuzma Minin, a burgher, and Prince Dymitr Pozarski. Their monument, untouched by the revolution, still stands in Moscow's Red Square.

A part of the garrison left for the west, as did Alexander Gosiewski. The command of the remaining garrison was taken over by Mikolaj Strus, promoted by the Potockis, who was eager to win fame by "holding the capital for the crown prince." Chodkiewicz's last attempt to bring supplies to the Kremlin failed, as he could not break through the fiercely defended gutted ruins of Moscow. As he withdrew to the border, the besieged garrison ate first the parchment church books, the candles, and the withered grass under the snow, then the leather saddles and harness, finally carrion, prisoners, the bodies of hanged men, and each other. They surrendered on November 7, 1612. Many lost their lives, for the conditions of the capitulation were not kept and all the infantry was slaughtered.

The king, slow in relieving the Kremlin garrison, was stuck in the snows near Fyodorovski, whence he sent a mission to Moscow, announcing his own and Prince Wladyslaw's arrival. He returned to Warsaw via Smolensk.

The fate of Maryna, daughter of Mniszech, the *voievode* of Sandomierz, and widow of two successive pretenders, merits some mention. She joined Ivan Zarudzki, a peasant from Zaruda near Tarnopol, the ataman of the Don Cossacks and a man of considerable ability and overriding ambition. The Cossacks had been giving Moscow at least as much trouble as the Poles and Lithuanians. The

Don and Zaporozhe Cossacks were roaming all over the country. After dealing with the Commonwealth forces, the Muscovites turned against them, moving southward. Zarudzki and Maryna with her son were captured on July 5 on the Bear's Island of the river Ural, known at the time as Jaik. The ataman was impaled in Moscow and the three-year-old child went to the gallows. Maryna's fate was the subject of many rumors: some said she was burned at the stake, others that she was drowned or strangled. The truth was probably that she died as a prisoner in the tower of Kolomna, a picture of which can be found in Alexander Hirschberg's book about Maryna Mniszech.

These sentences were approved by the new tsar of Moscow, seventeen-year-old Michael, son of Theodore Romanov. He was elected in February 1613 by the local council and his election was confirmed by the major cities, visited by special delegations sent for that purpose. The act of election constituted a consolidation of the state, though it was opposed by some members of the aristocracy.

Michael III, a modest and moderate man, belonged to an old family related to the house of Rurik. Anastasia Romanov was the first wife of Ivan the Terrible and was remembered for her kindness. She did not participate in Ivan's atrocities; on the contrary, she tried to protect her husband's victims. The Romanovs were not responsible for the crimes of Ivan or Boris, but suffered a good deal themselves under the latter and others. The young tsar's father, the metropolite Filaret, was still held in Poland, first at Gostynin and then at Malbork. The Russian people expected from the new dynasty stability, and revenge.

Moscow failed to recover Smolensk. Great Novgorod, seized in an opportune moment by the Swedes, was still in their hands. The war continued, and to make things worse the bands of Alexander Lisowski continued marauding all over Russia. The Seym rescinded the decree by which they were outlawed and Lisowski entered the king's service. Hetman Chodkiewicz issued what amounted to a letter of marque, stating that Lisowski's men were not entitled to pay for their services, which meant that they had to subsist on booty, corsairs on land. The black and red colors of Lisowski attracted desperadoes and adventurers of various backgrounds: Cossacks, Lithuanians, and even native Muscovites, but the core of the brotherhood remained Polish.

The boyars of Moscow were in no haste to advise Warsaw and

Wilno of the election and coronation of Michael III, judging it prudent to seek cover by informing first some more distant capitals, such as Istanbul and Vienna. In any case, public opinion in the Commonwealth viewed Zygmunt's endeavors in the east as a failure. Zbigniew Ossolinski wrote that they had cost Poland more than Moscow.

In 1613 Bishop Gembicki resigned the position of chancellor. He was one of the most dedicated royalists and had himself advocated the ascent of Zygmunt to the throne of Moscow. Gembicki had accompanied the king at Smolensk and then acted as viceroy during his absence. In view of the obvious fiasco of his policies, he relinquished his office to his rival, Felix Kryski, who also supported ambitious plans in the east, but in a more pragmatic manner.

Two years later Zygmunt appointed Gembicki archbishop of Gniezno and primate. A staunch champion of counter-reformation, he was nevertheless a man of wide learning and a patron of the arts. Domestically, he always placed the interests of the church first, while in foreign affairs he favored friendly relations with the Habsburg emperor, peace with Turkey, and an aggressive Moscow policy.

On April 7, 1617, he performed as the chief protagonist of a majestic spectacle held in the Warsaw cathedral. Before handing to Prince Wladyslaw a consecrated sword and standard, he addressed him in a speech that he concluded with the following words:

> The destiny which the Heavens hold in store for you is not for men to probe. If they command you, once elected, to sit on the throne of Moscow, ruling fairly that vast state, may you never forget the land of Piast and Jagiello, the land where your life started, where the ashes of your maternal forefathers rest and where your aged father reigns, the land of the Poles who love you.

Zygmunt III had relinquished at last his own candidacy and allowed Wladyslaw to claim the tsar's throne, pursuant to the Zolkiewski agreement, though the hetman himself declined any cooperation in the enterprise.

Wladyslaw and Jan Karol Chodkiewicz approached Moscow again, but did not enter it, though the one-handed Nowodworski displayed again his skill and courage by blowing up a gate with a petard. They were in a memorable spot—Tuszyn. In 1619 a truce was finally concluded and one of its clauses was Moscow's request for the return of the statue of Saint Nicholas the Miraclemaker, cast in pure gold and studded with jewels. Tsar Szuyski had tried to save it by moving it from Mojaysk to the Kremlin, but the holy relic fell into Polish or Lithuanian hands.

The Commonwealth kept Smolensk and the Sewiersk region, while a diplomatic evasion permitted both rivals to keep the contested title. Michael remained the actual, crowned tsar, but Wladyslaw continued to style himself tsar-elect.

What would have happened if he had become tsar and master of the Kremlin? The nagging question calls for an answer.

Since he had many enemies, his reign might have been brief and have had a sudden ending, as did that of Godunov. Another name would have been added to the long list of assassinated tsars. If that did not happen, however, a Moscow ruled by Wladyslaw would probably enter closer relations with Poland. The central figure, Wladyslaw himself, did not seem to care much for such a turn of history when he eventually became king of Poland. He was not overly fond of Poles or Lithuanians and constantly dreamed about the crown of Sweden. If he had become the tsar, the Commonwealth would have gained an ally of opportunity against Sweden and there would have been less hatred and resentment between Poland and Russia. Moscow would have escaped burning and Pushkin would have been short of a subject. Wladyslaw's reign would have favored western cultural influence in Russia and closer ties between the two nations, surely preferable to the chasm of enmity created by political blunders. The next Vasa king of the Commonwealth, Jan Casimir, would have started his reign earlier.

Leaving speculations aside, let us return to actual events. Bishop Pawel Piasecki insisted that the enlistment of some of the False Dymitr men in the king's army was harmful, as it diminished the disruptive forces in Russia.

The throne of Boris Godunov had shaky foundations, for the extinction of the Rurik dynasty provoked a major crisis in the Muscovite state. The scheming of the pretenders, dishonest and deceitful, exacerbated the situation. Vasili Szuyski could not cope with a congeries of crooks while threatened at the same time by popular uprisings and boyars' plots. The Polish magnates sponsored the impostors, but major national movements cannot be imported.

The crisis was deeply rooted in Russia itself. The Commonwealth had an obvious interest in prolonging the "smuta," a period of chaos weakening a potential enemy. The aggressive action of King Zygmunt III shortened the birth labors of the new order by stimulating a national consolidation and providing it with ready slogans and banners. While contributing indirectly to a strengthening of the Russian state, it also turned the anger of the people against the foreign invader. The king marched eastward in 1609; Michael Romanov, the national candidate, became tsar in February of 1613. It took only four years to terminate the "smuta." The recovery of Smolensk by the Commonwealth was hardly adequate compensation for contributing to the rise of a powerful adversary and to inciting his hostility.

The senators were soon telling the king that at only a fraction of the cost of supporting the first pretender, the Commonwealth could have secured from Boris major concessions. Zygmunt's adventurist delusions did more harm than those of Mniszech and the Wisniowiecki clan.

The idea of conquering the tsardom of Moscow was senseless. It was not enough to take the Kremlin and by doing so help the Swedes to hold Great Novgorod. It also would have been necessary to conquer Nijni Novgorod, Kaluga, Astrachan, Archangel . . . to depopulate the Commonwealth by recruiting garrisons for all the Russian provinces.

The fall of 1611 was rich in ceremonies. On November 5 Jan Zygmunt Hohenzollern, the Elector of Brandenburg, knelt before King Zygmunt III, seated on a high dais on the Krakowskie Przedmiescie avenue of Warsaw. He swore an oath of fealty and accepted a red standard with a white eagle and a parchment document. He was granted Ducal Prussia as his hereditary fief. Its mad prince was still alive, the last of a line to which King Zygmunt the Old had thoughtlessly and needlessly given Konigsberg nearly a century earlier. If the terms of the original grant had been respected, the city and the province would have become Polish. Zygmunt III gave them away to the Electors of Brandenburg, princes of the German Reich. Polish Pomerania was beginning to assume the shape of a "corridor."

How was that possible, when all the previous seyms had stubbornly refused to consider any transfer of fealty? Let us try to understand the psychological motives of that turnabout, visualize the mood of euphoria that made a small city on the Baltic coast appear unimportant.

A week before Warsaw had witnessed a triumph without precedent. In the same main avenue of Krakowskie Przedmiescie an enthusiastic crowd saw "His Majesty's great coach lined with leather and drawn by six horses and in it Tsar Vasili Szuyski in a white gold-braided coat and a tall fur hat." He looked "with a somber and severe stare" at the multitude lining the way. In the senatorial hall of the royal castle the hetman Stanislaw Zolkiewski surrendered him to the king and pleaded in a moving speech for royal mercy and respect for the prisoners. Vasili bowed his bare head, touched the floor with his hand, and kissed his own fingers. Dimitri Szuyski, the ill-fated commander at Kluszyn, touched his forehead to the floor once. His brother Ivan did so three times and wept.

The tsar was prisoner. Smolensk was recaptured, and the Referendary of the Grand Duchy of Lithuania was in command at the Kremlin. In the joyful atmosphere of victory, people hardly noticed that Polish Pomerania was becoming a rather slender neck in the still cautious hand of the Hohenzollern prince.

The Elector of Brandenburg made various promises for the future and in the meantime reinforced the bare royal treasury with three hundred thousand *zlotys*.

Turkey did not appreciate the Commonwealth's moves in Russia. Istanbul remembered well the old plans of Stefan I. Acting probably in accord with the sultan, the prince of Transylvania, Gabriel Batory, curbed Polish influence in Moldavia by removing Constantine Mohila in 1612. He was replaced by a certain Stefan Tomsha, who had previously served in the Hungarian infantry in Poland. Stefan Potocki's attempted private intervention failed and its author found himself prisoner in Turkey for a long time.

The influence of the Commonwealth in the southeast was dwindling precisely at the time when that region was acquiring greater importance. The Dimitriads and Muscovite wars enhanced tremendously the power and self-confidence of the Ukrainian Cossacks. Always highly agile, the Cossacks were seen everywhere, also at Smolensk, Moscow, and even further afield. It was their heroic era at sea as well as on land. Starting in 1606 the Cossacks attacked by sea Varna, Perekop, Trapezund, and Synopa; finally eighty of their light boats landed on the outskirts of Istanbul-Constantinople. The suburbs of Archioka and Mizevna were sacked and burned down, while the sultan Ahmed I watched helplessly. The Cossacks were masters of surprise. They defeated at sea the Turkish fleet sent in pursuit of the raiders and captured the Capudan Pasha, its admiral. This happened in 1615 and only the Persian front held Turkey back from going to war. The diplomats of the Commonwealth promised to restrain the Cossacks of the "Sich" and reduce the number of the "registered" Cossacks, that is those serving the Commonwealth for pay.

Yet when Crown Prince Wladyslaw and the hetman Jan Karol Chodkiewicz went to Moscow for the last time they were helped by Piotr Konaszewicz Sahaydaczny at the head of twenty thousand Zaporozhe Cossacks. No one asked him by what right he had recruited twenty thousand armed men, nor did anyone reproach him for his recent naval expedition against Kaffa. Konaszewicz looted mercilessly Muscovite cities and villages, burned down towns and butchered their population, refusing to go back to the Ukraine.

Sahaydaczny's antics hastened the conclusion of the Dywilin truce, signed in January 1619. In the following year the hetman Piotr Sahaydaczny visited Moscow with a Cossack mission, discussed with the Dyaks (priest) the situation of the Orthodox church in the Commonwealth and then escorted to Busha the patriarch Theophanes, knelt before him, and received absolution of the sins committed while in the king's service.

The Cossack expansion, the loss of the buffer state of Moldavia, and the Turks' rage did not augur well for the immediate future. All these developments occurred during the Dymitriads and the wars with Muscovy.

The troops returning home from the wars were not squadrons or regiments, but rather hordes of savage men inured to violence and plunder. There were among them the unpaid mercenaries from the Inflanty and Smolensk, volunteers who had joined the False Dimitris in the hope of rich booty, Gosiewski's men who left the Kremlin in time, soldiers of the *starost* of Uswiata, who "died in the tsar's chambers at the Kremlin," and many others. The Polish-Lithuanian occupation cost the capital of the tsars nine hundred thousand *rubles* and three hundred thousand *zlotys*. The rebellious troops demanded back pay in the amount of twenty millions. Some reckoned their pay due from 1604, when they left Lubniow with the first Pretender. The defenders of the Kremlin demanded double pay on the ground that noblemen were not obligated to serve "within walls," only in the field. Some of those claiming money joined the mob though they had never seen any action nor any part of Russia.

Confederacies were formed in Lwow, Brest Litovsk, and Bydgoszcz, creating a state within the state and computing the sums allegedly due to them. Their accountants calculated that half the revenue of the royal estates, as well as those of the bishops and abbots, would suffice to pay them off.

It was a return to the methods of Tuszyn and anarchy. No one was safe—neither the cities nor the country mansions, not even the peasants in the fields.

The Seym voted triple taxes and when that was not enough, it imposed taxes increased sixfold in Poland and fivefold in Lithuania. Stefan I could never get even a fraction of such contributions for his victorious wars.

The clergy also paid some of the costs, but only a very small share relative to its resources: three hundred thousand *zlotys*. Yet the Moscow expedition was hailed at the time as a crusade for the holy church. The clergy could surely have given more, if Bishop Gembicki alone contributed fifty thousand, without being unduly impoverished. Witness the splendor of his court and the affluence of his relatives whom he promoted.

In 1613 the Seym held two sessions. An important role was played by the castellan of Poznan, Jan Ostrorog, an independent politician without royalist ties. He managed to push through a resolution distasteful to many, but one which saved the country from a civil war. Voices demanding a new "rokosh" and dethronement already had been heard.

The legislation enacted with Ostrorog's help stated that the king would not be authorized in the future to declare war without the consent of the Seym and without explaining his motives to the county councils. It was another shackle on the nation's foreign policy, which was to weigh heavily on Zygmunt's son and successor. The hard-core pacifism of the gentry was becoming an allergy.

The second parliamentary session of 1613 was attended by four delegates of the confederacies, accompanied by many of their armed members. They were treated in Warsaw with much respect and some degree of fear.

"At night, in the dark, anything would pass, one was free to slash or kill without any questions asked. There was a saying at the time, heard whenever one of our men was engaged in some mischief, 'Seven thousand follow him, so let's leave him alone,' because that was the strength of our army."

The gentry and even the magnates were rather easily intimidated. The four "delegates" of the confederacies were assigned by the royal quartermaster five rooms on Mostowa street in a house previously rented by Prince Korecki. Although he had paid his rent in advance, the prince did not object to his new guests. Yet Mikolaj Zebrzydowski was mortally offended when, before the "rokosh," the king denied him accommodation at Wawel Castle in Cracow.

One can speculate that if the Commonwealth had been ruled by one of the Valois or Bourbons, he would have become the leader of the confederated soldiery and carried out a coup. Charles of Suderman or Gustav Adolph would probably have done the same thing. It was Poland's bad luck to get the least able member of the house of Vasa. Already in 1606 Zygmunt tried to threaten the Seym with force, but in the most inept manner. He had in Warsaw two thousand cavalry under Chodkiewicz and Weyher's German infantry. The ground floor and the cellars of the castle were full of armed men.

A decisive monarch might have used yet another weapon, if he knew how to seize the right moment. Piotr Konaszewicz Sahaydaczny had marched to Moscow, sailed to Kaffa. At the king's order he could find his way to Warsaw. Twenty thousand Zaporozhe Cossacks was a force to be reckoned with. The Confederates had only seven thousand, which enabled them to extort fabulous sums of money, recognized already by the ancients as the main instrument of policy.

Oddly enough, the pacifist gentry produced an abundance of first-rate soldiers. Let us examine the roll call of the successive commanders of the Lisowski brotherhood of the red and black banner: Lisowski, Czaplinski, Rogowski, Kleczkowski, Rusinowski, Strojnowski, Kalinowski, Noskowski, Gromadzki—most of them natives of the central provinces of Poland.

The country's population was growing rapidly, especially among the gentry, as the infant mortality was lower in the more prosperous families. There was often not enough land in the family to leave a good farm for all the sons. Some of the smallholders' farms were purchased by the magnates, not only in the eastern provinces, but also in Poland's heartland. The princes Zbaraski acquired estates in Pilica, Konska Wola, and Solec. Fields of rye sometimes had to make room for Italian gardens. The number of young noblemen without land or employment was growing and most of them sought military careers wherever they could be found, even in Turkey or in the army of Michael the Valiant, fighting against Jan Zamoyski. Many of the soldiers at Tuszyn and the Kremlin were such sons of the lesser gentry. They could have provided the king with a loyal force, at a far lesser cost than his vast grants to the magnates.

Zygmunt III was aware of the problem; he even wrote to Zamoyski about the swarms of restless youths raring for a fight. Yet he failed to turn their energy to the crown's advantage, but permitted them to join the pretenders in dubious adventures that did not serve the national interest.

After collecting the pay they had sought as their due, the veterans of the Muscovite wars solemnly burned the act of the Confederacy in April 1614 in the Lwow cathedral. Only some marauding bands were left, but they were soon under control. One of them was crushed at Halicz by Stanislaw Koniecpolski, another rising star of the military arts. The gang leaders were promptly impaled. Barbaric oriental customs were part of the heritage of the expeditions to the east, as was the demoralization of the troops.

Before finally dissolving their association, the Confederates pondered the disposition of their main booty. Let us hear again our friend from Kluszyn and the Seym misadventures, Maskiewicz: "We had heaps of booty from service within the walls in Moscow, but were not too happy about it, for we preferred ready cash. We offered to sell it to the king, he refused; to the Christian emperor, the princes of Brandenburg, the German Reich, the Gdansk burghers and everyone else we could think of. All was for nothing, so we decided to split the jewels among ourselves. Two crowns were broken up: one of Fyodor and the other Dimitri's; also a hussar's saddle set in gold and stones; three unicorns, but one of the horns remained intact with jewels. It went to Gosiewski and Dunkowski for their service within the walls, with a sapphire from the crown, two fingers thick, worth twenty-eight thousand *zlotys*. The stone alone was valued here at four thousand *zlotys* and in Moscow at ten thousand *rubles*, for their prices are higher, especially for diamonds. I got myself three diamonds, four rubies, gold for a hundred *zlotys*, two pieces of unicorn . . . worth three hundred *zlotys*.

Soon after the ex-confederate purchased at the Rzeszow fair two fine grizzled horses. They must have been good, for he traded in his "grey Samogitians" for one hundred twenty *zlotys*.

A year before, a crown carrying no tradition was placed on the brow of Michael Romanov. After the surrender of the Kremlin it was found in the sack of one of the Polish or Lithuanian starvlings.

VIII

"The entire Roman Empire and all the Christian realms and duchies were outraged by the reprehensible and disgraceful deed of two men of Czech origin and high estate, who acted in a shameful and unprecedented manner by throwing from a window into a deep moat two envoys of His Majesty, high dignitaries of Bohemia."

The famous Prague defenestration took place on May 23, 1618. It triggered a Czech national insurrection, which became the first stage of the Thirty Years' War, fought mainly in Germany. The pretext of a contest between the Catholic and Protestant camps provided an opportunity for a confrontation between the leading powers of Europe. The rising modern states were trying to build foundations for their future.

The document just quoted continued:

> Count Martinic, as he was falling, uttered ceaselessly the names of Jesus and Mary. He landed softly on the ground and thanks to the intervention of Virgin Mary suffered no injury despite his girth. Some devout and trustworthy people testified that they were passing in a procession over a nearby bridge and saw the Holy Mother of God supporting the falling man with her cloak and thus saving him from injury. Count Martinic did not see it, but during his fall he had a vision of heaven opening and the Lord welcoming him to eternal bliss. One of the knights, Ulrich Kinsky, sneered as he was throwing him: "Let us see whether his Mary will help him," and when he saw Count Martinic sitting on the ground unharmed, he cried: "I swear to God that Mary did indeed come to his rescue."

The Czechs rebelled when the none-too-tolerant, but still bearable Emperor Matthew gave them for king, Ferdinand, the brother of two queens of Poland, the late Anna and the still-living Constance. The archduke and, since 1619, Emperor Ferdinand, raised since his youth "in virtue and desire of eternal salvation," was a man of firm convictions, witness these excerpts from his letters, written long before the coronation:

"I would rather lose the country and its people, left in one shirt, than agree to any concessions harmful to religion . . . . I received the list of the game killed; there was quite a lot but, frankly, I had feared that the losses might be worse. I would rather see dead as many Protestant preachers or rebel leaders."

The ideological war was conducted with appropriate methods. The Swedish Council of State received an extensive report about the capture of Magdeburg by the Catholic side:

"The enemy treated the Evangelic pastors worst; they were killed in their own libraries and then burnt together with the books. Their wives and daughters were dragged behind horses to the camp, where they were raped and horribly mutilated. St. John's church was filled with women, then locked from the outside and set on fire. The Croats and Wallons were particularly cruel, they tossed children into the fire, the women of highest station and those most comely were attached to the riders' stirrups, so that they had to run with their horses; they spiked babies on their lances and after swinging them around a few times threw them into flames. Turks, Tartars and pagans could not have been worse."

The other side was not far behind. After the battle of Breitenfeld, Gustav Adolph, king of Sweden, "Thanked God for such a glorious victory, which served well the Protestant cause and swore that he had no other desire than the glory of the Lord, maintenance of Evangelic peace, freedom and prosperity for all countries under his guidance. He affirmed that he did not desire even a rod of land and would rather have the devil take him (which God forbid) than have even a particle of it cling to his cape. As he said so, he beat his breast with fervor."

Yet Sweden won in the Thirty Years' War Wismar and the estuaries of the three main rivers of Germany: the Weser, Elbe, and Oder, including Stettin (Szczecin). It was entering the brigand period of its history, a path that invited living off plunder and seeking ever new quarry.

Bidding farewell to his country, Gustav Adolph spoke as the most devout Protestant minister. As soon as he was abroad, on the Continent, he accepted from Catholic France a subsidy of a million *livres* a year. After his death, Cardinal Mazarin, the author of the foreign policy of "the eldest daughter of the church," wrote in an official document:

> The confidence which the Swedish lords place in the constant and total support of the allied cause by France could not be more justified or better founded. You can assure them that His Majesty will never abandon them and will only lay down arms when universal peace is attained.

This policy brought immense benefits to France, a Catholic power, which finally even gave armed support to the Protestant side. It was the great triumph of Paris diplomacy, never repeated again.

> . . . by the will and consent of the Electors, princes and estates of the Reich and in the interest of peace, it is resolved first that the sovereignty and full authority over the dioceses of Metz, Toul and Verdun, with the cities of the same name, which had hitherto belonged to the Roman Empire, will henceforth be vested in perpetuity and irrevocably in the crown of France. . . .

Alsace was another gain. But territorial acquisitions were not the main advantage won by France. The modern French historian Pierre Lafue writes: "The treaty of Westphalia of 1648 created in Germany over two thousand enclaves, republics, dioceses, duchies, and other entities, erecting a system of such complexity that it was called by the geographers "Calvary."

Cardinal Mazarin spent the staggering sum of three hundred million *livres* to secure the breakup of Germany into a multitude of separate principalities with hundreds of local rulers. The resulting chaos and corruption ensured France's security for centuries to come.

The Habsburgs consolidated their rule in the hereditary lands of their dynasty and in depopulated Bohemia, but they failed to achieve their main goal of turning Germany into a single monarchy. Zygmunt III supported the emperor's policy, which threatened Poland with the greatest danger. The Commonwealth should have formed a second front against the Habsburgs, instead of which it absorbed

225

the Swedish attacks meant for them and those of Turkey, which sided with the Protestants.

The posture of the majority of the gentry prevented at least the worst alternative—active support of Austria.

Nevertheless the Commonwealth was actually in the Habsburg camp. Aside from the earlier manifestations of friendship, two dynastic marriages and the honor of being the emperor's son-in-law, Zygmunt had tied Poland to Vienna by a new treaty concluded in 1613. The primate Gembicki openly opposed the Czech insurgents, thus helping the emperor and the youngest of his many brothers, Archduke Charles Habsburg, then the bishop of Wroclaw. All the adversaries of Emperor Ferdinand had to be suspicious of Warsaw and take against it political insurance. King Zygmunt actually helped them to do so.

The Commonwealth was only beginning to pay for the past thirty years of the royal doctrinaire's reign. It was at war with Sweden, which the Protestants wanted to bring into the German theatre of operations. The counter-reformation and its beloved offspring, the Brzesc union with Rome of a segment of the Orthodox population of the Commonwealth, had significantly weakened the moral bond holding together a multiethnic state. The loyalty of the non-Catholics, unquestioned under King Stefan, was increasingly in doubt. The Protestants and the Orthodox began to form a common front. Its leaders, among them the bishops of the Greek rite deprived of a legal political role, began to communicate without any scruple with foreign powers. It was an era when national identity was often defined by religious allegiance, which exerted a powerful influence on political orientation. This was particularly true in eastern Europe, where it would be indeed difficult, for example, to draw a line of ethnic or racial division between Ruthenia and Muscovy. They both used in their worship a Bulgarian dialect known as "Church Slavic."

The rapprochement between dissident groups within the Commonwealth was paralleled by events outside it. There was a trend toward a cooperation of the Protestants with all of the non-Catholics, which could find a political expression in plans for a coalition embracing Transylvania, Moscow, Sweden, and Turkey, opposing the easternmost bastion of counter-reformation, that is the Commonwealth.

226

The instructions given by the Vatican secretary of state to a nuncio assigned to Warsaw were quite clear:

"Poland is surrounded on almost all sides by enemies of the Catholic faith: Muslims, heretics, schismatics . . . . The king, the bishops, senators and ministers should therefore watch carefully the borders and prevent heresy from penetrating from them to the center. They should keep out foreigners and preachers spreading heresy, but support the missions and everything the clergy may devise for strengthening the faith. It is certain that the confusion of minds caused by the dissident sects caused discord among the citizens, which brought about insubordination, rebellion and ultimately damage to the power and authority of the kind and the Commonwealth."

The diagnosis was in error, though it has been often repeated even until our time. The harm was done by abandoning the ancient native tradition of pluralism allowing tolerance of other faiths and ethnicities, ensuring their harmonious coexistence. The main problem was not that of the new sects, but of the mossbacked Orthodox church, antedating Luther and Calvin by centuries.

The teachings of the fanatical clergy inspired by the counterreformation resulted in incidents such as the message sent in 1622 to the Kremlin by the Orthodox bishop of Przemysl, Isaiah Kopinski. He appealed for funds for a monastery and wrote: ". . . the Orthodox Christians and all the Zaporozhe Cossacks are ready to accept the sovereignty of Moscow because of the oppression by the Poles of the Orthodox church." Four years later Gustav Adolph promoted the same idea. There were plans of separating the Zaporozhe from the Commonwealth and establishing it as a republic under the protectorate of neighboring states. There was a tendency in Poland to treat the Cossacks as a parochial problem of a gang of brigands. Yet that problem evinced serious interest among the diplomats of the emperor, the Netherlands, England, France, Sweden, Transylvania, Turkey, and Muscovy. It had, in fact, wide European repercussions.

The foreign policy of the Kremlin was directed at the time by the patriarch Filaret, finally released from Malbork castle under the terms of the Dywillin truce. He heartily hated the Catholics, whom he described as "dogs and known enemies of God." The Kremlin, however, advised caution and waiting for an opportune moment, while others were doing its work.

227

An important role was played by a Cypriot Greek, Cyril Lukaris, the patriarch of Alexandria and since 1621 that of Constantinople (removed from office and reinstated several times by the Turks, to be finally strangled at the sultan's order). He knew the Commonwealth well. He had taught in the Orthodox schools of Ostrog and Wilno; he was present in Brzesc at the time of the union of the churches, which he naturally opposed. Lukaris encouraged the resistance to the union of Prince Constantine Ostrogski, enjoyed popularity among the Cossacks and was by conviction, almost openly, a Protestant. His writings were later condemned by Orthodox synods as heresy.

His Protestant leanings helped his contacts with the ambassadors of Protestant nations accredited in Istanbul. Lukaris promised them that he would incite the Cossacks to revolt against Poland. The leading western diplomat in Istanbul was the Dutch envoy Cornelius Haga, who had resided in Turkey for ten years and was thoroughly familiar with local conditions. He was the moving spirit of the plots aimed against the Commonwealth. The Habsburgs, with whom Zygmunt III had cordial relations, were the chief enemies of the independence of the Netherlands, thus making Ambassador Haga Poland's adversary. Had Warsaw pursued a different policy, he could be the Commonwealth's ally.

The Polish gentry's dislike of Austria, bordering on hatred, its tendency to separate policy from ideology, and its suspicions of the Vatican diplomacy were all sound principles. They were advocated by the better informed members of the Zebrzydowski "rokosh" movement, but rejected by the official policy of the crown. The Commonwealth did not oppose the Habsburgs in a second front and was thus forced into the position of a buffer state protecting Austria.

The Czechs called to their throne Frederick, the Elector of the Palatinate, later called the "winter king." Their situation improved considerably when a vassal of Turkey, Gabriel Bethlen, prince of Transylvania, incited in northern Hungary an uprising against the emperor, seized Koszyce and Presburg, finally besieging Vienna with the help of Czech forces.

Poland came to the rescue of Ferdinand. In view of the Turkish threat and the domestic opposition, Zygmunt III could not act overtly. He allowed, however, with the consent of part of the senate, the recruitment of Lisowski's men and their funding. Hieronim Kleczkowski, the head of the Lisowski brotherhood at the time, crossed the Carpathians with ten thousand of the best cavalry in Europe. On November 13, 1619, he crushed the Hungarians at Humien. The Lisowski horsemen were first-rate fighters as well as robbers and rapists. They reportedly killed seven thousand Hungarians and saved the emperor. Gabriel Bethlen lifted the siege of Vienna and the Lisowski units returned from Hungary to southern Poland, which they started plundering. The gentry of the ravaged province raised an outcry and the opposition took up their cause, helped by the princes Jerzy and Krzysztof Zbaraski, skilled in political advocacy. One of the pamphlets published at that time asserted that "the emperor will hold out with our help and defeat the Hungarians and Lutherans, on the other side the English and the Spaniards will take the Netherlands and we shall have Catholic faith, but as slaves of the Germans." That was a future threat, but the Turkish one was more immediate.

As soon as he left the ramparts of Vienna, Bethlen wrote to the sultan in Istanbul, representing the king of Poland as an ally of the emperor and Spain, bent on the destruction of Islam. Relations with Turkey, tense for some time, reached a crisis.

The young and bloodthirsty Sultan Osman II declared in the beginning of 1620 that anyone trying to dissuade him from war with Lechistan (Poland) would be hanged. In August the Cossacks captured Varna again and set it on fire. The recent agreement with Zolkiewski prohibited Cossack expeditions in the Black Sea, but the Cossack leaders argued that the letter of the treaty referred only to raids starting at the mouth of the Dniester, not those from other rivers.

Stanislaw Zolkiewski—by then not only hetman, but also chancellor of the crown—was seventy-three and his failing strength compelled him to apologize to the king for addressing the senate while remaining seated. There was some inconsistency about his positions at the time. On the one hand he warned against the Turkish threat and advised caution, but on the other he tolerated Zygmunt's pro-Habsburg moves (except for the Lisowski expedition). The old man carried out faithfully Warsaw's instructions, which probably motivated his decisions in the late summer of 1620.

Iskander Pasha crossed the Danube and joined forces with Kantimir Mirza, chief of the Budiak Tartars. They were ordered by the sultan to depose and punish the Hospodar of Moldavia, Caspar Gratiani, who sided with the Commonwealth. The army they headed exceeded by far the force needed for that mission and it was clear that they had other goals in mind after dealing with Gratiani. The sultan's open letter to King Zygmunt promised the leveling of Cracow and the extirpation of Christianity in Poland.

The Commonwealth forces, meager for want of time and money, had two options. One was to hold the line of the Dniestr, sending into the foreground Koniecpolski, eager to assume that task. The other was to cross the river and advance into Moldavia. The hetman chose the latter.

His decision may have been influenced by various factors, but many historians believe that the advice of "court counsellors" was decisive. They were afraid that the pasha would not attempt to force the defended line of the Dniester river, but turn instead westward against the emperor. Gratiani, who intercepted and sent to Warsaw Gabriel Bethlen's correspondence with the sultan, was compromised by Andrew Lipski, vice-chancellor of the crown. He sent to Bethlen one of his own letters, with bitter reproaches, revealing at the same time how he obtained it. Lipski's naivete as a politician and senior official was incredible. He was appointed vice-chancellor through the queen's influence and "being indebted to her, was strongly pro-Austrian." According to students of the period, Zolkiewski ordered the crossing of the Dniester immediately after receiving Lipski's message.

On September 2, 1620, an army eight-thousand strong crossed the river. The Cossacks defaulted, as their leadership was temporarily under the influence of a faction headed by Jacek Nierodowicz, nicknamed Borodawka, who was hostile to Poland. But there was among the few Cossacks who joined Zolkiewski a young man by the name of Bohdan Chmielnicki. The hetman encountered the Hospodar of Moldavia as he was fleeing to Poland and persuaded him to join his force. But instead of fifteen thousand or more, the Moldavian prince brought with him only six hundred men. The rest fled when they heard that Iskander Pasha was on the march.

Zolkiewski set camp on the same site near Cecora at which he had fought in a victorious battle under Zamoyski a quarter of a century earlier. He began to fend off enemy attacks on September 18. Two days later Gratiani sneaked out of the camp with some of the troops. The Polish force began a retreat toward the Dniester across steppes set on fire by the enemy. The border was close when the weary commander found a moment to write a letter which read in part:

> Gracious lady and my beloved and ever dear spouse. . . . Some kind of mutiny seems to be brewing in my camp, with a few of the knights plotting their own perdition by abandoning the cause, from which I barely restrained them. Iskander Pasha and Galga don't want to hear abut any negotiations and are readying for a major battle. But do not worry, my dearest wife, God will guard us; and even if I fall, I am old and of little more use to the Commonwealth, but the omnipotent Lord will see to it that our son, heir to his father's sword, will whet it on the pagans' necks and, even if what I said should pass, will revenge his father's blood. If that should happen, I entrust to my dearly beloved spouse the care and love of the children, the burial of my body worn out in the service of the country. . . . What God may grant so be it; may His holy will be done until the end of our lives, so I recommend myself to the prayers of my beloved lady wife and urge our children to always remember the Lord.
> At the camp near Cecora, *die 6 Octobris.*
> Yours unto death loving husband and father,
> Stanislaw Zolkiewski, Grand Hetman of the Crown.

Immediately after the writing of these words, the end came in the night of October 6. Panic broke out in the camp when some Polish soldiers who had lagged behind to get hay for their horses rejoined the camp after dark and were mistakenly taken for Tartars. The grooms unharnessed the horses from the wagons and rushed toward the Dniester carrying their loot. Chaos swept the camp and the Tartars had an easy task.

Kantimir Mirza sent Stanislaw Zolkiewski's head to Istanbul, where it was hung on a gate that the sultan passed every day on his way to the mosque. He could contemplate daily the trophy, with an open wound over the right ear. The body, with the right arm cut off, was left on the battlefield. The hetman of the crown had fought to the last.

On October 19 the Tartars reached Lwow, defended by a pitifully small force under Stanislaw Lubomirski. The Bernardine monks defended their monastery with muskets in hand. The city was not taken, but its environs were sacked and swept clean by the invaders.

The fears of the court counsellors never came true and Iskander Pasha did not attack the emperor. A month after Zolkiewski's death, on November 8, 1620, the army of Ferdinand II defeated the Czechs at Biala Gora (White Mountain), one hour's ride distant from Prague. An important role in the battle was played by the Lisowski contingent, which broke the Hungarian cavalry, drove it into the Czech ranks, and captured the standard of the "winter king."

The emperor's victory and the reprisals that followed reduced the population of Bohemia from four million to eight hundred thousand. The rule of the counter-reformation on the Vltava was not matched in brutality until Adolph Hitler's conquest of central and eastern Europe.

The November session of the Seym was held in Warsaw in an atmosphere of fear. It was obvious that Sultan Osman was going to return next year to complete his work. The capital was seized by hysteria when Michael Piekarski, a minor squire, wounded the king with a hatchet on his way to the Sunday service in the cathedral. The culprit was executed publicly after hideous tortures, but never revealed any confederates. He had none, for he was mentally unbalanced and officially declared incompetent, which was the reason for his grudge against the king.

The Seym voted unprecedented taxes, increased eightfold. Efforts to secure outside assistance proved fruitless. Ferdinand II was happy to see the sultan engaged outside Austria. The pope promised a subsidy of ten thousand *zlotys* a month, but the pay of the army amounted to a million *zlotys* every four weeks. Besides, the Vatican money did not arrive until after the war.

The sultan—the theoretical protector and actual political boss of the Orthodox patriarch of Constantinople—was to strike from the southeast, entering first the provinces of the Commonwealth inhabited mainly by an Orthodox population. Zygmunt III accordingly appealed to the patriarch Theophanes, who had just revived illegally the Orthodox hierarchy in Kiev. He asked him for moral support. Theophanes responded by a message addressed to the "glorious hetman, the senior officers and valiant Cossack warriors," whom he urged to defend Christianity and demand the royal approval of "your holy Ruthenian hierarchy in the Orthodox church."

The Orthodox deputies in the Seym called for a new Ukrainian policy, on the ground that at least half of the army facing the Turks would be Ruthenians. The Seym was willing to consider their request, but "the eagerness of the nuncio and the king's piety frustrated the endeavors of those opposing the union of the Catholic and Orthodox churches."

In June 1621 a tumultuous Cossack convention held in Fastow resolved to assist the Commonwealth. These were great days for the Sich of the Zaporozhe ("Sich" was the name of the Cossack community and "Zaporozhe" meant the part of the Dnieper basin below the rapids). The royal envoy mounted a dais built of barrels covered with carpets, while gun salvoes thundered and the ecstatic Jacek Borodawka cried: "Poland, Turkey, all the world trembles before the arms of the Zaporozhe." Anyone who witnessed such events could never return again to serfdom. The treatment of the Zaporozhe Cossacks by the Commonwealth was characterized by hypocrisy and shortsightedness. The Cossacks were courted in moments of danger, but as soon as the threat subsided they were maltreated or at least curbed.

Hundreds of Orthodox clergy participated in the Fastow convention. The first day was filled by their complaints and only later Piotr Konaszewicz Sahaydaczny assumed leadership and induced the Cossacks to follow him to the Commonwealth side. He then went on a mission to Warsaw, accompanied by three other delegates of the Sich. The content of their conversation with the king is unknown, but Zygmunt probably made some insincere promises, for the Cossack leader left the capital "very pleased."

In the meantime Jacek Borodawka discovered sacrilege in Biala Cerkiew. A desecrated likeness of Christ was "found" in the home of the richest Jew in that town. The enraged ataman (title of Cossack commander, equivalent to the Polish "hetman") responded by authorizing his men to plunder Jews throughout the Ukraine.

Sahaydaczny aligned the Cossack army against the Turks. The forces of the other two national components of the *de facto* tri-ethnic state were under the command of a Lithuanian. The night of October 6 had robbed the Commonwealth of both its military leaders. The great hetman of the crown was dead, while the field hetman, Stanislaw Koniecpolski, who also fought to the last, was wounded by an arrow and taken prisoner.

Hetman Jan Karol Chodkiewicz was much younger than

Zolkiewski, but at sixty his health was ruined. The hardships of war and the episodes of wild anger sapped the strength of an epileptic, whose tutor used to cover his eyes whenever an attack was approaching. The new marriage of the veteran soldier may have been the last straw. The widowed hetman married on November 24 Anna Ostrogska, aged twenty. He did not want to die without a male heir. His only son, Hieronim, died in childhood. The old soldier's dream was never fulfilled.

Chodkiewicz led his army to the Dniester and made there a very bold move. He crossed to the right bank of the river and set up a crescent-shaped encampment in front of the Chocim castle, with the river behind his back, cutting off the way of retreat. The purpose of this strange disposition of forces was to convince the Cossacks that the Poles and Lithuanians intended to fight and would not let them bear the brunt of the battle.

The river crossing was made possible by a Ruthenian of unknown name, a "simple and shabby looking man," who undertook to build a permanent bridge in a few days and kept his word. He "placed fairly heavy pillars in the water aslant, in pairs, binding them at the bottom with a third, thinner beam" and built the roadway on them. The homespun engineer was paid a hundred *zlotys* for his work. A hussar of noble birth was paid thirty *zlotys* a month, an enlisted man, fifteen. Rank and file Cossacks at Fastow received one *zloty* for two of them, but their main interest was in the booty.

The Cossacks arrived at the scene at the same time as the Turks. Sahaydaczny even encountered accidentally on the way the sultan's camp and was wounded by a shot, which did not take him out of action but cost him his life soon afterward.

The defense of Chocim displayed the fighting skills of the Cossacks, but they had competition, for the Polish and Lithuanian troops also gave a good account of themselves. The Lisowski men fought gallantly, as they had done at Cecora a year earlier (only a part of them had gone to Hungary and Biala Gora; the rest, under Walenty Rogawski, joined the Zolkiewski command).

On September 24, 1621, Jan Karol Chodkiewicz died at the Chocim castle, exhausted by recurrent epileptic attacks, which nevertheless did not prevent him from taking an active part in the battle. In the last days of his life he was disabled, but his mind remained alert. Unable to speak, he silently passed his hetman's

234

baton to Stanislaw Lubomirski, thus entrusting him with the command. The presence in the camp of the twenty-five-year-old Prince Wladyslaw was helpful. Some Lithuanians did not relish the idea of serving under a Pole, who did not even have official hetman rank, but the authority of the king's son dispelled their objections. This was all the more noteworthy as Wladyslaw was not formally heir to the throne, which had been elective for a long time. He had no official standing, but did represent the prestige of the crown. He was also well liked by the Cossacks, who had known him well since the Moscow expedition.

The troops learned about Chodkiewicz's death from the Turks, who spread the news secured by their spies. Lubomirski repelled two more assaults, backed by enemy artillery fire from both banks of the Dniester. On October 9 1621, a treaty was signed: the sultan promised to restrain the Tartar attacks, while Poland undertook to hold back the Cossacks. The Commonwealth implicitly renounced its sovereignty over Moldavia and promised to continue the "pay" of the Tartar troops, but refused the request for "gifts" to the sultan, which would have amounted to a tribute. Finally the Polish envoys paid their respects to the sultan, but they kept their heads covered. Thus both frontiers and honor were saved.

Each of the two armies went on its way. Lubomirski's men wading through early snow were a sorry sight. The Chocim garrison had gone hungry for a long time and was down to its last barrel of powder at the time of the cease-fire.

The French physician loaned to Sahaydaczny by Crown Prince Wladyslaw could not save him and the Cossack ataman died in the spring of 1622.

The Commonwealth managed to come out unharmed in the south. In the meantime, Gustav Adolph seized the opportunity in the north, landed with an army of twenty thousand and took Riga, Dyament, and Mitawa. The latter was soon recovered by Krzysztof Radziwill, field hetman of Lithuania, but he could do no more with his meager two thousand men—the rest had gone south with Chodkiewicz. The estuary of the Dzwina, for which Zygmunt August was the first to fight, was lost to the Grand Duchy forever.

Matters might have taken a much worse turn if the Kremlin had listened to the advice of Cyril Lukaris and attacked simultaneously with the sultan. Moscow still felt too weak and replied to the patriarch that it would act only if the king of Poland should break the peace. For the time being the Commonwealth was spared a third front.

Peace with Turkey, maintained with some effort since the days of Zygmunt the Old, had been broken and the green banner of the Prophet became a familiar sight to Polish soldiers. Let us cast a glance at that exotic world that attracted Poland's attention, bewitched her with its color, and exerted a cultural influence. Fortunately the members of the Polish embassy, sent to the Bosphorus to negotiate a confirmation of the treaty of Chocim, left no less than three separate diaries and memoirs. Two of them were in prose and the third in verse. One of the ambassador's aides was a poet, Samuel Twardowski, author of the *Embassy of His Highness Prince Christopher Zbaraski, Master of Horse to the King, from His Majesty Zygmunt III to the Turkish Emperor Mustapha*. Excerpts of this work have been included in the recently published anthology *The Poets of the Polish Baroque*. Thus we can see through contemporary eyes the Ottoman empire of the seventeenth century.

Prince Zbaraski, a former pupil of Galileo, was "given to literary pursuits" in his palace of Konska Wola and was reached there by the royal call to a diplomatic mission. The prince knew that he would be dealing with a new sultan, as the previous one, together with his Grand Vizier, was liquidated by a palace coup. The Janissaries, neglected by the ruler, suddenly surrounded the seraglio and dragged the sultan from the closet in which he was trying to hide. Osman was reportedly beheaded by Mustapha, his successor.

The sumptuous retinue of Prince Zbaraski traveled across Bulgaria, the inhabitants of which "regarded themselves as kinsmen of the Poles." The journey was rendered arduous by the horrible stench of countless corpses scattered along the highway. They were the victims of an epidemic of plague ". . . and the Turks are so blind that they regard the plague as an ordinary affliction and the death which it brings as a natural event, predestined and inevitable." He saw along the Black Sea "lands once fertile and populous, now empty and bleak, coated with the rusty mold of an all-embracing tyranny." In Adrianopol he admired the powerful columns of stone, which Osman had ordered carved to mark the new boundary of his empire—on the Baltic. In Istanbul the visitors caught only a glimpse of the Haga Sophia and Suleiman's Mosque, adorned with booty taken from Louis Jagiello in the battle of Mohacz.

The splendor of the ambassador's retinue impressed the capital

236

and his lavish gifts dazzled the sultan and his court. The prince, long a student in the land of Machiavelli, understood the use of opulence as a psychological weapon and knew that "pride without courage can only be curbed by fearless audacity." He reminded the hostile vizier of the recent plots and massacres, hinting that he could find his way to the Janissaries. Actually they were about to threaten the ambassador himself.

The Grand Vizier whispered to the guards demanding their pay that it was all the fault of the Lechistan's envoy, slow in paying the tribute to the sultan. The screaming soldiers rushed into the streets and the Polish embassy staff barricaded their house as night was falling:

> . . . we were getting ready to sell dearly our lives. Some were making excuses to God through their confessors, when pleasant music was heard outside the windows: the door opened and admitted Circassian maidens, who dropped their cloaks, revealing bodies and faces of the greatest beauty. Their shapely breasts could be seen through the translucent muslin, elaborate gold bands with jewels held their hair. Their faces were artfully painted, even the eyelashes of their large black eyes, and their tiny feet shod in morocco shoes. They had cithers and started singing a ballad about a princess sitting by the sea and mourning her country. Prince Zbaraski calmly listened to their song and watched their dance, then sent them away with generous reward.
>
> No one knew who sent the houris and why—was it to sweeten the last hours of our lives or to distract our attention?

In the morning a mounted Turk knocked at the gate, asking for baksheesh for bringing good news. The Janissaries had forced the sultan to change the vizier and elevate to that position Hussein Pasha, who was friendly toward Lechistan. The newly appointed dignitary had already paid homage to the monarch. He bent down and lifted a curtain, behind which the embalmed heads of the previous strangled and beheaded viziers were resting on cushions.

"May my head also rest there," he said, "if I do not serve you faithfully."

The sultan handed him the great seal and gave him a caftan as a token of his favor.

237

Samuel Twardowski described in poetic detail the festivities celebrating the appointment of a new vizier:

> The ceremonies last all of three days
> Hence the Turks have a saying
> Which subtly hints that three days
> Is the full term of a vizier's office.
>
> In truth few dawdle in that office
> As soon as another reaches the Divan
> They overthrow him for one reason or another
> And kill him if he does not reach a boat in time.
>
> Hussein, a man sensitive in such matters
> Always had boats ready in the Bosphor
> Which, when he sensed trouble, he loaded with gold
> And promptly took to sea on his way to Egypt.

It was with Hussein that Zbaraski reached agreement on the Chocim treaty. Relations with Turkey were to return to what they had been under the late Jagiellonians. Dniester would be the natural boundary between two peacefully disposed powers.

At the last meeting Zbaraski took out of a gold box the original of the former treaties between Poland and Turkey, which he had thoughtfully brought along. The Turkish dignitaries, deeply moved, crowded around him, eager to touch the parchment that had been handled by Suleiman the Magnificent himself. Here are the closing words of the pact concluded by the Lawgiver and Zygmunt the Old:

> I am seventy and you are old, too, the threads of our lives are running out. We shall soon meet in happier lands, where we shall sit, sated with fame and glory, next to the Highest, I on his right hand and you on his left, talking about our friendship. Your envoy, Opalinski, will tell you in what happiness he saw your sister and my wife. I commend him warmly to Your Majesty. Fare well.

The "sister" of Zygmunt was Roxolane, the beautiful daughter of an Orthodox priest of Rohatyn, seized by Tartar raiders and taken in shackles to Istanbul, to a career out of "A Thousand and One Nights."

Hussein Pasha must have been a reasonable man, for he told

Zbaraski: "What would it profit us to acquire more desert lands, most of the Ottoman empire is desert already, so we should settle it first before trying to get more from others. . . . Let us therefore live in peace."

The ebullient seventeenth century was rich enough to offer to one man a range of impressions from Galileo's study to the Ottoman court.

The envoy of the Commonwealth received substantial assistance from the ambassadors of England and France, who had a hand in the timely palace coup. Their governments wanted Turkey to leave Poland alone, so as to be able to turn against the Habsburg empire. The Thirty Years' War was still on.

Returning to his quarters, Zbaraski was delighted to find there several emaciated men with long beards, and sores left by chains on their legs. They were the leading prisoners captured by the Turks at the time of Zolkiewski's defeat and now released—but at a price. A ransom of fifty thousand *thalers* was requested and the ambassador's purse was by then depleted. He therefore ordered all his valuables, even the table cutlery, to be taken to the mint to be converted into money.

"It was sad to see," reported an eyewitness, "precious cups, gold beakers and mugs adorned with jewels, ornate basins and jugs, all the treasures of the ancient Zbaraski clan, so much antiquity and fine art broken up with heavy hammers and melted."

Zbaraski was later criticized for splurging too much and spoiling the Turks, who began to expect similar lavish generosity from other envoys. The prince himself paid all the expenses of his fabulous mission. Only the gifts for the sultan and his mother were supplied by the king. The precious ermine pelts, in bundles of forty, the "marvelously worked" marine compass, the various clocks (one of them with "goldfeathered parrots"), silver flasks, gold cups, a thousand Indian gold coins, capes of gold-threaded samite, mirrors, amber, "precious fragrances, delicious juices," bejewelled chessmen for the ladies of the harem, silver and gold trays for sweetmeats, cups for sherbets and coffee, Podolian greyhounds for hunters, guns with ebony butts, and countless other valuable gifts were supplied by the magnate himself, even though he was in opposition to the monarch he was representing. He paid, of course, all the expenses of his retinue. This was not unusual, for Zamoyski, Chodkiewicz,

Zolkiewski and the Radziwills served without salary and often paid the troops from their own funds. They could be valuable assets to the country, if guided in the right direction.

One of the ransomed prisoners was Stanislaw Koniecpolski, field hetman of the crown, who was soon to play an important role on the northern front.

That front could long have ceased to exist, for the loss of the Inflanty and Riga was not a matter of vital interest to the Commonwealth. Gustav Adolph was willing to conclude a peace treaty if Zygmunt III relinquished his claim to the Swedish crown and discontinued Catholic propaganda in Scandinavia. The Protestants of western Europe wanted to bring to Germany the man who was to prove himself the greatest military commander the continent had ever known. Henry IV of France worked patiently to bring about peace between Sweden and the Commonwealth, a policy continued by the French diplomacy after his tragic death. Cardinal Richelieu, who became the king's first minister in 1624, asserted that Sweden was closely bound to France and could be its instrument in dealing with the emperor and the German princes. Poland and Muscovy, according to that statesman, could be of little use to France, except for impeding some of the emperor's plans and for the fur trade.

The French mediation attempts were also supported by England, but only provisional truces were achieved, without a durable treaty.

According to the historian Waclaw Sobieski, Zygmunt III—an enemy of the Protestants and ardent champion of the Jesuits—could never abandon his claim to the throne of Sweden, for such a move would amount to yielding that country to Lutheranism.

Zygmunt's psychological makeup made such an abdication impossible. Fanatical doctrines find the most fertile ground in mediocre minds and can inflict on them terrible damage. Cardinal Richelieu backed Protestant Sweden against the Catholic emperor. He was joined in doing so by his aide and perhaps mentor, the man to whom we owe the term "grey eminence"—Father Joseph, a Capuchin friar.

The Commonwealth also had people who understood the difference between religion and politics, but they were not in power. In matters requiring flexibility, Zygmunt III adopted rigid postures typical of small minds.

240

Riga could have held out longer, waiting for Radziwill on his way with relief, but many of its Lutheran citizens:

> . . .both officials and commoners, wanted a new order, weary of the constant harassment they suffered from the Jesuits of the local college, who dragged them to royal courts on drummed up charges. . . .

During the Swedish siege, these malcontents "easily alienated the people from loyalty to the Commonwealth and the king." Gustav Adolph allowed the *voievode*, castellan, and garrison to go free with their arms and honor, but he expelled all the Jesuits.

The king of Sweden made some pertinent comments on the Commonwealth and the causes of its misfortunes. The perceptions of the great soldier and statesman were accurate:

> There are many valiant men in the Polish army, but God alone knows how they are led. It is no longer the same free and independent nation: because of their king they became the puppets of Austria.

Soldiers demanding their pay were again forming confederacies and marauding; the Lisowski bands were plundering whole towns; the peasants suffered dire poverty; the Seym ignored anyone advocating strong defense and refused to vote taxes, placing its hopes in peace negotiations with Sweden. The royal couple and their mostly foreign advisers listened to the counsels of the emperor and Spain, which promised the assistance of its navy in the Baltic! The royal faction was encouraged by Catholic successes in Germany. Zygmunt III did not appoint the capable Christopher Radziwill grand hetman of Lithuania because he was a Protestant. He named instead the eighty-year-old Leo Sapieha, who had been an astute politician when younger, but never a good commander. He had among his aides an experienced officer, Gosiewski of Kremlin fame, but appointed as his second in command his own inept son.

When the truce lapsed in 1625, Gustav Adolph invaded Samogitia (Zmudz) and took the castle of Birze. He sent immediately to Sweden the sixty guns and other booty seized there.

As in the days before King Stefan's expeditions, Lithuania kept only Dyneburg. It was defended by Alexander Gosiewski, with troops paid by Leo Sapieha and Christopher Radziwill, evidently not a man to bear a grudge.

Gustav Adolph always set his men an example by charging into the thick of the battle. This time he had a horse killed under him.

Faced with danger in the northeast, the Seym finally voted taxes for defense, but the senators continued to implore the king to abandon his claim to the Swedish crown and secure in return territorial concessions, yet Zygmunt remained adamant. Notwithstanding the Pacta Conventa, which he had confirmed after the "Rokosh" episode, the monarch still wielded considerable power in the Commonwealth as its anointed ruler. Jan Ostrorog was right when he told the Seym in 1605 "We should have either not invited the Swedish lord, or having elevated him, not abandon him in face of difficulties."

The gentry did not wish to humiliate its king by denying him his hereditary rights against his will. His ambitions were regarded as a utopian and harmful fantasy, but the principle of legitimacy was respected. The Commonwealth was a monarchy not in name only.

An enemy attack was expected in the Inflanty region and the warnings from Gdansk, loyally reporting to Warsaw suspicious Swedish naval moves in the Baltic, went unheeded. Gustav Adolph had already tried to blockade Gdansk before, interfering with the work on building a Polish navy.

In July 1626 the Swedish fleet effected a massive landing on the Prussian coast. The guns of Pilawa fired only blank charges and the city surrendered. Within twenty days Gustav Adolph took, mostly without firing a shot, sixteen forts, among them Frombork, Elblag, Braniewo, Puck, and Malbork. Gdansk, however, offered stiff resistance and did not surrender. Incidentally, by doing so it disproved the theories of those who claimed that King Stefan could have had forced Gdansk into submission. Gustav Adolph, a military genius, could not do so even though he had a fleet and did not have to face an Ivan the Terrible on another front.

The Swedes who landed at Pilawa looked like sappers rather than soldiers. Gustav Adolph dug himself in on the Baltic coast. He enlisted many Germans, while plunder and extortion supplied him with ample funds. The valuable library of the Jesuits at Braniewo was immediately shipped to Sweden and the cathedral of Frombork was ruthlessly sacked, including even the tombs of its canons. Oliwa and Pelplin were also ravaged.

Zygmunt III assembled a force of about eight thousand and the armies of the two kings, closely related to one another, clashed at Gniew. Zygmunt displayed personal courage, but proved to have even less military than political talent. He failed to appoint a commander-in-chief and left the officers commanding various units to act on their own. When the left wing was on the point of winning, Marshal Wolski ordered retreat.

Two weeks later the field hetman Stanislaw Koniecpolski arrived by forced march from the Ukraine and the hostilities continued with a seasoned soldier commanding on the Polish side. But twenty years had elapsed since the battle of Kircholm and forty since that of the lake of Lubieszow, while firearms had undergone considerable improvement in the meantime. The Polish armored cavalry no longer enjoyed marked superiority over the Swedes. Fortunately, Koniecpolski did not rely on cavalry alone and had mastered "Dutch style" warfare, using earthworks as well as skillful cavalry tactics. He also knew how to combine land and naval operations, by means of which he recaptured Puck in 1627. Two years later, toward the war's end, he performed a feat that evaded even the greatest European commanders of the period. He defeated Gustav Adolph in the battle of Trzciana, by pinning him down in front with Austrian troops and light cavalry, while outflanking the Swedes' left wing and artillery with a surprise charge of heavy hussar cavalry.

In October 1627 Poland won the naval battle of Oliwa, forcing the Swedish fleet to retreat with the loss of its admiral and two major ships. In the following year, however, the Polish fleet was lost at Wismar, seized by the Danes and Swedes. King Zygmunt had sent it there in accord with the Habsburg diplomacy, which bewitched him with visions of a Spanish fleet in the Baltic, a landing in Sweden and lavish subsidies. Such seductive illusions ruled out, of course, any peace treaty with Gustav Adolph. At that point he asked only for reimbursement of war costs and promised to return all his territorial gains except Estonia. But not a single ship from Cadiz was seen in the frigid Baltic and not a single ducat received. Consequently Sweden did not return anything, but captured Bronica—lost because of the treason of its French commander—defeated Stanislaw Potocki at Gorzno, and threatened Torun but did not take it.

It was a war of many victories and defeats, rich in dramatic moments. Both commanders fought in the front line and were involved in incidents that could have changed the course of the war. In one encounter Koniecpolski was felled with his horse and could not hold the animal, which galloped to the enemy camp. Convinced that the hetman was dead, Gustav Adolph attacked at the head of his men, but a Polish soldier concealed in a shack fired his musket and hit the king's left breast under the collarbone. It was the second wound suffered by the valiant king of Sweden in the campaign. The first was from a pistol shot fired by a Gdansk soldier. Many stories were told about the narrow escapes of Gustav Adolph in the battle of Trzciana. According to one of them, the king was seized by his shoulder strap but escaped by ducking his head under it and losing his hat in the process. It was also said that a Swedish soldier fired into the ear of a Polish hussar whose sword was already over the king's head. It was reported that Gustav Adolph was captured and about to be slain, but made his escape by pretending to be a common soldier.

The heroism of both commanders and Koniecpolski's feats of arms cannot obscure the fact the war was, from the Polish point of view, totally absurd and contrary to national interest.

Gustav Adolph was eager to get to Germany, the main theatre of the Thirty Years' War. He was to fight there for a goal extremely beneficial to the Commonwealth, more particularly to Poland proper, a goal pursued by France with every diplomatic, financial and ultimately military means at her disposal. That goal was the perpetuation of the weakness and parcellation of the German Reich. But before he could campaign in Germany toward that end, the king of Sweden had to cross Poland, with Zygmunt III trying to bar his way. Sweden qualified geopolitically to be Poland's natural ally both in the east and in the west. Yet the two nations had been at war for almost thirty years, with Poland the scene of the hostilities and their victim. Gustav Adolph was indeed right when he sneered, "God only knows how they are led."

In the final phase of the war, Austrian troops were seen in Prussia and Pomerania, helping in the battle of Trzciana and others. Their commander's behavior was so equivocal that he had to be recalled. The Habsburgs' mercenaries ravaged the country and sometimes crossed over to the Swedish side. The presence of these units was alarming and the Poles were aware of the danger. The Habsburgs wanted to rule all of Germany, as far as the Baltic and the North Sea. German regiments appearing in Gdansk, Torun, and

244

Malbork were an arm of a dynasty that claimed sovereignty over all of Prussia and Pomerania. In the event of the emperor's victory, the consequences could have been disastrous for the Commonwealth. Brothers of Ferdinand II (and of the queen of Poland) held high office in the Order of the Knights of the Cross, even as its grand masters.

Poland was fighting the war in Pomerania alone, for Lithuania had concluded earlier a truce with Sweden and kept extending its term. Lithuania also did not want to lose its grain trade and its exports fed Gustav Adolph's army.

That situation, incidentally, proves the utter falsity of the notion that the Lublin Union deprived the Grand Duchy of Lithuania of its independence and national identity. In the most critical phase of the war—as soon as the Lithuanian border was not in danger—Wilno made separate decisions, leaving Warsaw to its own devices.

These events antedated by a quarter of a century those described by Henryk Sienkiewicz in his great historical novel *The Deluge*. Christopher Radziwill was the father of Janusz, one of the chief protagonists of "The Deluge."

The policy of Zygmunt III, inspired by dynastic and missionary motives, undermined the unity of the Commonwealth not only in the denominational area. The Swedish wars that it initiated, destructive of the country and highly unpopular, jeopardized the very structure of the state. The abstention of Lithuania from a war in which Poland was engaged was a return to the situation under Casimir Jagiello, when Cracow had to fight the Knights of the Cross alone, defending the estuary of the Vistula and the Commonwealth's future. But the Union was still young then, while now the achievements of a century and a half of unity were at stake.

In 1629 a six-year truce was concluded at Altmark through French mediation, with the concurrence of England, Holland, and Brandenburg. Poland lost some of the conquests of King Casimir, but kept Gdansk and Puck, while the Swedes took Elblag and the Prussian ports, with the exception of Krolewiec (Konigsberg). The Elector of Brandenburg, acting in his own interest though a vassal of the Commonwealth, held in escrow Malbork, Sztum, and Zulawa Wielka, which he promised to deliver to Sweden if no permanent treaty was signed at the termination of the truce. The Inflanty—as far as the river Dzwina—went naturally to Sweden, while the prince of Courland took Mitawa.

In the spring of 1630, Gustav Adolph and Axel Oxenstierna,

who had acted during the war as the governor of the occupied provinces, entered an additional agreement with the city of Gdansk. It was charging a duty of 5.5 percent of value on all goods passing through the port. Three and a half percent went to Sweden, with the rest split between the city, the king, and the duke of Prussia. Thus Gustav Adolph financed his operations in Germany with Polish money, but the weakening of the emperor and the Reich were to the Commonwealth's advantage. The same benefits, however, could have been secured without giving up the revenue of the Gdansk custom house and the Pomeranian provinces.

The Austrian assistance cost Poland half a million *zlotys*.

In the final stage of the Altmark negotiations, when the envoys of both sides were talking directly to one another, Stanislaw Koniecpolski once entered unexpectedly the tent in which the talks were held. Axel Oxenstierna and the other Swedes rose and greeted the hetman with the greatest respect, which Koniecpolski had earned as their adversary.

The Seym was very critical of the terms of the truce, but the chancellor of the crown, Bishop Jacob Zadzik, told the deputies: "If you think that the state can continue the war, hand over to the Swedes us who have signed the agreement and go into field yourselves." Short of a reply to the chancellor's words, the Seym ratified the agreement.

The Commonwealth was actually unable to carry on, and needed a breathing space badly. It had seen little peace in the seventeenth century, then already thirty years old. First the rumblings of war were heard from afar, during the Inflanty campaigns and the False Dimitri episodes, leaving most of the country unaffected. But the "memorable Seym" and the "Night of the Jesuits" stirred up the "rokosh" rebellion, bringing civil war into the heart of the Commonwealth. The year 1606 was a watershed. A precarious balance of order can be upset very easily, even in twenty-four hours. But, frail though it may be, a precarious balance is better than none.

Under the terms of the truce, large sections of Pomerania remained occupied by foreign forces. In the final moments of the negotiations, Zygmunt wrote to Jacob Zadzik that inflexibility in matters of religion was more important than holding Frombork or Braniew. He was preaching to a bishop.

Special commissions surveyed the damage done by the enemy in the provinces recovered by the Commonwealth. It turned out that in every village that had a church, the local school was burned down. The existence of so many schools had been taken for granted until then and amazed only foreign visitors. The country was swept by epidemics brought by the Swedish army, while an economic crisis worsened the situation. Modern economists explain that the crisis was caused by improper distribution of national income. The privileged class, mainly the magnates, made few purchases in the domestic market, for they imported luxury goods from abroad and had staples produced by their own subjects in estates and privately owned towns. The progressive devaluation of the currency was dealt with by increasing the export of grain, at the expense of the peasants, who could not afford to buy much. The economic problems were actually a by-product of the political system and the dominant role of the magnates favored by the king, who had little interest in the prosperity of the townsmen and the lesser gentry. The Jagiellonian tradition of an unwritten alliance between the king and the middle class, both gentry and burghers, designed to curb the power of the aristocracy, was being abandoned. Yet during the Zebrzydowski uprising, the "rokosh," some of its wiser leaders championed the interests of the urban middle class, neglected by Zygmunt III.

After the truce of Altmark the royal army returned to the Ukraine, where the clergy tried to use it for a crusade against the Orthodox church. The Dominican friars of Lwow consecrated the sword of Stanislaw Koniecpolski and displayed it in processions as the symbol of the militant Catholic church. When he had marched north three years earlier, the hetman left behind him in the southeast a complex and ominous situation. Let us review briefly the events that followed the battle of Chocim.

The forty thousand Cossacks who had participated were not disposed to lay down their arms. Piotr Konaszewicz Sahaydaczny died on April 20, 1622, and the Cossack community (known as the "Sich") was thrown into chaos in the absence of his leadership. Two years later the Tartars launched an invasion that surpassed all their previous raids. People started to count their attacks from the "first Tartars," that is those who appeared in June 1624 and ravaged the country as far west as Iwonicz. Koniecpolski crushed them at Martynow near Halicz and set free a large number of civilian prisoners they had seized for the slave markets of the Middle East. His next task was the pacification of the Cossacks, whose naval expeditions in the Black Sea and connivance in Crimea's revolt against the Turks threatened to unleash a war with Istanbul.

After a brief and indecisive confrontation, an agreement was concluded at Kurukow. The Commonwealth enlisted as permanent mercenaries six thousand men, known as "registered Cossacks." They were supposed to be a legitimate army charged with maintaining peace and order, preventing Tartar incursions and the expeditions of the Zaporozhe Cossacks in the Black Sea. The "registered Cossacks" became a privileged elite, leaving outside tens of thousands of others. Those not enlisted in the "register" remained freemen if they resided in royal estates, but had obligations of servitude in private ones. The solutions offered to the Cossack problem were paper solutions, while the reality remained uncertain. The ranks of the Cossacks began to grow rapidly as they were joined by runaway serfs. As he was leaving for Pomerania, Koniecpolski was well aware that the Ukrainian cauldron was not likely to settle down in the meantime.

Some events during the hetman's absence, however, hinted at a path that could and perhaps should have been taken. Koniecpolski left behind him as his deputy Stefan Chmielecki, an outstanding officer, though not the equal of such great commanders as Zolkiewski, Zamoyski, Chodkiewicz, or Koniecpolski himself. He defeated at Biala Cerkiew a Tartar force far superior in numbers, in a battle of several days, in which the "registered Cossacks" performed well. At the decisive point of the battle, torrential rain swept the battlefield. It softened the Tartars' bowstrings and soaked the powder of the Polish troops. Lances and swords decided the outcome. The Cossacks were commanded at Biala Cerkiew by Michael Doroszenko, who fell three years later in the Crimea, where he went to defend the khans Mehmet and Shahin Girey against the Turkish forces of Kantamir. These local conflicts offered to the Commonwealth an opportunity that it did not use. Only twenty years later King Wladyslaw IV would have given much to have had that chance.

Khan Mehmet Girey, removed from power by the Turks, asked for Poland's assistance, offering to become its vassal. The moderately favorable response confined itself at first to giving him asylum in the Ukraine. More positive acceptance was signalled by three major Cossack expeditions to Crimea, carried out with the knowledge and approval of the hetman's deputy, Stefan Chmielecki, as well as those of Jerzy Zbaraski and Mikolaj Potocki.

Before he fell at Bakhchysaray, Doroszenko took and destroyed the fortress of Islam-Kermen, built by the Turks on the lower Dnieper as a bastion against the Cossacks and the Commonwealth. But Poland was waging at the time in the north a war started some thirty years earlier for dynastic and religious reasons, so it could not offer significant support to the Cossacks in the Crimea.

Some historians claim that the concept of turning the Tartar khans of the Crimea into vassals of the Commonwealth was unrealistic, as they had a tradition of living off the plunder of the Ruthenian provinces. Yet there is no reason to believe that the Tartars could not change their ways or find other targets for their raids.

The Ukraine was part of the Commonwealth. The Ruthenian nobility became culturally assimilated to Poland and Catholicism, leaving only the Zaporozhe "Sich" of the Cossacks as the champion of a separate Ukrainian identity. The Commonwealth was faced with a crucial problem, which could be resolved either by some form of political understanding with the Cossacks or by the abandonment of the Ukraine.

Koniecpolski returned to the Ukraine in the fall of 1629 to find it even more turbulent than before. Poland was surrounded from the north, east, and southeast by a crescent of states of various religious faiths, all engaged in political propaganda campaigns exploiting inflamed religious emotions. A peace with Sweden was concluded, but Zygmunt III remained a staunch friend of the Habsburgs. Immediately after the termination of the hostilities in Prussia some Polish units went to fight on the Catholic side in Germany, with the king's knowledge and blessing.

In March 1630 the Zaporozhe Cossacks murdered the commander of the "registered Cossacks," Hrycko Sawicz, nicknamed "The Black," who was loyal to Poland. A new uprising was headed by Taras Fedorowicz. The forces of the crown suffered some reverses and lost the town of Korsun, the inhabitants of which supported the Cossacks. Koniecpolski crossed the Dnieper and on May 17 attacked the fortified Cossack camp of Perejaslaw. But the commander who had defeated Gustav Adolph managed only a draw with the Zaporozhe. Pawel Piasecki, a participant in the battle, reported in his memoirs that about three hundred "noble knights" fell at Perejaslaw, not counting common soldiers. Both sides saved face and some accommodations were reached. The hetman no longer demanded Taras dead or alive and the number of "registered Cossacks" was raised to eight thousand. The Zaporozhe promised again to obey the king, live at peace with its "registered" brethren, abstain from raids into the Black Sea, or any provocations of the sultan of Turkey. The Cossacks even agreed to burn their pirates' boats.

The compromise was not due to the hetman's benevolence or generosity of spirit. It was Stefan Chmielecki, the son of a tenant squire, who climbed from poverty to high command and the rank of *voievode* of Kiev, that knew how to coexist with the Cossacks and the people, treating them with understanding. Koniecpolski was not a man inclined to yield. Owner of vast estates in the Braclaw region, a fearless soldier of giant stature, he was capable of enforcing his will with the gallows of a headman's axe. His physical strength was such that he could pierce armor with an arrow at a considerable distance. He stuttered and there was a saying that "Sir Stanislaw will strike before he speaks." But not before giving serious thought to the matter in hand. A stern soldier and master, he never acted in war or in politics without careful reflection. He attacked the Cossack camp, but the resistance he encountered caused him to accept a compromise. Eighteen years later, Mikolaj Potocki and Jeremi Wisniowiecki, members of the same class, acting in the same region of Korsun and Perejaslaw, failed to display such sound judgment.

Bohdan Chmielnicki, captured by the Turks together with Koniecpolski, was by then free, released after two years.

Theoretically, a third way of resolving the problem of the Ukraine was to crush the Sich by overwhelming force and destroy the power of the Cossacks. Koniecpolski's experience at Perejaslaw did not suggest it as a viable option. Let us recall that Russia only managed to achieve that objective a century later.

In September 1631 the "Elder" of the Register Cossacks, Ivan Kulaha Petrazycki, reported to the hetman that two "Germans" had arrived in Kaniow and he enclosed, still unsealed, the letters they had brought with them. The mysterious Germans turned out to be Frenchmen sent by Gustav Adolph. They reached Kaniow by an oddly circuitous route via Transylvania, Istanbul, and Moscow. In Turkey they were entertained by Cornelius Haga, the Dutch diplomat we have referred to before. A contemporary Polish writer summed up the political philosophy of the indefatigable travelers as follows: "The cause of all the evil in Europe is the king of Poland, who is guided by the Jesuits and supports Austria." Gustav Adolph intended to use the Frenchmen to establish contact with the Cossacks. He promised them protection of the Orthodox religion and increased pay if he should be soon crowned king of Poland. He urged the Cossacks to attack the emperor to help to bring about that event.

Koniecpolski thought that the best way to deal with the foreign agents was the old Cossack custom of throwing inconvenient people into the rapids of the Dnieper, but he shared that idea only with the chancellor, advising Petrazycki to send them to Warsaw. The chancellor directed them in turn to Oxenstierna, complaining about their plotting.

The Frenchmen had brought from Moscow the tsar's message to the Orthodox clergy and another from the Patriarch of Istanbul. The archimandrite of the Lavra Pecherska monastery near Kiev intercepted both documents and told their bearers: "You deserve to be impaled for these letters."

Poland could still find political partners in the Ukraine of 1631, but not if the country was to be turned into a plantation worked by serfs.

Gustav Adolph was evidently thinking about the Polish crown. The time was ripe, for Zygmunt III was sixty five.

The royal couple always set an example to their subjects by participating in the Corpus Christi procession regardless of the weather. This time the obese Queen Constance, oblivious of the sultry heat, walked the streets of Warsaw bareheaded beside her husband. She developed "an inflammation" and was treated with cold baths, but the fever did not subside. On July 10 as was her daily custom, Ursula Gienger, entering the bedroom of her mistress in the morning, found her dead.

The main pillar of the pro-Austrian policy, next to the king himself, was gone. By a coincidence, the main opponent of that policy, Prince Jerzy Zbaraski, also died in his sleep soon after. The prince had been waiting for the demise of the king, aspiring to the throne himself. Jerzy's brother, Galileo's disciple and ambassador to the court of Istanbul, had died earlier. A great family was extinct, its estates inherited by the Wisniowiecki clan.

The king did not expect to survive his wife, twenty years his junior, named in his will as the main heiress of the royal fortune. After the queen's death Zygmunt, always solitary by nature, became a virtual hermit and state documents reached him almost

251

exclusively through the intermediary of Ursula Gienger. Dignitaries waiting in the antechamber received from her the parchments already signed by the king.

Moved by sympathy for the widowed monarch, public opinion accepted such practices with indulgence, as time mellowed former animosities. Zygmunt even made his peace with Christopher Radziwill, his adversary and the leader of the Protestants.

Stanislaw Koniecpolski became at last the grand hetman of the crown, a post vacant since Zolkiewski's death.

No one doubted that a tumultuous throng would soon again fill the electoral field near Wola. Zygmunt III was fading away and obviously recognized it, by admitting physicians, hitherto rejected with disgust. They began treatment of the gout that tormented the king, the method being the application of red hot iron to the afflicted parts.

The problem of electoral reform was discussed and in October 1630 the chancellor, Jacob Zadzik, recalled Jan Zamoyski's proposal made forty years earlier. There was again talk about electing a crown prince or a candidate "of Slavic blood and speech" by majority vote. Only Ruthenia had reservations, while Poland proper favored a special parliamentary commission to study electoral reform.

The last Seym session under the reign of Zygmunt III opened on April 1, 1632. The hall was swathed in black and all the senators and deputies wore mourning for Queen Constance. The Speaker had barely finished reading the draft of a resolution concerning provision for the king's offspring when voices were heard asking the monarch to bring in his children. They entered in order of seniority and sat at the foot of the throne: Jan Casimir, Jan Olbracht, Karol Ferdinand, Alexander Karol, and the thirteen-year-old Catherine Constance. The solemn silence was broken by the king's feeble voice:

> These are children born in Poland, my offspring and yours, they have already lost their mother and are about to lose a father. I entrust them to the Commonwealth, may it take care of them and be generous.

The resolution awarding to the princes high offices and royal estates was adopted unanimously.

The scene witnessed at the Warsaw castle, its patriarchal and almost religious character and mood were expressions of a historic fact. The House of Vasa was accepted by Poland and inherited a

252

precious legacy of the Jagiellonians: the attachment of the people to the monarchy. It was clear that the father would be succeeded by the son, so that the reform of electoral procedures became redundant. Jan Zamoyski wanted to strike the iron while it was hot, in the aftermath of the battle of Byczyna.

The children present in the Seym chamber were all those of the recently deceased queen, but Wladyslaw, the son of Anna, was absent. He was busy hunting in the district of Plonsk.

His firstborn caused Zygmunt III much concern. The insane profligacy of the thirty-seven-year-old prince reached such extremes that a delegation complained about it to the king, who immediately ordered sealed the famous Kazanowski palace in close vicinity to the royal castle.

Wladyslaw received from his father forty thousand *florins* annually, in addition to which he collected, with the consent of the Seym, the revenue of the duchy of Siewiersk and eight counties. He was nevertheless always short of funds. A free spender, he neglected the management of his affairs and, worst of all, could refuse nothing to his cronies and allowed himself to be robbed by them.

This was happening in a state that was constantly short of money for the army, causing such victories as Kircholm to be wasted, while confederacies of unpaid soldiers spread chaos and anarchy.

Let us glance indiscreetly at the last will and testament of Zygmunt III, drawn up in 1624. It lists riches that we usually visualize in our imagination when thinking about maharajahs. There were sixteen solid-gold statues of saints, with ebony bases (plus others, as yet unfinished), silver altars, gold shields set with diamonds, vast quantities of chains with rubies and pearls. Here are some examples: "The chain bequeathed to us by our Aunt Anne, with diamonds set up in the shape of roses . . . a triple chain of diamonds, four of them of large size . . . a triple chain similar to the former, with four rubies on each link . . . thirty-two diamond necklaces with nineteen diamonds in each . . . a necklace of Urian pearls numbering one hundred and fifty . . . a chain of diamonds in oblong links, in each of which there are three major diamonds of triangular shape, as well as many smaller ones . . . a similar chain of rubies . . . a gold chain with diamonds, rubies and pearls, with a pendant bearing the letters S. A. surmounted by a crown and a huge pearl above . . .

Enough of chains. Let us pass up swords set with gold and jewels, precious rings, diadems, and other items. The king also earmarked fifty thousand *florins* in ready cash for "devout donations," not counting church vestments studded with gold and pearls.

"Reflecting on the immense wealth described in this testament," wrote the eighteenth-century historian Julian Ursyn Niemcewicz, "one asks the obvious question: Where did it all go? Let the invaders reply."

Who was responsible for opening the borders of the Commonwealth to the invaders?

Nor were the Poles blameless. We have referred earlier to the "unicorns" and Moscow crowns. There must have been an ample supply of them at the Kremlin, since Zygmunt left one to Wladyslaw and was laid out on the bier in another.

The Seym, stingy when voting funds for the army, was profligate when the dynasty was concerned. The magnates received from the crown lavish land grants, but they sometimes spent their money generously in the national interest, always voluntarily and not in the form of a tax.

Let us return to the sealed palace in the main avenue of Warsaw. Its owner, Adam Kazanowski, was the most favored of the crown prince's sycophants. He received from Wladyslaw precious gifts and sums of money and finally simply started taking works of art from the royal castle to his nearby palace. Advised of the royal order, he returned hastily from Krolewiec and started looking desperately for protectors, bowing obsequiously to people who "were later lucky to be recognized by his lackeys."

Fate saved Kazanowski in his distress. On April 23, 1632, Zygmunt fell ill in Opacz, where he had gone to test his strength. He wanted to find out whether he would be able to escort to Cracow the body of his wife, still remaining in Warsaw. The papal nuncio was the first to notice signs of mortal weakness in the king's countenance.

The agony, though not particularly painful, lasted a week. A stroke paralyzed the left side of his body, distorted his face, and almost deprived Zygmunt of speech. Ursula Gienger announced to the dignitaries gathered at the bedside the latest appointments and then treated them to a lecture on the gratitude they owed to the dying monarch for his benefactions. Asked by the chancellor whether the promotions announced by Ursula were indeed his will, the king responded with a wave of the hand, whispering, "Yes." On the same evening of April 25 he gave his blessing to Wladyslaw and placed on his head the crown of Sweden.

The most devout of all monarchs received extreme unction and all the religious rites were duly performed. When on April 28 both chancellors, Jacob Zadzik of Poland and Albrecht Radziwill of Lithuania, entered the royal chamber at the head of the entire court to kiss for the last time the king's hand, they saw by his bedside about a dozen Jesuits "yelling into the dying man's both ears, ordering him to repent his sins."

The scene was the very image of the counter-reformation: overbearing, brutal, and pathetic.

Zygmunt III died at dawn, on April 30, 1632.

He had assumed in his early youth the leadership of a nation that in the course of the preceding fourteen years had dealt with the crises of three interregna, won three campaigns against Muscovy and one against Austria, was fully capable of growth and reform, and was enjoying a freedom of expression greater than other European nations. In the forty-fifth year of his reign, he left a Commonwealth in a state of lethargy, moral disarray, and physical exhaustion, held in the tight grip of religious fanaticism.

People are easily demoralized by witnessing ineptness, slipshod work, laxity. Some of the gentry approved the Moscow wars, others opposed them. None could remain indifferent, however, when they heard that only cavalry and infantry went to fight at Smolensk, while the artillery was left in Warsaw, Tykocin, and Wilno. Outrage is short-lived and often succeeded by the acceptance of mediocrity as the norm.

The long reign of Zygmunt III was full of examples of bumbling incompetence. The king's policy, in opposition to the prevailing public opinion, was furthermore executed in a clumsy and inept manner. Smolensk and the Siewiersk region were taken, but the returning soldiers ransacked the country and extorted millions in tribute. The average citizen had reason to regard himself as the loser in that victorious war.

Yet few other reigns saw such a sequence of dazzling short-term triumphs. The Commonwealth held as a prisoner of war an Austrian archduke, a brother of the emperor. The overthrown tsar of Moscow and the father of his successor met the same fate. Polish and Lithuanian soldiers camped at the Kremlin, installed *hospodars* (princes) in Jassy and Bucharest, won the battles of Byczyna, Kircholm,

Kluszyn, Chocim, Trzciana, not to mention numerous lesser victories on land and at sea or the taking of scores of fortified castles. Yet the record shows that the military effort of the Commonwealth was wasted. The great deeds that Nicolo Machiavelli recommended to princes should achieve real, visible, and durable results. They should not be in the nature of fireworks.

The crown of Sweden rested on a table next to Zygmunt III lying in state and that of Moscow was on his head, but the impressive display did not reflect political reality. A Swedish governor administered large sections of Polish Pomerania, while many citizens of the Commonwealth looked to the Kremlin for the protection of their Orthodox faith.

In the course of forty-five years the Commonwealth had placed at its ruler's disposal resources that could have been used to strengthen the structure and defense ramparts of the national home shared by all its inhabitants. That was the significance of the long list of military victories just enumerated. Historic achievements are nothing but the sum total of fruitful endeavors. Efforts which produced no results cannot be summed up.

Under the reign of Zygmunt III the Commonwealth crossed a watershed. From 1606 on, the way was downward.

CHAPTER 5

THE COMMONWEALTH'S
INDIAN SUMMER

*Our happiness is in remaining whole within our
frontiers and each man's and our own welfare are our
treasure.*

Stanislaw Lubienski
Bishop of Plock, 1634

I

The fourth royal election to be held in Poland took an unexpected turn. It lasted half an hour. The deceased king's son was elected unanimously, notwithstanding the fact that he could not be described as a crown prince, since he became since the moment of his father's death the hereditary king of Sweden. Zygmunt III favored more the children of his second marriage and Queen Constance preferred among them Jan Casimir, but the gentry handed the crown to the firstborn.

257

"His highest ambition was to recover the lost throne of Sweden, yielding that of Poland to one of his brothers," wrote the historian Wladyslaw Czaplinski.

Traditional loyalties supported the monarch who became master of a country with an area of 390,000 square miles. Recent research has thrown new light on the personality of Wladyslaw by discovering the written instructions he had given to his envoy to the emperor in May 1632. He stated openly that "since his early youth he disliked Poland and dreamed about Germany." A mature politician approaching forty would not have committed such sentiments to paper.

Six months later, on November 8, 1632, the author of that declaration became the monarch of the country he did not like. His candidacy was backed by all three components of the Commonwealth, but only two of them were heard: Poland and Lithuania. The Ukraine, which volunteered to participate, was not admitted to the debate.

A delegation from the Zaporozhe appeared at the electoral convention. The Cossacks declared that, being warriors and subjects of the Commonwealth, they wished to participate in the election, giving their vote to Prince Wladyslaw. The response they received was almost literary in its graphic imagery. Yes, they were told, you are part of the Commonwealth's body, just as nails are part of the human body and need trimming from time to time. But the convention and royal election are matters for the nobility. Commoners should not meddle in them and had better remain silent.

The "Elder" of the cossacks was still Ivan Kulaha Petrazycki, who had recently displayed commendable loyalty by sending the French agents of Sweden to the chancellor and handing their letters to the hetman. The richest and perhaps the most powerful lord of the entire Commonwealth was at the time a countryman of the ataman, Prince Wladyslaw Dominik Zaslawski, who had inherited the vast land holdings of the Ostrogski clan. But his vote was counted exactly like that of Koniecpolski, as a Polish, not Ruthenian vote.

In the summer of the same year 1632 Ruthenia and the Orthodox church suffered a painful loss. The twenty-year-old Prince Jeremy Michael Wisniowiecki, the last of the great Ruthenian lords of the Orthodox faith, converted to Catholicism. He was the only one of the magnates to live beyond the Dnieper rather than in central Poland and resembled in his tastes and style the Cossacks more than the learned statesmen of Cracow with their Latin books. It is true that the Czetwertynski, Kisiel, and many other Ruthenian noblemen remained Orthodox, but they were no match for the Wisniowiecki or Zaslawski clans, who surpassed the Radziwills in wealth and power.

The Orthodox metropolite Isaiah Kopinski tried to dissuade Prince Jeremy, invoking the memory of his deceased parents:

". . . the Church of God, our mother, is in tears and laments being rejected by Your Grace. . . . They say that the Greek faith is that of peasants: if so, the Greek emperors, other great monarchs and the apostles were also of peasant faith. . . ."

He used the past tense. There was no denying that within the Commonwealth the "Greek faith" was indeed one for the peasants.

No one would have spoken about nails if a Wisniowiecki or a Zaslawski had pleaded the cause of the Ukraine before the Seym. Lithuania, with Radziwill her spokesman, was respected. But what would have happened if its representative were a mere . . . Mickiewicz?

After his conversion, the prince always stressed his Polish nationality and Catholic faith, while his chancery conducted correspondence only in Polish. Yet the documents sent by the royal chancery to the eastern provinces continued to be in Ruthenian. No one compelled the magnates of the Ukraine to abandon their religion or language. Nor was there any force capable of compelling them to anything.

Poland was, of course, not the only country in which class distinctions could override national interest.

In February 1615 the youthful Louis XIII called to Paris the General Estates of France. The delegates were rather crowded in the vast hall of the Palais Bourbon, as the best seats were taken by two thousand courtiers. In accordance with French custom, the first to speak was the representative of the clergy, Armand du Plessis de Richelieu, bishop of Lucon. Before speaking, he honored the throne with a light bow. The representative of the nobility, Baron de Sencey, was spared that effort, as the king dispensed him of it with a wave of the hand. But the aged mayor of Paris, Robert Miron, had to speak on his knees. For three hours he pleaded, kneeling, for the rights of the people, which actually meant the elite of the burghers. On the following day the monarch prohibited any separate meetings of the Third Estate, judging them detrimental to the state. The next session of General Estates was held one hundred and seventy four years later, on the eve of the Revolution.

In Paris the old, wealthy, and educated mayor of Paris on his knees; in Warsaw the valiant and dynamic Cossacks dismissed with a sneer. Contempt for the lower orders was universal throughout the Continent. But class problems were infinitely more complex in the eastern provinces of the Commonwealth than in western Europe. The division of social classes was intertwined with differences of religion, language, and cultural tradition—all the components of a national identity.

The conclusion is obvious: the polonisation of the Ukrainian magnates at that stage of historical development was a major tragedy. They alone could have demanded with authority the conversion of the state into a Commonwealth of Three Nations, which it was in fact though not in law. By relinquishing their leadership of the Ruthenians they condemned them first to futile rebellion and eventually to absorption by Russia. They could not have become vassals of either Moscow or Istanbul, neither of which would have granted them the freedoms of the Commonwealth.

The curt dismissal of the Cossack delegation to the Seym was greeted in the Ukraine with rage, but it was soon forgotten under the pressure of more momentous events.

During the interregnum Tsar Michael seized the opportunity and attacked the eastern border of the Commonwealth, breaking the truce. Several forts and cities were lost and on November 14 Michael Szejn attacked the ramparts of Smolensk, which he had defended twenty years earlier. In July 1633 the Muscovites took Polock and then Wielin, Iswiat, and Ozierzyszcze. The Commonwealth forces were assembling slowly, the offended Cossacks were not eager to help, and the Tartars had to be watched. The hetman of Lithuania, Christopher Radziwill, lived up to his difficult task. He broke twice the ring of the siege and brought reinforcements to the small garrison of Smolensk, which held on staunchly. Szejn blew up with mines one of the towers and a section of the wall; he bombarded the fortress with two hundred guns, but could not take it.

On September 4, 1633, the king himself came to the rescue with an army of twenty thousand and the Zaporozhe Cossacks, indispensable on such occasions. Wladyslaw did not waste any time and, together with Radziwill, proved himself a talented commander.

260

Within one month the situation was totally reversed. Szein's forces, surrounded, were trapped and in November the tsar began to seek peace. During the summer the Tartars had ransacked the southern part of his realm and their advance guards were seen within ten miles of Moscow. Soldiers from the invaded provinces simply left the ranks and the tsar was compelled to proclaim amnesty for deserters. The treasury was empty and taxes were coming in no faster than in Poland and Lithuania. The Russian commanders at Smolensk feuded and could not agree on anything, while their adversaries advanced.

Historians rate that Smolensk campaign as one of the best-executed military operations of the Commonwealth, stressing the thorough preparations and excellent equipment. One unexpected aspect of the campaign merits attention: its cosmopolitan character. Generally speaking, western Europe was at the time ahead of the Commonwealth in military technology, while nations to the east were behind it. But in this instance the situation was reversed. Chroniclers claim that Szein's artillery at Smolensk was of English origin and his heaviest mortars were supplied by Amsterdam foundries. Mercenaries spoke various European languages and represented the military skills of fully developed countries. The army of the Commonwealth had to face on the upper Dnieper the power of Moscow assisted by western technology.

The Polish-Lithuanian state was never noted for successes as an aggressor, but when hard pressed it sometimes performed remarkable feats in defense. This seeming contradiction was no doubt due to the pacifist tendencies of the ruling class, the landed gentry.

On February 25, 1634, Michael Szejn surrendered and did obeisance to Wladyslaw IV, mounted on his horse. The king could see from his saddle enemy banners spread on the ground, over a hundred pieces of artillery, and a vast array of other equipment. "The tsar-elect of Moscow" triumphed at last, but he no longer dreamed about the Kremlin. He preferred to make common cause with the defeated adversary and seek with his help the crown of Sweden, now his foremost goal. The motto at the beginning of this chapter quotes lines written by Bishop Lubienski two weeks after Szein's capitulation, on March 11, 1634. The Commonwealth wanted to recover the losses of the Grand Duchy of Lithuania and that objective was achieved. Further conquests were judged futile and King

Wladyslaw's dynastic ambitions were neither approved nor supported by the gentry. After all, the Pacta Conventa required the king to abdicate his claim to the Swedish throne.

And Moscow? It did not take the king's proposals seriously, even though royal envoys promised that Wladyslaw as king of Sweden would return to Russia all the conquests of Gustav Adolph, thus opening her way to the Baltic.

Both sides now sought not a truce but a peace treaty for perpetuity, which was in fact concluded on June 14, 1634, on the banks of the river Polanowka. A quarter of a century earlier an exchange of prisoners took place on the same site and the new agreement provided for a similar exchange, but that clause of the treaty encountered obstacles in its implementation. Lists of prisoners were submitted by the Commonwealth envoys, but even the tsar's orders failed to produce results because of sabotage in the lower echelons. Moscow did not want to lose men in their prime, good soldiers, artisans, or farmers. It also failed to deliver, contrary to the terms of the treaty, some of its own boyars, Wladyslaw's supporters who had been captured in Lithuania, but they were kept for different reasons.

The treaty of Polanowka gave to the Commonwealth in perpetuity Smolensk and the provinces of Siewiersk and Czernihow, bringing the area of the state to a million square kilometers.

Actually, from the Moscow point of view, territorial arrangements were less important than the relinquishment by Wladyslaw of his claim to the throne of the Kremlin. One of the clauses of the treaty required that the actual document of election, drawn by the boyars and Stanislaw Zolkiewski at the walls of Moscow, be returned to Russia.

In March 1635 a "great embassy," headed by the governor of Suzdal, Prince Gregory Mihailovich Lwow, arrived in Warsaw. The senators were greatly embarrassed when it was discovered that the document was nowhere to be found. Zygmunt III, as noted earlier, "rejected the diploma with contempt" as it was handed to him by Zolkiewski and it had not been seen since. The chancellor informed the Russian envoys confidentially of the situation and then:

> Prince Lwow, as if thunderstruck, grew pale and suddenly froze, then after a deep sigh said, "My lord bishop, I had believed you like a God's angel, but you lied and

perjured yourself, together with the other commissioners, when you promised to return the script."

A special messenger was sent to the tsar and finally, on May 3, 1635, Wladyslaw IV, kneeling at the great altar of St. John's Cathedral, solemnly swore that he renounces the title, but cannot return the lost document. He then kissed the cross and the senators did likewise, repeating his oath. The Moscow envoys watched and listened in breathless suspense.

Unable to fulfill his promise in the matter of the act of election, the king sought to appease the Russians with a friendly gesture. He allowed them to take to Moscow the remains of the Szuyski brothers, deceased in Poland and buried in a chapel built for that purpose close to the Church of the Holy Cross in Warsaw.

Five days after the royal oath "the Muscovite envoys left Warsaw, while some of their servants who had tasted Polish freedom defected and stayed behind; but those they found paid dearly for their flight."

Moscow was not alone in having Tartar problems in the course of the war. There were many Tartar hordes, acting separately on their own. Since 1627 a secret treaty between the Kremlin and Istanbul governed their joint actions against the Commonwealth, ostensibly independent of one another. The first Tartar incursions coincided with the interregnum, but in the following year, when the operations in the northeast intensified, Moscow diplomacy managed to induce its clandestine allies to initiate a full-scale campaign. It was conducted in proxy by Abazy, a Ruthenian assimilated in Turkey, the pasha of Widyn. The impressive remnants of his fortified castle can still be seen on the northern border of Bulgaria. The walls, rising from the Danube, offer a panorama of southern Rumania. At the time of the events we describe, a new type of icon began to appear in the cottages of the oppressed Balkan peasants. The picture of St. George bore a striking resemblance to the features of Wladyslaw IV. One can still see in Widyn the well-preserved massive gate and the cells enclosed with bars, located so that the ruler passing through could observe the prisoners.

Abazy Pasha acted against Poland on orders from Sultan Amurat, who was engaged himself on the Persian front. Moscow diplomacy reached there, too, trying to mediate and restore peace between Persia and Turkey. The Kremlin promised to the Padyshah of Persia as reward some hitherto contested lands on the Caspian Sea shores. The tsar had little interest in territorial gains, as he already had an abundance of undeveloped land. His dominant goal was the consolidation of his authority within the territory already theoretically belonging to Russia.

In the summer of 1633 the Tartars crossed the Dniester near Chocim and invaded the province of Podole. Stanislaw Koniecpolski took them by surprise by attacking their rear, at the camp of Sasowy Rog on the river Prut, deep into Moldavia. The horde was routed and the hetman did not break the law by taking his army abroad, as his action was clearly defensive. He had to punish the aggressor and set free the prisoners he had taken.

Abazy Pasha advanced in the fall. Koniecpolski was waiting for him in the well-fortified camp at Panowce, near Jamieniec Podolski, on an elevation from which there was a wide view of Chocim and the bend of the Dniester. The enemy's assaults were repulsed. The Moslems fought gallantly, but "the Moldavians and Valachians, driven into battle with clubs by the Turks, did not want to fight against Christians with the pagans and immediately fled."

Koniecpolski did not pursue the escaping pasha. His forces were small and he was mindful of the second front. It was October 1633 and the Smolensk confrontation remained still undecided. The pursuit of Abazy might have degenerated into a full-fledged war with the sultan himself and the hetman was not eager to accept responsibility for such a development. He subscribed to a political principle and observed it strictly: he refused to conduct military actions unless they were sanctioned by the Seym. He wanted to act constitutionally, but his authority was such that he was capable of influencing Seym resolutions. Stanislaw Koniecpolski was in this respect a worthy successor of his eminent predecessors, the grand hetmans of the crown Jan Zamoyski and Stanislaw Zolkiewski, who supported and implemented the same policy.

Abazy Pasha lost at Panowce, but he took the village of Studzienice, though it was stubbornly defended by the peasants. In proof of his victories, he sent prisoners to Istanbul, among them a beautiful girl whom he presented to the sultan as Koniecpolski's daughter. Poor communications made such deceptions possible at the time. Sultan Amurat, because of lack of information, was not aware of the changed situation on Commonwealth's northeastern front. Believing that the Polish-Lithuanian army was still tied up in the northeast, he mounted an expedition against Poland as soon as he had concluded a peace treaty with Persia. In April 1634 he started to assemble an army at Adrianopol. In the meantime regiments from Smolensk kept arriving in Kamieniec and Koniecpolski's force soon grew to thirty-five thousand, exclusive of the Cossacks. The Seym voted funds for the pay of the soldiers in the Moscow campaign. This was all the more necessary as the units marching south followed their old practice of ransacking towns, even monasteries.

A major confrontation was brewing on the Dniester. The gentry demanded that a Seym session be held in Lwow and the king arrived in the city in September.

Sultan Amurat, who had not a long time ago drawn his sword against the Commonwealth's ambassador, Alexander Trzebinski, demanding the conversion of Lechistan (Poland) to Islam, now sent Sehin Aga as his envoy and desperately sought peace. He realized that the astute Moscow diplomacy made him its instrument and did not relish the prospect of carrying on alone the war he had started himself.

In October the Commonwealth concluded a treaty with Turkey more favorable than that negotiated on the Bosphorus a few years earlier by Christopher Zbaraski. Turkey undertook to remove the Tartars from the Budziak and Bialogrod steppes and to appoint as *hospodars* of Moldavia and Valachia only persons acceptable to the king of Poland.

It was a victory for the Commonwealth, but a Pyrrhic one. At the very beginning of his reign, Wladyslaw IV was offered an opportunity, the absence of which fourteen years later, toward the end of his life, brought disaster.

Late in October Wladyslaw left Lwow for Warsaw and wrote to Koniecpolski: "We pray to God that this peace should be durable." At the same time Bishop Piasecki confided to the nuncio in a letter that the Poles "signed reluctantly and only because the truce with Sweden expires within a year and it was expedient to settle with Turkey before that time."

Stockholm, Moscow, Istanbul—that was the triangle within which the Commonwealth's attention wandered. However, its monarch was actually interested only in Sweden and his own career.

Tsar Michael honored his diplomats returning from Polanowka with a treaty that consolidated the power of the founder of the

Romanov dynasty. He condemned to death Michael Szejn, the gallant but unlucky commander. In Istanbul Abazy Pasha was strangled at the sultan's order, ostensibly as punishment for inciting friction with the Commonwealth.

Only two years had passed since the election. No other king of Poland had defeated two major powers at the very outset of his reign. The eyes of Europe were turned toward Wladyslaw IV.

"As black is different from white, so is Zygmunt's son Wladyslaw unlike his father," the Gdansk potentate Zygmunt Kerschenstein told a French visitor. "Zygmunt had a prickly pride; he never returned the greeting of a commoner. He stuck obstinately with his opinion, right or wrong, and never changed it. Those who lost his favor could never win it back. What he promised or even only indicated to be his will, he kept faithfully. He either liked the Austrians, to whom he was connected by marriage, or feared them—and that was why he did not want Wladyslaw to visit France. Zygmunt was more skilled in the arts of peace than those of war, in which he had little luck. Wladyslaw, on the contrary, is both brave and lucky. He has a more human touch and pleasing manner, ready to laughter, while his father never laughed. He listens willingly to his friends or dignitaries, yields to sensible argument, does not bear grudges or seek revenge. He is always glad to see the people and soldiers, but not the clergy. . . ."

It was an early opinion and we do not know whether the Gdansk scholar had occasion to revise it later. There is in it much truth, but it misses several vital points.

Wladyslaw certainly did not resemble his father in appearance, personality, or character. He was free of the old king's complexes, his bigotry, clericalism, and excessive concern with protocol, typical of the upstart. But Wladyslaw had no desire to ignore the Austrians, his relatives. Earlier, as the young crown prince, he expressed to Philip IV his warm affection for "our common house" of Habsburg. In January 1633 within a month of his election, he renewed his father's treaty, which profited only Austria. The emperor was assured of Poland's friendship, had the right to recruit soldiers in the Commonwealth, and was promised that the Commonwealth would abstain from any attempt to acquire territories under Habsburg rule. They included, however, both Upper and Lower Silesia. Wladyslaw was inconsolate when Ursula Gienger died in Warsaw, influential to the last and the official intermediary of both

Zygmunt and his son in dealings with Austria and Spain, carrying on their behalf correspondence with the court of Vienna.

What was a conspicuous irritant under the first reign was now concealed by pleasing appearances. The new king had personal charm and an amazing talent for winning friends. He was well liked by the Cossacks, though he never did anything for them. Yet he was skillful in making the right gestures: He offered to Sahaydaczny his personal physician and received courteously in Warsaw the Zaporozhe envoys. Wladyslaw could get along with almost anyone, with Christopher Radziwill as well as with a simple peasant, whose hospitality he did not disdain. Well educated, familiar with western Europe, fluent in Latin, German, Italian, and Swedish in addition to Polish, a patron and connoisseur of theatre and ballet, he was liked and admired by all. Only the most perceptive of them managed to realize that the king's genial, even folksy manner concealed a secretive, unpredictable, and obstinate character. He had his personal goals well set as he ascended the throne and never deviated from them, even though his policy appeared to be zig-zagging. The historian Victor Czermak asserted seventy years ago, without being much contradicted since, that "his ambition was to bring the maximum of glory to his name and power to the house of Vasa. . . ." The Commonwealth was to serve as a springboard for its ruler, who had dazzling plans for himself, but none for the state. The zig-zag swings of his policy were evidence of that posture.

Zygmunt III had set his goals high and his son surpassed him. While some of the father's projects were simply not viable, his heir's were sometimes not even worthy of serious consideration. The king of Spain once appointed Wladyslaw *el capitano general* of a Spanish armada in the Baltic. The then crown prince was delighted with the promotion and eager to become the admiral of the north. These fantasies cost the Commonwealth the loss of its fledgling fleet, which had already scored a victory at Oliwa. Its seven ships enlarged the Swedish navy.

Undeterred by the setback, Wladyslaw dreamed of himself as the arbiter of Europe, the conqueror of Constantinople, heir to the imperial crown. His plans and ambitions often switched from one track to another, dragging behind the galloping horse of his imagination the fate of the country he ruled.

At the very start of his reign he thought he had an opportunity worth grasping.

The Thirty Years' War was still in progress. On November 16, 1632, a week after the royal election in Poland, another battle was fought near the German town of Lutzen. The field was crossed by deep ditches, which impeded the advance of the Swedish cavalry. Gustav Adolph, at the head of a regiment of Smaland horses, was the first to leap over the obstacle, turning the tide of the battle and receiving a serious wound in the shoulder. Bleeding heavily, the king asked the duke of Saxony "to take him from the battlefield to a secure place." The duke did so, but when he had moved some distance from the Swedish troops through fog, smoke and the chaos of battle, he accidentally encountered a squadron of Austrian cavalry. Two shots, one in the abdomen and the other in the head, killed King Gustav Adolph, but the emperor's men did not recognize him and left the body behind them.

Six-year-old Christina was the king's heiress. Wladyslaw IV had assumed the title of king of Sweden immediately after his father's death, but with Gustav Adolph removed he felt his chances greatly improved. He was overlooking two things: the overwhelming majority of his Polish and Lithuanian subjects were firmly opposed to any dynastic adventures in the north, while the Swedes disclaimed the Polish branch of the house of Vasa. Furthermore, no one in Sweden was as eager to remove from power men of talent as Zygmunt did in Poland. Axel Oxenstierna remained chancellor after the death of Gustav Adolph and concluded sixteen years later a peace treaty sanctioning his conquests. He was more fortunate than Jan Zamoyski, who survived King Stefan I by nineteen years, but was no longer allowed to serve the country with his outstanding ability and experience.

The truce with Sweden was due to expire in September 1635. Negotiations were opened and the Commonwealth endeavored to recover its losses—the Pomeranian and Prussian ports and the province of Inflanty. King Wladyslaw wanted war and was preparing for it. That was why he thanked God for the settlement with Turkey and moved the army to the north. Stanislaw Koniecpolski had to leave the Ukraine again and return to the scene of his earlier battles against Gustav Adolph.

The negotiations in Sztumdorf, between Sztum and Parbuty, dealt with problems of high interest to the rest of Europe. The emperor wanted to break them off, while other nations took the opposite position. Representatives of England, Holland, and France appeared on the Baltic coast. The second secretary of the French embassy, Charles Ogier, was the author of the famous *Diary*, which soon became a literary sensation and a bibliographic rarity. An excellent translation was published recently in Poland.

The Frenchmen landed in Gdansk "one of the leading cities of Europe" and were amazed to find out that the diplomatic talks were conducted entirely in Latin, just as in ancient Rome. Some artisans in Pomerania and enlisted men in the Polish forces were fluent in the language of Caesar, as were all the noblemen. The visitors enjoyed a colorful cosmopolitan spectacle, as both sides came to Pomerania in force. The dazzling, exotic attire of the Polish cavalry was among the striking features of the multinational assembly. The camps of the Germans looked like well set-up villages, with the wives and children of the soldiers keeping them company. The German *knechts* regarded their profession of war as they would any other trade and saw no reason to be separated from their families. Unlike the German camps, those of the Scots were rather like cemeteries, while the Swedish camps were "the image of human misery and madness." Scandinavian soldiers were poorly paid, with moldy, wet bread rationed by weight. That may have been one of the reasons for the rapacity with which the Swedes looted conquered cities.

They had not been faring well lately and had suffered several defeats in Germany, so they demanded from the Commonwealth, if not a perpetual peace, at least a fifty-year truce. Wladyslaw IV was willing to give them twelve years. The negotiators laboriously extended the existing truce on a day-to-day basis. Sometimes batteries not advised of the extension opened fire on the enemy positions on one side of the Vistula or the other. War was hanging by a thread and on one occasion, in August, it very nearly broke out. The Polish commissioners barely managed to stop a hussar charge, risking being trampled themselves. The Scandinavian infantry, uncontrolled even by the officers' canes, was restrained by Field Marshal Herman Wrangel himself.

The Swedes were adamant in refusing to tolerate Catholic religious practices in the Inflanty and the violent dispute over that point nearly triggered an armed confrontation. It is true that the representatives of the child queen, Christina, were in a difficult situation, since under the laws of their country any concession on matters of religion was punishable by death.

A book about Poland, a predominantly Catholic country, deals inevitably with Catholic excesses, thus presenting a somewhat distorted view of the facts. In Protestant countries the conflict between religious denominations assumed often a more virulent and violent form. It is true that Poland and Lithuania were gradually abandoning their earlier tradition of total tolerance, but despite the existing friction the situation was one observed with surprise by Charles Ogier. In Malbork, for example, the Lutherans appropriated a former Catholic church, as there were only a few Catholic families left in town. They used one of the altars, leaving the other two for the Catholics. From dawn to 9 A.M. Catholic services were held, then a bell was sounded and the Lutherans took over until noon. The French visitor was astounded by that reasonable arrangement, unthinkable in his country.

Jacob Sobieski, who rejected on behalf of the Commonwealth commissioners the conditions set by the Swedes, took a liberal view. He declared that freedom of belief was not enough.

". . . for it is a natural right, inalienable because no one can control a person's thoughts and religious beliefs. But such an expression of faith is not enough, for faith must also take an outward form of cult, to worship the Lord with soul and body. Therefore if the Swedes allow freedom of faith, they should also permit religious observances, at least those performed in private homes."

In Stockholm, Ogier reports, even Frenchmen were driven away from their own ambassador's door "so that they could not attend Mass." "But there never was in Stockholm any massacre such as in Paris," replied Jan Nikodemus, a Swedish diplomat. Yet the learned secretary of the French mission objected, "It was not a massacre, but an act of justice, as the members of the new religion were regarded in our country at the time as murderers and criminals."

It was not an argument likely to promote Swedish tolerance. While we report here accurately the misdeeds of the counter-reformation in Poland, they should be viewed in the right perspective. Such an exchange would have been impossible in Poland, since there were no facts that could provide that kind of argument.

Acting under the pressure of his own subjects, Wladyslaw IV added some years to the dozen he had proposed at first. The Swedes agreed to a compromise and on September 12, 1635, a twenty-six-year truce was signed, but it was not a permanent peace treaty. The Baltic ports and the occupied parts of Pomerania reverted to the

Commonwealth, while the other side kept the Inflanty. One of the clauses of the agreement stipulated, "The river traffic from the grand duchy of Lithuania on the Dzwina river shall not be impeded and the tolls will be at the same level as before the war."

That was the outcome of the action started some eighty years earlier by Zygmunt August and regrettably entangled in complications by his nephew. The last of the Jagiellonians tried to bar Moscow's way to the Baltic, a goal that was achieved by the Swedes to their own advantage. The huge loss of lives and treasure by the Commonwealth had to be written off, though it could have kept Riga at the cost of renouncing claims to the crown of Sweden.

The major blunder was in spending much blood and money fighting for the Inflanty, but not one musket cartridge on the port of Klaipeda, at the mouth of the river Niemen.

The Lithuanian export trade assured the prosperity of both Klaipeda and Krolewiec (Konigsberg). The Inflanty campaign was initiated by a king of Lithuanian descent, but Lithuania did not profit by it, because of a political miscalculation.

The hetman Krzysztof Radziwill wanted to keep the Inflanty for Lithuania and suggested giving to the Swedes instead some ports on the Polish Baltic coast, but the Poles rejected that idea. Nevertheless the same Radziwill maintained excellent relations with the Hohenzollern master of Klaipeda, an Elector of the German Reich.

Wladyslaw IV doubted that the negotiations would succeed and did not wish them to. He was preparing for war, in Poland as well as in ducal Prussia, where the king of Poland had more influence than might at first appear on the basis of the treaties. The military superiority of the Commonwealth counted for more than the parchments. That was also the reason for the neglect by the Polish gentry of the potential danger of a separate duchy, independent though a vassal of the Polish crown. Great foresight would have been required to perceive the future consequences of such an arrangement, which laid the foundations of German imperialism when the Commonwealth was weakened by reverses on other fronts.

Wladyslaw IV created an accomplished fact by seizing military control over ducal Prussia, which Brandenburg was at the time powerless to prevent. Some of the population of Prussia favored Warsaw more than Berlin and the city of Krolewiec was in open opposition to the Hohenzollern duke.

In July 1635 Wladyslaw arrived in Krolewiec with two thousand soldiers and half as many members of his court. He traveled via Olsztyn and Ilawa, accompanied by the hetman Stanislaw Koniecpolski and vice-chancellor Jerzy Ossolinski, as well as other senators, soon joined by Krzysztof Radziwill. The entire political elite of the Commonwealth was assembled in Krolewiec.

The historian Wladyslaw Czaplinski writes:

> The seat of the grand masters of the Order of the Cross, founded by the Slav prince Ottokar Mons Regia, became for eight days Poland's capital. The old gothic chambers of the Knights of the Cross and the more recent Renaissance rooms heard Polish speech and served the monarch of the Commonwealth. The powerful castle dominating the city was the scene of decisions concerning the Commonwealth and its *membrum*, the Duchy of Prussia.

Wladyslaw rejoined his army at Grudziadz and left in Krolewiec as his deputy Jerzy Ossolinski, giving him wide authority to act in the national interest. The vice-treasurer of the crown, one of the ablest statesmen of his time, a skillful diplomat and administrator, carried out many constructive moves. He raised funds and used them wisely. The mercenary regiments, commanded by foreign officers, were joined by the purely Polish Zoltowski regiment, twelve-hundred strong. In August, Prussia saw unusual visitors. At the king's order ataman Constantine Wolk brought to Krolewiec through Grodno a thousand Zaporozhe Cossacks, for whom a specialist had prepared boats of the same kind as they used in the Black Sea, the "Chaika." The Cossacks sailed out and immediately seized a Swedish freighter, an event that impressed the Scandinavians.

Jerzy Ossolinski remained in Krolewiec briefly, only until September 17 of the same year. He was replaced in his position of royal "legate" or viceroy by the castellan of Parnawa, Magnus Ernest Denhoff, but the situation remained unchanged. The Commonwealth was holding Krolewiec firmly, in accordance of the political law of *Beatus qui tenet*. Several thousand royal troops garrisoned Prussian fortresses and there was an ample supply of superb fighting men from the Zaporozhe.

The Polish Seym, composed of landlubbers, began for the first time to take some interest in the sea. No power either wished or could dislodge Poland from Prussia and Krolewiec. After the truce of Sztumdorf, Wladyslaw had an uneasy peace with Sweden, while both the emperor and France tried to win him over to their respective camps. The Elector of Brandenburg, deeply involved in the Thirty Years' War, could not intervene in the east. The Commonwealth could easily have annexed Ducal Prussia and the previous conduct of the Knights of the Cross and the Electors of Brandenburg would have justified such an act, which would not have required any military operations since the Polish forces were already in Prussia.

But Wladyslaw was after more spectacular political moves and dreamed of assuming the role of arbiter in the European dispute rather than of taking Prussia. He even tolerated the provocative behavior of the Elector of Brandenburg, whom he did not want to antagonize in view of his ambitious European plans.

A few years later, on October 7, 1641, the successive duke of Prussia paid homage to Wladyslaw in the courtyard of Warsaw Castle. No one realized at the time that it was to be the last of these ceremonies, initiated under Zygmunt the Old. The Hohenzollern prince who knelt before King Wladyslaw IV and ostentatiously gave precedence to Crown Prince John Casimir, was called Frederic Wilhelm and history knows him as the Great Elector. About a dozen years later he seized the opportunity of setting his duchy free of fealty to the Polish crown. His son and successor, Frederic, was the first *konig in Preussen*—king in Prussia. His grandson, Frederic II the Great, was the main author of the first partition of Poland, whose governments seemed to have made a practice of wasting political opportunities in the north.

As to Wladyslaw IV, his ambition of becoming the mediator and peacemaker of Europe was never fulfilled. Both feuding camps deceived him, playing on his naive but boundless personal aspirations. Both history and the literature of the period tend to the view that it was the peace-loving nation that curbed the dynamic monarch's far-reaching plans and tied his hands. All the major nations of Europe were then fighting for their futures, with the Commonwealth alone stagnating in lethargic sloth.

Let us evaluate that opinion in the light of facts seen in the perspective of history. According to the conventional view, Poland should have joined the Thirty Years' War on one side or the other. That may have been true, but only at the very outset, when such a move was still feasible.

Toward the end of the reign of Zygmunt III the Commonwealth was finally concluding its own thirty-year stretch of hostilities. The war with Sweden was started in 1600 and concluded by the Altmar treaty in 1629. There were also the Muscovite and Turkish campaigns. The victory of Kluszyn and the defeat of Cecora were both costly in lives and funds. Later, under King Wladyslaw, Poland fought the Smolensk campaign and another against Abazy Pasha, winning both. The seventeenth century had already reached Christ's age, but the Commonwealth had not known peace. Its resources were depleted and a rest was needed. Scholars deploring the pacifism of the gentry at the time are theorizing in the void. A society exhausted by war, or even more so by a succession of wars, reaches a saturation point that may well influence the course of history. Toward the end of the Napoleonic era the French peasant had to give to the army the fifth of his sons and that was why the Corsican was cursed as he was sent to the island of Elbe, despite the glory he brought to France. Even the emperor's marshals, who made dazzling careers in the wars, were weary and failed their leader. In World War I the French fought magnificently, but in 1940 they displayed an inertia that was perhaps condemned too hastily. Even engineering knows the phenomenon of metal fatigue.

The Commonwealth lost the Inflanty, for which most of its citizens cared little; it recovered earlier losses in Pomerania, maintained its frontier on the river Dniester in the southeast and even improved its position there. At Szturmdorf the Commonwealth commissioners knelt before their king begging him to moderate his personal claims, likely to drive the country into another war. The eminent historian Wladyslaw Konopczynski wrote about that period: "Poland never had a better opportunity to recover—and perhaps improve—the position it had held under Batory." He could not forgive the gentry's reluctance to continue the war with Sweden. It is true that Poland's position on the Baltic could have been improved and the errors of Stefan I corrected. But this could have been achieved not by fighting the Swedes, but by remaining in Krolewiec, whose ruler was at odds with Sweden and joined its enemies. Actually the Swedish wars helped the Hohenzollerns of Prussia to sever their ties with Poland and thus lay the foundations of Prussian imperialism.

The Thirty Years' War provided Poland with an opportunity for profiting by the European conflict without participating in it, by seizing East Prussia, while France and Sweden engaged the emperor's attention and helped the breaking up of Germany into a multitude of political entities.

Profligacy in the home is like consumption:
it acts slowly but brings certain death.

Anselm Gostowski,
Husbandry, 1589

The king forbade the ringing of bells to celebrate the truce, but the Seym ratified it within two weeks. Wladyslaw persisted in his plans for recapturing the crown of Sweden, or at least trading it for a hereditary duchy, while the gentry of the Commonwealth breathed relief and awaited a period of comfortable peace. The aspirations of the monarch and those of his subjects were clearly contradictory and both sides were well aware of it. The king, using mostly foreign intermediaries, was pursuing his political schemes abroad, which were viewed with suspicion by the citizens, anxious to protect their rights and privileges.

In the meantime the country flourished as a monarchy, though the theory of a "republic of the gentry" was gradually superseded by the actual hegemony of the magnates.

The new capital was growing. The castle of Zygmunt III remained its center, but a new palace, later known as Casimir's, was built on the Krakowskie Przedmiescie avenue, on the site of the former zoological gardens of the princes of Masovia.

Below the terrace of the castle, on which the royal family dined in the summer or played billiards, two gardens descended toward the river. The upper flower garden, embellished with statues and towers with gold-plated copper roofs, offered a panorama of the Vistula below. The lower garden was a park roamed by deer, with fountains and a pool supplied with running water. Further south, in the suburban Ujazdow, a new stone building was erected next to the old wooden mansion of Queen Anna Jagiello. The Niepore palace, however, remained as it was under Zygmunt III, "a magnificent piece of woodwork." A visiting Frenchman noted: "It lacks for nothing, with many chambers, a large courtyard, garden and chapel. It leaves nothing to be desired, except to be built of more durable material: it is like a ship that requires frequent repairs."

Though it referred to an actual building, that judgment could also apply to the structure of the entire Commonwealth.

The palaces and castles were richly decorated. The Ujazdow palace was filled with marble statues from Florence and furniture of forged silver, the envy of Poland's northern and eastern neighbors and later their booty, though not equal to the treasures of Italy. Only in one respect were the halls of the king and his more prominent subjects unmatched anywhere.

"The royal wall draperies," wrote a much-traveled foreign visitor, "are the most beautiful not only in Europe, but also in Asia." The walls of the Ujazdow palace were covered with gold-threaded tapestries from the Netherlands and the Cistertian friars of Oliwa had no fewer than one hundred and sixty magnificent tapestries.

There was a passion for carpets and wall coverings. The only walls left unprotected were those at the Commonwealth's borders.

The castles of the powerful lords proliferated and they, rather than the royal residences, set the style of the era. Stanislaw Lubomirski, of Chocim fame, rejected toward the end of his life the king's offer of the highest office in the state, that of castellan of Cracow. He did not crave advancement, writes the historian Victor Cermak, "for he felt equal to the king and did not care for his favors, indeed considered himself above the crown."

The *voievode* Lubomirski, holder of five rich counties, erected twenty churches and purchased from the Stadnicki clan Lancut with all its lands. He also developed splendidly Wisnicz, founded by the extinct Kmita family. He lived there like a sovereign and was regarded as such, since the emperor of the Roman Empire granted him twice princely rank.

Yet the Lubomirskis had started their ascent quite recently, under Zygmunt III. We referred earlier to Sebastian, the modest owner of four villages, who was the father of the prince.

Instead of contemplating the power of the Radziwills, let us consider the splendors displayed by the new aristocracy, evidence of the economic potential of the Commonwealth, mobilized in a relatively short time. It was the harvest of the favors enjoyed by the court favorites of Zygmunt III.

There are two versions of the sad end in the nineteenth century of the castle of Ossolin, of which only a bridge and an arcade are left today. According to the first version, the owner had it pulled down to discourage his son from the temptation of restoring it to its former splendor. The second version claims that he demolished the walls in search for hidden treasure. The castle was built by Jerzy Ossolinski, the short-lived governor of Krolewiec, later chancellor of the crown. He also had a residence in Warsaw, so sumptuous that his apartments were served not only by stairs but also by elevators (though used only for descending). In Ossolin he was content with a small castle of twenty-two rooms and two large halls. Its roof was adorned with gables and tall statues representing Wisdom and Virtue, visible from afar, with incredibly long inscriptions of philosophical nature on their pedestals. The castle was filled with works of art. The chancellor purchased abroad paintings by Raphael, Veronese, Guido Renni, Titian, Durer . . . not all of them in the chancellor's Warsaw palace.

The Swedes took from the Wisnicz palace of the Lubomirskis works of the same masters, as well as others. A gobelin tapestry with the coat of arms of Jacob Zadzik, founder of the still existing bishop's palace in Kielce, also found its way to Stockholm.

The capital was at that time not necessarily leading in opulence, especially in the Commonwealth, where the city of Gdansk had an income equal to that of the royal treasury and some senators were richer than the king.

Incomparably more spectacular than Ossolin was the castle of Krzyztopor, near the village of Ujazd and the town of Opatow, built by the *voidevode* of Sandomierz, Krzysztof Ossolinski, brother of the chancellor. The "Year in Stone" had three hundred sixty-five windows, fifty-two rooms, twelve halls, and four towers. The outer walls were embellished with large fresco portraits of the owner's ancestors and marble plaques praising their deeds and accomplishments. The feeding troughs in the stables were also of marble.

Krzyztopor was fortified according to the current state of the art, but some of its features suggested that its lord anticipated enjoyable peace for his successors. In the north section of the castle an octagonal rotunda housed a banquet hall with a glass ceiling, which was the bottom of a huge aquarium. The sight of exotic fish swimming above them added an artistic touch to the *voievode's* guests feasting below. The founder evidently did not anticipate visitors equipped with howitzers firing eighty-pound shells.

Completed in 1644, Krzyztopor lasted in its full glory eleven years. It was reported to have cost thirty million *zlotys*. Its character and its fate were a paradigm of its era.

The castle of Nieswiez, built by Radziwill "the Orphan," had time to age gracefully, as did the castles of Baranow and Krasiczyn. But the Podhorce of Stanislaw Koniecpolski, the most opulent in the south of Poland, as well as several others, were brand new. The Gladysz family, modest by comparison with the great lords, had its handsome Szymbark on the river Ropa. The heritage of the Middle Ages and the Renaissance, mostly intact, was enriched by new additions and the Commonwealth gained splendor. Yet those living in that never-to-be-repeated time of peace, prosperity, and luxury behaved like a pack of hungry wolves.

Toward the end of the reign of Wladyslaw IV two potentates—Jeremy Wisniowiecki and Alexander Koniecpolski, the hetman's son—started their feud over Hadziacz, which belonged to the crown, but was often leased to one of these clans. A local war broke out. Prince Jeremy besieged the object of the dispute with a private army of several thousand and took it by assault "with awful cannon and howitzer fire." The sequence of that event brought even more startling developments when Wisniowiecki was requested by the Seym to swear that he had failed to appear in court because of illness.

"In the evening before the session," related one of his courtiers, "Prince Wisniowiecki assembled all the people in his service, numbering nearly four thousand. When they were all there, except for the infantry and lesser servants, he addressed them, asking them to stand by him and watch, ready to finish what he may begin. He added that if he should be compelled to swear the oath, he would immediately rise, slash Marshal Koniecpolski with his sword, and fight all those who might oppose him, including the king himself. And all of you serving in my court squeeze into the senate hall and bring me reinforcement."

Sword play was avoided when Koniecpolski, under pressure from the other senators, no longer insisted on an oath. But Wisniowiecki did not fall out of favor with the king. He soon received another royal grant—the isle of Chortyce on the Dnieper, which had been long ago the site of the first Cossack "Sich," or fortified camp, founded by his ancestor. The actual takeover of the grant was prevented by the events described at the end of the present volume.

Not all the magnates sought lucrative *starosta* appointments as ruthlessly as Wisniowiecki did that of Hadziacz, but they were ever hunting for wealth in an endless race. There was nothing to restrain them, since they were themselves the dominant political power in the state.

A few years after the new king's coronation the Commonwealth had to pay his huge debts, amounting to four million *zlotys*. His second spouse declared soon after the wedding that Wladyslaw could easily amass a large fortune, if only he did not spend recklessly. The royal estates were mismanaged rather than managed and vast sums were spent on favorites of both sexes, ranging from Adam Kazanowski with his magnificent palace to various small-fry. The king conducted for some time an affair with two sisters, the daughters of a Grodno burgher. He rewarded them by finding them husbands and making each of them a *starosta*. Even the court jester of Prince Zaslawski had several servants in livery, held his own banquets, and owned the leases of half a dozen villages.

Some polite historians describe King Wladyslaw as sensitive to feminine charms, surely an understatement. A Swedish diplomat reported to Stockholm that the king of Poland spent little on his army, more on his residences, the theatre, his father's statue, "but most of all on women." When the Seym opposed the king's ambitious foreign plans and ordered some regiments disbanded, Wladyslaw said to his courtiers: "Why don't we just say that I spent that few hundred thousand *zlotys* on my whores?"

The king was constantly on the lookout for money, which he squandered as soon as he got it. Both activities often interfered with policy. After the truce of Sztumdorf, the government of the Commonwealth decided, in consultation with the maritime powers, to institute customs duties on the Gdansk trade. They were to be less than those extorted by Sweden, but would nevertheless help the treasury. The city of Gdansk was about to agree, but it then seized the last chance of avoiding the levy: it offered to Wladyslaw eight hundred thousand *zlotys* if it was not imposed. The king eagerly agreed and collected half the amount on the next day, with the next fifty thousand payable in the following year and the balance from the Commonwealth treasury, which happened to owe Gdansk that precise amount.

"That monarch is extremely gracious and polished in manner, also very generous, but the sources of his largesse are mostly dried out. . . . It is said that he will see himself little of that sum, already earmarked for legal creditors or favorites," noted the observant Charles Ogier.

The year was 1636. In the following year the situation changed and the agreement with the Sztumdorf mediators was less important. Wladyslaw suddenly returned to the problem of customs and ordered them collected. On December 1 a Danish naval squadron intervened. The ships of Christian IV sailed into the harbor on a moonlit night and opened fire on the Polish ships, whose foreign crews surrendered without offering resistance. Soon afterward Gdansk received from Louis XIII of France a letter in which he promised support, while the French ambassador declared officially in the Seym that the king of France "urges and requests Your Majesty and you noble lords to discontinue in the future the collection of these customs duties." Discouraged by the pro-Austrian policy of Wladyslaw, France seldom missed an opportunity of giving him trouble.

The crown lost revenue and the Commonwealth was publicly reprimanded as a result of Wladyslaw's greed and volatility.

In 1644, under the reign of Wladyslaw IV, the work of Anselm Gostomski (father of the royalist Hieronim, mentioned earlier) saw its third printing. The book, entitled *Husbandry*, was a classic agricultural-management guide. Its author, the *voievode* of Rawa, was a devout Calvinist, but even the most fanatical papists profited by his wise counsel. He advised, for example, that the men loading wheat on river barges should work barefooted, as shoes could damage the grain, even though it should be placed on straw mats.

One of Gostomski's counsels reached beyond domestic economy: "The peasants' labor is the squire's main source of income and profit, so he should organize it so as not to impoverish the peasants, but bring them more prosperity every year."

The literature of the period reported some heartrending cases of dispossessed peasants ousted from their cottages. Actually such explusions were rare, for the landlord usually gave to the peasant some less desirable piece of land, as driving him away would deprive the estate of labor.

Yet there was no doubt that the peasants were getting poorer, squeezed between the burdens of servitude and the dwindling of farms caused by population growth. The typical peasant now had fewer horses, but he still led in cattle raising. He not only sold dairy products, but consumed them himself. Gostomski advised butter and cheese on the bread of the manor staff, but in carefully measured amounts. The pantry master should have a wide assortment of wooden measuring vessels, for accurate distribution for two, three, or four persons. Lard should be provided for the boatmen carrying grain to Gdansk on river barges.

Not all squires fed their servants as well and not all peasants ate their fill. The wide economic gap between various levels of the nobility existed also among the commoners. Some peasants farmed on a large scale and hired outside help, also others—even after supplying daily a team or two to the squire's farms—managed to live quite well. Others suffered poverty, due not only to their overlord's greed, but also to local conditions. Jan Pazdur, an expert on the subject, insists that until the middle of the seventeenth century about 40 percent of the rural population in the industrialized sections of what is today the province of Kielce enjoyed considerable prosperity despite the feudal impositions.

The well-being of the peasants varied depending on certain local conditions. They fared better in the royal estates, where they could appeal to state courts, and in estates managed or at least personally supervised by their owner. The worst conditions prevailed under leasehold landlords or any kind of administrators. They had to squeeze out profit for themselves as well as for the absentee owner. The squire's deputy, often not a member of the gentry himself, seldom heeded Gostomski's wise counsel "not to impoverish the peasants."

There were few medium-size estates managed by their owners in the Ukraine. The large estates were managed by bailiffs of various backgrounds, including Jews. The mysteries of agricultural management had far-reaching political consequences.

A century had gone by since the time when Zygmunt the Old declared that he did not want to stand between the gentry and their subjects. The state had long relinquished its jurisdiction over 60 percent of its prospective citizens, leaving it in the hands of the landed gentry. Gostomski's book offers generous advice on organizing surveillance and recuiting informers. Peasants were not allowed to play cards or spend a night in town. They were permitted to visit the inn only after completing the day's work and properly disposing of all equipment. Their own as well as the squire's. If a peasant failed to keep his house in good repair, the bailiff was advised to damage it further, so that the negligent tenant would learn diligence by seeking shelter under others' roofs. Offenders had to run the gauntlet of their neighbors with rods, so that each of them would give them a stroke "the shame hurting more than the punishment."

The only state legislation concerning the peasants dealt with fugitives. The very number of such ordnances attests to their ineffectiveness. There was still plenty of room for hiding in the vast

Commonwealth, either in the Ukraine or in the estates of a powerful lord who could defy the law, or a bishop.

Passive and active resistance, even rebellions, did occur from time to time, but—except for the Ukraine—not on a scale comparable to other countries, including Muscovy. The degree of oppression was widely differentiated and many peasants remained fairly prosperous. The more ambitious and aggressive among them managed to sneak into the "noble estate," which was easier than one might think, owing to the absence of an official heraldry office.

Some historians calculated that there was a sword-carrying guardian for every six or seven peasants, but that was only theory. In actual practice that guardian was assisted by a swarm of plebeian climbers, eager to serve with a view to improving their own position.

With the gentry comprising 10 percent of its population, the Commonwealth was in that respect far ahead of the rest of Europe. Every tenth citizen was a dedicated guardian of the existing order, in fact of his own property. Any revision of the social structure of such a state was not easy. It was even less so when the man at the top of the pyramid did not wish any change. A numerous privileged class is not easy to dislodge.

The existing system was guarded also by a far-better organized body, with numerous instruments at its disposal. In central Poland the rural land holdings of the clergy were larger than those of the king, in Masovia even double. This does not mean that the church was absent from the cities. Bishops and religious orders owned some towns outright. The city of Kielce, now a province capital, belonged then to the diocese of Cracow, which also owned nearby Ilza.

Chancellor Oxenstierna, understandably interested in the Commonwealth, said that it could become a threat to all its neighbors if it had richer cities and confiscated all the church estates for the crown. The first condition seemed more feasible. The creditors of kings were mostly urban merchants.

A hundred years earlier, Marcin Zborowski organized a plot, reportedly joined by seven hundred members of the landed gentry. They swore to refuse to recognize Zygmunt August, though he was already crowned, until he confiscated and promised to turn to defense purposes one third of the land holdings of the church. After the death of Zygmunt III even devout Catholics raised alarm at the

282

NORTHEASTERN TOWER OF THE CASTLE OF KRASICZYN

COUNTRY MANSION OF PODDEBICE

W. HONDIUS. PORTRAIT OF WLADYSLAW IV

R. NANTEUIL. PORTRAIT OF
CARDINAL RICHELIEU

J. SCHUBELLER. PORTRAIT OF
JACOB SOBIESKI

TOWNHOUSE IN CRACOW

KRZYZTOPOR CASTLE

PETER DANCKERS
DE RIJ. PORTRAIT
OF QUEEN CECILY
RENATA

ZYGMUNT COLUMN IN WARSAW

TOWNHOUSES IN KAZIMIERZ

PARISH CHURCH IN RADZYN

FIREPLACE AT WAWEL CASTLE IN CRACOW, WITH VASA COAT OF ARMS

CELEJOW TOWNHOUSE IN KAZIMIERZ

PORTRAIT OF A LADY

MONASTERY OF KALWARJA ZEBRZYDOWSKA

JACEK BARYCZKA,
WARSAW BURGHER

COMMEMORATIVE MEDAL
OF THE WEDDING
OF WLADYSLAW IV
AND CECILY RENATA

FRANCISZEK I, PRINCE
OF POMERANIA

LOUISE MARIE AS PRINCESS

electoral convention: "It is to be feared that Poland may turn into an ecclesiastic state." Jerzy Ossolinski was sent to Rome to seek a papal prohibition of further land acquisitions by the clergy.

The envoy, a graduate of the Jesuit schools of Pultusk and Gratz in Austria, basing his career on the backing of the Catholic church, managed to eliminate that clause from his written instructions. He dazzled Rome with his opulent entry into the city. He wore clothes studded with diamonds and his horses lost along the way their gold horseshoes, deliberately loosely attached. He brought back to Poland decisions that disappointed the gentry. Only the religious orders were told not to buy any new estates. Some interpreted this to mean that they could still receive them as gifts.

Chancellor Oxenstierna did not have to fear any undue growth of the Commonwealth's power. He still deplored the fact that young Polish landless noblemen, as well as ambitious plebeians, enlisted in the army of Emperor Ferdinand II and, later, III. That practice should have concerned the Polish government more than the Swedish chancellor, but that was not the case.

The forges of Samsonow and Suchedniow alone produced an income of about a hundred fifty thousand *zlotys* a year. In the present village of Bialogon a foundry with five furnaces, a metallurgical plant unmatched in size at the time, was built at the beginning of the seventeenth century. The Old Polish Industrial Region between the rivers Vistula, Nida, and Pilica was then far ahead of Silesia. It belonged to the bishop of Cracow, except for the royal armory on the Dobrzyca river, built in 1598. But the mills of Samsonow, Suchedniow, and Bialogon belonged to the Cracow diocese.

Steel began to be produced in Poland in mid-seventeenth century and the smelting of non-ferrous metals was developing. Western Poland supplied grain for export; Lithuania, lumber and wood products; the Ukraine, livestock, but there were many exceptions to that division. Stanislaw Koniecpolski established at Brody a weaving mill that used techniques borrowed from both Persia and the Netherlands. The famous military commander did not shun industrial enterprise. The industry was concentrated in the central region, but there were also smelters near Czestochowa and elsewhere.

The great poet Kochanowski complained that:

My home was always where the forest was thickest
But you have digged so diligently in Poland

That you drove out the poor Satyr from the woods
Wherever he looks trees are falling
Beeches for the smelter, fir for tar or oak for the ships.

There is no doubt that wood-fire furnaces depleted the forests. Many among the gentry shared the poet's concern, others used it as pretext. Since the end of the sixteenth century, when the Seym under Zygmunt August annulled all contracts for perpetuity, forges and smelters were under two kinds of attack. Some were neglected or demolished and converted to simple farms, while others, more numerous, passed into the hands of the squires. This was damaging to the social structure of the country, for the freemen working in the forges became serfs. A peasant who earned money performing auxiliary functions at the plant now had to give away days of free labor.

Nevertheless, the country had a significant metal industry and was by no means exclusively agricultural. There was considerable potential for development and many citizens advocated its efficient management.

The interaction of historical events is unpredictable and sometimes those motivated by human passions or impulses, however ill-founded, produce very practical results.

The wars that the Commonwealth had waged almost constantly since the beginning of the seventeenth century were motivated either by national interest or, more often, by missionary fervor and dynastic ambition. But they all required weapons and equipment. As a result, an important armament industry developed, both royal and private, directed by foreign experts or native lords. Among the owners of the armament factories was Stanislaw Koniecpolski, expert in the end use of the product if not its manufacture. Some at least of the muskets and pistols were imported from abroad, but the cannon and hand weapons were made locally.

It is thought that only the wealthy could afford foreign arms, while the mass of the cavalry and infantry had to depend on domestic weapons. Some role was played also by the peculiar armament of the Polish cavalry, which used sabers and not rapiers, heavy lances and swords, also the hussars' wings, hardly known outside Poland. They served other purposes aside from frightening the horses of the enemy. It was next to impossible to lasso a rider with tall feathered

284

wings rising above his head, used by the Tartars and Cossacks and called by them "arcan." The hussars were mostly well-heeled noblemen, whose capture could bring a handsome ransom. Hetman Koniecpolski loved the bow above all other weapons and attained rare mastery in archery, but was not alone, as the bow was widely used by the cavalry.

"Sword works" were established throughout the country and the Seym advised city councils to promote "artisans skilled in making military gear."

Wladyslaw IV went to Jaroslaw specially to see its fair, the largest in the Commonwealth and second in size only to Frankfurt in eastern Europe. The monarch's linguistic talents enabled him to talk to the Italian merchants in their own language, but he probably had to use interpreters with the Persians.

The king visited the town after the fire that had destroyed it in 1625. Jaroslaw declined, but not entirely, since the famous Orsetti town house, which still stands today, was built eight years after the fire and was not the only major building erected at the time. The churches and monasteries of the Dominicans and Benedictines were built anew or restored. Jaroslaw has one of the earliest Jesuit churches in Poland.

The best known and widely admired town houses: the Prelate's house in Cracow, the Baryczka in Warsaw's Market Square, the Cecejowski, St. Nicholas, and St. Christopher's in Lower Kazimierz were all built in the first decades of the seventeenth century. Yet the Polish cities could not match the finest of Flanders, Germany, the Italian republics, or France. Only Gdansk was declared by Charles Ogier to be equal to the best in Europe.

Snubbed in the political arena, underprivileged by law, the cities still maintained standards of which future generations could only dream. The traditions of the ancient guilds and their specialization in a variety of crafts ensured high levels of quality. For example, Opatow, which now retains only the Romanesque Collegiate and the Renaissance Warsaw Gate as relics of its centuries-old heritage, was then famous for its lace. Many other towns also had artisans highly proficient in a specific area.

Many new cities were chartered in the first half of the seventeenth century. It is true that in the Ukraine they owed their rank of cities only to their fortifications, as the country remained mainly agricultural. But in central Poland they were genuine urban centers, sometimes in competition with existing ones.

The Seym occasionally attempted to regulate city life, for example by trying to control excessive luxury and extravagance, witness the rhymes of Adam Jarzebski about the ladies of Warsaw:

> One walks like a manikin
> Another wears white-laced
> shoes with edgings.
> The third pantaloons
> Over a white shirt.
> Her stockings are laced with gold
> Her gloves studded with pearls.

The Seym ordnances proved, of course, futile. The magnates' palaces, carriages, and way of life tempted with evermore opulence. It is normal for the upper class to set a model to which other classes aspire and finally try to achieve by any and every means. No warnings or prohibitions can compel people living in the same community to accept meekly austerity while they see luxury around them.

Some prominence was achieved at the time in Ruthenia by a certain Yhnat Wysoczan, a peasant from Wiktorowo. He took booty from the Tartars, looted what he could during the war, and when he settled down near Bednarowo he did not become a democratic egalitarian leader. He built himself a splendid mansion and became a "peasant magnate" on the model of the aristocratic ones.

The summit sets the example. Ihnat Wysoczyn was a miniature copy of Jeremy Wisniowiecki. If an Amsterdam merchant could find at the Jaroslaw fair buyers for six hundred thousand *zlotys* worth of jewelry, why should a Warsaw burgher's wife not wear gloves stubbed with pearls?

The Seym also tried to protect domestic trade and native merchants. It enacted legislation to control profit. It was set at 7 percent for resident Christian merchants, 5 percent for nonresident Christians and 3 percent for non-Christians, which meant Jews. Such a law could obviously never be enforced, as there was no way of checking actual profits.

The attempt to control commercial activities, made by a body of noblemen holding trade in contempt, was pathetically naive. Importers and exporters of goods were supposed to declare their value and be charged customs duties accordingly, without any examination of the shipment. Let us recall Graziani's statement that in Poland an oath in court constituted sufficient evidence of truth. The learned diplomat surely did not mean to apply that principle to trade, in which the concept of truth tends to become flexible.

In the third decade of the seventeenth century, under Zygmunt III, concerned businessmen purchased and destroyed copies of an economic treatise that knowledgeably described various form of fraud, offered ways in which the treasury could prevent them, and demanded sensible reforms, notably taxes on the gentry and clergy. An assault against these privileged classes could evidently threaten more serious consequences than the burning of some books, so the author chose to remain anonymous. He is believed to have been Wojciech Gostkowski, a squire who was also a talented writer on economics and acquired his expertise when working in the office of the royal treasury. He was not known to have traveled abroad. Gostkowski was the first to discuss the balance of payments, pointing out that large sums were spent abroad for other than commercial purposes, among them education at foreign universities, church donations, and ransom paid for prisoners held by the Turks.

Stereotypes are no more adequate in characterizing the gentry than any other class or group of people. The naive ordinance enacted by the Seym reflects the pressure exerted in the defense of the status quo, but should not be interpreted as evidence of absence of rational thought among the nobility. Some of them were content to look after their crops, but there were others deeply involved in the same problems that engaged the attention of intellectuals in other European countries.

In the first half of the seventeenth century a protracted debate on economics was in progress in Poland, with some writings signed by their authors and many anonymous. Among the known writers were Szymon Starowolski and Wojciech Gostkowski, whom we have quoted. The German citizens of Gdansk and Ducal Prussia adopted the posture of patriots eager to restructure the foundations of the common home of several ethnic groups—the Commonwealth. The polemic on economics was triggered by a monetary crisis, but it dealt also with the broader problem of economic reform.

In his recently published *The Economy and the Beginning of the Commonwealth's Decline in the Seventeenth Century*, Zdzislaw Sadowski writes: "The progressive Polish economists of the early seventeenth century, observing the regressive trends of the national economy, set as the goal the enrichment of the community. Their merit was in realizing that development required industrialization, which in turn needed a more rational and efficient foreign trade policy. They wanted to break Poland out of the vicious circle of the export of grain and the import of manufactured products, to build a native industry based on domestic raw materials and pursue firmly that goal."

In western Europe such objectives were actively pursued by a numerous and dynamic urban middle class, but in Poland they could only be promoted by a rational government policy, that is by the king. Gostkowski makes many veiled critical remarks in his writings about Zygmunt's policies, aimed mainly against the privileges of the powerful lords.

The government of the Commonwealth had a choice to make, but it made the wrong one. Instead of backing those interested in progressive development, it sided with those who, suffering the least from the economic stagnation, blamed it on dishonest merchants and Jews. The *voievode* Hieronim Gostomski, a pillar of the official royal policy, declared that the shopkeepers could leave the country if they did not like the taxation of goods enacted by the gentry. He was also hostile to the Jewish shopkeepers on religious grounds.

The law controlling the profit margin of merchants was largely aimed against the Jews, but it actually gave them an advantage instead of curbing their profits and by doing so incited the antagonism of the Christian merchants who were faced as a result with stronger competition. Some books about the alleged ritual murders perpetrated by the Jews were published at the time and in 1618 Zygmunt III ordered one of them confiscated, even though he was himself a militant Catholic.

When the personal physician of Marie Medici, queen of France, died, he had to be buried in Amsterdam, as there was not a single Jewish cemetery in France. The Thirty Years' War was a dark period for the Jews. Armies of Christians, aroused against one another and flying religious banners, were eager to revenge the crucifixion, the more so as the Jews were generally well-heeled. These armies consisted of mercenaries, ready to fight anyone for pay and to loot anything in sight. Still, such activities have always and everywhere welcomed an ideological justification.

Some years earlier Prince Radziwill "the Orphan" had a significant experience in Egypt. He sailed along the Nile to Cairo with some companions, incognito, pretending to be a French merchant. The sultan's customs men searched the travelers thoroughly, including their pockets, as Frenchmen were reputed at the time to be talented and dedicated smugglers. The search proved fruitless and it was not until then that the chief of the customs house overheard the conversation of the suspects. He immediately pushed his men away and approached Radziwill, addressing him in Polish. He introduced himself as a Jew, "a countryman from the town of Chelm in Ruthenia," and after apologizing for the search "offered his services in anything we might have needed and frequently visited us afterwards."

This happened in 1582. Some years later the Commonwealth shocked the papal legate, Cardinal Hippolito Aldobrandi and his retinue, by the laxity in its treatment of the Jews. The Jews in Poland did not wear any distinctive attire or identifying emblems, so that they could only be recognized "by their faces, unwashed with holy water," as the Italian member of the mission put it in his diary.

Many of the traditions and customs long established in the country must have survived into the counter-reformation era, since during the Thirty Years' War Jews fled Germany to settle in Poland.

In the Ukraine the fate of the Jews was shaped by the economic structure of the country. The Jews were known as tough rent and tax collectors, who purchased from the government or the magnates tax or toll-collection rights and then squeezed from the people as much as they could get to double or triple their investment. They reportedly even held a lease on church keys, which they only released to Orthodox parishes for payment. The fortune of a magnate or a squire and that of his Jewish agent grew together and shared the same hazards.

When Jeremy Wisniowiecki began his forced withdrawal from the Zaporozhe in the Ukraine, his hussars and dragoons were followed by a long train carrying five hundred Jewish families and their possessions. They were the lucky ones who survived.

III

In July 1636 in the church of the University of Wilno, Wladyslaw IV honored a poet whose Latin works were known throughout Europe at the time and remained remembered long after. Matthew

Casimir Sarbiewski received the hat of a doctor of theology, poet's laurels, and a precious ring for good measure. The ceremony was assisted by the academic senate, the royal court, and the papal nuncio, paying homage to the master, who had been crowned earlier in Rome by Pope Urban VIII.

Wladyslaw was openhanded in cultural matters and displayed a keen interest in the arts. Natives watched the royal theatre and ballet with somewhat naive amazement. Foreigners recognized them as the best in Europe. When Rubens died in 1640, his family held an auction of his works in Amsterdam that was attended by agents representing four monarchs. The Polish king was second only to the king of Sapin in the volume of his purchases. In the halls of the royal castle of Warsaw one could meet artists of many nationalities, not only those already familiar, but also the Dutch painters in their distinctive garb, who were a novelty. Unlike his father, the king was not unduly prejudiced and received the Protestants from Flanders without fear of contamination.

Soon after honoring Sarbiewski, Wladyslaw participated in the ceremony of the transfer of the relics of Saint Casimir. The Wilno chapel, the Torun tomb of Anna Vasa, and Zygmunt's column in Warsaw are considered the outstanding monuments of the period. All three have survived to this day and that may be the reason for their high rating. Peter I of Russia did not manage to take to St. Petersburg Zygmunt's monument, but he looted all the sculptures in Casimir's palace spared by the Swedes. It is impossible to evaluate today the vast collections of art assembled by father and son, Zygmunt and Wladyslaw, both dedicated collectors and patrons of the arts.

Anne Catherine Constance, the king's sister, married Philip Wilhelm, the Elector of the Palatinate. She had a dowry of four hundred fifty thousand *thalers* and many valuable works of art.

In the bishop's palace of Kielce, an architectural treasure even without its adornment, we see the frescoes described cautiously by experts as "from the workshop of Tomas Dolabelli," which means painted by the master's pupils under his supervision. One of the ceilings carries a picture of the trial of the Arians.

On April 20, 1638, the king ordered under a verdict of the senatorial court the closing of the Rakow academy. It was the end of a school founded in 1602, which could accurately be described as an institution of higher learning with several hundred students, excellent professors, and a European reputation. Among its graduates was Stanislaw Lubieniecki, historian and astronomer, author of the *Historiae Reformationis Poloniae* and the treatise *Theatrum cometicum*. The closing of the college, the intellectual center of Polish Arianism, was responsible for the fact that Lubieniecki continued his scholarly activity in Denmark. He brought with him from Poland a perfect command of Latin, which was a major component of the Rakow college curriculum.

The Rakow students were not compelled to emigrate after the closing of their college. They could move to Luslawice in the Carpathian foothills, or to Kisielin in the Wolyn region, where schools of their denomination continued to function. Religious services were also held on the estates and in the homes of Arian nobility and no one had the right to interfere with them. The law expelling the Polish Brethren was never enforced. Even at the court of Jeremy Wisniowiecki, an eager convert to Catholicism, the Domaradzki family not only professed Arianism, but protected and promoted it. Gabriel Domaradzki even held public services in the estate of Warwa on the east bank of the Dnieper, which he leased from the prince.

The decree condemning the Rakow college was widely publicized as evidence of religious persecution. Yet even after that legislation the Arians—detested by all the other denominations—enjoyed far more rights in the Commonwealth than the Catholics in Sweden or the Inflanty, where they had none.

Jacob Sienienski was the owner of Rakow. The royal decree threatened him, in case of noncompliance, with a heavy fine but not with death. In other countries the protector of a condemned heresy would have received other treatment. That is why the Swedish diplomats at Sztumdorf were so adamant in refusing even modest Catholic demands.

Rakow was taken from the Arians by official order, backed by force. But that fact alone does not account for the rapid progress of counter-reformation in Poland.

Three years after the verdict terminating the Rakow college, Father Bonaventura Dzierzanowski was appointed the pastor of the local Catholic parish. The peasants found a patron and protector in the dynamic priest, who visited the villages on foot, showed concern in the life of his flock and helped them. Father Dzierzanowski also

291

visited foreign countries, attending the conventions of his order. He went four times to Rome and once to Toledo, walking all the way. Like Saint Francis of Assisi, he did not take bread with him.

The counter-reformation was capable of attracting and enlisting in its ranks men of outstanding ability and character. Dzierzanowski was not an exception, there were others working selflessly for the cause. Piotr Skarga exerted a significant influence on the policy of a major nation, but lived like a pauper. Both talent and character are needed to capture the imagination of the masses and their trust. The first generation of Polish Jesuits had stars such as Jacob Wujek, Piotr Skarga, and Matthew Sarbiewski.

Among the causes of the successes of the counter-reformation was one particularly well known to the Jesuits. They were sworn to blind obedience. Each of them was to be to his superiors "as a cane in the hand of an old man, a dead object." Compliance with doctrine and its goals, coupled with wide freedom of initiative in the choice of means used, proved a very effective policy. That latter privilege permitted effective action and helped to attract brilliant minds.

Counter-reformation did not shun either innovative art or strong personalities among its supporters.

During the election there was some concern in its ranks about the royal candidate's personality. Wladyslaw was far from devout and differed in that respect from his father. He was even suspected of religious indifference, largely on the ground of his friendship with Protestant leaders such as Rafal Leszczynski and Krzysztof Radziwill. Wladyslaw was indeed no crowned missionary and managed to set himself free of his father's inhibitions and complexes. The historian Victor Cermak observed that a man whose chief ambition was the throne of Sweden could hardly persecute the Protestants if he was of sound mind. Wladyslaw's foreign and domestic policies were both subordinated to that goal, to which he gave first priority. It was to cost the Commonwealth dearly soon afterward, but in this particular instance its side effects were beneficial. The monarch no longer provoked the religious dissenters and he even tried to curb the growing intolerance. He did so even when he had to give consent to injustice. He yielded to pressure, but immediately tried to offer some degree of compensation.

One year after the verdict against the Rakow college, religious disorders broke out in Wilno. The local Calvinists were accused of shooting arrows at the holy picture in front of the Bernardine church. A royal decree expelled the Helvetian congregation beyond the boundaries of the capital of Lithuania, but peace was not restored, for Jesuit students attacked Protestant ministers visiting the city. The king reacted sharply: he threatened the bishop with restricting the rights of the Catholic academy and ordered the *voievode* to maintain order.

If Poland was fated to have Wladyslaw IV for its king, he should have come sooner. He would not have allowed the deterioration of interreligious relations in a multidenominational federation. His purely political mind was bored by theological argument. The king realized the need for peaceful coexistence, but upon his ascent to the throne he inherited too many accomplished facts perpetrated with the consent and blessing of his dead father.

During the interregnum the Protestants requested various guarantees of religious freedom, but they heard in response from the Catholics that "Protestantism is an itinerant vagrant who, having begged shelter in Poland, cannot enforce anything on the true masters of this land and its ancient heirs. Whatever is accorded to the dissidents, meager though it may be, should be accepted by them with gratitude. Should they choose contest, the Commonwealth will not be short of determination and force to hold on to its native rights and to save the ancient faith."

The more militant adherents of Rome even advised the merging of the private armies of all the Catholic magnates to stamp out the heretics.

The dissidents were told startling news: they were second-class citizens, who could only enjoy such rights as they had as a favor from "this land's true masters." The consequences were not long to come. On August 6, 1632, the hetman Krzysztof Radziwill met at his own request with the Elector of Brandenburg. Thoroughly incensed, he proposed on behalf of the Protestants a formal alliance, to which he planned to attract also the Orthodox, including the Cossacks. He also wanted intervention by England, Holland, Denmark, and even Sweden.

Such an initiative was manna from heaven for the Elector, for it offered him a footing within the Commonwealth and assisted him in his difficult task of emancipation from its sovereignty.

Let us not judge Radziwill's action by present-day standards. Men of the seventeenth century identified religious with national allegiance and did not regard as legitimate a government that oppressed their faith. Fervent Catholics thought the emperor's political interests to be the supreme good and no one charged them with treason for doing so, nor should we. The hetman Stanislaw Koniecpolski knew the military weakness of the country, was aware of the enlistment of Poles in the emperor's army and tolerated it, yet he was surely no traitor. Krzysztof Radziwill has the right to be judged by the same criteria.

The state ruled by Wladyslaw IV was on a slippery slope. The counter-reformation had eroded its internal cohesion. Citizens acquired the habit of following alien ideological banners and the king was powerless to undo the harm already done. His tolerant attitude, however, did slow down the disruption of the bonds holding the federation of three—formally two—nations.

Radziwill and Leszczynswki were on Wladyslaw's side to such an extent that they even supported his plans of war against Protestant Sweden, with a view to increasing the importance of the religious dissidents within Poland.

A minor but significant incident reflected the evolution of the relationship between Poland and the Vatican. It was connected with Jerzy Ossolinski's embassy to Rome in 1633. Earlier Seyms had quarelled persistently with Zygmunt III over the ownership of the magnificent Flemish tapestries of the last of the Jagiellonians. The king regarded them as his personal property and the Seym as that of the crown, but not the monarch. Yet now it did not object when three out of five major tapestries in the "Moses" series were to be taken by Ossolinski to Rome as a gift for the pope.

Later the senate and the gentry took Wladyslaw's side in his feud with the Roman curia. They were incensed over the unresolved problem of the prohibition of land acquisitions by the clergy. Urban VIII treated the king of Poland condescendingly, as not equal to hereditary monarchs, while the nuncio tried to throw his weight about in Warsaw in an offensive manner. He opposed the demolition of a few houses purchased from the Bernardine nuns to make room for a column commemorating Zygmunt III. Finally the houses were pulled down, the column erected, and Mario Filonardi had to leave Poland without receiving the king's farewell. Until the death of Urban VIII in 1645 the Commonwealth had no diplomatic relations with the Holy See.

The arrogant language of the nuncio, Wladyslaw's formal order to intercept his mail, and the royal guards posted in front of the bishop's residence placing him under virtual house arrest were the outward symptoms of a conflict over basic principles. Urban VIII demanded the abolition of all the rights of the non-Catholics and the establishment of Catholicism as the state religion, which would have been tantamount to a declaration of civil war. The verdict against the Arians was one of the king's concessions, as was the expulsion of the Calvinists from Wilno, forced by the local fanatics. Wladyslaw yielded under pressure, but used delaying tactics. The death of Urban VIII was a blessing for the Commonwealth, for his successor, Innocent X, discontinued the pressure.

In 1632 the Cossacks sent delegates to the last Seym session under the reign of Zygmunt III. They declared their loyalty to the crown, but complained about religious persecution, which did not as yet affect them directly but "caused our Ruthenian nation suffering . . . in almost all the lands of the duchy of Lithuania, in the Przemysl region and Wolyn, drawing closer to us lately . . . in the Siewiersk district near Czernihow and elsewhere." Zygmunt responded by promising an investigation and admonished the petitioners not to interfere in the affairs of the grand duchy of Lithuania.

He was formally right: the Cossacks were the subjects of the Polish crown. But their appeal was significant insofar as it proved that the Cossacks of the Zaporozhe were beginning to act as spokesmen for all the Ruthenians within the Commonwealth, not only in the Ukraine but also in Bielorussia in the grand duchy of Lithuania.

Two evolutions were in progress, acting in different directions but compounding each other: the Ruthenian national consciousness was growing in the east, while the Jagiellonian tradition of equality of nations and faiths was declining in the west.

The errors in the treatment of the Orthodox church were so glaring that even Zygmunt III moderated them somewhat in the last years of his life and reign. He received warnings from devout Catholics, among them Albrecht Radziwill and Stanislaw Koniecpolski. Both statesmen pointed out that the maltreatment of the Orthodox served the interests of Moscow and inflamed the Cossacks, further instigated by foreign powers. There was much talk about "pacifying the Greek religion" at the Seym and throughout the country, but the matter was postponed from one session to another and finally nothing was done until the death of the servant of doctrine.

The first years of the reign of Wladyslaw brought some important but casual concessions, ordered by the king himself or by commissions acting on his behalf. Several local disputes were resolved in favor of the "Greeks" and it was decided to establish in the Grand Duchy two metropolitan sees: an Orthodox one in Mohylew and a Uniate one (the branch of the Orthodox church recognizing the authority of the pope) in Polock. Finally, in 1635, the metropolitan see of Kiev was revived under Piotr Mohila.

The nephew of the *hospodar* of Moldavia had already proved himself loyal to the king and the Commonwealth, but that was not his only asset. Piotr Mohila was dedicated to the dominant culture of the Commonwealth. Educated in the west, fluent in Latin, he certainly had no intention of betraying Ruthenia or the Orthodox faith. On the contrary, he wanted to bring them out of their lethargy and low standing. He realized that this could be accomplished only by catching up with the Poles and Lithuanians in education, knowledge, and creativity. Mohila had to fight stubborn resistance to that idea among his own people and his life was at times in danger while he was evolving the concept of a college, later to become an academy.

Conditions in the Ukraine were characterized by the statement of the previous metropolite of Kiev, then still illegal, Piotr Borecki: "A fairly well-educated man is here like a diamond amidst rocks, gold amidst rough stones." Borecki wrote those words in Polish, the preferred language of the upper strata of Ukrainian society, including the Cossack leaders, mostly descended from lesser Polish gentry. The process that had started long ago in Lithuania was repeated in the Ukraine. But the use of the Polish language and culture did not mean in either case any desire to abandon distinct national identities within the framework of the Commonwealth. Piotr Mohila's school taught Latin and followed the organizational patterns set by the Jesuits, but it remained Orthodox and Ruthenian. That was why its activity served the best interests of the federation, helping to make it a reality.

Piotr Mohila was authorized to act in 1635, but nothing could reverse the damage done during the previous forty years, when the law of the Ukraine and Bielorussia denied legal standing to the Orthodox faith.

In 1623 Krzysztof Zbaraski dealt with that problem in a Seym speech which does him credit:

For if they want to abolish Ruthenian nationality in Ruthenia, that is impossible. No argument and no violence can accomplish it. Whoever breaks the law drives a dagger into our fatherland's heart by destroying the peace among the nations constituting the Polish Commonwealth and killing it. That is the dispute which they started with the Ruthenian nation, our blood brothers.

Krzysztof Zbaraski, son of the *voievode* of Braclaw Janusz and Anna, née Princess Czetwertynska. Yet his was a voice addressing the Ukraine from outside. The great lord's plea would carry quite a different political weight if he had been in a position to say: "This is a quarrel started with us, the Ruthenian nation, your own brothers and kin, gentlemen of Poland." That quarrel would never had occurred if the Zbaraskis, Zaslawskis, and Ostrogskis had remained what their ancestors had been under the Jagiellonian kings.

Konstanty Wisniowiecki had addressed Zygmunt August, outlining the condition of peace, "Let no one be held lower because of a different faith, especially Greek, and no one dragged to another religion."

Now in the seventeenth century, Krzysztof Zbaraski protests against "harassment in the courts, seizure of priests, expulsion of monks," but agrees that the Orthodox be persuaded to accept the Catholic faith as "the only good and secure, with uncontrovertible truth."

The prince was totally absorbed by Polonism and Catholicism. This voluntary conversion harmed him and his people by removing the main pillar of the unity of several nations, the powerful lords of other than Catholic persuasion.

IV

The truce of Sztumdorf, which brought much glory to some magnates and peace to the gentry at large, did less for the king and thereby for the state.

The problem of the Gdansk customs duties was handled with amazing ineptitude. The king and his advisers forgot that iron has to be struck while it is hot. As a result, Denmark intervened militarily and France diplomatically to secure major advantages. Yet the Polish crown and treasury could have kept the Gdansk revenues if only appropriate action had been taken a year earlier.

The attempts to build a Polish navy in the Baltic were ineffectual. They started in a pathetically comical manner when a Scotsman enjoying the king's confidence was sent to the West on a secret mission, with funds for the purchase of ships. Instead of buying ships he vanished together with the money. Too many foreigners seeking their own profit and totally indifferent to Poland's national interest were involved, while native efforts were inadequate.

The best and only way to build sea power was starting from a strong land base, from Warsaw to Krolewiec, from Wilno to Klaipeda. The Commonwealth did send there a governor and a soldier, the hetmans of both Poland and Lithuania were in Krolewiec. Then, because of the king's fantasies and his dreams of becoming the arbiter of Europe, that key strategic position was abandoned, no doubt to the delight of the ghosts of the Knights of the Cross of old, none of whom when alive were in the habit of leaving voluntarily any spot taken by the force of arms. The ghosts may have been in hell, but their political achievement survived to bring later hell on earth.

Let us repeat that Poland and Lithuania could have become a maritime power only the same way Russia did, by first becoming a continental power and then gaining adequate access to the sea. Russia achieved the status of a maritime power at Poltava, far from any sea. The tsars had two fleets: one in the Baltic and the other in the Black Sea, but they only built the latter after taking possession of the Crimea.

The king built on the coast the forts of Wladyslaw and Kazimierz. He also bought from the Gdansk merchant potentate Hewel some ships, used for trading when not assigned other missions. When Hewel died and his heirs demanded payment, the ships had to be sold at a loss.

Wladyslaw never abandoned his dream of the Swedish throne, or at least compensation for renouncing it, in the form of a hereditary duchy for the Polish branch of the Vasa dynasty. Inflanty was considered first and then Wladyslaw turned to other parts of Europe. He thought that by becoming an architect of peace he could win renown and also a duchy for himself and his heirs. In his endeavors for achieving that goal he used almost exclusively non-Polish agents.

The dynastic objectives of the king influenced his position during the Sztumdorf negotiations and also the plans of a navy. They played an important role in his matrimonial projects.

Wladyslaw planned to marry a Protestant, the daughter of the "winter king" who died in exile, Princess Elisabeth. He hoped to secure in this way an alliance with England, but the Polish bishops were of course outraged. The only one among them to abstain from opposition was Pawel Piasecki, quoted earlier. Other candidates for the queen's crown were a mother and daughter: Gustav Adolph's widow, Maria Eleanora, and the young, extravagant queen of Sweden, Christina. Finally Wladyslaw followed a well-beaten track and married on September 12, 1637 a Habsburg, Cecily Renata, his own cousin and sister of Emperor Ferdinand III, who had just ascended the throne of Vienna. The king thus became the emperor's brother-in-law, a fact that incited dreams of imperial heritage and also sent a very clear political message to the chanceries of Europe.

Cecily Renata was crowned in St. John's Cathedral of Warsaw. The Seym protested this break with tradition and constitutionally endorsed the rights of Cracow as the coronation city.

The cousins' marriage was not a happy one. The king did not like his spouse and she had good reason to disapprove of his conduct. Needless to add, Cecily Renata followed the example of her grandmothers, wives of Zygmunt August, as well as her two aunts, who shared successively the bed of Zygmunt III. Like they, she was an unofficial but very real agent for the promotion of Austrian interests. She performed her function, however, far less ostentatiously than the late Constance.

The year 1637 brought an agreement known as the "family treaty" between Wladyslaw IV and the Habsburgs. Some of its clauses border on audacious fantasy. For example, in the event of the Polish branch of the Vasa dynasty becoming extinct, its rights to the Swedish throne were to be passed on to the Habsburgs. The authors of the treaty overlooked the fact that the Swedish parliament had resolved quite formally after Gustav Adolph's death to banish the descendants of Zygmunt from Stockholm and in fact proclaim them morally and physically outcasts in Scandinavia. The "family treaty" also established an aggressive alliance against Turkey, with the provision that the lands to be eventually taken from the sultan were to become the hereditary property of the Polish branch of the house of Vasa, except for its member currently ruling Poland.

The emperor's diplomats endorsed such daring projects, but

that did not mean that they proposed to help in their implementation. Austria wanted to keep the Commonwealth in a lethargic state, which permitted the recruitment of troops for the emperor's army. It was afraid that the Commonwealth might seek a rapprochement with France and try to recapture Silesia with her backing. The main purpose of the treaty was to alienate Poland from France. Paris understood it very well and Wladyslaw immediately started to encounter at every step obstacles placed in his way by the French. Louis XIII was not helping Gdansk out of compassion and the archcatholic king's ambassador interfered boldly and openly in the Commonwealth's domestic affairs.

Important units of Polish troops had served the emperor under the reigns of Zygmunt and Wladyslaw, with their knowledge and consent. The goal of French policy was therefore the weakening of the royal authority in Poland, which could prevent the enlistment of Polish mercenaries in the emperor's army.

In May 1622 some squadrons of Lisowski's private army appeared on the Rhine and later even in northern Italy. In 1635 Pawel Noskowski from Masovia and Jan Gromadzki from Sandomierz led their cavalry into regions seldom visited by Polish soldiers. Their regiments crossed the Rhine at Worms and invaded Champagne, scoring several victories over the French. These were among the last exploits of the Lisowski bands, which vanished from the scene of history soon afterward.

It was then that one of Lisowski's men, probably sent to Amsterdam on some errand, attracted Rembrandt's attention. The "Polish Rider" is a masterpiece evoking a dark period.

The French maneuvers against Poland were not without cause. They were simply the consequence of Wladyslaw's attachment to Austria.

In August 1638 Wladyslaw IV left Poland, heading for Baden in Lower Austria, ostensibly to take care of his health at the baths. His real purpose was a meeting with the emperor for a discussion of Polish-Austrian relations. The Seym was not consulted in advance and the protests of several senators, amongst them hetman Koniecpolski, were ignored. The king was accompanied by Queen Cecily Renata and an impressive retinue: the chancellor of the crown, Piotr Gembicki; both vice-chancellors: Jerzy Ossolinski and Stefan Pac; Jacob Sobieski; the inseparable confidant Adam Kazanowski; and the Brandenburg envoy Jan Hoverbeck; not to mention lesser dignitaries. The monarchs met in October in Nikolsburg. Receiving his royal brother-in-law in his country, Ferdinand III, contrary to previously arranged protocol, ostentatiously took the first place. The Polish royal couple were assigned a second-rate apartment facing the courtyard.

The emperor refused to help his brother-in-law in an embarrassing situation, for which he was himself largely responsible. Since May 9 of the same year the crown prince of Poland, Jan Casimir, was held in a French jail and treated harshly there. The guards allowed him to speak only in French and very loudly. At the time of his arrest a crowd demonstrated in approval of the action of the French government.

The half-brother of Wladyslaw IV had served previously in the imperial army with the rank of colonel, participated in the Lorraine campaign, and escorted Cecily Renata from Vienna to Poland. His close and cordial relations with the Habsburgs were well known to the French, who had an excellent intelligence service. In January 1638 Jan Casimir set out on an interesting journey. He reached Venice—via Vienna, of course—and boarded the ship "Diana" bound for Spain.

His official capacity was modest, as a private member of the retinue of the Polish ambassador, Jan Karol Konopacki. His real mission was to start upon his arrival in the Iberian peninsula, where he was to be appointed, by agreement with Emperor Ferdinand, viceroy of Portugal and admiral of the Spanish fleet. The traveler knew what rank awaited him as he strolled on his way in the ports of Toulon and Marseilles. Cardinal Richelieu was not unreasonable in suspecting Prince Jan Casimir of espionage on behalf of Spain. There was no hard evidence to support the suspicion, but the crown prince was arrested by the order of the governor of Provence and held successively in the fortresses of Salon and Cisteron. Only in August 1639 was he transferred to the castle of Vincennes near Paris, where the conditions were better. The prince's freedom was won in February 1640 by the embassy of Krzysztof Gosiewski, *voievode* of Smolensk. He had to sign a document on behalf of the Commonwealth pledging abstention from treaties hostile to France and the termination of recruitment in Poland for the imperial army.

Louis XIII then admitted Jan Casimir to his presence, receiving him in accordance with the protocol for "princes of the second rank." The audience was held in the royal bedroom.

Pleas for the freedom of the admiral-to-be were made by Pope Urban VIII, Charles I of England, the cities of Venice and Genoa. Only Ferdinand III, brother-in-law and ally, failed to do anything or even promise to help. Gustav Adolph's remark about the Commonwealth, "God only knows how they are led," proved accurate again.

Three years after his release, Jan Casimir conceived a new idea: when in Loretto he suddenly discovered a vocation and entered the Jesuit order. Urban VIII confirmed his admission, to spite Wladyslaw. The candidate for viceroy of Portugal became a cardinal instead.

The head of the dynasty could find comfort in the fact that since Palm Sunday of 1640, which happened to be the first of April, he had a presumptive heir to the throne, Prince Zygmunt Casimir. The imperial couple, Ferdinand and his spouse, were to be the godparents. They were represented by the uncle and aunt of the newborn prince and no banquet was held, for the overjoyed king could not rise. He was plagued by gout, with pain so severe that his screams were sometimes heard all over the castle and he had to be carried on his bed to assist the Seym sessions.

Wladyslaw was only forty-five, but his health was poor. He turned obese early, was sluggish and ailing. He ceased to wear Polish attire, as the foreign style shoes were easier on his swollen feet. Unlike his father, he liked to sleep late and transact state affairs in bed. He suffered some kind of particularly vicious rheumatism and bladder stones. It is not known whether those who blamed his ailments on the excesses of his youth were right. Let us examine contemporary memoirs. Every now and then one of their protagonists suffers simple or "tertiary" fevers, sudden accesses of "shakes" and an assortment of other strange afflictions. Present-day medical associations should publish these memoirs to make people appreciate the blessings of modern medicine. In 1624 the archduke Charles Habsburg, bishop of Wroclaw, died suddenly when traveling in Spain with then Crown Prince Wladyslaw. He fell ill because of "drinking strong wine" and died because "the Spanish physicians, unfamiliar with the diseases of northerners, drained too much of his blood."

Hygienic conditions were then atrocious, even Paris was plunged in unbearable stench. Drinking and gluttony reached unbelievable proportions. The Poles and Lithuanians were no different in that respect from other nations, with the possible exception of

Italy. England, the Scandinavian countries and Germany, Moscow, and Vienna—all were alike. The Elector of Brandenburg, when receiving Wladyslaw in Szczytno, relieved himself at the table, so that his courtiers had to drag him out hastily, to avoid soiling the other guests. In the famous Arthus Hall of Gdansk heavy drinking of beer went on day and night, without any food being served. It was normal routine at various royal courts to place vomiting vats on the landings and in antechambers. Some preventive measures were taken in France: Louis XIII threatened excessive gluttony with a punishment to fit the crime—confiscation of the table silver and all the dining room equipment. The only culinary innovation in Paris at the time was the adding of hot spices and scent to the dishes, which had been popular in Poland even earlier. No one was shocked by grabbing food with the fingers or replacing on the serving plate pieces found less attractive.

Wladyslaw showed displeasure when only a few dishes were served. The only moderating factor of his diet was an occasional shortage of cash, but Queen Cecily Renata was reported to have saved in a short time eight million *zlotys*, half of which she sent to her family in Vienna.

Time went on, the king was nearly fifty and the successes of his early years were not repeated. We will not attempt to list all his wild projects, among them that of starting a war with Sweden. The gentry were becoming increasingly distrustful and suspected that even in the matter of the Gdansk customs revenues Wladyslaw was acting under the emperor's influence and in his interest. It was suggested that the revenues, if any, should be channeled to the state treasury, not the royal purse. The action against the Arians alarmed many, even among the Catholics, as the procedure used had no precedent in law and no legal justification. Everyone was careful not to be accused of favoring the heretics, so Rakow found few defenders, but the affair generated more suspicion.

The plan for establishing a "knighthood of the Order of the Immaculate Conception" was eventually dropped. Perhaps an educational reform might have been more useful, as the existing schools taught mainly rhetoric, respect for the status quo, and bigotry.

The projected "Knighthood" would have comprised seventy-two domestic and twenty-four foreign members appointed by the king. It would have become another version of the royalist party under Zygmunt III, which failed to bring any benefits to the country. The two leading senators: Stanislaw Lubomirski and Stanislaw Koniec-polski, thanked politely for the honor, but declined it. Krzysztof Radziwill opposed the project vehemently, as only Catholics could be members of the Order. The concept was basically contrary to the character of the Commonwealth, as it would have created an official privileged elite associated with a single religious denomination. Such an elite already existed unofficially, but to give it legal sanction would have aggravated the political situation.

Jerzy Ossolinski was a supporter of the "Knighthood of the Order of Immaculate Conception" project and probably one of its authors. He was an able man and a brilliant diplomat, but lacked skill in domestic politics. His staunch monarchist philosophy was no doubt justified at the time, but his tactics were faulty. Disregard of the ancient laws and traditions of the Commonwealth contributed to the decline of royal authority.

Wladyslaw IV inherited from his father two lieutenants of out-standing ability and character: Jerzy Ossolinski and Stanislaw Koniecpolski. The first, a civilian politician, used high-handed meth-ods to achieve his goals, trying to terrorize the deputies and ignor-ing Seym resolutions. He was the principal instigator of the Rakow and Wilno decrees aimed against the Protestants. The second of the two men, a soldier, ruthless to the point of cruelty, observed meticu-lously the law and shunned any illegal methods. That was why he could have played a crucial role in the approaching crisis.

In the meantime, Koniecpolski had his hands full in the Ukraine. He was acting there in accordance with the law, though it was a law in conflict with the reforms required to ensure the survival of the federation.

The system of servitude was spreading in the Ukraine, putting an end to the period when fugitives pursued elsewhere were given there the status of free men. Conditions remained more relaxed beyond the Dnieper, which was understandable, as the drive for "order" was advancing gradually from the west, from the more densely populated regions settled earlier. The unrelenting drive for wealth among the upper classes made the lot of the plebeians pro-gressively harder. But, lest we congratulate ourselves on that in-sight, let us hear a contemporary, Pawel Piasecki:

"Various Polish lords who gained either by purchase or by royal grant vast estates in the Kiev region, the principal seat of the Cossacks, tried to increase their revenues by persuading the senate and the king that the excessive freedom of the Cossacks, which they saw as an obstacle to the the their designs, should be curbed."

Let us not pretend that no one understood at the time the real interests of the state. They formed a tangled web in the Ukraine, requiring a farsighted policy aware of its ultimate goals. The non-registered Cossacks were seen by the landed gentry as prospective serfs and by the state as a reserve of military manpower, to be used anywhere, even in Prussia. Yet the same state contemplated unperturbed the Cossack raids in the Black Sea, over which it had no control whatsoever. After the treaty concluded with Turkey in 1635, so appreciated by a king looking toward Stockholm, disturbances in the southeast were to be avoided.

The treaties with Moscow, the Sultan, and Sweden stabilized to some extent the situation in the major components of the Commonwealth, Poland and Lithuania. In the third, the Ukraine, basic problems were still to be resolved and should have been the main concern of the government, which engaged its attention elsewhere.

Poland proper recovered after Sztumdorf its ports and the Grand Duchy Smolensk, the Siewiersk and Czernihow regions, with the right of navigation on the Dzwina for its export trade. This was a satisfactory situation, but in the Ukraine the border was a fluid line across the steppes. The Zaporozhe claimed the right to receive both royal commissioners and envoys of foreign powers. Some maps show the customary paths of Tartar incursions: the Valachian, Kuchmen, and Black. Each of them reached far west, to Zbaraz, Krzemieniec, Lwow, Sanok, even Iwonicz. It could only be achieved by a well-planned, sustained effort.

In 1635 the Seym resolved to build on the Dnieper the fortress of Kudak. Its garrison was supposed to watch the Zaporozhe, cut off its communication with the rest of the Ukraine and thus prevent "disorders."

The decision was a wise one. It could be faulted only for planning one fortress instead of a dozen. Kudak symbolized a concept, but failed to carry it out. It was an irritant, but not an adequate instrument of control. It annoyed not only the Zaporozhe Cossacks but also the Tartars. Only a day's march from its ramparts, the narrows of the Dnieper allowed an easy crossing.

Casimir the Great might have been right or wrong in conquering "Red Ruthenia," the region on the west bank of the Dnieper, but he was surely right in starting immediately to build there a network of defensive castles. There is much to be learned by observing Sobien on the river San. Beside the rock crowned by the ruins of the castle, the Germans built during World War II a powerful bunker, with a field of fire covering the river valley. It was exactly the same spot picked six hundred years earlier by the king of Poland for his fortifications.

The construction of the Kudak fortress was funded partly by hetman Stanislaw Koniecpolski from his own resources. A state whose ambassador dropped gold horseshoes in the streets of Rome was too poor to pay for the defense outpost alone.

Computing the debts of Wladyslaw IV or the savings of his wife, actual or exaggerated, historians talk about millions of *zlotys*. Yet the wages of the "registered Cossacks" amounted to about one hundred fifty thousand *zlotys* a year. The government was often in arrears in their payment, thus antagonizing the Cossack military elite, embittered by poverty.

Various structural reasons prevented the conversion of the Commonwealth from a binational into a trinational federation. Nevertheless it had the means of controlling the situation by force, at any rate until the disposition of the Tartar problem, which would have allowed a broader settlement.

The Kudak fortress, still under construction, was attacked by Cossacks under Sulima. They were men at the lowest level of the Cossack community and their "ataman" would be described in twentieth-century terms as a populist leader. Social relations in the Ukraine were fluid at the time and evade any attempt at classification. The historian Wladyslaw Tomkiewicz unearthed recently the sensational fact that the same Sulima was a creditor of Prince Jeremy Wisniowiecki, in the amount of four thousand *zlotys* that he had loaned to the magnate.

The people of the Ukraine were surely unhappy but those who incited them to rebellion were thinking of their own advancement and profit rather than social justice. The major error of the Commonwealth was in failing to elevate the entire upper echelon of the Cossacks to noble rank. Coats of arms, estates, and the role of squires would have pacified them very effectively.

The registered Cossacks helped to suppress the Sulima rising, which nevertheless managed to destroy the walls of Kudak, slaughter the military detachment guarding the construction, and impale its commander, the French mercenary officer Morion. Sulima was soon captured and beheaded in Warsaw, His widow still held as security of the Wisniowiecki loan the village of Pulince near Lubnie, while Sulima's aide, Pawluk, whose death sentence was commuted, led another major rebellion in 1637.

Shortly before its outbreak the royal commissioners, headed by Adam Kisiel, managed to win over some of the registered Cossacks by paying them arrears of their wages. This alone doomed the Sulima rising to failure. The operation against the rebels was led by Mikolaj Potocki, field hetman of the crown. Koniecpolski, ill at home, supervised the campaign, which was carried out strictly according to his orders.

The hetman's proclamation announced ruthless punishment for those who failed to surrender within two weeks. They were to be punished also "in their wives and children" and their homes demolished, "for it is better that nettles should grow there than traitors to His Majesty and the Commonwealth have their breeding ground."

After taking Kudak, Sulima and his men were not content with slaughtering the soldiers, but murdered also their wives and children. Koniecpolski promised revenge in kind, but did so only after his negotiations with Pawluk failed.

The latter also did not spare his enemies. He captured and ordered executed all the senior officers of the registered Cossacks, notably Colonel Sava Kononowicz and the military scribe Theodore Onuszkiewicz. The ataman's proclamation, issued on August 12, 1637, appealed to the nonregistered Cossacks and the peasantry. It called for war against the lords and traitors but did not attack the king at all, quite the contrary. Pawluk promised to the monarch assistance in need. No far-reaching conclusions should be drawn from this statement, as the peasants and lower-rank Cossacks were already at that time beginning to look toward Moscow. The Commonwealth could only count on the support of a relatively small Cossack elite. Those of its members who managed to escape Pawluk sought asylum in the camp of the royal forces.

The campaign against Pawluk was soon over. The easy victory may have turned Potocki's head and made a commander of middling talent overconfident. The hetman paid dearly ten years later, when he had to face an adversary worth alone more than all the leaders of the Cossack risings before him. Figures familiar to the readers of Sienkiewicz's great historical novel, *Fire and Sword*, were then beginning to appear on the scene.

The ominous proclamation of Koniecpolski was issued in September, after that of Pawluk, but it was not until November that the army arrived from the Dniester region, which it had been guarding against an expected Tartar attack. As soon as they arrived on the . banks of the Dnieper, the troops formed a confederacy and demanded payment of wages in arrear. Potocki had to negotiate with his subordinates, treat them courteously and make promises. On December 10 he left Rokitno for Bohuslaw and Korsun. On December 16 he won the battle of Kumejki and four days later he besieged at Borowica the remnants of the Cossacks, who surrendered and delivered Pawluk to the hetman. It was a ten-day winter campaign.

The Polish forces performed at Kumejki an uncommon feat by breaking through a Cossack wagon ring with a cavalry charge. The casualties were heavy, but the result was overwhelming. The French engineer Beauplan, who designed the plans for the Kudak fortress, left us a testimony that throws light on this exploit. He stated that two hundred Polish cavalrymen could deal in the field with two thousand mounted Cossacks, but a hundred Cossacks could defend successfully a ring of wagons against ten times as many Polish troops. This time the hussars broke through the ring.

The morale of the defeated Cossacks was such that they simply gave up the fight. Pawluk tried to escape surreptitiously from Borowica, but was captured by his own comrades, who delivered him to Potocki. Adam Kisiel, who sincerely desired accord with the Cossacks, personally promised them that Pawluk's life would be spared, but he was executed in Warsaw later.

The humble, obsequious act of surrender was signed at Borowica by the scribe of the Zaporozhe forces, Bohdan Chmielnicki. Eleven years later he was negotiating terms of peace with the same Adam Kisiel, whose pledge was disregarded and broken by others.

Mikovaj Potocki did not confine himself to military operations. He had rebels beheaded and their heads placed on public display. The hetman did so in Kiev and the principal towns and the local lords on their estates.

Koniecpolski and Wladyslaw IV approved Potocki's actions, as did the spring session of the Seym of 1638. The Cossack "Register" was limited to six thousand men, carefully separated from the peasants and burghers, under the command of a commissioner and officers of noble birth.

All the nonregistered Cossacks were declared by the Seym to be "rabble turned into peasants." Wladyslaw IV, generally considered a staunch friend of the Cossacks, had approved Koniecpolski's moves even prior to the Seym session. This was demonstrated in Adam Kersten's book about Stefan Czarniecki, who had fought against Pawluk as a lieutenant of hussars and took part in the Kumejki charge.

The ataman was beheaded and his body quartered, while the Ukraine witnessed the second, even bloodier, phase of the uprising led by Jacob Ostranica, Dymitr Hunia, and Carp Skidan. This time the rebels against the Commonwealth were assisted by subjects of the tsar of Moscow, the Don Cossacks. Several hundred of them served under the command of Putywlec in a detachment which, hard pressed by Potocki, surrendered only to be immediately butchered contrary to promises given before the capitulation.

Prince Jeremy Wisniowiecki was very active in the suppression of the second phase of the rising. He could not participate in the first as he was then wooing the young Griselda Constance Zamoyska. This time he brought with him his private army, and proved himself a courageous and skillful commander, winning popularity among the gentry.

Ostranica and Hunia abandoned their men and fled eastward, where they later heroically defended Azev against the Turks, together with the Don Cossacks. On August 10, 1638, the siege of the Cossack camp at the juncture of the rivers Sula and Dnieper, defended with extraordinary tenacity, was ended. The remnants of the defenders had to surrender unconditionally to Mikolaj Potocki. The field hetman scored another triumph, earning perhaps more credit than he deserved.

The Kudak fortress was completed. Its commander was Krzysztof Grodzicki, a military engineer and artillery expert trained in the Netherlands and tested in Germany in the emperor's service, under Wallenstein himself.

The victories over the Cossacks were the only successes achieved by Wladyslaw IV after the truce of Sztumdorf. All his other enterprises failed. An uneasy peace returned to the Ukraine—until the time when it was upset by the king's policy, which turned its attention to the southeast at least ten years too late.

V

Wladyslaw's plans of a war against Turkey were the subject of many scholarly and literary works. The latter tended to promote the view that a wise and dynamic king's admirable designs were thwarted by the sluggish pacifism of the gentry.

The plans were rather like the Loch Ness monster, popping up from time to time and then vanishing so completely that its existence was in doubt. This went on for thirteen years. It was only toward the end of the reign that the plan of a crusade against the Crescent surfaced permanently and almost immediately grew to proportions beyond all reason, reaching a gigantism likely to frighten not only the home loving squires but anyone of sound mind.

If the crowned head of the government had been concerned with national interest rather than his personal ambitions, he would have returned to the southeast immediately after Sztumdorf, that is, after securing the northern and northeastern borders and settling fairly satisfactorily the problems of Lithuania and Poland proper. Let us not forget that at the very beginning of the reign the sultan had made a move and the Seym responded by voting substantial taxes. Even later Koniecpolski reported "fair weather," which in his language meant an opportunity for action. But the royal policy was lost in fantasies, looking all over Europe for spectacular effects. It neglected deplorably the problem of Prussia and only remembered the Turkish—actually Tartar—problem in the last moment, when the Ukraine, always smoldering, was about to burst out in flames.

Wladyslaw IV was reported to have said, "If only the Poles were like the Spaniards, who prepare plans years before an expedition, assemble resources and wait for an opportunity. . . ." The king should have addressed the admonition to himself.

In matters of foreign policy and war, a nation can act only through its executive. It it fails to perform, the nation remains helpless.

The Pacta Conventa clearly obligated the king to defend the Commonwealth with his own means. They also stated specifically that the provision referred to the Tartars. Every incursion of the horde could bring a broad response, reaching as far as Budziak, even the Crimea, assuming tactics of hot pursuit. After all, Koniecpolski had once taken the royal army as far as Sasowy Rog in Moldavia. Soon afterward the sultan promised to remove the Tartars from the Budziak steppes, but failed to do so.

Two things were required. First, a concept, not necessarily a new one, for it could revive the old plans of Jan Zamoyski, whose successor and champion was no other than Koniecpolski. It was a matter of ensuring the security of the Ukraine against outside attack. Second, funds were needed to support the army in the first phase of operations before the Seym had voted taxes. It was a question of creating an accomplished fact.

When, during the Sztumdorf negotiations, Wladyslaw sailed down the Vistula, he could see only the roofs of the houses on the right bank of the river, which was in full flood. The luxury of the royal court and those of the magnates swept the country with an even greater flood of opulence. According to a French diplomat, no country in Europe endowed its queen as generously as Poland. Yet after deciding on war with Turkey, Wladyslaw started desperate appeals for subsidies from Venice and the Vatican.

After the unfortunate exploits of Abazy Pasha, the Tartars behaved rather erratically. The feuds among the worshipers of the Prophet caused the khan of Crimea to collaborate occasionally with the Commonwealth, even to submit to it. The hordes were then so quiet that "not even a chicken was missing in Your Majesty's domains." At other times it was not so.

According to popular view, the Tartars organized their raids only in the spring and summer, when the steppes grew green and the population could be taken by surprise in the fields during harvest. That was often true of the Valachian and Kuchmen trails, but the Black Trail was used mainly for winter incursions. The Tartars invading by that route seized tens of thousands of civilian prisoners in 1640. The pursuit came within sight of the Tartars with their human booty, but a sudden blizzard or fog halted the Polish cavalry. It was surprised by the raid, as Polish envoys were negotiating at the time with the sultan in Istanbul and he did not want any disturbance of the peace.

Four years later Koniecpolski, informed by his spies, knew about a planned raid in advance and waited for the superior forces of Tuhay Bey. He confronted them on January 30, 1644, at Ochmatow on the river Tykicz, having unerringly calculated the route the invaders would take. Supported at a crucial moment by Wisniowiecki, the hetman won a decisive victory. The commissioner for the Zaporozhe forces, Mikolaj Zacwilichowski, chased the defeated Tartars and caught up with them on the Siniucha river. The ice could not hold the escaping horde and many Tartars drowned, others reportedly crossing the river on a bridge of their bodies.

Turkey did not stand behind her vassal. Four years earlier it was unaware of their plans. A war against the Tartars risked provoking the sultan, but not necessarily to the point of war, as there were possibilities of political maneuver.

These two incursions were among the major ones, the smaller raids could hardly be counted. The Budziak Tartars made their living by regularly bleeding the Commonwealth with small pinpricks.

The Ochmatow encounter triggered a reaction and the war plans mentioned occasionally by the king surfaced again. In 1645 the forthcoming war was already discussed at the county councils.

Wladyslaw's policy was drifting at the time toward France. That move was assisted by an unexpected event—the death of the thirty-three-year old Queen Cecily Renata. The pregnant queen was active until the end, taking a keen interest in politics. On March 23, 1644, she gave birth to a dead child and died herself on the following day. The bereaved king lost no time in thinking of a new marriage. The Habsburgs sent him sixteen portraits of princesses from which to choose. France sent only a quarter of that number, but chancellor Jerzy Ossolinski counselled a French connection, desirable for several reasons.

Wladyslaw did not want to quarrel with the Habsburgs or disturb the family ties. In 1645 he even made a deal with them whereby he took duchies of Raciborz and Opole in Silesia as a pledge for the dowries of his late wife, mother, and stepmother. Two years later he took title to them, but for the house of Vasa rather than the crown of Poland. This was made clear in the agreement and no Polish administration was to be introduced in Silesia.

The king's rapprochement with France was motivated by his hopes of seizing with its help the Swedish throne. Like all his other schemes, it never materialized. Only one path to great deeds and glory was left, the southeast. Wladyslaw turned to it with the blind passion of an aging and ailing man seeking his last chance. This concatenation of circumstances had disastrous consequences, for it drove the king to a wrong choice of means used to achieve his goal. It is also true, however, that luck was definitely against him.

The matrimonial choice was Louise Marie Gonzaga, princess of Mantua, Montferratu, and Nevers, descended from the Paleologues, who had once ruled Constantinople and heiress to their tradition. Such a bride, or rather the memories and moral claims of her breed, gave wings to Wladyslaw's imagination and launched it on hazardous

312

flights. The superstititious monarch was also influenced by prophecies predicting the crown of Greece for the princess. Louise Marie's father, Charles Gonzaga de Nevers, had been active years earlier among the Christian subjects of the sultan, inciting them to rebellion.

The bride, a lady with an eventful past, a year older than Cecily Renata, kept a cool head in the situation. She sold all her lands to the king of France and as a result had eight hundred thousand *thalers* in her private purse as queen of Poland. She knew that one cannot make bricks without straw.

Preparing for war by all possible means, the king quite sensibly sought peace and even a close alliance with Moscow. As an inducement, he agreed to minor border adjustments in Russia's favor, disregarding the protests of the Grand Duchy, which Poland pacified by giving Lithuania other territories as compensation. The Polanowka treaty went beyond merely establishing peace; it set the ground for future collaboration. On both sides of the frontier new generations were growing up, which only knew secondhand about the era of the False Dimitris, the Moscow massacre, or the Polish occupation of the Kremlin. Political rationality was beginning to take over from emotions. Tsar Michael died on July 23, 1645. On his deathbed he entreated his son Alexy to keep peace with the Commonwealth, under pain of withholding his blessing.

Moscow was a good candidate for an ally against the Tartars. It preferred to pay and give away the spoils rather than antagonize the sultan. It ordered the Cossacks to abandon Azov, which they had taken and defended with incredible tenacity. Helped by the Zaporozhe, the Don Cossacks repulsed twenty-four Turkish assaults, with several hundred Cossack women fighting on the ramparts together with the men. The tsar preferred to have the fortress razed and the territory returned to the Turks.

In the winter of 1645 the Tartar horde attacked Muscovy. Mikolaj Potocki marched to the rescue at the head of a substantial Polish army. He accomplished little, as his troops were ravaged by the cold, but his march meant more than a mere exchange of embassies between Warsaw and the Kremlin. The cooperation was taking actual shape, in accordance with the king's plans and orders.

In January 1646, when the field hetman was freezing in the steppes, the hetman of the crown, Stanislaw Koniecpolski, paid a brief visit to Warsaw. He had little time, as he was about to marry for the fourth time. The aging, recently widowed lord developed a passionate love for sixteen-year-old Sophia Opalinska.

Nor did he neglect public affairs because of romance. Koniecpolski brought with him a carefully phrased "Discourse" on war against the Tartars and a "league" with Moscow. He presented it to the king, Chancellor Ossolinski, and a few trusted senators at a secret meeting.

"As to a military alliance with Moscow against the Tartars, especially now when they have ravaged half of that country, who can doubt its use and need?" were the opening words of that historic document.

The hetman, just as Jan Zamoyski several decades earlier, did not trust exotic alliances, but thought cooperation with the tsar useful. He did not indulge in euphoria and was well aware of the danger presented by a neighbor grown too strong; but after weighing the pros and cons, he advised the conquest of Crimea, to be yielded to Moscow in return for some territorial compensation elsewhere. He thought it better to have in the Crimea "Moscow, a dubious friend, than infidels, avowed enemies." As to the security of the Commonwealth, once it was secure in the east, ". .we would have a border on the Danube or further. We have the means of achieving that, by gaining in return for the Crimea Valachia and Moldavia, perhaps also Transylvania, lands so rich that they could wage war against the Turks themselves, leaving our country secure from the enemy, without taxation or foreign missions for our forces."

He was following the footsteps of Zamoyski, who advised control of the foreground by creating a buffer between Poland and Turkey.

The hetman of the crown was not a militarist. He won renown in many wars as an outstanding commander and he regarded the army as a necessary evil. Such a statesman and soldier could find common ground with the gentry.

Wladyslaw IV had his way open to constructive feats of arms on a regional scale. Ossolinski was also in favor of action, but in a slightly different direction. He wanted to attack Moldavia directly, instead of the Crimea. But the real difference between the hetman and the chancellor lay elsewhere. We have referred to the basic difference in their characters, in odd contradiction to the offices they held. The soldier refused to consider any action contrary to the will of the Seym. The chancellor disregarded such subtleties and was ready to ride roughshod to his goal.

Koniecpolski knew the defenses of the Crimea and had secured sketches of them, using a spy who pretended to be a merchant but was actually an engineer. The hetman was confident of the result, provided that the Crimean campaign was conducted efficiently, with the full knowledge and consent of the Commonwealth. After presenting his views he left promptly for Rytwiany, where he was married on January 16, 1646.

It became widely known that "the Cracow lord was enormously pleased with his wife," for the castellan of Cracow, *voievode*, and commander-in-chief, pushing sixty, reported his pleasure in letters to his friends.

In the meantime a brother of his bride, the *voievode* Krzysztof Opalinski, and Bishop Jerzy Leszczynski brought from Paris Louise Marie, the king's bride. Wladyslaw IV had another attack of gout, so the French lady had to wait a week in Falenty near Warsaw for his recovery. On March 10, still ailing, the king sat on a chair placed in front of St. John's Cathedral. He was in a bilious mood, for he had received from Paris reports of his fiancées earlier romances. "Is this the beauty about whom you told me so much?" he coarsely asked Viscount de Bregy, the French ambassador. That was all the greeting Louise Marie heard from the king, while Ossolinski welcomed her courteously as his deputy, trying to smooth over his master's rudeness, "The Polish crown will add new luster to your glorious breed, which carries the last drops of Paleologue blood and will, with God's help, recover its ancient might."

These meaningful words were uttered early in the day of March 10. Stanislaw Koniecpolski died in Brody on the following night.

"You Poles do not know what you have lost," said the *hospodar* of Moldavia, "but in two or three years at most not only you, but all Christendom will mourn the loss of such a great senator and hetman."

Two years! Actually it took exactly two years and two months to prove that, contrary to popular wisdom, there are in this world some men who are irreplaceable.

The hetman was not the victim of poison or an epidemic. He died of "too much love." He was about fifty-six. War does not unduly tax the health of a man of that age, especially when he is the commander. But there are more stressful tasks, though more pleasant ones.

At the outset of the war the commander in chief was missing. On the eve of actions that could determine the future of the Ukraine, a strong man, whose authority was recognized on both sides of the Dnieper, was gone. There was nothing to control the king's wild fantasies.

The untimely death of Stanislaw Koniecpolski was one of the most tragic events of Poland's history. It is not widely known, for the action of *Fire and Sword*, the great historical novel of Henryk Sienkiewicz, Nobel prize laureate and author of *Quo Vadis*, begins nineteen months later. Koniecpolski's death would not have had as great significance had the enterprise in the southeast not been indefinitely postponed by foolish adventures. It should have taken place earlier, in the lifetime of the hetman's previous wife, Christine Lubomirska. The fate of nations can sometimes be determined by a few names. In this instance the fate of not one but three nations was at stake. The hetman's death allowed others to unleash such a congeries of blunders that coexistence with the Ukraine and the transformation of the Commonwealth into a federation of three nations became impossible. A severe crisis broke out in the spring of 1646.

The king returned on May 9 from a hunt and declared his intention of starting a war against Turkey. Its ultimate goal was not the Crimea, Valachia, or Moldavia. It was no less than Constantinople, Istanbul, the capital of the Ottoman empire.

The campaign was to start in the same year, 1646. Stanislaw Koniecpolski was one of the strange breed of Polish and Lithuanian warriors of the Silver Age. Zamoyski, Chodkiewicz, and Zolkiewski liked to charge ahead heedless of obstacles but only in the field. In matters of state they held back more impetuous politicians. The departure of the hetman removed a major block in the way of the king's fantasies, an authority with which he had to reckon. Wladyslaw IV immediately committed a major blunder, an act of political suicide.

His action was a flagrant breach of the law. He was not authorized to declare war or enlist troops without the consent of the Estates—the Senate and the Seym. He could, acting cautiously, obtain their agreement to dealing with the Tartars, who harassed the Ruthenian provinces. But a war of aggression against the sultan

316

was unthinkable for the Commonwealth, as it was bound to end in defeat. Whoever protested against it was right. The only success on the Turkish front, the battle of Chocim, amounted to barely saving the Polish border. Everyone knows that after countless efforts by the Russian tsars and a world war in which Turkey was on the losing side, that country still remains independent.

Wladyslaw was seduced by the idea of a crusade. He looked for allies as far as Morocco and Persia. Venice was at the time contesting against the Turks the island of Crete, and an agent of the Republic, Battista Tiepolo, roamed Warsaw and incited the king by every imaginable means. The pope was the natural patron of a crusade.

He could not offer money as he did not have any. The revenues of the Holy See were absorbed by the service of its huge debt. Venice promised some funds, but was actually only waiting for the outbreak of Wladyslaw's war with the sultan to conclude a peace treaty with him. The queen of the Adriatic was looking for a diversion that would allow it to disengage itself.

Wladyslaw borrowed from his wife the money for enlisting his first soldiers. He was out to conquer the world with an empty purse,

The king's advisers at that time were almost all foreigners. The senators saw the closed doors of the king's chamber and knew that the most important matters of state were decided without their knowledge. The outsize egos of the magnates were hurt, but so also was the principle of constitutional government. The king held secret councils and carried out their decisions, openly enlisting troops. These actions were in violation of the basic principle of the Commonwealth's government, requiring approval of policy by the Seym and the Senate.

Jerzy Ossolinski was the only native Pole among the king's advisers, but the chancellor was not burdened with much scruple. Always at the top of his class in Jesuit schools, favored by the Habsburg archdukes, he did not fit into the pattern of the democracy of the gentry and was inclined to force his decisions without consultation. He backed the idea of a campaign in the southeast, but his plans did not reach beyond the Budziak steppes and Moldavia. Ossolinski was not without faults, but he was a statesman and did not want a major battle with the sultan.

"I was betrayed by the chancellor like Christ by Judas, not out of anger or hate," the king complained to a Venetian. It was true that Ossolinski was not guided by emotion, but simply refused to break the law and did not sign the recruitment documents.

Wladyslaw was left alone and could go no further. He could not afford to. Even the troops that he would have needed to carry out a coup had to be paid.

The senators opposed the king's plans. Jacob Sobieski, the father of the future king Jan, who had been appointed castellan of Cracow after Koniecpolski's death, was so upset by the controversy that he fell ill and only managed to get to his estate of Zolkiew just before dying.

Faced with pressure, Wladyslaw changed course. He now declared that he only wanted to deal with the Tartars, but he did go to Lwow and ordered artillery to be moved there. It had been long rumored across the country that this would be the signal for war against Turkey.

On December 6 the Seym resolved not only to disband the units recruited by the king but also to reduce the royal guard. According to some, Wladyslaw did not resist these moves much because he wanted to win popularity among the gentry for his son, Zygmunt Casimir, the presumptive heir to the throne. The crown prince, however, died on August 9, 1647, after a brief illness.

The houses of the Seym had held a session earlier, in May, and resolved to allow the government to use certain reserve funds kept for an invasion emergency. This amounted to increasing the "quarter troops." The Seym also decided to refuse to offer "gifts" to the Tartars, which meant a challenge to the horde. No embassy was sent to Turkey.

There is no doubt that a more sensible and straightforward policy could have avoided many disasters and permitted an expedition against the Tartars of Budziak and Crimea. The Commonwealth was constitutionally opposed to wars. Instead of inducing it to carry out necessary protective military measures, it was urged to reach for the sun but not given any means of doing so.

In August the castellan of Kiev, Adam Kisiel, arrived in Moscow as ambassador, with a retinue of five hundred, all of them Orthodox. The envoy managed to reach a provisional agreement of mutual assistance against the impending Tartar invasion. The tsar's troops began assembling at Putywel. They received explicit orders to pay cash for anything they needed after entering Commonwealth territory, to abstain from violence, and generally to behave as allies.

There was also a promise of assistance from the other end of Europe. Cardinal Mazarin of France undertook to pay two hundred thousand *florins* annually from the beginning of a war with Turkey. He soon reduced his requirements and promised the same amount for a war against the Tartars only. Paris preferred Wladyslaw's energy and that of his subjects to be expended far away from France and the area of its immediate interests. It did not want to see any more Polish cavalry in the Champagne region.

Late in the fall Alexander Koniecpolski and Jeremy Wisniowiecki carried out, on the king's order, deep raids into the steppes. The former reached the region of Perekop, seized some herds and a few scores of men. The latter visited Chortyca, which he was recently granted, and erected there a rock mound, without encountering any opposition. The Tartars avoided provocation. Crimea was ruled by a new khan, the tempestuous and cruel Islam-Girey.

The year 1647 seemed at first to untangle the knots tied in the preceding year, but that was only an illusion. Actually it was already too late.

On his return from the expedition, Alexander Koniecpolski arrested and intended to sentence to death Bohdan Chmielnicki. The war council vetoed the order, as the accused was a scribe of the Zaporozhe Cossacks serving the crown and therefore subject to the hetman's jurisdiction.

Chmielnicki was a contemporary of King Wladyslaw, over fifty, but he had not distinguished himself in any way so far. Stanislaw Koniecpolski knew him well and remembered the time when he came to Warsaw for consultations in January 1646.

The hetman had used then a convincing argument. He realized that the attempt to curb the Cossacks by force had failed and that the Ukraine was starting to simmer again. He also had reports of an impending alliance of the Zaporozhe with the Tartars. He thought that it was time to attack the Crimea before that "league" had time to materialize. For the same reason Koniecpolski advised that the Cossack war boats should be let loose in the Black Sea. The author of the threatening proclamation against the Pawluk uprising was now concerned with dissipating the energy of the defeated side. He wanted to direct it outwards, which was certainly in the interest of the Commonwealth. Once the Crimea and the Budziak region were conquered, the Ukraine would be free of the constant menace of invasion and thus render superfluous the armed readiness of the Zaporozhe. After victory over the Tartars, which would open wide economic opportunities, the Cossacks, skilled in various crafts, might find a place for themselves under the new order. Those who acquired coats of arms could become squires, the others merchants, artisans, or burghers in other trades. Control over the Ukrainian coastal area would ensure the security of all of southeastern Ruthenia. Koniecpolski realized that the tsar and future master of Crimea would have a serious chance of bringing the Orthodox Ruthenians to his side and he spoke about it at the Warsaw conference. This well-founded conviction provided a motive for the solution of the Ukrainian problem within the Commonwealth.

All the complex threads of the Cossack lair of Zaporozhe and the Ukraine at large were in the hands of Koniecpolski as he left Warsaw for his ill-fated wedding, carrying with him a plan of action that remains unknown to us. The only man with a wide experience and a profound understanding of the situation was gone, leaving on the scene the king, who had little knowledge of Cossack affairs.

In April 1646 a strictly secret mission of the Zaporozhe army was received in Warsaw. It was probably brought there by Hieronim Radziejowski at the king's order. Four men arrived at the royal castle at night. They were Ivan Barabasz, Ivan Eliaszenko, Nestorenko, and Bohdan Chmielnicki. The king talked to them in the presence of seven witnesses, only one of whom, Adam Kazanowski, was Polish. Even Ossolinski was not admitted to the meeting, the content of which others tried three years later to extort by torture from Cossack prisoners in the belief that they may have heard about it at the time.

The four Cossack delegates were told about the planned war. They received eighteen thousand *zlotys* for building war boats and the number of "registered" Cossacks was doubled to twelve thousand. These grants were confirmed by written documents.

It was not much, but every Cossack could dream of becoming one of the lucky six thousand new recruits or a member of the crew of one of the "Chayka" boats about to sail for glory and booty. The mere fact of royal favor was a potent factor, as the news of it could generate legend.

The king requested secrecy and his partners observed it for a long time. Both documents rested in the chest of colonel Ivan Barabasz until the following winter.

320

The night meeting was held no later than April 20, when only an expedition against the Tartars was contemplated. Three weeks later the king announced that he intended to march against Istanbul. The situation had changed completely, but the documents remained. They contained tempting and concrete promises, now having become *de facto* invalid, instead of firm authorizations. The letter of the parchments remained the same but their meaning, since the Seym resolution cancelling the plan, was now different.

The widely publicized and then immediately dropped plans created an upheaval throughout the country. Contrary to the simplistic views of some writers, not all the "feudal lords" were raring for conquest. Most of them preferred to profit by what they already had without taking further risks. That was particularly the view of the lessees and all kinds of bailiffs, who exploited the peasants for their own advantage as well as that of the landlord. For them, war was a disaster to be avoided at all costs.

The bailiffs and estate managers were running wild so much that the king himself wrote to Alexander Koniecpolski urging him to curb the excesses of the "masters by proxy." This had little effect and the complaints sent to Warsaw could "fill a whole chest." Jerzy Ossolinski received a letter from a man who could not be suspected of softness or any great love for the plebians:

> The Zaporozhe army are constantly complaining to me about the outrageous wrongs they are suffering from the bailiffs, servants, and leaseholders: haystacks, granaries, beehives, and other property is taken from the Cossacks, who are beaten or killed; this may cause that militia [the registered Cossacks] to dissolve or bring about a civil war, for they must get tired of such lawlessness, and brought to the point when they must either become the serfs of the leaseholders or start a rebellion.

The author of the letter was Mikolaj Potocki, grand hetman of the crown amd castellan of Cracow, the victor of Kumejki and the ruthless pacificator of the Ukraine. The date is as eloquent as the writer's name: November 21, 1647.

At the political summit negotiations were at the time in progress with Moscow and France, while reason finally prevailed and cooperation with the Cossacks was planned. Yet the lower echelons, practically out of control and motivated by personal gain, frustrated all plans and triggered a national disaster. Authority out of control in the hands of petty and stupid people is bound to bring misfortune.

Stanislaw Koniecpolski fell into lethargy in the last hours of his life and did not have time to dispose of his assets, which was rare among people of that era. Nevertheless, he found time to express regret for having left Bohdan Chmielnicki alive. Earlier, then in full health and vigor, he had promoted him from a junior officer in the Czehryn regiment to scribe of the Zaporozhe army. "Great things will come from this man, good or bad. There is much to be feared," he then observed. The hetman formed that view from the moment when Chmielnicki, asked his opinion of the powerful fortress of Kudak, replied, "My lord, what human hands built, human hands can destroy."

It seems a simple maxim but we do not know in what tone it was spoken. We can only guess that the brilliant commander, therefore a good judge of men, read the message in the Cossack's eyes.

The hetman was evidently confident in his strength. He felt that he could deal with Chmielnicki and work with him. That was why he did not wipe out a man "from whom great things would come." But parting with this world, he was appalled to realize that his successor could not handle the Cossack leader.

Unlike Koniecpolski, a certain Daniel Czaplinski had no inkling of the character of the man with whom fate brought him into contact. He was of Lithuanian descent, had served under Alexander Koniecpolski as deputy *starosta* and squadron leader. He was mentioned in passing in Sienkiewicz's *Fire and Sword*. His life story vividly confirms the theory that civic and military virtues seldom go together.

It is possible that Czaplinski earlier had managed one of the estates of the Kiszka clan in Lithuania and tortured rebellious peasants there. After the outbreak, Chmielnicki included among the terms of major political agreements a clause demanding that his enemy be delivered to him. One shudders to think what would happen to him if he had been. Czaplinski did not flee from the Ukraine. He took part in the defense of Zbanaz, then fought at Beresteczko, escaped the nightmare of Batoh, and finally vanished out of sight.

It was a time when passions reached an intensity that is difficult for us to understand. Czaplinski took away from the widowed Chmielnicki a woman he loved, born Komorowska, and married her.

Later the hetman of the Zaporozhe managed to seize the beauty and married her with the permission of the Orthodox church. After a time the lady turned unfaithful to her fierce husband. Chmielnicki ordered his eldest son, Timothy, to carry out an investigation and if the adulterers were guilty to hang them. The son found that his father had indeed been deceived and the sentence was carried out in the gate of the family estate of Subotow, the guilty couple hanging lashed to one another so that they would die together as they had sinned.

Let us not underestimate the reflexes of the seventeenth century in evaluating the historic role of the private feud which started in 1647 near Czehryn.

Chmielnicki's personal feelings were not the cause of the uprising, but they did play a key role in the development of events. They incensed and pushed to extremes a man who had hitherto behaved cautiously, like a farmer rather than a commander. Pawel Pawluk scorned men such as Bohdan Chmielnicki . . . as he was until the Czaplinski incident a typical member of the senior staff of registered Cossacks, loyal to the crown.

Chmielnicki was a member of the gentry and a fairly prosperous squire, managing his estate well. Being Orthodox did not stop him from attending a Jesuit college, where he learned Latin and rhetoric. The time he spent as a prisoner of war, later ransomed by his mother, gave him an opportunity to learn the Turkish and Tartar languages. Polish and Ukrainian were his mother tongues.

He had known Warsaw and the king for a long time. In September 1638, after the suppression of a rebellion in which he had not participated, he went to the capital to pay homage to the monarch, as member of a delegation of Cossack loyalists.

As late as August 1647, according to the Ukrainian writer Miron Korduba, he was not inclined to take any risks. Jerzy Ossolinski appeared in the Ukraine on a mysterious mission. The chancellor surely did not go there merely to discuss the cooperation of the Catholic and Orthodox churches. He was probably encouraging the Cossacks discreetly to organize some raids in the Black Sea. It was at his instigation that Chmielnicki engaged in "cautious agitation."

Daniel Czaplinski took his woman, invaded and ravaged his property. He took savage revenge for the complaint to Alexander Koniecpolski. He ordered Chmielnicki's ten-year-old son, Ostap, flogged so severely that the boy died a few days later. He then accused Bohdan of insubordination. The charge was based precisely on what Chmielnicki was doing on instructions from the chancellor of the crown, that is, agitation for a naval raid.

Personal revenge? One may assume that a man of brilliant organizational talent, then still dormant, was brought out of his slumber by the shock of pain and realized that the Ukraine was heading into a morass. He knew that after Stanislaw Koniecpolski's death he had no one to talk to seriously, no one whose word he could trust and no one he needed to fear. Then he decided to seize the rudder himself. He was not yet thinking of breaking away from the king and the Commonwealth. A bold stance by the Zaporozhe might even have benefited it by placing the problem of a Duchy of Ruthenia on the agenda and forcing change. Chmielnicki said soon afterward that he wished the king to be king and "cut down the dukes and princes."

The war council did not allow Alexander Koniecpolski to sentence Chmielnicki to death. He was placed in the custody of Krzyczewski, colonel of the Czehryn regiment of the registered Cossacks. An old friend of Chmielnicki, he allowed him to escape.

It is by no means certain whether, as some writers have alleged, Chmielnicki once again visited King Wladyslaw and heard from him the legendary words of advice about the sword being the best instrument of vengeance. He certainly remembered well the royal charter obtained at the secred conference in April of the previous year. He invited Ivan Barabasz to a feast and treated him with liquor. When the colonel passed out, he took off his belt. Barabasz's wife recognized it and delivered to Chmielnicki the royal parchments.

On December 17 Chmielnicki fled from Czehryn to the Sich of Zaporozhe.

No one was much concerned. The year 1647, the last of the Commonwealth's Indian summer, ended peacefully, though various "signs in heaven and on earth," as for example an exceptionally mild winter, were said to augur great and dire events.

Yet letters exchanged by the gentry at that turning point of an era breathed confidence in the future. They dealt with money matters, family affairs, and plans for new buildings to be erected in the coming year. One of them, by a senator from western Poland, contains a phrase that rings with the snigger of history:

"So, by the grace of God, we have concluded it all *feliciter*."

VI

Chmielnicki removed from the Sich the Czerkasy regiment of the registered Cossacks, which was serving there its turn of duty. He started negotiating with the Tartars the agreement that had been hanging over the Commonwealth for at least three years. The king undertook a joint march with the Cossacks to the Crimea and Budziak too late and made his preparations with criminal negligence. By doing so, he aroused among the Cossacks high expectations that were not fulfilled and thus facilitated the alliance of his Zaporozhe subjects with the intended enemy.

Many prominent people showered hetman Potocki with letters advising moderation. The victor of Chocim, the aged Stanislaw Lubomirski, discouraged an expedition against Chmielnicki. Recent experience taught that Koniecpolski tried at first to negotiate with Pawluk.

"I marched to terminate the war by casting fear," wrote to the king the commander of the royal army, "and so far the Cossacks have not spilt one drop of blood of Your Majesty's troops and they will not, if the enemy submits."

He did not "march" very far. At the end of April 1648 a small force of no more than three and a half thousand went into the steppes. It was commanded by the hetman's son, Stefan Potocki, a young man of twenty-four. Reinforcements sailed down the Dnieper. They were all registered Cossacks, comrades in arms of Bohdan Chmielnicki. There were also many Ukrainians in the units under young Potocki, mainly in the dragoons.

The hetman justified his move with various arguments. He heard the cries of despair of the gentry after the removal of the Czerkasy regiment from the Sich of Zaporozhe. He could not allow the rebels to enter the more densely populated areas, where his and Wisniowiecki's men confiscated in villages thousands of firearms and cannon in the towns. A region under permanent Tartar threat was armed to the teeth. Everyone who wanted to live and did not relish the prospect of pulling an oar on a Turkish galley had to have arms. The hetman agreed with the need of a naval Cossack raid, but felt that the boats had to be readied first and their crews brought to heel. The letter of Mikolaj Potocki, hetman of the crown, took victory for granted.

His confidence was based on the memory of his quick victory

over Pawluk and the unconditional surrender of the Cossacks, begging for mercy. Mikolaj Potocki had been intoxicated by the easy success he had achieved ten years earlier and, unlike Koniecpolski, he never sobered up.

He sent his son against Chmielnicki, thinking that the old Zaporozhe warrior, remembering the battle of Cecora, would be intimidated by a youngster.

Stefan Potocki's force encountered the Cossacks and the Tartar horde on April 29 at Zolte Wody and fought gallantly for almost three weeks, although the enemy had by the final phase of the battle a ten-to-one numerical superiority. The registered Cossacks sailing down the Dnieper murdered their colonels and joined the rebels, soon followed by the dragoons and Cossacks of the land troops. Tuhay Bey proposed negotiations and promptly imprisoned the envoys, among them Stefan Czarniecki, attached to the young Potocki as a "director." Chmielnicki demanded the delivery of guns as a condition of the release of the prisoners and immediately started to take them from the Polish train.

The hetman received news of the situation and his scouts reported that gunfire was heard in the steppes. The reinforcements did not arrive, Stefan Potocki's corps was wiped out; he died of wounds; and many of his staff were taken prisoners.

On the day of young Potocki's encounter with Chmielnicki at Zolte Wody, Wladyslaw IV left Wilno for Warsaw. The king was slow to recognize the danger. He thought little of it when early in the year he left the capital, sick and almost incapacitated. His order to abstain from action against Chmielnicki, sent from Wilno, did not reach the hetman in time because it had to be first signed by the chancellor in Warsaw. The absence of the king in the capital compounded the disaster, but that was not all.

Wladyslaw stopped on his way in Merecz, held back by the sudden illness of his wife. He felt better than in the winter and early spring when doctors feared for his life. The dysentery and leg stiffness had disappeared. On May 5 the king rose early to go hunting. He hunted all day and then, displeased with his driver's caution, pushed him off his seat and did what he always had done in politics: seized the reins himself and rushed madly over rough ground.

At night he felt pains in his side and after two days he felt terrible pain in the kidneys. The medic prescribed nine grams of

"Antimonium," but since there was none in the traveling apothecary, they took some from the bag of an unknown itinerant barber. The reaction was violent. Within three days the court physician counted one hundred and fifty bowel movements. The king was seized by "febra maligna" and hiccups. Blood letting was, of course, the remedy of choice. The blood was thick and "not of the best augury."

His retinue did not dare tell their lord the truth. The vice-chancellor of Lithuania and the king's favorite, Leon Sapieha, who just arrived in Merecz, did. When asked by the king, he said: "Yes, Your Majesty, there is no cure for death."

Wladyslaw ordered him to affix the seal of the Grand Duchy to his testament, a priest heard his confession, but he could not take Communion for a long time because of the hiccups. On May 20 in the middle of the night, "He yielded his soul to the Lord with piety and contrition."

In the post mortem "a large oblong stone was found in the right loin and several smaller ones."

The corps commanded by Stefan Potocki did not exist any more. The hetman, advised of the disaster by the commander of the Kudak fortress, was retreating toward Korsun, sending to the already dead king and the chancellor messages asking for reinforcements.

About four thousand men were lost in the steppes, either killed, passing over to the enemy, or taken prisoner. But the power of the twelve-million-strong Commonwealth was as yet untouched. The main army of the crown had not yet met Chmielnicki. Wisniowiecki with his regiments was still beyond the Dnieper and the Lithuanian army remained in its quarters.

The interregnum paralyzed the central command of the state. The army had to defend a headless realm, whose fate was now in the hands of the hetman of the crown.

It is idle to speculate on what might have happened if the forces of the Commonwealth in the Ukraine in the spring of 1648 had been under the command of the warrior who died two years earlier from too much love. The man who had once faced Gustav Adolph and had more recently defeated at Ochmatow the Tartar Tuhay Bey, who now joined forces with Chmielnicki. One thing is sure: the orders given in that dark spring could never have been approved by Koniecpolski.

Overconfidence soon turned to panic. A contemporary chronicler wrote about Mikolaj Potocki: "Because of constant drunkenness he wasted the army, brought eternal shame and dishonor to the crown of Poland, lost sons of the crown, old soldiers and many others."

The hetman did not extend help to his son perishing in the steppes, though he was aware of his tragic situation. Later, contrary to the advice of the war council, he refused to stop in Korsun and wait there for Prince Wisniowiecki, who had already sent a message asking where he should go with his six thousand first-rate soldiers. These private forces, together with those of the crown, would have formed a twelve-thousand-strong army, well equipped and led by experienced officers. Chodkiewicz had one-third of that number at Kircholm.

Potocki decided to withdraw to Bohuslaw, but not immediately on Monday, as he regarded that day as unlucky. He started on the next day, a "lucky Tuesday." Everyone in the camp knew the time of departure and the destination, so the information also reached the Cossacks. They hastened to "block the road to Bohuslaw at a point where there was a deep ravine called Kruta Balka, about a mile from Korsun." They dug a trench across it, while Chmielnicki hid in the undergrowth and waited with his force.

Not only Koniecpolski, but any sane commander would have sent a cavalry patrol into the ravine before entering it with the entire train of the army.

"But how could there be any good sense when the lord of Cracow, the hetman of the crown Mikolaj Potocki, drinking vodka all the time, was then also drunk in his coach, while the field hetman, Kalinowski, was not listened to when he suggested other action. Besides, his sight was not too good, for when someone was within an arrow's range he could hardly recognize that it was a man."

When caught in an ambush, one had to act instinctively and with lightning speed. Marcin Kalinowski at least had courage. He was wounded twice.

The infantry marched into the ravine with closed ranks, followed down the steep slope by the guns and supply carriages. The trench, which had not been there the previous day, stopped the head of the line, while the guns and carriages, driven by momentum, crashed into the soldiers. The salvoes of Cossack muskets raked a mass of overturned guns and carriages mingling with swarming men. The battle lasted four hours. The squadrons of Krzysztof Korycki, Konstanty Klobukowski, and some others disregarded the hetman's order, mounted their horses and broke through the Tartar throng. Potocki had forbidden the cavalry to respond in the traditional manner, by charging through the enemy ranks. He had evidently forgotten Kumejki.

The fleeing men were not pursued too eagerly because a magnet of gold and silver kept the Cossacks by the supply carriages where the loot was. "The noble lords, as it behooved their station, went to war with all they needed for their comfort." Especially the young Hieronim Sieniawski, who was taking his baptism of war, carried in his train treasures "which the enemy cleared out in one hour, leaving not a trace." Both the hetmans and many of their men were taken prisoners.

The messenger of "Prince Jeremy" reached the Potocki camp safe and sound only by finding an opening in a garden fence and dashing through it into the steppe. The settlements he passed were either empty as if after the plague or packed with an armed mob. After the defeat of the royal forces the entire population joined the rebellion. Wisniowiecki was left cut off beyond the Dnieper "like a bird in a cage." All the ferries on the river disappeared. The only retreat route was to the north and the prince took it.

Far behind him the sad relic of the Commonwealth's rule over the steppes of the Ukraine, the fortress of Kudak, was still holding out, confident in its heavy guns. After a spirited defense, its garrison ceased resistance in late September. Krzysztof Grodzicki held back several Cossack regiments as long as possible but he could not stop the flood. On the broad highway to the Vistula, Chmielnicki had only two major obstacles left: Lwow and Zamosc.

In the meantime an election had to be held in Warsaw, by the grace of the nuncio Hannibal of Capua and Zygmunt III still under the same rules of freedom and unanimity. The Wola field was waiting for the throng of armed electors, the feuding of the parties, and the foreign intrigues. Old Cardinal Lubienski was the interrex. Chancellor Ossolinski was charged with deliberately provoking the Cossacks and being responsible for all the misfortunes of the Commonwealth. The country was faced with a civil war which had already brought down one of the walls of the common home, seized all of the duchy of Ruthenia, threatened the lands of Poland, and nibbled at the southern border of Lithuania. The Commonwealth became at that point actually a federation of only two nations, both on the edge of a precipice.

The allied Muscovite army, assembled near Putywle, had already started moving toward the Dnieper. The Tartars were seen within the Commonwealth borders, an invasion by Islam-Girey had been expected since the beginning of the year and the *casus foederis*, under the terms of the alliance, was clearly operative. But the news of the king's death and the defeat of Korsun stopped the advance of Tsar Alexey's regiments. They stopped and then started to withdraw gradually to the east.

In the four weeks that had elapsed since the departure of Stefan Potocki, the image of eastern Europe underwent a profound change, darkening for some, dazzling others with tempting color. It revealed brutally the truth concealed under the cloak of ancient glory and glittering appearances. It soon became obvious to all that the vast Polish-Lithuanian state was a giant with a weak bone structure and poor blood circulation. With all the perquisites of a major power, the kingdom was neither a desirable ally nor an enemy inspiring respect, but rather prospective booty for its neighbors.

The spring of 1648 was rich in tragic developments. Wladyslaw IV died immediately after the first defeat of his armies in the field and on the eve of another, far worse. But the most ominous of all was the see-saw movement of the tsar's army. It backed away from the alliance to gain space for a leap forward.

CHAPTER 6

OTHER PERSPECTIVES

*The realm prospers when the king's interest is identical
with that of the nation.*

Jean de la Bruyere
Characters, 1688

Historians have calculated that the revenues of the treasury
were the same under Casimir the Great and under Wladyslaw IV.
They were, of course, taking into account purchasing power, not
monetary units, the value of which varied widely.

Under Casimir, Poland had an area of about two hundred fifty
thousand square kilometers, a population of less than two million,
and no access to the sea. It was recovering after a prolonged and
exhausting period of political division. Wladyslaw's realm was quad-
rupled in size and one of the largest in Europe, it had Polish
Pomerania and had enjoyed centuries of peace and prosperity.

Since the Piast era the country had gained much glory, culture, people, and renown, but not money in the treasury. Since Casimir the Great, that is over two hundred seventy years, there has been no military reform consistent with the nation's needs.

The bone structure of the huge body of the Commonwealth was indeed frail, its arteries constricted. They were adequate centuries earlier when the load was far smaller. They had served well until Grunwald, but not since.

The international situation must have favored Poland for centuries for the collapse to be postponed so long. No one can blame the Good Lord. His patience was abused.

The facts and figures on the treasury and defense explain it all. Persistent neglect of the two pillars of any state had to result in ultimate disaster. But the basic question is: How was such neglect possible?

The traditional answer to that question blames the national character, flawed by an inborn leaning to anarchy and devoid of organizational talent. Such a judgment seems odd in a country noted for its mathematicians and logicians.

Let the prosecutors decide which of the nationalities they want as defendants: Poles, Lithuanians, White Ruthenians (Byelorussians), or Ukrainians? Should a Zamoyski, Radziwill, Sapieha, or Wisniowiecki stand in the dock as representative of his group? Any impartial tribunal would also include among the guilty two Swedes and quite a number of Germans. The respected Polish families of Bazenski and Czema used to spell their names von Beisen and von Zehmen. Weihers and Denhoffs held the offices of *starosta* of Puck, Czluchow, Koscierzyna; *voievodes* of Pomerania, Malbork, Chelmno; castellans of Gdansk and Parnawa. Descended from Cracow burghers, the Szembeks climbed to the offices of castellans of Sanok and Biecz. Emilia Plater, the patron of all the heroic Polish women, was not descended from a Polish Piast. The Russian writer Pobiedonostzev complained later that too many Zyberks and Weyssenhoffs were boldly Polonizing the thoroughly Russian Lithuania.

The German nobility of Pomerania, Prussia, and the Inflanty found a comfortable shelter in a Commonwealth free of any discrimination, in which they were regarded at first as equal co-citizens and later as brothers. The Germans assimilated rapidly and learned the Polish language. The *voievode* of Pomerania, Gerhard Denhoff, was appointed marshal of the court of Queen Cecily Renata. Noticing the queen's apartment crowded, he reprimanded the throng in very colloquial Polish vernacular: "Don't crawl over the queen, gentlemen. Her Majesty is much annoyed when people are all over her." He had been seeking his court position for a long time, because the queen, who was German herself, did not like him. Some contemporaries reproached him for lack of polish and "Dutch coarseness" but not for being German.

The Commonwealth was the home and property of the gentry of all its nationalities. Within the knightly estate there was no differentiation by ethnic origin. Anyone claiming that the Commonwealth was ruled by the Poles would only display ignorance or ill will.

A mystical analysis of national character cannot explain why the small kingdom of Casimir the Great, comprising a part of Poland and Red Ruthenia, could be protected by a multitude of castles, while the huge Commonwealth comprising Lithuania, Pomerania, Ruthenia, and the Kiev region could not afford to do so. Historical facts must give the answer rather than theoretical speculation.

Let us consider a document written at the time of Wladyslaw IV, but far away in France. It may explain how that country became consolidated and developed harmoniously, enabling its own citizens and countless others to engage in cultural activities.

The political testament of Cardinal Richelieu strikes a familiar note. It deals with the domestic situation in his country.

> . . . license was France's sickness. The king's majesty was loved, but not his power. The king was afraid of his subjects, who sinned to inspire fear; he paid them for services which should have been free; ransom in gold was taken for crimes that deserved execution; pensions were granted to prevent rebellion. There was a laxity of conscience and compulsion to crime. The sickness was treated with gifts and exacerbated by such permissiveness.

"I taught blind obedience," said the great statesman, "so that it should be almost a religion to the French."

He did teach it. He cut down dukes and princes. But his instruction was not lasting. After the cardinal's death, eminent Frenchmen took up arms against the king. On the eve of the Revolution, Louis

XVI encountered a rebellion of the privileged, who refused reforms proposed by a perfectly reasonable government.

Let us listen to Richelieu some more:

> My first concern was then the royal majesty—and the second the greatness of the state. I found a France smaller than herself. Everything shrank, except for the reach of the language, which remained French even when it crossed the borders of France. Nations that were once our subjects now denounced us—in our own language. They were French and yet France's enemies. France was arming against herself; the enemy used us against ourselves; and the Frenchman was both victor and defeated, as valiant for others' glory as for his own downfall.
>
> Therefore the goal of my policy was to restore to Gaul the frontiers given to it by nature. To give to Frenchmen again a French king, identify Gaul with France, and revive a new Gaul wherever the ancient one had reached.
>
> Three obstacles stood in the way of my design: France resisted, hostile to herself; Spain resisted because it wanted to make all the world its home and France one of its parts; the border nations resisted because they were the friends of Spain, unable to be its enemies.
>
> To overcome these obstacles, I reconciled France with itself, so that it would see the enemy outside; I employed Spain at home, so that it could not be active abroad; I showed freedom to the allies and compelled some of them against their will to become free.

One thing strikes us when reading these words. The substance of the argument of Armand du Plessis de Richelieu could easily be signed Charles de Gaulle. The royal school of political thought left a durable legacy.

The dominant feature of the principles set out in Richelieu's testament was down-to-earth realism, a certain narrowness of horizons—all characteristics despised by Vistulan snobs, posturing as the "Frenchmen of the North," who like to visit Paris but give little thought to how it became what it is. The political ideology of cardinal Richelieu can be summed up in one word: France.

Many books have been written about the decline and fall of the Commonwealth, but few point out how seldom since the extinction of the house of Piast had Poland or the commonwealth been the master of its own policy. Since the time when Casimir Jagiello started planting his sons on the thrones of neighboring countries, such instances were rare. What should have been the rule became the exception. That was the basic reason for the neglect of the key interests of the state, for which the nation paid so dearly.

The cruel and cunning tribe of Piast established the same relationship to the state as that of a Polish peasant to his hereditary homestead. The humane, generous Jagiellonians, especially the later ones, had their own dynastic patriotism and were cool to the attempted reforms proposed by the gentry. What happened under the Swedish dynasty of Vasa can only be described as a crime and a political nightmare. The victory of the counter-reformation in Europe and the throne of Sweden were their first priorities. For several decades the Commonwealth lavished blood and vast funds in pursuing goals in total opposition to its own interests. It was the victim of theories that served only the Habsburgs, but were for Poland and some other European nations only deceitful propaganda. France was not caught in that whirlpool, for its government watched its national interest alone. We can be sure that in Paris a nuncio would not be permitted to veto an already enacted law on the election of kings, nor would a parliamentary resolution be submitted for approval or rejection to monks responsible to no one in the country.

An error without consequences is a stroke of luck. But when the entire conduct of policy is one glaring error, luck runs out.

Historians commented: The nation failed, proved incapable. . . .

That "nation," as others at the time, had no idea of political parties with permanent professional staffs in the capital, offices in the provincial and county seats, with a list of membership, monthly dues and organizational discipline. The "nation" of the gentry was dispersed in thousands of country houses and if somewhere twenty-five people could be found in a square kilometer, that region was thought to be heavily populated. No nation can conduct its common business, especially that of the treasury and defense, otherwise than through its executive.

All the four royal elections we have dealt with so far were concluded successfully, that is by a victory of the majority, sometimes even by unanimity. Despite the freedom of choice, the principle of heredity, even in the female line, was observed. These decisions were taken by the "nation," unorganized and assembled ad hoc at Kamien or Wola. The same "nation," represented by its deputies, had been striving since the beginning of the sixteenth century for a comprehensive reform of the structure of the state and was ready to reduce in favor of the treasury the excessive holdings of the clergy. The majority of the citizens of Both Nations protested against the False Dimitri affair, which nevertheless became fact, with the consequences we know. The idea of a war of aggression against Moscow was promoted by only a few individuals, but it did take place. The highly unpopular and harmful wars with Sweden were paid for with taxes increased twelvefold. Yet only the government wanted these wars and provoked them.

It was not the nation but the rulers who treated their subjects as instruments of their ambitions, who were responsible for the decline and fall.

The gentry guarded jealously its "freedoms," but to understand its position we should determine the meaning given to that term at the time. It comprised not only the class privileges but also the sovereignty of the state. The landed gentry were against any enhancement of royal authority not only because they thought it might restrict their rights. They knew that, even within their powers circumscribed by the Pacta Conventa, the kings pursued political goals harmful to the Commonwealth and were even ready to trade its crown for another one better to their liking.

The deputies to the Seym cried that their "liberties are violated" when the king decided, against popular will, to marry an Austrian princess and conspired secretly with Habsburg archdukes.

The nations of the Commonwealth did see their interest served under Stefan I, with whom they could communicate only in Latin. Batory was even more of an outsider than the Vasa kings, but he belonged to the race of honest men. Zygmunt III tried to use a multidenominational state as an instrument of Catholic indoctrination, destroying the priceless heritage of harmonious coexistence of faiths built over centures. Wladyslaw IV served only his own personal ambition and glory. Both squandered resources, each in his own way, but with the same final result.

There was no attempt to save every penny for the vital needs of the state, nor to improve its structure, if only by small increments.

Neither was there any consistent policy line. Zygmunt August started the Inflanty campaign in order to push Moscow away from

336

the Baltic. He offered his sister in marriage to the king of Sweden, with a view to securing an alliance in the north. Stefan accepted his predecessor's inheritance and carried on his design, fighting in the northeast until he secured all of the Inflanty. He did not antagonize Sweden and even respected its interests. Zygmunt marched to Moscow in order to gain its support in his campaign for the crown of Sweden. Wladyslaw pursued the same goal and promised to return to the tsar the lands conquered by Gustav Adolph, that is, access to the Baltic (anticipating by several decades the most ardent wishes of Peter the Great). In the sixty years that had elapsed since the death of Zygmunt August the commonwealth's policy was turned around, but in a direction totally oblivious of the actual national interest.

Cardinal Richelieu sought for France the boundaries given to Gaul by Julius Caesar, who died in the year 44 B.C., and strived stubbornly for their restoration.

When Zygmunt III decided to fight Moscow, Stanislaw Zolkiewski demanded his assurance that he was seeking the national interest not his own. During the Seym debate that culminated in instructing Wladyslaw to disband the regiments he had enlisted aganst Turkey, one of the deputies said, "Your Majesty wants to take Constantinople, but whose property will it be after victory: the Commonwealth's or Your Majesty's?"

This was no idle rhetoric. We have referred to the family pact concluded by Wladyslaw with the Habsburgs. The territories conquered from Turkey were to become a hereditary duchy under the "Polish" branch of the Vasa dynasty, excluding its member reigning in Warsaw as king of Poland. In other words, the Commonwealth was expected to engage in a murderous war with the sultan and receive nothing in return even in the event of victory. This was what Richelieu called "valor for others' glory and one's own perdition."

There was a full awareness of the parting between the interests and policies of the rulers and those of the Commonwealth. The handling of foreign affairs on behalf of the king of Poland and grand duke of Lithuania was largely in the hands of foreigners, civilian soldiers of fortune. The kings of the Vasa dynasty never interfered with the personal freedoms of the nobility, but continuously violated freedom in the sense of the primacy of national interest.

The two last Jagiellonians practiced olympian detachment. These men of the Renaissance seemed to have adopted the philosophy of a sage of the antiquity, who taught that happiness consists of avoiding trouble. The Vasa kings, on the other hand, simply did not care much for the Commonwealth or its interests.

It was a situation that produced tragic absurdities and was hardly conducive to constructive political action. Genuinely loyal to their monarchs, the members of the knightly estate contributed freely to their and their spouses private expenses, but turned stingy when the needs of the state were concerned. It was an era of political madness.

Such blunders might not have brought down a state such as Poland was prior to its union with Lithuania, a relatively small kingdom with a homogenous population and few domestic problems. But the Commonwealth of Both Nations was a unique phenomenon, a magnificent structure looking to the future, but also a complex and delicate mechanism requiring constant care of its many gears and levers. It had to its credit a tremendous achievement: the on-the-whole harmonious cooperation on equal terms between Poland and Lithuania, based on mutual acceptance and tolerance between citizens of Catholic, Orthodox, and Protestant faiths. The later rulers of the Commonwealth poured sand into that hitherto smooth-running mechanism.

All the nationalities of the Commonwealth participated in the establishment and consolidation of a multinational state. The contributions each of them made to that end remain the highlights of their history. That difficult task was accomplished with a fair measure of success so long as past experience and tradition were the guide. Disaster was brought about by men who were kings of Poland, grand dukes of Lithuania and Ruthenia in law, but not in their hearts.

"POLISH HERITAGE SERIES"

BOOK CLUB

AMERICAN INSTITUTE
OF POLISH CULTURE

1440 79th STREET CAUSEWAY, SUITE 403
MIAMI, FLORIDA 33141
(305) 864-2349

The American Institute of Polish Culture was founded in 1972 by Mrs. Lewis S. Rosenstiel as a non-profit, non-sectarian, tax-exempt Florida corporation. The aims of the Institute are twofold: first to share with all Americans the rich heritage of Poland, which made an important contribution to Western civilization. Second, to establish a center of educational facilities and resources for the encouragement and promotion of the current scientific and aesthetic endeavours by Americans of Polish descent.

Toward this end, the Institute has presented artistic events, concerts, lectures, radio and television programs, film presentations, art exhibitions, art and history tours of Poland and has published books, scholarly works and catalogues.

To become a member simply complete, sign and return the order card along with your check made payable to A.I.P.C. We publish two books per year and your membership will authorize you to buy as many editions as you wish at membership prices which are far below publishers list price. Shipping charges are included.

INTRODUCTION TO POLAND
by Olgierd Budrewicz

Introduction to Poland is a highly personal, emotional but extremely informative introduction to Poland, Polish towns and villages, historical places and history of the Polish nation. It tells you—or reminds you—of Polish humor, hospitality, sense of time, ghosts, mathematics, vodka, mushrooms, etc. More than 50 towns and villages worth a visit are mentioned in the book which has five sub-chapters. The titles of the chapters are "What To Know", which explains some of Poland's history; "What To Understand", which puts recent Polish history into perspective; "What To Discover", which explains Polish customs; "What To See", which tells the reader about the beauty of Polish towns and the countryside, and "What To Remember", which gives the traveler useful tips.

List Price $12.00   Membership Price $9.60

JAGIELLONIAN POLAND
by Pawel Jasienica
Translated by Alexander T. Jordan

The high noon of Poland's history, the period which brought the nation to the pinnacle of its political growth and its culture to a golden age, setting the pattern for centuries to come, is brilliantly described by Pawel Jasienica.

A bestseller in Poland, packed with facts, rich in vivid anecdotes, this historical book describes the turning point in Poland's history—its union with Lithuania, whereby Poland became at one stroke the largest country in Europe at that time. It is a fascinating journey into another era, probing the thoughts and motivations of Polish people, pondering the choices they had to make, and their consequences—some of them reverberating to this day.

The Jagiellonian era was the time of the Renaissance and the Reformation—two movements that changed the face of our civilization. Jasienica analyzes perceptively their impact in Poland and the unique manner in which that country shared in the mainstream of West European thought.

List Price $16.50   Membership Price $13.20

THE CONSTITUTIONS OF POLAND AND OF THE UNITED STATES
by Dr. J. Kasparek-Obst

Dr. Kasparek-Obst's study reveals many hitherto little known aspects of the growth of constitutional principles which found expression in both the Polish and American constitutions and provides fascinating insights into intellectual trends shared and exchanged between Poland and America even prior to the Declaration of Independence.

Polish Americans in particular will find here much of interest and may be gratified to discover that the contribution of Polish political thinkers, though less known, might have been as significant as that of the soldiers, such as Kosciuszko and Pulaski.

List Price $17.50   Membership Price $14.00

MADAME CURIE—DAUGHTER OF POLAND
by R. Woznicki, Ph.D.

The biography of the world famous scientist, Maria Curie Sklodowska, who spent the first twenty four years of her life in Poland, traces her life through hardship, tragedy and moments of dazzling success.

She won two Nobel prizes in physics, her daughter one. Collectively, they are the greatest mother and daughter team in the history of science.

Dr. Woznicki's life of Maria Curie Sklodowska is a vivid narrative, with many illustrations, which add an extra dimension to the biography of this extraordinary Polish woman, who did not wait for our times to prove that genuine achievement is open to both women and men—providing they have genius.

List Price $9.50   Membership Price $7.60

CONRAD AND HIS CONTEMPORARIES
by J.H. Retinger

Probably few of his contemporaries had as intimate a relationship with Joseph Conrad as his fellow Pole and lifelong friend, Joseph H. Retinger. Retinger's life paralleled closely that of Conrad. They were both born in Poland and came as young men to England, where they met when Conrad was beginning to carve for himself the literary career which lifted him to heights of world renown. The two friends moved in the same circles and shared intellectual interests. Their friendship lasted until Conrad's death.

Conrad showed to his friend Retinger a side of his life unknown to other contemporaries and biographers. Their common roots and language formed a strong bond between them, and it was Retinger who brought Conrad back to Poland after an absence of forty years. By an odd coincidence, Conrad's homecoming occurred when war was declared in 1914.

List Price $11.50   Membership Price $9.20

SELECTED TALES
by Henryk Sienkiewicz

The present collection of short stories is a good introduction to Sienkiewicz for those not ready to face his major multi-volume historical sagas.

These are light stories, a random selection including that well known classic, "The Lighthouse Keeper". Some of them allude to the author's visit in the United States, when he was a guest of the famous Polish actress Helen Modjeska on her California ranch, in the eighties of the last century.

List Price $11.50   Membership Price $9.20

TRUE HEROES OF JAMESTOWN
by Arthur Leonard Waldo

"True Heroes of Jamestown" is a fascinating foray into the earliest era of European settlement in North America and further back into relations between Poland and England, which led to the presence of Poles in Jamestown, Virginia in 1608.

In 1581 there were 500 permanent English residents in the Polish city of Elblag on the river Vistula. Poland exported to England grain, lumber for shipbuilding, tar, hemp and flax. When the English started colonizing North America, it was natural that they enlisted the help of Polish artisans, expert in tar making and glass manufacture. A group of them was brought to Jamestown by Captain John Smith. "Heroes of Jamestown" is the story of their struggle against nature and the Indians, their hardships and achievements. The Polish settlers were the first Americans to strike for their civil rights, demanding equality with the English and thus initiating the pluralistic society which was to become the United States.

List Price $15.00   Membership Price $12.00

PIAST POLAND
by Pawel Jasienica
Translated by Alexander T. Jordan

Piast Poland is the family saga of the House of Piast, which ruled Poland from the 10th to the 14th century. It is also the story of the four centuries during which the Piast princes and kings forged out of the many tribes between the rivers Oder and Vistula and their numerous principalities a single, homogenous nation.

Jasienica describes in vivid detail that long drawn process of coalescence, the relapses into regional parcellation and the tenacity with which successive generations of Piasts struggled for 'The Crown'—a symbol of national cohesion.

List Price $19.50   Membership Price $15.60

I wish to enroll in the
"POLISH HERITAGE BOOK CLUB".
(Membership may be cancelled any time by notifying the Institute.
No dues are required).

Print Name and Address ————————————————————————————

——

——

Signature: ————————————————————————————————————

		Membership Price
I would like to order	List Price	−20%
☐ SELECTED TALES by Henryk Sienkiewicz	$11.50	$ 9.20
☐ TRUE HEROES OF JAMESTOWN		
by Arthur Waldo	$15.00	$12.00
☐ JAGIELLONIAN POLAND		
by Pawel Jasienica	$16.50	$13.20
☐ CONSTITUTIONS OF POLAND AND U.S.		
by Kasparek-Obst	$17.50	$14.00
☐ CONRAD AND HIS CONTEMPORARIES		
by J.H. Retinger	$11.50	$ 9.20
☐ MADAME CURIE-DAUGHTER OF POLAND		
by R. Woznicki, Ph.D.	$ 9.50	$ 7.60
☐ INTRODUCTION TO POLAND		
by Olgierd Budrewicz	$12.00	$ 9.60
☐ PIAST POLAND		
by Pawel Jasienica	$19.50	$15.60

Enclosed is my check for $——————— in payment for above order (shipping charges are included).